SPIRIT Dancer
THE CRYSTAL LEGACY SERIES

SHARON SILVA

SPIRIT DANCER
A novel of Romantic Suspense with Paranormal Elements

ISBN 978-0-9906196-0-4 electronic format
ISBN 978-0-9906196-1-1 print format

Cover and Book Design by THE KILLION GROUP
www.thekilliongroupinc.com

DEDICATION

This book is dedicated to my husband, the love of my life and my own true soul mate, and to my four grandchildren who bring love, laughter and sunshine into my days. And to my daddy, who so lovingly taught me to never ever give up.

This book series is purely a creation of my heart and mind. It is a product of my imagination and the pictures that exist only in my mind's eye. It is not intended to precisely depict historic facts or to specifically replicate in any way the beliefs or actions of any ethnic group or sector of the population. It was written solely for the purpose of entertainment and for those who enjoy the adventure of exploring the depths of possibility. And it is to you, too, that I dedicate this book.

ACKNOWLEDGEMENTS

Though writing is indeed a solitary profession, no book is ever created without sacrifice and the work of many hands. My deepest gratitude to all those who helped bring this dream of mine into being. A book begins with a story and untold hours of research and hard work. I want to thank my family, especially my husband, for tolerating my absence sometimes physically, and frequently mentally, during the creation of this book. Thank you all for the love you have showed by supporting and believing in me.

And thank you to my dearest friend and writing sister in heart, Jude Willhoff, for sharing her time and always being there with help and encouragement when I didn't know if the journey would be worth it all. You were right, as always.

THE CRYSTAL LEGACY SERIES

The Crystal Legacy began a thousand years ago in the canyons and on the mesas of the desert Southwest, when an ancient secret was passed to a peaceful people destined to become the messengers that will help save the Earth Mother and all mankind.

For the unsuspecting members of a modern day family, the fulfillment of that legacy began with a mysterious letter written by their grandfather's shaky hand.

> *To my grandchildren,*
>
> *Expect a package in the coming days. Each of you is about to receive a piece of your heritage, a gift from my brother in the form of family heirloom. Forgive my hesitation in passing these on to you. I am not a superstitious man, but your great uncle's writings give me cause for concern.*
>
> *A secret, long kept, is somehow associated with these gifts, and I fear my brother left us before it could be passed along. I am unclear on their significance but I do not believe it was a coincidence that he passed from this world on December 21, 2012, the very day of the ending of the Mayan calendar. Though it did not bring the end of the world as many thought, more than one indigenous people believed in the ending of an era, and I for one believe that passage into the next one will not come without an upheaval in the spirit world of monumental proportion.*
>
> *Go forward with care.*
> *Grandfather Nakai*

THE ANCIENTS

Oh, ancient ones, I hear you speak
I hear your voices still
And among the crumbled ruins seek
The spirit of your undying will

The bits and pieces of your past
Call to me from this place
A place where ancient spirits cast
The shadows of a long lost race

You walk the paths of ancient lands
Your whispers carry on the wind
The imprints of your ancient hands
Touch my soul, oh ancient kin

Along the crumbled walls I hear
The echoes from beyond
Your lives held hardship, pain and fear
But it was here that you belonged

I feel your eyes from far away
Watching over these sacred sands
Trying to teach us in our modern day
The truth of these native lands

And so I walk the canyons deep
And mesas where you dwelled
And seek to find before I sleep
The secrets that you held

Sharon Silva

PROLOGUE

Spirits lingered on the canyon rim that morning rising as clouds of mist from the waking earth. If archaeologist Alex Nakai had believed in that sort of thing, he'd have recognized their presence as surely as he felt the sand shift beneath his feet.

He squinted into the sun that peeked through an apricot cloud above the mesa top and surveyed the almost mystical landscape around him. Light sparkled in the water droplets that clung to the nearby piñon and juniper trees from last night's rain. The thin spines of a yucca plant cast their shadow next to his on the canyon floor.

For months his mind had been preoccupied with thoughts of this place and this excavation, yet he'd never pictured it quite like this. Perhaps his imagination had been skewed by the seriousness of the question burning in his core. At last he was here in Southwestern Colorado with an opportunity to investigate the theory that he dared not share with another living soul, not until he was sure it could be proven.

He reached into the pocket of his jeans and fingered the pottery shard that had started it all. He'd discovered it in Southern Mexico, among some trinkets spread on the blanket of an old man on a street corner.

"Buy it. It will bring you good luck," the old man had told him. But the shard had brought with it a lot more than that. The chip was distinctly Anasazi in its markings.

When he'd pressed the old fellow about its origin, he told Alex he'd found it down by the Mayan ruins. It was too bizarre a story for the man to have made up. Could there truly have been a connection between the Mayans and the Mesa Verdans? He pushed the shard back into his pocket. Only time would tell.

He dropped to his knees in the moist earth and resumed his tedious task. With a gentle, determined hand, he brushed at the cool dirt in the crevice between two sandstone slabs. Bit by bit, each parting grain of sand fell away to reveal the skeleton he labored over. He'd thought it was the remains of a small animal, possibly a rabbit. Now with each stroke of the soft brush, the realization came.

The perfectly preserved skeleton of an ancient infant, its tiny spine, arms and legs curled in a fetal position, lay exposed to the warming rays of light. A burst of air escaped his lips as a mixture of sorrow and wonder ran through him ending with heaviness in his chest. His jaw clenched against his gut reaction. He put his hand to the bridge of his nose and pushed at the corners of his eyes, defying a tear to escape.

Remnants of an ancient burial cloth clung to the bones and a thin strip of beaded rawhide was still visible around the skull. Next to the delicate bones lay a crushed, but still distinguishable piece of pottery. Fragile, like the child itself, the vessel was no doubt intended to carry the nectar of the gods into the next world.

He picked up a small shard of the pot and rubbed it between his fingers. Examining it with a careful eye, he squeezed it tight to his palm. It was strikingly similar to his. Though, much like his goal, it was so close, and yet so far away. One piece, with a matching pattern could prove to be the key to the mysterious connection that had haunted his mind for months. But as he stared down again at the grave, a torrent of unexplained emotions poured through his heart and his obsession faded into oblivion next to another storm brewing in his soul.

Kneeling in the heartland of his ancestral past, he felt his native history for the first time. Sketchy as his own knowledge of it was, strange thoughts and feelings vibrated through him. *Life. Death. Roots. Beginnings and endings.* The premonition of a rebirth of the spirit, his spirit, that seemed destined to begin. Brought to the surface by this internal storm, images of things that were, and those yet to be, walked on moccasin-covered feet through his mind. The remains of a long dead civilization were intertwined here with his own ancestral dawning, in the sanctity of a tiny grave.

Ashes to ashes and dust to dust. It gave new meaning to his oneness with the earth. Yet it symbolized a new beginning that festered in his soul, unidentified and nagging. Here lay undeniable proof of ancient suffering, of his people's painful history and of the loss of not just life, but of a way of life. It touched him, slammed him face first into his own mortality, into his own fragile existence, and into his own heritage.

He moved his dirt-covered finger gently down the tiny skull and arm then carefully covered it again, returning the sands of many ages to their rightful home.

"I'll not disturb your sleep, little one," he whispered as he patted the earth, sealing the secret away for eternity. For a moment, he studied the piece of the vessel in his palm then pushed it deep into the earth. Sitting back and looking up into the morning sun, a haunting picture formed in his mind's eye.

*The buckskin-clad chieftain rubbed the dark wisps
of hair on the baby boy's head and smiled as he
brought the soft roundness to his lips and kissed it,
savoring the smell of the child's newness. Holding him
skyward, to the full moon overhead, he offered his son
for the blessing of the gods. "Sin atsa, you shall be
called," the chief said with great love and pride. "Song
of the Eagle. It will be your song that will one day
carry the prayers of the people to the gods. For one day
you will lead our clan."*

*The chief placed the baby in his mother's arms and
she cuddled the child to her breast beneath the
warmth of the buffalo robe that encircled her
shoulders. The man chanted and danced around the
fire that burned in the fire pit of the great temple.*

*"Hay na na. Hay na na," the chief repeated over and
over as the flames reached skyward, sending tiny
sparks along with the hope of the future high into the
smoke-filled night air.*

Alex sat with eyes closed and face to the sky. The
vision in his mind was gone now. The imprint of this
moment and its emotion on his soul would not vanish
so quickly.

CHAPTER ONE

Don't die with the music still in your soul. The words of a popular motivational speaker rang in Jessica Sinclair's ears and sent the pain of a razor blade through her heart. Though she'd listened to the speaker before, this time the truth pierced her being. As she pulled the ear buds from her ears, she turned off the MP3 player. She couldn't bear to hear this right now and didn't need anything else to bring on her tears.

She tossed the device aside and pushed a thick strip of packing tape tight against the flap of the cardboard box—the last box. The truck would be here momentarily to cart the whole pile off to a worthy charity, all but a small box of keepsakes. She turned toward the old empty house and sighed. Three more weeks rattling around in here alone and she might not keep her sanity. With all of her aunt's things removed, the house seemed empty and sterile.

The chime of her cell phone jarred her from her thoughts. She glanced at the display and brought the phone to her ear.

"Simon," she said into the phone, forcing a cheerful lilt into her voice.

"Hey, Jessica. How are you? You sound better."

"Better than what?" One corner of her mouth crept up awkwardly at the feeble attempt at humor.

"You know what I mean. You've been through a lot lately. I've been worried." Simon Forbes, her long-time friend, spoke with sincerity.

"Thanks for the concern, Simon. I just finished packing the house." The words caught in her throat. That sounded more like she was moving away, than just moving on.

"Give yourself a break. Healing is going to take some time. Helen and you were very close. And the last year has been hell for you."

"I'm glad I could be here and take care of her." Painful memories welled up in her eyes. "She'd been like a mother to me since I lost my parents."

"And we both know it's taken a toll on you." Simon cleared his throat. "Maybe that's why I've had you on my mind. Jessica, something's come up. That's why I called."

"What sort of *something?*" she asked cautiously, not sure she was ready for any excitement just yet.

"I got a lead this morning on a discovery in Southwestern Colorado that sounds pretty exciting. It seems there's a new archaeological site in the Four Corners area that could be the oldest ruin ever discovered in the U.S." He paused. "The magazine might want to use it as a feature next month and I need someone down there. You haven't done an article for us in a long time and I'd love for you to do this piece."

"Well, I do have three more weeks—" She considered the offer for a moment. *Don't die with the music still in your soul.* Simon's timing was profound. After watching the lid of a casket close on her Aunt Helen's dreams of a dance studio, Jessica wasn't sure she could go back to her accounting job when her leave of absence was over. Accounting was a job that paid the bills, but it had never been her dream. She was hesitant—and curious. "Where is it exactly?"

"The site is in a canyon that borders Mesa Verde National Park. Right there in the heart of all those ancient ruins, hidden away under their noses all these years."

The inevitable questions had to be asked. "Simon, I know you have freelancers better versed on the subject. So why me?"

"You could stand to get out of Denver for awhile. And besides nobody deserves a break more than you do. This could land you a full-time job at the magazine, if you pull it off."

"Really? Wow." The gods of the universe worked in mysterious ways but they must have been piped directly into her thoughts this morning.

"But there is one thing," Simon's voice sounded strained. "I had to pull some really big strings to get you this assignment. My butt and my job could both be on the line if we aren't the first ones with this story."

"Simon. Why would you put yourself in that position for me?" she scolded.

"Because you're a damn good reporter and I believe in you and your dream."

"Oh, Simon—"

"You've got two weeks to pull it off, all expenses paid. How soon can you leave?"

"Two weeks?" She heard the truck outside in the driveway and glanced at her watch. It was just after eight a.m. Oh, what the hell. "I'm half a room full of boxes, and a suitcase away from hitting the road. I'll be there tonight."

She ended the call. He was right about one thing. She needed to get away, but, archaeology? And Simon's job could be riding on it? *What have I gotten myself into this time?*

Alex examined the package and read the return address. He'd half-expected it after his grandfather's letter days earlier, but it still boggled his mind for his grandfather to track him down here in Cortez. A strange uneasiness ran through him.

After crossing the post office parking lot back to his SUV, and placing the box on the seat, he carefully tore the brown paper to reveal a plain cardboard box. Alex's hands trembled as he pulled back the flaps, but he couldn't explain his reaction. Some folded sheets of beige stationary lay on top of more plain brown paper and bubble wrap that was cinched securely around an object about a foot long.

After some less than gentle encouragement, the wrappings fell away to reveal a carved wooden statue. Alex recognized it immediately as a kachina. A customary Hopi statue like many he'd seen in gift shops across the Southwest. He examined it in detail.

This wasn't an ordinary kachina. Carefully carved by a craftsman's hand, it was clothed in a white ceremonial costume trimmed in turquoise and red with intricate designs painted on the breechcloth and it's brown bare chest. A headdress of black and white feathers crowned the head and ran down its back. Tiny turquoise beads adorned the neck and ears and strips of white fur and feathers had been added along with a small, carved bell in its hand.

Most strikingly to Alex, this kachina had no face but a large blue star outlined in red was painted in place of facial features. Carved at the feet of the figure were two details that made Alex's heart rate kick up a notch, a broken pot bearing a black and white design, and a round green disk with tiny designs carved in it.

Turning it over he read the inscription on a small metal plate "Spirit Dancer, Chasing Star." He held it firmly and rubbed his hand across the base. An odd feeling ran through him. He closed his eyes. An image flashed through his mind, the intense image of a huge blazing blue star. It came and went so quickly, it dizzied him. He shook his head, and gave the somewhat eerie statue another glance, then sat it on the seat next to him. He unfolded the stationary and began to read.

> *Alex -*
>
> *I knew when I first saw you as a boy you were destined for something special. Your brothers have strong spirits, too. I have felt their energy even though I have never met them. I believe the Great Spirit's hand has brought this kachina safely through many generations of our family and has now delivered it to its purpose. Since I will see the sun rise only a few more times, I now entrust it to your care.*
>
> *With this passing, there are things you must know. Every kachina represents a spirit, a dancer in our Hopi ceremonies. A being from the supernatural world, perhaps one of our own ancestors, whose spirit will one day rise again. But this kachina is not ordinary. Guard it well and its power, for it was delivered to your hands not by chance but by destiny. Many mysterious things have occurred over the centuries, brought about by the power of this kachina, and more shall come to you in the days ahead. Just remember you must concern yourself with only this day of your journey.*
>
> *Secrets have been kept from ancient times, from generation to generation. Secrets that those of us entrusted with these family heirlooms, do not understand ourselves. Ours is an odd mixing of bloods,*

the Hopi and the Navajo. Each has their distinct prophecy of the fall of evil and the return of peace. And many believe the end of Mayan calendar shall mark the beginning of this new era.

I, too, believe a great change is about to take place, beginning with a shift of great significance in the spirit world. A shift like nothing the world has ever seen before. Those of us in touch with that realm have felt it. And know that evil will not release its hold on mankind easily.

Do my words frighten you, Alex? They should. Go forth and keep this spirit dancer with you for guidance and protection. You will rely upon him in the days ahead as the sands beneath your feet shift in a new direction.

Your great uncle,
Hosiah Nakai

Alex folded the pages, the words feeling strange as they roamed through his mind. Was his uncle in possession of all his faculties? The letter gave Alex cause for doubt. It was down right bizarre. He stared at the kachina. It was a mere piece of wood for God's sake. That was all. And yet the star on it's face seemed to bore into his soul again, his hands were unnaturally warm as if it emitted heat, and an odd unsettled feeling hung over his heart. He thought of his own emotions and actions earlier, there at the tiny grave.

The words echoed in his mind. *A shift in the spirit world.* His hand trembled again. Again, unexplained. He wrapped the kachina back in the brown paper and returned it to the box. Tucking it away in the back of the SUV, Alex tried to direct his mind back to his real reason for coming here. *The Mayan connection.*

But the thoughts persisted. What was the chance more than one theory hinged on a single ancient civilization would come together with such bizarre timing and in such an odd way as Alex's quest and the two letters referring to the Mayan calendar. Not to mention the objects he was certain were replicated in the carvings at the kachina's feet.

It was too crazy. He glanced at his watch and chided himself for even considering such superstition. And for even considering something that was nothing more than a strange coincidence. He sure as hell didn't have time for nonsense like this.

Alex slammed the tailgate shut and tried to shake off the lingering tightness in his gut. It was a nice gesture on his uncle's part and a unique piece of his family's history. And it was a damn good thing he was grounded only in scientific principle or a thing like that could mess with his head.

Nine hours after hanging up the phone, Jessica turned off the main highway. The initial adrenaline rush had faded and uneasiness seeped into her being as she started through the switchbacks of the steep winding road into Mesa Verde. She tried to explain it away as fatigue, but it grew, building as she climbed higher, almost as if the sensation and the incline worked as one. It was like a presence, as if the small trees and rocks provided shelter for eyes watching from hidden places.

The fine hairs at the back of her neck prickled. She ran a hand through her short dark hair and brushed it down. "Nonsense," she muttered as she turned off the air conditioner and rolled the window down, filling her lungs with the fresh mountain air.

She forced her focus to the scenery, to the visual part of the experience, hoping to ground herself in reality. The view was awe-inspiring. The mesa overlooked piñon and juniper forests and canyons where ancient rivers had carved their winding pathways. Holy cow. If a land could speak, what a tale this place could tell. Her heart warmed as the profound spiritual effect of it all washed through her and touched something deep within.

The car climbed nearer the top of the mesa, and the breathtaking view revealed New Mexico's Shiprock in the distance. Small wonder some fifteen hundred years earlier the Anasazi, the ancient people of the Southwest, had chosen this place, close to the gods, for their home.

Rounding the next hairpin turn, she caught a glimpse of snowy fur against the sandy hillside among the yucca and deer brush. She looked again. A white wolf stood poised on the embankment to the right. The wolf's eyes met hers just as the animal lifted its paws and leaped onto the roadway. She slammed the brakes to the floor as rubber squealed.

The seat belt cut into tender flesh and her heart caught in her throat. As the car skidded to a stop, she heard a sickening thud hit the front bumper. Shoving the gearshift into park, she gave the door handle a quick yank, and jumped from the car. The smell of hot tires and dust stung her nose. With trepidation, she peered over the hood expecting to see the injured wolf.

"Oh my God." Her hand clasped her mouth. Horror stole her breath. A young man lay in the dirt. His eyes were closed, his long dark hair splayed on the ground around his head. "Where did you come from?" she whispered.Her knees went liquid and her feet wanted to run away. Forcing her body into action, she moved around and stood over him. *Is he dead?* Her hammering heart burned against her breastbone.

Kneeling, she put a reluctant hand on his chest. It rose and fell beneath her touch.

Adrenalin kicked in.

She jumped to her feet and ran back to the car. Grabbing the cell phone from the seat, she forced shaking fingers to press 9-1-1 and rushed back to the man in the road.

"Montezuma County Sheriff's Department, what is your emergency?"

Jessica couldn't respond. The phone fell away from her mouth. In the spot where the man had lain, there was nothing.

Quickly, she glanced around. Where could he have gone? She hadn't taken her eyes off the road for more than a second. The voice on the phone asked again.

"Sorry, there's been a mistake," her voice quivered as she disconnected the call. She stood rigid and stared in silence at the crack that ran across the right headlight and the dent in the bumper beneath it. She ran a shaky hand across it. Neither had been there before.

She took a deep breath and pressed her fingertips to her eyelids trying to compose herself. Weakly, she walked around and slid behind the wheel. What had just happened? The knot in the pit of her stomach had an all-too familiar feeling. She hadn't had an experience like this since she was a child. The return of the bizarre visions that had haunted her then wouldn't be a welcome surprise.

She wasn't sure how long she sat there, but she eventually realized she was parked on the turn—a dangerous place to be. This incident couldn't set the tone for her trip. She was finally realizing how important this opportunity could be to her life and her career. She shook her head. No. Whatever had happened or whatever hallucination she'd just had, it was over. Taking another cleansing breath, she pulled back onto the road and drove on up the mountain.

By the time the silver Ford sedan rounded the final turn at the mesa top, Jessica had beaten her jangled nerves into submission. She stopped at the ranger's station at the park entrance, paid the park fee and glanced through the map that was part of the handout at the gate. Deciding to take a quick tour of the Mesa Top Loop road, she followed the signs.

Within a few minutes, she caught sight of a row of dwellings built into the canyon wall to her right. Braking, she pulled into the parking area. She climbed from the car, muttering a few words of encouragement to herself, then gathered her camera and walked with focused determination toward the canyon.

Her steps slowed, as that sense of a presence around her grew stronger than ever. Just as she reached the viewing platform, a springtime wind that had tugged at her shirt stopped abruptly. A chattering jay nearby ceased his song.

She hugged her arms attempting to shrug off her discomfort, determined to ignore the sudden silence. It was mid-May and midweek, and her car was the only one in the lot. Perhaps the quiet magnified her senses. She scanned the area and listened, engulfed by the eerie silence.

Forcing herself to her purpose, she turned toward the canyon. Awe flooded her as she looked upon the ruins. The dwelling place of a long-dead generation of primitive peoples emerged from the sandstone cliff. A small village lay camouflaged in its alcove, crumbled walls all that remained of an ancient civilization.

She wasn't prepared for the emotions that encompassed her. Wonder at their accomplishments was tempered with sadness at their passing. The ancient people were gone, but they'd left behind a legacy of stone and spirit. Something in the wind still carried their voices. The canyon walls seemed alive with the eyes of old souls watching over their ancestral home.

These people had left behind their imprint on the world. What legacy would remain when she was gone? *Life—definitely not a permanent situation.* And it was time she made the most of hers.

She glanced at her watch. It was after five. Her gut gnawed in anxiousness, she had her work cut out for her this time. The small pile of books in the back of the car she'd grabbed from the remains of her aunt's library would help her with the history of the area, but what she really needed was a hands-on feel for the place. Maybe a tour of one of the ruins would give her some clues to what had happened here fifteen hundred years ago.

She wanted to have something under her belt before she questioned the archaeologist in charge of the dig. She'd done these interviews before, and was well aware she needed enough knowledge to get his attention or he wouldn't be willing to share much with her.

A cold wind blew down the back of her flannel shirt, causing her to shiver. Yes, this place had a genuine uniqueness, unlike anything she'd experienced.

Turning back to the structure for one last look, Jessica was flooded with the eerie feeling of being transported to another time. A picture formed in her mind of the deep bronze skin and black shining hair of the ancient people who lived and died here. Hauntingly clear, as if their shadowy spirits had the power to call them to life. Wanting to somehow capture the moment, she snapped a picture with the camera that hung from her neck. Slowly, she turned away, forcing herself to return to reality.

Back in the car, Jessica situated herself in the driver's seat, casting a quick glance in the rear-view mirror. The dark circles under her eyes looked hollow above her high cheekbones. The contrast against her fair skin and hazel eyes made them seem all the worse. She slipped on sunglasses in exasperation and disguised her fatigue behind them. It was just another reminder of the strain of the past months. She thought about the incident on the road. Perhaps that strain had affected her more than she realized. It was definitely time to move on.

The sun hung in a blazing orange sky, just above the purple horizon to the west. The temptation to watch the sunset was overridden by her desire to get settled in her cabin before dark. Driving back toward the park entrance, she spotted the Visitor's Center.

Jessica parked at the center to have a quick look around. She scanned the beautiful tan stone building with its expansive windows as she approached then reached for the heavy glass door. She stopped short. From the corner of her eye, she caught a glimpse of a man seated on one of the benches shaded by a large pillar next to the entrance. She could have sworn the bench was empty a second ago. Attempting to camouflage her surprise, she pretended to check her jeans pocket for the car keys as she studied him briefly behind her dark glasses.

He appeared to be in his early thirties. Long raven hair was pulled to the side and hung down onto his pale denim shirt. Folding his arms, he leaned back against the wall. Wasn't he the man she saw lying on the ground in front of her car? Or had she really seen anyone at all? God, her mind must be playing tricks on her.

The man cast a glance in her direction. His dark eyes set against bronze skin were intent upon her. Long lean legs stretched out in front of him and crossed at a pair of worn cowboy boots.

Suddenly uncomfortable, Jessica gave him a quick smile and a nod then turned away. An odd feeling hung somewhere between her heart and the pit of her stomach as she opened the huge door and walked inside. She shook off the discomfort.

Jessica took a quick look around and scheduled a tour for the following morning. She picked up some information about a research library in the park, and scanned the brochure as she walked outside.

The Indian man was still seated on the bench. He hadn't moved. She pretended not to notice him. As she passed him on her way out, an undeniable urge made her look in his direction.

"Watch yourself, Missy," he said in a low, deep voice.

Startled, she turned to face him. "Excuse me?"

He pulled himself upright and looked directly at her. "You must be very careful," he said, his face stern. His dark eyes shone with an odd light.

"What do you mean?" She glanced around, expecting to see some immediate danger. She saw nothing. When she looked back at the man, he had leaned back against the wall, his eyes closed and his arms folded.

"Were you talking to me?" Now she was annoyed.

He didn't move or give any sign of hearing her question.

"I don't understand," she prodded. *What's this guy's problem?*

Still, he said nothing. He raised one hand and motioned for her to go. The knot in her stomach returned and the prickling sensation ran up the nape of her neck once again.

Shaking her head, she turned and walked away. *How weird.* She must have misunderstood. Why would he have told her to be careful? Something strange was at work in this place. She'd felt it from the beginning.

The brilliant pinks and purples of the morning sky greeted Jessica as she looked to the east from the parking lot at the cabin. It was small and quaint and just a short distance from the park entrance. Best of all, no phones, no television, just peace and quiet; a perfect spot for a getaway where she could focus on her story. Anxious to get to the ruins, a surge of exhilaration ran through her, for the first time in a long time. This story was going to be a challenge and she relished it.

After a small breakfast at the empty cafeteria, she headed for the Cliff Palace ruin. A slender blond woman in a khaki ranger's uniform waited on the observation deck above the canyon. Her cap was pulled down until it met the sunglasses she wore. Beneath it she flashed a friendly smile.

"Good morning," she said. "It'll just be the two of us today. Hope you don't mind."

"Not at all. What could be better than a private tour?"

The guide grinned. "I had a school group scheduled, but they were hit by a case of chicken pox this morning, so they packed up and went home."

Jessica smiled. "Too bad they had to cut their trip short. But I'm here doing some research and their misfortune may turn out to be a godsend."

The ranger extended a petite hand. "I'm Michelle."

"Jessica Sinclair, with the *Colorado Explorer.*"

"So, what sort of research are you doing?" Michelle opened the gate above the metal stairway leading to the trailhead.

"I'm working on an article about the recently discovered ruin near the foot of the mesa," Jessica replied as they began their descent on the steep trail.

"Thought I'd do a little homework before I move on to the site."

"I'd be happy to help any way I can. I live just a few miles away in Cortez."

A local could be useful. Jessica made a mental note and stopped periodically to snap pictures as they made their way down the rocky trail into the canyon.

"I haven't heard much about the new site yet," Michelle commented. "I believe they're only doing preliminary studies."

"All the better. Being first with the story is what we want. I really want to do this article justice, but this is all new stuff to me." She felt her face flush at her own honesty. Maybe she should at least pretend she knew her subject, but "faking it" just wasn't her style.

Michelle didn't appear to notice. "I know an archaeologist arrived a week or so ago. He's probably your best bet."

"I'm headed out there as soon as we're done. And I plan to meet with the rancher who brought in the artifacts, too."

"McCabe?" A frown crossed Michelle's face. "Watch yourself if you do."

"What do you mean?"

"Well, don't put this in your article, but he has kind of—shall we say—a reputation around here."

"Really?" Jessica asked, curious about Michelle's tone of apprehension. "Sounds like an interesting character."

"Interesting isn't the word I'd choose, but you're the writer. I'll just say he's not a very nice person and leave it at that." Michelle seemed anxious to change the subject and took the lead. "Watch your step here," she cautioned. "The gravel can slide under your feet."

"You said his name's McCabe?" Jessica picked her way across the patch of loose rock.

"Yes, Jonathan McCabe. He's been in the area a long time. Inherited the ranch from his father."

"You don't think he'd cooperate even if it meant getting his name in print?" Jessica felt confident she could find a way to get what she wanted.

Michelle shook her head. "Haven't heard of him being cooperative about anything lately."

"Well, hopefully, I'll be able to work with the archaeologist." Jessica refused to let the gray cloud cast a shadow on her plans.

Michelle smiled. "I'm sure you'll enjoy working with *him*." She shot a sideways grin in Jessica's direction and raised her eyebrows.

Intrigued, Jessica couldn't keep the corners of her mouth from turning upward. "Care to elaborate?"

"I haven't met him, but I've seen him around town. Jet-black hair and blue eyes. Quite attractive."

"Well, I am here on business, but I guess there's no harm in enjoying the scenery."

Michelle grinned. "My sentiments exactly."

Approaching the ruin, Jessica maneuvered down the rocky slope to snap some more shots of the main structure. "Amazing, isn't it? Hard to believe it's been here almost a thousand years."

"Actually, Cliff Palace was built around twelve hundred A.D., although the mesa was inhabited by the Anasazi more than nine hundred years earlier. This ruin is especially well- preserved because of the shelter of the canyon wall."

"Why do you suppose they built it here?"

Michelle shrugged. "Maybe they moved here from the top of the mesa during a drought. They'd have been closer to the water in the bottom of the canyon and garnered some protection from the heat." Michelle shaded her eyes with her hand as she scanned the rocky walls. "Or maybe wars with other tribes drove them here. Who can say for sure?"

Jessica ran her hand across one of the stone walls. "Fascinating." She hesitated, noticing an odd warmth flow through her hand along with a faint pulsating sensation. What a strange feeling. It was almost as if the walls themselves had something to say.

Jessica stooped low and entered one of the small rooms. "They weren't very large people, were they?"

"No. Four feet or slightly taller."

"Any idea what each of the rooms was used for?"

"The larger round rooms were gathering rooms." Michelle pulled a brochure from her pocket and unfolded it, exposing a diagram of the structure. "The smaller ones were probably sleeping rooms and food storage."

Jessica pointed to the drawing. "What about this area between the structure and the cave wall?"

"Refuse disposal mostly. Sometimes in the dead of winter it was used as a burial place."

Jessica made a face. "Oh, yuck. That's gross."

Michelle shrugged. "That was life back then."

"How about this round room in the front? It looks like it's below ground."

"That's the kiva." Michelle motioned toward the ladder a few yards away. "It was a ceremonial chamber."

"Wow." Jessica walked over to the ladder, snapping several photographs as she moved toward it.

The radio on Michelle's hip buzzed noisily. "Michelle, you copy?" Michelle motioned to Jessica as she pulled the two-way from its holster. "Go ahead and go down. I'll be along in a minute."

Jessica grasped the top rung of the ladder and descended into the dark hole. A tiny stream of light came from the opening in the roof where the ladder stood.

The room was small, and a wide stone ledge skirted part of its circumference. In the center, a circular depression in the stone marked where ceremonial fires once burned.

The air was heavy, the light dim and eerie. Sensations of the presence she'd experienced yesterday were very strong here. She snapped a picture. The flash sent an uncomfortable feeling through her, a sense she was disturbing the sanctity of the place or some dark secrets of its past. She stopped and let the camera hang from the strap around her neck.

Drawn into the mood with mental pictures of rituals that had taken place here centuries before, she sat on the cold stone bench and beckoned her imagination to journey into another world. A chill ran through her as a cool, damp breeze hit her. Goose bumps rose on her arms beneath her flannel shirt. She rubbed them away. Her heartbeat quickened.

She glanced around the room, visualizing the bench lined with half-clothed beings, bronzed from days in the sun and weathered by the elements. Closing her eyes, she saw a clear picture in her mind. She could see herself seated among them. Dark eyes glistened in the firelight as a hum began in her ears. The chant of the primitive group called to the spirits. "Aaahmmm, aaahmmm." The whispered droning parted her lips and flowed through her memory.

She opened her eyes and her gaze was drawn like a magnet to a small hole near the fire pit. A pinpoint of blue light formed in the center of the opening. Slowly, it grew larger. The light, like reflections through a prism, changed from blue to white then became multi-colored. Spinning in the circle, the light intensified, mesmerizing Jessica with its hypnotic effect. Gradually, the colored light expanded until it covered the dirt floor.

A deep male voice broke the silence and spoke barely above a whisper. "You hear me speak, Daughter of the Ages?"

Jessica looked around warily. "Who—who's there?" She glanced at the square opening above her. She saw no one there.

Her eyes went back to the light that now vibrated and fluctuated in size. An odd calmness settled in.

"I knew one day you would come," the voice spoke again, emotion thick in its tone.

"Is this some sort of cheap trick?" This must be part of a sideshow for the tourists.

The light grew larger then moved rapidly around the room. Faster and faster it spun, forming a funnel cloud. As it spun, it created a wind that pushed Jessica back against the wall. Surprised by the events, but strangely having no desire to flee, she allowed herself to be enveloped by the spinning cloud. The light from it was now blue and lavender and she shielded her face from the fierceness of the wind with her arms. Her hair whipped into her eyes as the cloud whirled.

"I have waited long for you, Daughter of the Ages." The voice surrounded her totally.

Her heart beat faster as the realization set in that this was no joke. Who was here with her? "Why are you calling me that? Who are you?" *What the hell is going on?*

"You ask too many questions. It is best simply to listen."

She opened her mouth to speak but could not. Some power outside of herself controlled her vocal chords. Powerless to do anything but sit wide-eyed and observe, her mind filled with confusion.

"You ask why I call you Daughter of the Ages. I have waited for nearly seven centuries to be heard. You are the one I have waited for." His words carried on the howling wind and echoed through the chamber. "You ask who I am. I am the spirit of the four winds that whisper across native lands. I am the spirit of the

eagle that flies overhead and looks down upon the
generations who have passed before us."

An image formed of an eagle in flight. The eagle
then dissolved into many small birds that flew at
Jessica, barely missing her. Their wing tips grazed her
face as they brushed past and vanished into
nothingness.

"I am the spirit of the dove whose mournful cooing
speaks of injustice for the passing of a civilization. The
passing of my people."

The cloud grew light and translucent and a forceful
wind blew, carrying with it tiny particles that stung
Jessica's face. She raised her hand to shield her eyes
as the debris pecked at her cheeks and the light grew
brighter still.

"What do you want with me?" Jessica squeaked at
last. "Why do you speak to me?"

The voice thundered in the tiny space. "You are the
Daughter of the Ages. The one who has come to hear
my voice."   Then softly it said, "You have come to me
after so many years."

Bewildered, Jessica fumbled for an explanation.
"I'm here doing research, there must be some
mistake."

"The spirit of all spirits makes no mistake, young
one."

"What is it you're talking about? What is it you
want?"

"Questions. I knew you would have many. You must
be patient, for not all can be revealed to you now. You
must first understand why."

"If you can speak to me, why can't I see you?"
Jessica persisted, grasping for a logical explanation.
"Show yourself."

Silence hung in the air as the wind stilled and the
cloud grew smaller and hovered at the end of the room.
Bit by bit, the wrinkled face of an Indian shaman

formed in the haze, the headdress of a white bison upon his aged head. Black horns curled upward in the woolly mass. Long white hair flowed from beneath the head gear and down onto the faded buckskin that covered his shoulders. The pelt of a coyote with its shriveled eyeholes and white teeth hung ominously next to his wrinkled neck.

"This is my image as you would recognize me, young one," he said.

Jessica sat back, stunned. Why was this ancient thing, this—spirit speaking to her? "But you're an Indian spirit. What do you want with me?"

"You carry the blood of your native mothers."

"I don't know what you're talking about." She held her hands to her temples and the words flowed from her more out of confusion than anything else.

"It brings me sadness to know that the blood of the ancients has been so thinned you do not even know of your ancestry, young one."

"Stop calling me young one. I'm a grown woman, for God's sake."

"You are very young in the scheme of things. Your spirit is fresh and new. You are not here of your choice, but of the choice of destiny. You have heard my voice. You have been called here to help the souls of many."

"What do you mean *called*? How do you know you have the right person?"

"You hear my voice, therefore, I know."

A shiver ran through her. The answer struck a deep chord. There was a heavy silence then Jessica numbly asked her next question. "What is this helping of souls you talk about?"

"In time it shall be revealed to you. Go now. Come to peace with what you have seen and heard. When your spirit understands, you will seek me again."

The cloud dissipated as quickly as it had appeared. Jessica watched, spellbound, aware only of the hammering of her own heart. The cloud moved toward her, enveloped her then faded away, leaving its mist upon her face. She reached up and touched the tiny droplets and rubbed them between her fingers, the moisture bringing the dream world crashing into reality.

CHAPTER TWO

"Everything okay down there?" Michelle's voice echoed through the stone chamber, pulling Jessica back to this world. She blinked, leaned forward on the stone bench, and ran a cold hand through her hair. Her stiff fingers brought the realization of the chill that had crept into her bones.

Jessica finally found words and sputtered her response. "Uh, yeah. Yeah, everything's fine." What else could she say? Had she just experienced the most unbelievable hallucination of her life? Or had she truly stepped through some supernatural portal and come face to face with a bonafide ancient spirit?

"You were so quiet, I was beginning to wonder," Michelle called. "Hang on. I'll be right down."

"Don't bother. I'm coming up." Jessica grabbed a rung of the pine ladder and climbed on trembling legs back into the warm sunlight.

"You see a ghost or something?" Michelle asked laughingly, her eyes meeting Jessica's as she emerged through the opening.

The look Jessica shot back must have said it all.

Michelle raised a questioning eyebrow. "I was only kidding. You look a little pale and wide-eyed."

"It's a little bright out here." Jessica pulled her sunglasses from her shirt pocket and hid her eyes behind them. For the moment, she'd like to keep her secrets to herself.

Michelle gave her an odd look and leaned closer then lightly touched Jessica's shirtsleeve. "You look kind of clammy. Sure you're okay?"

Jessica resented the prying. "Nothing to worry about."

"Don't you want to hear about the kiva? It's one of the better parts of the tour." Michelle stepped toward the ladder and put her boot on the top rung.

"Yeah, but I think I'll listen from up here if you don't mind." She wasn't sure what had happened, but she damned sure wasn't going back down. Not now anyway. Jessica rubbed the chill from her arms, grateful for a few minutes to get her wits about her, while Michelle rattled off a tour-guide monologue.

"Like I said earlier, the kiva was an underground chamber used for religious ceremonies." Michelle unfolded the map and spread it on a short wall then pointed to a diagram of the kiva.

Jessica half-listened to the hum of Michelle's voice as she went through her tourist version of the architectural aspects of the structure. Each kiva has six pilasters on the inside wall which helped support the structure. This bench-like ledge the pilasters rest on stored pottery or ceremonial objects. This large hole in the center of the room was the fire pit."

Jessica's interest peaked, she pointed at the map with a trembling finger. "What about this one? The small hole here?"

"That's called the *sipapu*. The spirit hole. It was believed to be an entrance to the underworld."

A chill ran through Jessica's body that touched her to the bone and surfaced in a shiver.

"Are you cold?" Michelle asked. "Sorry I left you down there so long. I had to take a call on the radio. The boss. You know how it is."

"Don't worry about it." Jessica rubbed her clammy palms on her jeans. "You know, I need to get out to the site, if you don't mind cutting this short." Much as a part of her was fascinated by this place, an overwhelming need to get away from the kiva engulfed her.

"No problem. You've seen most of the ruin anyway." Michelle took several long strides back toward the trail.

Jessica followed close, casting a final wary glance over her shoulder. Whatever, whoever she'd seen, she just wanted to put distance between her and it. The two climbed the steep incline in silence.

Michelle clamped the metal gate lock into place at the head of the trail. "Let me know if I can be of any help."

"What's the best way to get out to the site?"

"Go back toward Cortez and take the first dirt road to the left about half a mile down the highway."

"How far is it from the main road?"

"I'd say at least five miles. Pretty rugged. You weren't planning on driving *that*, were you?" Michelle tipped her head in the direction of Jessica's car. "It takes a four-wheel drive to navigate the back country."

Great. "Maybe I'd better hike in instead."

"You could. You'd better be ready if you do." Michelle paused, rubbing her jaw thoughtfully. "You know, there's a place in town that does Jeep tours. I think they also have rentals."

Jessica let out a small sigh of relief. "I'll check it out. Thanks. You've been a great help."

"Good luck with your story. You can reach me anytime through the Visitors Center. Call if you need me." Michelle checked the lock on the gate one last time as Jessica started toward her car. "You be careful out there."

Be careful.

An eerie feeling ran through Jessica as the words echoed in her ears once more. "Thanks," she called over her shoulder. It wasn't likely she'd forget.

Half an hour later, Jessica drove down the narrow street that wound through the old downtown section of Cortez. Quaint buildings displayed signs depicting an assortment of tourist attractions. The scattered appearance of pickup trucks and bronzed faces beneath cowboy hats were visual reminders the little town nestled in the heart of a rich farming community.

Jessica had been through this area several times when she was traveling, and had never so much as stopped for a cup of coffee. She grinned as she passed the city park where a huge white and red banner announced nightly Indian dancers. She'd stepped into a different world—and she liked it. It provided a refreshing escape for her scalded soul. This place was alive, and she had thought of nothing but death for so many months.

The charm of the town's old brick buildings soon gave way to a newer section with the typical chain stores. A half block ahead, she spotted a sign that read Mountain Jeep Tours.

"This must be the place." The row of shiny black Jeeps with tan rag tops and gold lettering on the doors didn't leave much doubt.

A cowbell announced her arrival as she stepped inside and let the heavy glass door close behind her. Curtains made of wooden beads covered a doorway behind the counter constructed of rough lumber. The curtains rustled and a tall form appeared. She could barely believe her eyes as the Indian man she'd seen the previous day at the Visitor's Center approached.

"Well, good afternoon," he said with a smug smile.

Perhaps she should pretend not to recognize him. "I need to rent a Jeep," she said quickly.

"I know."

The quiet stare from his dark eyes with their strange light pierced through her. She shifted, frowned, and cocked her head to one side. "What do you mean, you know?"

"I've been expecting you." He reached under the counter, pulled out a form and laid it before her.

"What are you talking about? You couldn't possibly have known." She hadn't known herself. Frankly, she wasn't in the mood for his foolish games.

"How long?" he asked.

"How long?"

"How long do you want the Jeep?"

She leaned over the counter toward him. "Why don't you tell me? You seem to know everything else."

"Ma'am, I'm just trying to rent you a Jeep," he said, unsmiling this time.

"I need it for the afternoon."

"I only have a daily rate," he replied. "Not a half."

"Then I'll pay for a whole day." She eyed him suspiciously. She'd had about enough of his smug attitude. "I remember you from yesterday at the mesa."

He shrugged, pulled a pen from a drawer behind the counter and pushed it in her direction. "Forty dollars."

"Excuse me."

"Forty dollars for the day," he repeated.

"Why did you tell me to be careful?"

He pushed the form toward her. "Fill out the paperwork and you can be on your way."

He pulled a set of keys from the pegboard behind him and placed them on the counter.

Hurriedly, she filled out the form, aware of his mysterious eyes on her.

"Going into the back country?" he asked.

"Yes." Not that it was any of his business.

"Best to be careful."

She stopped short. "I believe you said that before. I'm quite sure I can take care of myself, thank you." She signed the form with a flourish and shoved it back across the counter.

"Lots of danger out there," he persisted as he placed the keys in her hand and pressed them in her palm.

"Danger?" She bit the inside of her cheek in annoyance and looked at him as if she hadn't the slightest clue what he was talking about.

"Forty dollars," he said as he pushed the buttons on an antique cash register. A bell rang and the drawer popped open.

"Yeah. Forty dollars." Exasperated, she reached in her purse, pulled out two twenty-dollar bills and placed them on the counter. "Do you always speak in riddles?"

"As time goes by, you will see." He put the money in the cash register and handed her the receipt. Turning on the heel of his boot, he walked back through the curtained opening and was gone.

Jessica sighed and looked at the keys in her hand. She hoped the archaeologist wasn't as strange as this guy, or she was in for some trouble.

The Jeep dipped into a large rut that jarred her so hard her teeth slammed together and her neck all but disappeared for a moment. Why were the best stories always in some godforsaken place? She shifted back in the seat.

Was this why everyone was so damned concerned with her safety? Well, it would take more than a few rocks in the road to turn her away. They hadn't been where she'd been for the last three years. No one here had a clue how important this story was to her. She'd put her life on hold for far too long. Now the universe had thrown her a chance at her dreams, and nothing, absolutely nothing, was going to stop her.

Eager to get to her destination, she smiled. Mister Gorgeous Archaeologist, huh. God. How long had it been since she'd had time to think about a man? A few more months and she could have been officially declared a nun. With everything riding on this story, the last thing she needed was some great looking guy to set her neglected hormones into hyper-drive. Like hell, she'd let that happen.

The Jeep hit another rut and the jolt sent a stab of pain down her spine. She'd come more than five miles on what was little more than an old wagon trail cut through rugged wilderness. Surely it couldn't be much farther.

She pulled to a stop. Just ahead, the trail ended at the rim of a canyon. Navigating the deep ruts and protruding rocks, the Jeep bounced at every turn of the wheels. Jessica eased the vehicle down the incline and into the small gorge that lay at the foot of the mesa.

She scanned the area, at first unimpressed. Weathered sandstone formations jutted upward and formed the canyon walls. Mother Nature's camouflage did its job so well any evidence of ancient life was hidden almost completely. As the Jeep bounced down into the canyon, Jessica could make out the faint outline of what could once have been a wall at the foot of a massive rock formation. Wow. No wonder it had remained hidden for so long.

A dark green SUV was parked next to what appeared to be a huge rockslide. A large rectangle of metal stakes marked with caution tape surrounded an area at the base of the slide. Well, this must be the place. Her searching gaze took in the canyon wall that hid the ruin. The mass of rock protruded from the hillside and neatly wrapped itself around the base of the mesa. She grabbed her camera and snapped a few shots.

"Something I can do for you?" a male voice called out. From behind the rock formation stepped the tall silhouette of a man with the sun at his back. The sun's rays highlighted the form in tight-fitting jeans and a khaki shirt that moved in a gentle breeze.

She squinted, trying to make out his face. The sunlight blocked out the view until he stepped closer. His black hair reflected steel-blue highlights in the afternoon sun. His striking blue eyes drew hers in like a magnet. She couldn't pull her gaze away from their deepness. They held her almost hypnotically and left her standing there, staring and momentarily speechless.

He waited for a minute in silence. "Something I can help you with?" he repeated.

"Oh." She realized her hands had gone sweaty as a warm rush jetted through her body. "Ah. Jessica Sinclair—with the *Colorado Explorer*." She made a quick pass across her jeans before reaching to shake his hand.

"Alex Nakai." His large rough hand encompassed her small one. A warm tingle shot up her arm as they touched. He let go slowly, a trace of a smile on his face, a distinct twinkle in his eyes.

At that moment, a large male golden retriever with a red bandana around his neck bounded from behind the rock and sat next to Alex. He pushed against Alex's leg with his nose as if requesting an introduction of his own. Jessica acknowledged his presence with a smile in the dog's direction.

"This is Yellow Dog." Alex pushed the dog's nose away and gave him an affectionate pat on the neck.

Jessica extended her hand and the dog stepped forward wagging his tail. "Quite a road to get into this place," she said, scratching Yellow Dog behind the ears.

"Yes, it is. You've gone to a lot of trouble to get here." He glanced around her at the Jeep parked next to his vehicle. "What brings you?"

"Like I said, I'm with the *Colorado Explorer.* I was hoping I could have a little of your time to talk about the ruin."

"*Colorado Explorer?*"

"Yes. The magazine. I'm working on a story about this site."

The color left his tanned face and the blue eyes went hard and steely. "A reporter?" he asked through a clenched jaw.

"Yes. Do you mind if I ask you a few questions?" She paused, her eagerness waning. "If this isn't a good time—"

"I'm extremely busy," he said with a scowl. Crossing his arms, he turned partially away from her, obviously avoiding her gaze. He looked down at the ground then back at her with a set jaw before he turned his attentions in the direction of the ruin.

"I won't take much of your time," she said, mystified by his sudden change of demeanor. What had happened? She damned sure couldn't afford to alienate him. Without his input, her story was dead in the water before it got started.

"We're not ready for any press releases yet. Contact the University in a month or so. They may be willing to give you a statement then."

"But it was the University that told me I could come out here and take some photographs." She looked away, contemplating how to handle this switch in attitude. She wasn't going to let him brush her off so easily. "They told me you were the expert." She shot him a flirtatious smile that evaporated in the icy barrier he'd thrown up.

"There are no findings to report. This study is strictly preliminary and strictly confidential."

She shifted her feet in the sand. He wasn't going to make it easy for her. But she'd come too far to be put off by some guy with a chip on his shoulder and a stubborn attitude. Maybe all he needed was a little prodding. "I understand this site may predate any other discovery on the mesa," she said as she fiddled with her camera and contemplated taking one more quick shot.

Turning to face her, he stonily stepped in front of her. "I wouldn't know about that."

"Funny, I was told you were doing the carbon dating here."

His eyes flashed. "I don't know where you got your information, but why don't you go back to your magazine and maybe later on the University will have a press release for you."

"Press release? Dammit, I've come here to get a story." The words no more left her lips than she regretted them. She sucked in a deep breath as if by doing so she could retrieve her statement. She had to get a grip. "I don't understand your objections. My magazine is well respected in the scientific community for appropriate representation of things like this."

His brow furrowed and with long strides he stepped to the Jeep and opened the door. He motioned for her to get in. His message was loud and clear. "Maybe you've just got the wrong archaeologist, lady. And be careful driving out of here. There are some really nasty ruts in that road."

All the magnetism of their first look evaporated into thin air as she climbed into the vehicle. She wanted to push the issue and confront him, but she didn't trust herself or her emotions at the moment. What the hell was wrong with her? This was her big chance and she'd behaved stupidly. Another slip-up and any hope she had of getting her story would be lost. Her best bet was to get out and regroup.

She slammed the door and turned the key in the ignition. A cloud of dust engulfed her as she whipped the Jeep around and headed back in the direction of the highway.

Alex watched the taillights of the Jeep make its way up the hill. *Damn the luck. A reporter.* If that wasn't just what he needed right now.

"Hmmph," he grunted. His experience with reporters was enough in itself to leave him cold. Even the scenario was the same. A sexy, good-looking woman trying to schmooze him into telling her everything he knew. Well, he wasn't stupid enough to make the same mistake twice.

The last time he'd gotten hooked, hooked really good. He'd even slept with the woman, and damned if he didn't wake up the next morning with his picture on the front page of the local paper. She'd made him look like an ass. And that was probably only half the complications this one could cause.

He was on this dig because he'd cut a deal with the head of the archaeology department. Offering to supervise the project, he'd only asked for three weeks here—alone. To his surprise, they'd accepted his proposal. Though last summer's forest fires had them desperate for experienced people, his trump card was his expertise in carbon dating. At this site specifically, that made him invaluable.

The fires had devastated Mesa Verde and its surrounding forests as well as thousands of acres in New Mexico. The flames had laid bare hundreds of ruins and archaeological sites in their wake. With manpower short, only the most promising sites were under consideration for immediate excavation. The unusual nature of the artifacts at this one put it at the top of the list. And those artifacts were the reason he wanted some time here—without interruptions.

In only two-and-a-half weeks, this place would be crawling with the crew from the University. He'd also agreed to do some preliminary work while he was here. When the team did arrive, if he couldn't come up with some solid reasons for them to proceed with the excavation, they'd get orders to catalog the site and seed it over.

What they were looking for here wasn't what interested him. The early findings suggested it could be one of the oldest sites to be discovered in the area. That could be significant. He had a very small window of time to prove a theory that could rock the archaeological community to its foundation. And this woman, this reporter, had the potential of blowing it all to hell.

Who at the University had told her he was here? He was supposed to be in charge of this project and he'd asked for it not to be made public knowledge yet. If she did write a story, checked into his past and came up with the other article. Damn, if she didn't potentially hold his future in her hand—a soft, feminine hand.

Why did they all have to be so good-looking? His mind stopped at the picture of her as she'd climbed into the Jeep a few feet in front of him. That woman needed to buy a pair of jeans with a little sag in the backside. She'd been close enough he'd caught the sweet smell of her as she stormed past.

Alex, you've been in the field way too long. He'd spent six solid months in southern Mexico before this, nobody but him, the dog and the guys for weeks on end. It was enough to make a man a little crazy. It didn't matter. This time he'd save his heart and his career.

He couldn't afford the distraction. There was too much on the line, and he didn't have time for this nonsense.

Reaching into the pocket of his jeans, he pulled out the chip of black and white pottery once again. One square inch of pottery from the past had started a landslide in his life. It had made him a driven man, changed his career path and started a fire in his belly that wouldn't rest.

Since that day, the piece had haunted Alex. The possibility had kept him awake nights. He'd told a colleague about it, and the colleague had laughed. He'd trusted a reporter with his speculation, and she'd fabricated a story that made him look like a fool to the rest of his profession.

Now this woman— He had to protect his secret until he could prove it to the world. And he had to protect it from yet another nosy reporter. For somebody who was, by nature, a logical, slow-moving kind of guy, he'd somehow landed himself a lap full this time.

He glanced around and turned back toward the ruin. The only thing he'd never anticipated was the feeling in his soul this place churned up. But he couldn't take time to dissect it. He had to move on. Time was too valuable and too limited.

Alex looked up at the sky as the sun made its way toward the mountains to the west. Yet another precious day was about to pass. He walked back to the ruin trying to wipe the imprint of Jessica Sinclair from his mind.

—◆—

Minutes later, Jessica slammed the heel of her hand against the steering wheel hard enough to send a shot of pain up her arm. "How the heck am I going to get a story out of that guy?" she asked herself. First, she had some ancient ghost trying to tell her she was here to save her ancestry, and now Mister Gorgeous had turned out to be some neurotic schizophrenic. *So much for squeezing in a little rest and relaxation on this trip.*

One minute the guy was all smiles and flirting eyes, and the next he was ordering her back into her Jeep. Okay, he was a great looking guy, but looks weren't everything. Well, maybe they wouldn't count for as much without those devastating blue eyes—but they certainly weren't everything.

Jessica slowed. *What the heck is this?* A few hundred yards ahead, a black pickup truck was stopped crossways in the steep rutted road. A tall thin man in a cowboy hat leaned against the driver's door. He was as scraggly as the water deprived pine trees protruding from the rocks above him. His haggard and weather-beaten face looked intimidating. When he motioned to her, she stopped. A bit apprehensively, she locked the door and rolled down her window as he approached the Jeep.

"Good afternoon," she said.

"This is private property. Ain't no tourists allowed up here," he growled.

"I'm sorry. I didn't realize I was trespassing. I'm not really a tourist. My name's Jessica Sinclair and I'm with the *Colorado Explorer*." She offered him her hand then retracted it, when it was clear he wasn't going to shake it, then shifted nervously beneath his withering gaze. He made her feel like a guilty child making excuses to the principal. "I came out here to interview Dr. Nakai down at the site."

"Nakai, huh? Well it's my land you're drivin' across to get there," he snarled through clenched teeth. "I want you and all these other nosy people out of here. Now!" He threw her a hateful look as he ground his boot into the dirt for emphasis and stormed to his truck.

"No reason to get upset. I'm leaving," she called after him as he jumped into the truck. He spattered the Jeep in a hail of pebbles as he spun the tires and drove away at a frightening speed on the narrow winding trail. She looked after him in amazement then let out a long breath. If he hadn't left, she would have. She wasn't arguing with a madman in the middle of nowhere.

"Jonathan McCabe." The realization hit home at almost the same time the dust lifted. He said it was his land. It had to be. Not a very charming guy. Not that she could say much for Alex Nakai's manners either. What was the problem with the two of them? What a stroke of luck, not one but two jerks to fight her way through to get her story. "Oh, God, why me?" she moaned. Steering the Jeep up the rocky incline, she climbed the rutted road and rounded a steep turn before starting a slow descent toward a treed area several hundred yards ahead. A shower of small rock pelted the hood, followed by several larger pieces and a cloud of dust.

Then she heard it. Jessica glanced up the hillside to the right. A massive boulder careened down the mountainside headed straight at her. Terrifyingly close. She pulled the steering wheel to the left. The Jeep skidded toward an embankment. Its wheels bottomed out in a huge rut. The Jeep tipped, slamming her into the door.

A spinning sensation followed. The world seemed to move in slow motion. The seat belt cut painfully into her collarbone. Her stunned brain at last got the message she was rolling down the hillside. She bounced around like a piece of popcorn in a harness. One final jerk launched the side of her head into the window. Smashing glass and blinding pain were followed by a warm gush down the side of her face.

A fleeting glimpse of someone on the road above her registered, just before it all blurred and faded to blackness.

CHAPTER THREE

"Awaken, Daughter of the Ages, you have much to do before you sleep." A hazy image spoke through the foggy cloud in Jessica's brain. She shook her head and blinked, trying to focus.

"Miss Sinclair. Miss Sinclair." The male voice came from a tanned face framed by long dark hair. A blue cloudless sky showed tinges of pink behind him as she drifted in and out of a fog struggling to regain her bearings. The realization crept in that she lay sprawled in the dirt. *What the hell happened? Where am I?*

"Miss Sinclair, you okay?" the man asked as he knelt with Jessica's head resting on his lap. Her vision clearing, she recognized the face hovering above her as the man from the Jeep rental.

"I think so," she said, confused and shaky. "What happened?"

"You're very lucky. Your Jeep is at the bottom of the ravine. Good sized boulder on top of it."

"Oh my God." Jessica put a hand to her head and struggled to clear her brain. Her heart jumped to her throat as she remembered the boulder careening down the hillside. The rest was a blur.

"Move slowly," he cautioned.

Taking his advice, Jessica rolled her shoulders and moved each limb, expecting to be in pain. Strange as it seemed, she was completely unharmed. When she raised herself up on her elbows in the gravel, something jabbed into tender flesh.

"Ouch."

"You need a doctor?" Concern wrinkled his brow.

"No, just a pair of tweezers." She pulled a large pine needle from her shirtsleeve. Sitting there in the dirt, she looked curiously at the man who'd appeared in her life three—or was it four times in two days. "Who are you, anyway?"

"Excuse me?"

"Everywhere I go you're there."

"This is true. Everywhere I go I'm there."

Jessica rolled her eyes. His limericks were too much for her right now. "Oh fine. Do you have a name?"

He gave her a sideways smirk. "I've been called many things, but you can call me Nechi."

What a peculiar person. "Nechi. Somehow that suits you. Do you have a last name?"

"Yes. But you can call me Nechi."

Grinning, he rose to his feet and offered an oddly soft hand. Jessica accepted and he pulled her to a stand. Gingerly she brushed at the dust that covered her, still half-expecting to find an injury.

A sharp mental picture of the accident flashed through Jessica's brain. Pain shot through her head and her hand instinctively went to where she'd taken the hard blow into the window. There had been a warm gush—she knew she was bleeding, but now there was nothing, not a trace—not a bump or a scratch. How could that be?

Nechi seemed to read her thoughts. "Spirit did a good job for you, did he not?"

"Huh?" *Spirit.* Jessica shot him a questioning glance, but was taken back by the serious expression in his eyes. "Yeah. I guess I was pretty lucky." Wishing to change the subject, she studied the tire marks in the gravel. The deep gouges ended at the edge of the road. She grasped her stomach. A knot formed at the very thought of going over.

"The Jeep's down there." He pointed toward the embankment a few yards ahead.

Stepping near the edge, Jessica peered into the ravine. Only the tires of the Jeep, which was now buried in an evergreen cove, were visible. The vehicle lay on its side with a huge boulder resting on the passenger door.

"I should scold you for not wearing your seat belt, but it may have saved your life."

"I had it on," she replied, a sudden wave of emotion washing over her. The soreness in her collarbone confirmed that.

Nechi raised his eyebrows and smiled. "Then Spirit did a *very* good job."

"Why do you keep saying that?" She rubbed her shoulder in annoyance.

He only shrugged in response. His comments rang uncomfortably close to those of the ancient in the kiva. Perhaps sometime, when she felt a little less close to death herself, she would question Nechi about this spirit he referred to.

"What are you doing out here in the middle of nowhere anyway?" Jessica asked, hoping to force away the eeriness of the silence that had fallen upon them.

"Taking care of business," he replied. With that, he began a rapid descent down the embankment toward the Jeep. Gravel scattered beneath his dust-covered boots. "I'll check to see if your camera equipment is salvageable," he called over his shoulder. "Then I'll give you a lift back into town."

How did he know she had camera equipment? She couldn't recall mentioning it to him. Standing at the top of the hill, she watched him maneuver his slender frame into the back of the vehicle. Moments later a sigh of relief escaped as Nechi gave her a thumbs-up and waved the camera case.

Who was this strange man who constantly kept appearing? And what the hell was he doing out here? She rubbed her temples where a dull ache was beginning and dropped to her knees in the dirt to rest. She'd had enough excitement for one day—more than she'd bargained for.

———

Jessica bit her lip. "I'll be just fine, Miriam. I told you I'm all but back to normal."

"Are you sure? You sound a little strained to me." The voice on the other end of the pay phone was Miriam Westmoreland, a grief counselor from Hospice who'd taken a special interest in Jessica and her aunt. Actually, she'd more or less made Jessica her own private project. "You know I can see right through you when you're not telling me the whole truth, Jessica." The two had become quite close and Jessica had shared a lot with Miriam. *Maybe too much.* Miriam seemed to sense something weighed heavy on Jessica's mind.

"I'd say it's been an interesting trip so far, to say the least." Jessica struggled to make conversation, but it was definitely time to change the subject. She was squeamish about sharing the strangeness of the past two days with anyone, including Miriam.

"You know me, I just wanted to check on you. The movers are coming in the morning and I wanted to talk to you before I left for Washington." There was a long pause. "You sound tired—or something." Miriam was fishing, darn her and her intuition. She referred to herself as a "borderline" psychic. Jessica knew how hard it was to hide anything from her.

She fingered the handwritten telephone message she'd found tucked under her door. She glanced over her shoulder to see if anyone was in earshot. The rustic cabins at the lodge had no phones or televisions and her cell was cutting in and out because of the mountains. The pay phone in the lobby of the lodge didn't provide much privacy.

"There have been some rather odd things happening." Jessica spoke in a low voice.

"I'm sorry, hon, I can barely hear you."

Great. She wasn't going to shout it in a public place. "Uh—never mind. I'll call you when you get settled."

"Now, Jessica," Miriam prodded. "I know Aunt Helen's passing brought back a lot of bad memories for you. I've told you it's normal to grieve for other lost loved ones all over again when things like this happen."

Subconscious grief. Was that what was causing all this strangeness? "Something seems to have brought back more than memories."

"I have no doubt it's dredged up some childhood fears of being left alone and such. We've talked about that. Remember?"

"Of course I do. But tell me Miriam, can it cause— have you ever heard of—"

"Yes, what is it? Talk to me."

"Has anyone you've worked with mentioned seeing apparitions—or things that weren't really there?"

There was silence on the other end. "Jessica, a lot of strange things can happen when you're in an emotional state. And consider where you are. The desert Southwest is one of the most spiritual places on earth."

Maybe Miriam was right. The incident on the road, the voice in the kiva, even the strange feeling she'd had after the accident, they could all be reasonably explained. Were they really so different from the visions and voices she'd experienced after her parents were killed? Not really. Only different because they were likely influenced by her surroundings.

"I suppose you're right. I probably just need some rest."

"I'm sure you do. But Jessica—" There was hesitation in her voice. "Things happen for a reason, don't be too quick to turn your back completely on this. It's possible for grief to elevate our awareness to a higher plane. There may be a message."

Oh dear. Psychic Miriam was about to speak.

"You know, Miriam, I'm glad you called. Now, you stop fussing over me and get back to your packing. Everything is just fine here. We'll keep in touch."

"Now you sound like the Jessica I know. Take care of yourself, girl, and try to relax and have a good time. That will help more than anything. Bye now."

"Bye." Jessica hung up the phone. She let out her breath. No matter what anyone said, there was only one path she was going to take, the one leading straight back to her story and a fresh start. It was time to put everything out of her mind and climb back into the driver's seat of her own life. As for the rest of it, in Miriam's words, this too would pass, it had before and it would again.

Jessica ate dinner and walked off the funky mood the phone call had pulled her into. The past was gone and she was prepared to leave it behind. Back in her cabin, she slipped into a hot bath her achy muscles and exhausted mind both needed the comfort of the soothing water. She leaned her head back against the tub, rubbed her neck and let out a huge sigh.

As she relaxed, her mind went to work, attempting to put together the pieces of the day's progress, if there had been any. It had been a rocky start, literally, but tomorrow would be a new day. A quiver of enthusiasm ran through her as she delved into the possibilities that had unfolded in the past twenty-four hours.

The fright of the accident had placed her frustrations on the back burner, but she had to have her focus back on the story first thing in the morning. Nothing that happened today was going to stop her. Except maybe Alex Nakai—he intrigued her—in more ways than one.

Something in the course of their conversation had turned him one hundred and eighty degrees. He'd thrown up deflector shields that would have put the Starship Enterprise to shame. She didn't know what his problem was, but there were ways to get the information she needed. He might be a challenge, but she'd find his soft spot.

A grin claimed her mouth. She'd like to see some of his soft spots. On a scale of one to ten, Alex was about a fourteen. Damn, those amazing eyes were downright hypnotic, even when he was angry— She stopped. *Yeah, six-feet tall with a ten-foot chip on his shoulder.* But she'd have to watch herself. Even when he'd behaved like a jerk, there was still persuasiveness written all over his smile. Jessica's challenge would be to keep swallowing the knot he'd instantly put in the pit of her stomach. No matter. Whatever it took, she'd find the story around him and that site.

McCabe was her other concern. Now there was a man who could cause some real problems. She wasn't about to drive that dangerous road again and chance meeting up with that slug. What made him so wild-eyed and angry, almost like a rabid animal? She'd do some checking around about him. No two ways about it, the next trip into the site would have to be on foot. She could deal with that, too. She'd backpacked in the Colorado mountains many times.

That resolved her direction for tomorrow, although it didn't stop the images bombarding her brain. The whirling picture of the accident still clutched at her throat. It could have all ended there. But it hadn't. Somehow, she had walked away unharmed. It was almost impossible, as if some invisible hand had plucked her out of the Jeep and laid her gently in the dirt. Now she sounded like Miriam. But it seemed too much of a coincidence. Although her logical mind couldn't prove another realm existed, another side of her had always refused to deny the possibility.

The bath water cooled and she wrapped herself in a fluffy white towel wanting only to crawl into bed. The sensual effect of the warm folds of terry cloth on her bare flesh drew the picture of Alex back into her mind. God, those hypnotic blue eyes were stuck in her head and wouldn't leave her alone. A vision of Alex's muscular arms around her flashed in her imagination. She savored the thought for a second then let it go. It had been a very long time since she'd been with a man. *A very long time.* Surely one never forgot how to—

She'd come here to get her story and she couldn't afford this distraction. She ran her hands through her wet hair and let the towel drop to the floor. A smile tugged at the corners of her mouth as she reached for her robe and allowed her imagination to have its way for another fleeting moment. It was all in her head. What could it hurt?

"So you're the reporter who went off the mountain yesterday, huh?" The chubby deputy smiled at her across the counter. A white-haired woman at the dispatch desk turned and inspected Jessica over the top of her wire-rimmed glasses.

"Yes. I need to fill out an accident report," Jessica said. She'd planned to be on her way to the site by now, but it was after ten o'clock. An aching body had kept her awake and demanded some rest this morning. Since she'd gotten such a late start, she might as well take care of this annoying detail today.

The deputy reached under the counter, pulled out several forms and snapped them to a brown clipboard. "I was up there earlier this morning. Damn near a miracle you're still alive."

Jessica grinned. This was what she loved about small towns. The people. Everyone knew everybody else and their business. Anybody new who came to town was a curiosity and an object of the latest gossip. "I was very lucky," she said.

She took in the deputy's appearance with a quick and unobtrusive glance. The khaki uniform barely fastened over his broad mid-section and patches of a white T-shirt could be seen between the buttons. His short stubby hair was unevenly cut and stood up comically in a cowlick at the back.

"They pulled her out of there with a tow truck." Puckering his lips, he whistled between his teeth. "I don't know how you got yourself out in one piece."

"I must have been thrown clear. I woke up at the top of the embankment lying in the dirt."

He looked at her questioningly. "First time I ever saw anybody thrown out of a buckled seat belt." He rubbed his chin. "That sucker was buckled up tight as could be and wouldn't come undone. Looked like something came through the windshield and smashed it together."

She rubbed her shoulder and squinted at him, unable to make any sense of what he was saying. "I have the bruises to prove it was fastened. It almost broke my collarbone when the Jeep rolled."

"Whatever you say, ma'am." The deputy shuffled paperwork on the counter and looked up at her with a twitch of his wrinkled brow.

Puzzled, she took a chair and began filling out the forms. The chatty deputy was only quiet for a few minutes.

"Yep, you're about as lucky as anyone I've ever met. Right next to a miracle someone came along and gave you a lift. You could've been stuck out there on that road for a good long time. Ain't anybody ever goes out there except that archaeologist fellow, and he camps out there a lot of the time."

"I was fortunate that nice young Indian man from the Jeep rental place came by and brought me back."

The deputy let out a loud horselaugh. "Injun? You mean Mr. Nagasaki?" He threw his head back and roared. "He ain't no Injun. He's as Japanese as they come. Came here straight from Japan, him and his wife."

"No. The one named Nechi. He must be one of their employees. He rented me the Jeep and brought me back to town after the accident."

The deputy shrugged. "Nagasaki ain't got no employees, ma'am. Just a small family business. His wife and his boys run the place."

Jessica was becoming annoyed. The man seemed bent on correcting everything she said. But maybe this gossipy deputy could be of some use. "That road is pretty remote," she baited him. "Guess it only goes to the site and Mr. McCabe's land, of course."

"Yeah, McCabe. Ohhh—lucky you didn't run into him up there. Anything goes past his cattle guard, he thinks is fair game for target practice."

"Really? I did run into him on my way out and he wasn't very friendly."

"No, ma'am. Not anymore. Funny thing about him though is he used to be plain hospitable to folks.

Something's gone wrong with him since he started findin' them pots and stuff."

"You mean he hasn't always been like that?"

"Oh hel—heavens no. He's gotten so ornery even his old lady couldn't live with him anymore. She up and left him six weeks ago when all this stuff about the ruin started up."

"Is she still around?" she asked, taking mental notes as she pretended to be engrossed in the paperwork.

"Oh, yeah, she moved into town here. Too bad. Mrs. McCabe's a real nice lady."

She had a hot one here and she was going to milk him for all he was worth. The deputy seemed hell bent on telling her everything he knew anyway. "Know anything about the archaeologist? I only talked to him briefly."

"I don't know much about him. He breezed into town last week. Spends most of his time out at the site. I only see him once in awhile. Guess he's got a room at the Best Western, but camps out there a lot with that dog of his."

The white-haired woman had been engrossed in a romance novel, but perked up and removed her headset. "A right good lookin' man," she chimed in.

Jessica held back a chuckle as she finished signing the papers. Alex seemed to have gotten the attention of all the local women.

"Seems like a nice fellow, if you can get him to talk to you," the deputy went on. "Kind of a quiet sort, you know."

"Really?"

"Why I'd heard some of them old pots and stuff McCabe dug up and tried to sell dated back beyond 400 A.D. That was the rumor 'round town anyways. Why that's older than any of the dwellin's on the mesa. This could be something big, really big."

"I'd heard they were very old."

"Why of course you have, ma'am. You come here to write about this stuff. You probably already know all of this. I tend to run on at the mouth too much."

"And that's the truth," the lady said, looking at Jessica over her glasses once more, this time throwing her a wink.

"I've enjoyed the conversation." Jessica handed the deputy his clipboard. "If you need anything else, you can reach me at the lodge up on the mesa."

"Ma'am, if you don't mind, could you drop a copy of this accident report off at Mountain Jeep Tours? Mr. Nagasaki needs this for his insurance folks."

"I'd be glad to. In fact, I was headed over there to thank that nice young man for his help yesterday."

"Okay, whatever you say." He gave her a patronizing smile. "You take care of yourself now and watch out for those falling rocks."

"I'll do that."

A few minutes later, Jessica opened the door at Mountain Jeep Tours and the cowbell rang just as it had the day before. She stood at the counter waiting for someone to appear through the bead curtains. In a few moments, they rattled and a small Asian man appeared.

"Good morning," he said, cordially bowing his head. "May I be of assistance?"

"You must be Mr. Nagasaki," Jessica said, returning the gesture.

"I am Nagasaki."

"I have these papers for you," she said. "The deputy over at the police station asked me to deliver them."

He quickly scanned the sheets. "Ah, yes, you must be Miss Sinclair."

"Yes, sir. I'm very sorry about the accident yesterday. I know it totaled your Jeep."

"Not to worry. It was insured, so I see no problem. We are thankful you were not hurt or killed. There seemed nothing you could have done to prevent what happened with the boulder."

Jessica smiled at the kind and gentle man who stood before her. "Is the young man here who brought me into town yesterday?"

"Pardon?"

"The one who works for you. He brought me back here after the accident. Nechi was his name."

"I do not understand. I did not see who brought you here last night."

"The one who rented me the Jeep."

"Oh, person who rented Jeep. One moment. I get for you."

Jessica smiled and leaned on the counter. Perhaps Mr. Nagasaki didn't understand. She waited for a few seconds until the rattle of the curtain came again. Looking up, she was surprised to see a petite oriental woman with beautiful long black hair.

"You wish to see me?" she asked.

"No. I was looking for the man who rented me the Jeep yesterday."

"I rent you Jeep yesterday."

Jessica blinked and looked at her in disbelief. "There was a young man here—yesterday—when I rented the Jeep. There was an accident and he brought me back to town."

"Yes, I know someone bring you back after accident. I no see that person."

"But he must work here, he rented me the Jeep."

The woman reached under the counter and pulled out some papers. After leafing through them, she pulled out the form with Jessica's name across the top. A frown furrowed the woman's brow as she pointed to the bottom of the paper. "I rent you Jeep. See. I sign right here."

Jessica scanned the paper and looked at the line at the bottom. The signature was clearly legible. Osun

Nagasaki. Jessica's jaw dropped. "No, there's some mistake. The man who works for you must have forgotten to sign this. The man with the long black hair."

Mr. Nagasaki had stood quietly behind his wife during the discussion between the two. "Miss," he said softly. "I have two sons who work here, neither has long hair. I have two summer guides who start next month. No one else works for me."

"I only wanted to thank him for his kindness," she said, bewildered.

"That very nice," said the woman. "But he no work for us. You no see him here."

Jessica ran her hand through her hair. The two stood on the opposite side of the counter and stared questioningly. "Someone here is really confused," she whispered.

Mr. Nagasaki gave her a small smile and bowed graciously. It was obvious who he thought was confused.

Jessica would say no more. "Well, thanks anyway." She turned and opened the door.

Deep in thought, Jessica reached for the car door. "There you are." A deep voice stopped her in her tracks. Turning, she came face to face with Alex Nakai.

"Good God, you look good for someone who should be dead right now." He smiled and shook his head as his eyes took her in from head to toe.

"You scared the hell out of me," she uttered then blushed at his admiring look. "Thanks for the compliment—I think."

"On my way in from the site this morning I saw them pulling your Jeep out of the ravine. I came straight here to see what had happened to you." He rubbed his hand across his chin. "I have to say I don't know why you're still walking around."

"So I keep hearing. But I'm fine, thanks." At least she was fine physically, although she was beginning to wonder about her mental side.

"I just stopped in to see if you were okay." His obvious relief at her condition faded a little. "Well, I came for supplies, I need to get going."

Recovering from the surprise, she realized she had Alex's attention. Maybe she could play this to her advantage. She shot him a warm smile. "That's a pretty rugged road out there. I hope you're careful driving it all the time like you do."

"Yeah. No problem." He backed up a few steps and put his hands in the pockets of his jeans. "Like I said, I wanted to be sure you were okay."

She knew he was retreating, afraid she'd try to question him again. And she planned to, but she needed to be careful and mend a few fences first. The ice had broken between them for a fleeting moment. One wrong word and he'd run like a scared rabbit.

"I appreciate your concern."

He nodded his reply. His eyes met hers. That damned hypnotic blue.

"Sorry if I came on too strong yesterday." She fished for his reaction. "I didn't mean to interfere with your work. I am really interested in the site."

"That was obvious." He glanced toward his SUV where the furry head of the golden retriever appeared through a half-open window. "Well, I need to be going."

"Maybe I'll see you again—I mean before I leave. I'll be here a couple of weeks, if everything goes well."

"Maybe." He walked a few steps then turned back in her direction. "I'm glad you weren't hurt." He climbed into his vehicle and pulled from the parking lot.

Jessica watched as he disappeared down the street. "Damn," she whispered under her breath. Alex could prove to be her biggest challenge—in more ways than one.

CHAPTER FOUR

Alex drove the quiet stretch of highway back to the cutoff, appreciative tonight of the lack of traffic. His mind was where he'd rather it not be, on a woman. *A woman reporter.* Jessica churned up emotions he hadn't allowed to surface in a long time.

Sure, he was alone. That was okay with him, at least for the present. He was at peace with his soul. The traveling and months away from home at various digs didn't suit a family man. Sometimes he loved the solitude, like now when he was alone at the site, just him and Yellow Dog. The peace of the land got into his bones and settled there and could almost make him forget there was an ache in his heart.

Love hadn't been a friend to him in the past. He let out a heavy sigh. Truth was, he'd been very good at choosing the wrong women. Maybe that was why he'd chosen so few along the way. The problem was, when he fell, he fell hard. It wasn't going to happen again. Next time he wouldn't let his guard down until he was sure. The hurt wasn't worth it.

Jessica Sinclair was going to be a challenge. She brought out a longing for the touch of a woman, the smell and softness of her skin next to his. Dammit, he hoped she hadn't read anything into him tracking her down after the accident. After seeing that Jeep, he had to know she was all right. It was an impulsive action. Maybe he should have thought it through.

The way things were he'd have to keep an eye on her and her story. Running her off like he did yesterday might not have been the best way to handle the situation. He wasn't sure exactly how to manage this, but he had an idea. If he simply played along and fed Jessica just what he wanted her to know, maybe she wouldn't go digging around in his past. He could have some control over what she sent to press. She was hungry for a story, so why not give her what she came for—a story—on his terms. But he damned sure would have to keep his hormones in check.

As he steered the SUV over the rutted road, another thought occurred to him. He drove this road every day. It might be wise to check the rock pile at the top of the mountain for any other loose boulders.

Alex pulled his vehicle to the side of the narrow road. Stepping from the car, he let Yellow Dog run up the steep embankment ahead of him. The gravel scattered as the animal took long heavy strides, weaving his way up the soft slope toward the rock formation at the top. Alex dug in the toes of his boots, imitating the dog's zigzagging method to keep from sliding back down the hill. At the top of the gravel slope was a massive rock formation comprised of varying sized boulders.

"No wonder one of these babies came down," Alex said to the dog that intently sniffed the ground. Alex surveyed the rock pile with a keen eye. Climbing a short way up the rocks, he checked a few stones for stability, his feet slipping on the slick pine needles. The mass seemed pretty solid. Brushing the dirt from his hands, he jumped back to the ground.

Alex made his way around to the other side, to a huge gap in the mass of rock. This had to be where the boulder had given way yesterday. He stooped and picked up a handful of fresh earth. Compacted indentations appeared in a circular pattern all around the perimeter of the impression. Pretty unusual.

Turning toward a stand of pine trees opposite the rocks, he saw a freshly cut pine tree a few feet away. The sharp end of the four or five-inch tree was deeply scarred and broken in several places. The axe marks were worn away, suggesting it had been used to pry something heavy.

Alex kicked the wood chips at the base of the stump and looked around. There were myriad footprints on the hillside. Embedded in the soil were the imprints of a man's boots. Leaning close, he noted the faint outline of a star on the boot heel.

He rubbed his chin in contemplation. Yellow Dog sat at his feet. A deep throaty growl brought Alex from his thoughts. He turned toward the sound coming from among the trees. Laying high up the slope, in the shadow of the woods, was a white wolf, its pale opalescent eyes focused on Alex. Yellow Dog growled and barked twice. Alex reached for his collar and gave it a quick jerk. The wolf lay motionless. Contrary to all he'd been taught about animals in the wild, Alex allowed his eyes to meet the pale blue ones of the wolf. Not reacting to the nearness of Alex and the dog, he made no effort to move away. Yellow Dog grew silent, watching with ears up as if mesmerized by the wild creature.

They stood motionless as the wolf rose to his feet and walked to the stump, no more than two yards from Alex. Breaking his stare long enough to sniff the remains of the tree, his eyes went back to meet Alex's as if punctuating an understanding between them. Then the wolf turned away and trotted into the woods.

Several yards up the hillside, the animal stopped and looked back at Alex. A message had been delivered, along with an omen of things to come.

Questions haunted Alex as he made his way back down the hill. Why had someone pushed that boulder down the mountain? Who was it really meant for—Jessica Sinclair or him? This was no accident, and it was serious business. Was someone trying to frighten one of them away? Or did someone want one of them dead?

Questions haunted Alex as he made his way back down the hill. Why had someone pushed that boulder down the mountain? Who was it really meant for—Jessica Sinclair or him? This was no accident, and it was serious business. Was someone trying to frighten one of them away? Or did someone want one of them dead?

The air was crisp and cool and the sun was bright in a cloudless sky as Jessica pulled the backpack firmly onto her shoulders and began the hike toward the site. She checked the button on the shirt pocket that contained a map Michelle had sketched for her and leaned into the walk with enthusiasm.

The beauty and wildness of her surroundings magnified her feeling of connection to this land. It seemed as if it were somehow part of her, and had been part of her for a very long time. The pungent smell of sage and juniper tingled in her nostrils, and the exhilaration of unbridled freedom stirred in her soul with a familiarity she could not explain.

She'd spent a lot of time in the outdoors, but something here was different. Something indefinable. There was comfort in the unspoiled naturalness of the place, but there was also a presence. And there was a peacefulness that led one to wonder if the land itself had a spirit, a soul—or maybe many souls.

She felt better knowing the trail didn't cross McCabe's land. Instead, it took her into the opposite side of the site. The trek would be long, but well worth it if she didn't have to see that wild-eyed rancher again. Something about McCabe frightened her. If she did attempt an interview with him, he'd have to meet her in town. Encountering him on his property again was something she'd avoid at all costs.

She kept to the existing trail for about two miles then headed due west through rough terrain that varied from piñon trees and junipers to rough craggy rocks. A little over a mile farther, she came to a hill she judged to be about an eighth of a mile from the site. Through her binoculars she could see it clearly.

Hot, tired and thirsty, she dropped her backpack onto a large boulder at the top of the hill and took a drink of cold water from her canteen. Wiping her mouth on the sleeve of her shirt, she mopped her brow and looked around. The top of the boulder provided a perfect vantage point to view the site, yet offered cover among the trees and the scrub oak.

Pulling herself up onto the rough rock, she scooted to a place of comfort and scanned the area through binoculars. Alex's vehicle was partially hidden by the huge rock formation that towered over the ruin. He was kneeling at the base of the slide area, working over a small square hole in the ground. The dog stood several yards away, at first sniffing the ground on the trail of some rodent then raised his ears and looked in her direction. As the dog stood at attention, Jessica squirmed. Could he see her at this distance? Had he caught her scent? He watched for a moment and barked twice. The sound echoed through the small canyon and faded off into the distance.

Alex turned and looked at the dog then rose to scan the hillside. Jessica sat motionless hoping she hadn't been spotted. Alex patted the dog's head and turned back to his work. Letting a sigh of relief escape, Jessica lowered the binoculars.

The sun shone bright and warm, the day was nearly perfect. She let the breeze blow through her hair as she ran her hands through it. To the east, a band of clouds formed over the blue mountain peaks threatening an afternoon storm, but for now the sky overhead was deep blue and cloudless.

Pulling out her camera, she snapped her strongest lens into place. Zooming in, she took several shots of the ruin. With the help of the lens, she could make out the faint lines of some rooms in the area where Alex was working. The stone had crumbled, but the lines of the ancient walls were surprisingly distinct.

The surrounding area looked like a giant sandbox. At the foot of the rocks was the slide area where part of the formation had fallen away. Alex worked at the edge of that area, painstakingly brushing at something in the earth. The dog now lay contentedly nearby stretched in the warm midday sun.

She discovered the view was better through the camera lens than the binoculars, and she could study the photos at her leisure. To be perfectly honest, she was more interested in Alex than the landscape. He removed his shirt, baring his broad shoulders to the noonday sun. They glistened with moisture, as did the smooth rippling muscles across his back. Admiring the meticulous way he worked, the pit of her stomach tightened. Did Alex do everything in this slow sexy style?

Her mind wandered, but she forced her attention to something Alex was placing in a small plastic bag. It was far too tiny to identify at this distance, but, wow, the tender way those hands worked made her wish she was an artifact. She took a picture then another. Later she'd have them blown up and study them for details— of the artifact, of course. She smiled.

Something rustled in the scrub oak, startling Jessica. A large jackrabbit darted across the hilltop and into a juniper bush a few feet away. Laying down the camera, she leaned back on the large warm rock and enjoyed the warmth of the sun on her body. It had been far too long since she'd allowed herself even such a simple pleasure. After her vigorous hike, it wasn't long before she was drifting in a half-asleep state. A gentle breeze stirred the pine trees and carried the soft scent to her nose as the bright sunlight faded behind her eyelids.

"Awaken, my daughter." A soft voice came from somewhere in the dreamy mist. "There is something you must see."

Jessica's eyes fluttered for a second, but she pinched them closed against the brightness. She believed the voice came from somewhere in her imagination and sleep quickly recaptured her.

"Daughter," the whisper came again.

Then came another voice, this one soft, feminine and distraught. "Oh, my love." It spoke just above a whisper. Then the sound of sobs, quiet nearly silent sobs, tugging at her dream state. Jessica pulled herself back to reality gradually realizing the sound came from outside of her own mind. She blinked her eyes at the sunlight and raised herself onto her elbows.

The noise came from behind her. Turning, she stopped in disbelief. Several yards up the slope, on a nearby rock, sat a young woman with long dark hair. A band of rawhide with a long gray feather was tied around her head. Her small frame was clad in a faded buckskin dress that flowed all the way to the ground and appeared to sprout up out of the earth. She held her chin in her hands and tears glistened in the sunlight. They ran down her face and hands and sparkled in the sun before they dripped onto her buckskin garments. Fine beadwork decorated the top of the dress in blue, white and red sunburst designs. At her feet lay a large white dog. No. A wolf. Its pale blue eyes stared back at Jessica.

Jessica spun around and slid from the rock onto her feet. "Hello?" she said, as if testing her vision for reality. The woman only looked at her, tears ran down her tanned cheeks. The Indian maiden rose to her feet, the buckskin falling in rolls to the ground. Raising one arm, she pointed in the direction of the ruin.

"My love," she said, her pleading eyes tearing at Jessica's heart. "Help me," she whispered. "Please, help me."

Jessica could only stare. "I—I don't understand," she stuttered. "What can I do?"

The woman nodded. "I need to be with him." Her voice trailed off. Before Jessica's eyes the maiden evaporated, disappearing into a mist that lingered for a few seconds and was gone. The white wolf remained. He looked into Jessica's eyes then ran into a clump of trees.

Jessica stood like a statue for an undetermined amount of time. She finally became aware of the boulder gouging into her leg as she leaned against it for support.

Clearing her throat, she looked around. Wow, this time she couldn't dismiss the vision. Maybe she was still asleep. God, she hoped she was still asleep. She pressed her eyelids tight together and tried to force the issue. But the spears of bright sunlight forced their way in, proving what she already knew.

Positioning herself on the rock, she sat like a wary animal. Who was that woman? What was she asking of Jessica? Normal people didn't just have visions much less have conversations with them. Maybe it was the sun, the exertion from the long hike—

The sound of a vehicle in the distance triggered her to reach for the binoculars and look again to the site. A black truck topped the hill on the adjacent road and wound its way down to the ruin. Startled by the sound of distant thunder, she glanced over her shoulder. Letting out a stress-relieving sigh, she shuffled on her rocky perch and tried to get a better vantage point.

Was there a connection between Alex and McCabe? If not, why was McCabe out here paying Alex a visit? Another boom of thunder cracked and Jessica stuffed the camera equipment into her backpack and jumped to the ground. *I guess I won't be finding out today.* The smell of rain was heavy on the air and she wasn't stupid enough to get caught out here in a thunderstorm. She'd love to know what the two of them were up to, but for now she had a race to win with Mother Nature.

—◆—

A knot formed in Alex's stomach as the black truck made its way down the hill and stopped next to his vehicle. The knot tightened as McCabe stepped from the driver's seat. Rising to his feet, Alex rubbed his soil-covered hands together then down the rough denim of his jeans. Squaring his shoulders, he met McCabe halfway.

"Afternoon." McCabe extended a friendly hand. "How's things goin' out here?"

Alex stood with thumbs hooked in his back pockets, ignoring the gesture. His gaze was locked on McCabe and his jaw was set. "Something you need?" Alex asked in a cold voice.

"No. Just stopped by t'see how you were doin'," McCabe replied.

"I don't see it as any of your concern."

McCabe frowned. "Just curious. After all, I found this place. I feel like I have a vested interest here." McCabe's tone grew deep. His eyes flashed, momentarily revealing the anger that lay beneath the false smile pasted on his face.

"Not likely," Alex said.

McCabe shot a fiery glance and popped open the snap on the pocket of his western shirt. He pulled out a cigarette package and offered Alex a smoke. Alex didn't move. McCabe shrugged and put a cigarette between his lips then lit a match on the seam of his jeans. McCabe eyed Alex nervously, his gaze darting to the place where Alex had been working.

McCabe looked at the ground and kicked the dirt with the toe of his boot. "You ain't very hospitable today. Somethin' eatin' you?" he asked without looking up.

Alex hesitated as he surveyed the man before him. McCabe was nervous about something. Why was he here sniffing around? Alex sure as hell wasn't falling for this 'old buddy' crap. That weasel-like face and those beady eyes that wouldn't meet his had left Alex with an uneasy feeling from the start. Well, he had a few questions of his own that needed answers.

"You see the accident on the road yesterday?" Alex gritted his teeth.

McCabe shot a suspicious look in Alex's direction then looked back at his worn cowboy boots. "Yeah. Sheriff called and said there was a wreck up on the east end of my land." He set his jaw and shot another steely glance at Alex. "Why? Somebody you know?"

Alex rubbed the stitching on his jeans pocket with his fingers, holding his angry suspicions behind clenched teeth. "Nobody I know. Figured you knew something about it. After all, it happened on your land."

"Damn people." McCabe spat on the ground and wiped his mouth with his sleeve, as the ash from his cigarette grew long and gray in his opposite hand. "Ought not to be trespassing."

"Was somebody trespassing? I seem to recall you gave the University permission to cross your property." Alex's cold stare held McCabe's before McCabe nervously looked away.

"Ain't just anybody got my permission to be there," McCabe growled. "Anybody without my permission is a trespasser."

"And just how do you handle trespassers, Mr. McCabe?"

McCabe's face went pale as he shot a look at Alex. The ash from the unfiltered cigarette in his hand finally burned its way to flesh and McCabe flinched and threw the cigarette aside. "Dammit," he said, but was distracted only for a moment from Alex's question. Glancing down at the smoldering cigarette butt, McCabe stepped forward and ground it fiercely into the sand before he spoke. "I got things to do." He turned and stormed back to his truck. Slamming the door, he glared at Alex and backed up throwing dirt in all directions.

Alex watched him drive away without moving from his stance. There was something wrong with McCabe's actions. His eyes followed the trail of footprints that led away from him, but to no avail. The soft sand had filled the heel prints as soon as McCabe's foot left them. He couldn't prove who sent that boulder down the mountain, but his gut told him McCabe didn't want him or anyone else here for some reason. Maybe it was time he had a little talk with the sheriff. Letting out an annoyed sigh and glancing up at the darkening sky, Alex turned and went back to his work. One thing he knew for certain, his time was too precious to waste on McCabe.

———

Jonathan McCabe put his rough, dry finger to his mouth, sucking at the cigarette burn as he steered the truck over the rocky road and back toward his ranch. That wiseass archaeologist was just in the way. He'd like to show him what he did with trespassers. "Bastard," he growled. His hands itched for the feel of the rifle that hung in the back window and his dry lips curled into an evil grin.

He rubbed his whisker-roughened chin and pushed back his hat. There was too much for him to gain to let his temper get the better of him. He had to play the game, but when the time was right he'd have his chance to settle the score.

CHAPTER FIVE

Jessica surveyed the place through a dim cloud of smoke that hung over the bar.

"Table for one?" asked the waiter, adjusting the clean white apron that encircled his hips.

"Yes. Something over there, please." She pointed to the wall opposite the bar, hoping for something out of the range of the cigarette smoke.

"Sure." He shrugged and motioned to her with a large red menu.

She followed him past several empty tables and chairs. The smell of fried food was noticeable on his clothes as he pulled out the chair for her.

It was late. Exhausted from her hike, she'd fallen asleep and awakened ravenous. Nothing at the lodge was open so she'd journeyed into Cortez in search of a hot meal. This place wasn't her first choice, but it would have to do.

She ordered a drink as she tucked herself into a booth with a black Formica top then browsed through the variety of barbecued meats on the menu. Country music droned in the background and several men sat at the brass and oak bar drinking beer and talking loudly.

"Bud Light?" The bartender placed a tall frosty glass of beer in front of her.

"Thanks," she replied with a smile. Glancing past him, she caught a glimpse of a man seated alone at the end of the bar. The dark hair and broad shoulders had an immediate familiarity. They should, she'd watched them through binoculars half the day.

Alex Nakai sat with the heel of his boot hooked over the wrung of a bar stool, one sun-browned arm draped over his thigh. His chin rested in his palm and his thoughts seemed a million miles away.

Jessica's heartbeat went up a notch. Over the top of the menu her eyes scanned every detail of his tall muscular form. Her hands went clammy and a slow burn started somewhere between her heart and her throat.

At that moment the waiter popped his head over the top of the other side of the booth. "Ready to order, ma'am?"

"Uh no. I'm still looking at the manu—er—the menu."

A blush warmed her face as she wrapped her fingers in the back of her short hair and looked away. It had been a long time since anyone had made her feel like a schoolgirl.

Okay Jessica, tuck your hormones in your briefcase and act like a professional. She bit the inside of her cheek and debated approaching Alex and striking up a conversation. Maybe she could get him to talk about the site, but how would he react?

Alex eyed her from the end of the bar. Now he'd seen her. Jessica pretended not to notice him. Heat crept under her collar. He looked away. She fanned her face, hoping to cool the heat that burned her cheeks hotter than ever. She couldn't talk to him in this state, even if she could gather intelligent words, which she doubted, she'd likely trip over her own panting tongue. She'd done hundreds of interviews and wheedled more information out of unsuspecting people than anyone could count. That was her job. Why was Alex so different? The knot in the pit of her stomach was strangling back her words and frankly she found it kind of funny.

She took a sip of the beer and crossed her arms on the tabletop. Maybe she should sit here for a while, collect herself, and enjoy the view. He didn't appear to be paying much attention to her anyway.

Jessica savored a small tasty meal of barbecued chicken and potato salad while she kept an eye on Alex's quiet form. He appeared to be deep in thought, contemplating something, as he sipped at a cold frothy mug.

A hand touched Jessica's shoulder and a voice spoke in her ear. "Like t' dance?"

Jessica turned to see the bronzed face of a cowboy uncomfortably near hers. The band of the young man's white cowboy hat was stained yellow with perspiration and he smelled of a mixture of cheap cologne and beer.

"No thanks," she said.

"Oh, c'mon, honey." A smile touched his lips as he pushed the hat back on his head.

Jessica smiled and shook her head. "No. Thank you."

He grasped her upper arm. "Ah, come on. This dance was made for the two of us," he whined, leaning closer.

A large hand grasped the man's shoulder and pulled him backward. "The lady's with me." Alex's deep voice was unmistakable. He flashed her a quick smile. His pale blue eyes twinkled.

"I only want her to dance with me." The cowboy gave Alex a pouty look then challenged him. "If she's with you, why ain't you payin' her no mind?"

"This dance is mine. Find somebody else." Alex stood a head taller than the cowboy's Stetson hat.

The man opened his mouth as if to argue, sized up his opponent and stepped back. "Well, go ahead." The cowboy stood aside and looked expectantly at Alex.

Alex narrowed his eyes then turned a smiling look at Jessica. "I guess this must be our dance."

"That's not necessary," she stammered.

"I think it is." He glanced over his shoulder and raised his brows. Hands on hips, his challenger waited in the wings.

Jessica surveyed the smirk on the greasy face of her other option. The tension was thick and the outcome was riding on her response. "Okay." She got up awkwardly from the booth and the cowboy turned and walked away.

Alex put his large hand in the small of her back and escorted her to the dance floor. Pulling her near him, he wrapped her hand in his and held her tight to his chest.

Jessica swallowed hard. "Thanks for rescuing me from that guy." She was unaccustomed to such a show of chivalry.

"No problem. I specialize in damsels in distress."

"Really." She looked up into his amused blue eyes, but was unsure what was really going on behind them. She could take care of herself. A knight in shining armor wasn't necessary to save her from a drunken cowboy. She'd have handled him just fine. Still, she wondered what Alex was thinking.

"You been here before?" His question interrupted her thoughts.

"Not in this lifetime. You?"

"I was hot and tired and looking for a cold beer. Not much open this time of night."

She laughed. "Well then I guess we have to chalk it up to fate."

Alex shot a glance over his shoulder at the cocky cowboy who was still watching them. He gave her an odd look but pulled her closer, his breath feather soft on her neck. The warmth of his strong hand around hers was commanding. A slow country song droned on the juke box and she resisted the temptation to lay her head against the broadness of his chest.

"God, I hate country music," he whispered.

"Yeah. Me, too," she whispered back, allowing the music and the moment to pull her into their magic.

Alex's strong embrace held her fast as she followed his lead and their bodies swayed to the beat as they moved around the dance floor again. His strong arms pressed her closer. She gave in and nestled against him. His heart beat next to her ear. He was silent, not giving away what he was thinking.

Warmth built in Jessica's shoulders and spread through her rib cage washing down through her insides and into her thighs. His smooth even breath grew warm against her neck as they moved slowly back and forth.

"How long you plan to be around?" he asked as he brought his mouth close to her ear.

"Till I get my story." Her mind should be on that story right now, but if she tried to push it he might bolt. Maybe if she played her cards right, there would be another opportunity. This dance could make sure of that.

"How about you? How long will you be here?"

"Till I get my answers."

"I see." Jessica raised her eyebrows. A little discomfort had suddenly seeped into their closeness.

"I thought maybe you'd gone home when I didn't see you today."

"Oh, I've been around." She grinned slyly.

"Really? Even though you've hit a dead end?"

"Dead end? Why, I'm only getting started." She smiled at him assuredly.

"Oh," he replied, stiffening at her answer.

Alex's breath on her neck grew quicker and he pushed her away from him. "It's getting warm in here. I really need to go."

"Yeah. Me too."

The magic had waned. The cowboy at the bar had left in disgust. "I think your admirer went home, too," Alex chuckled.

"Guess he gave up." Jessica smiled relieved to see that Alex still had his sense of humor.

"Come on. I'll walk you to your car."

"Thanks. I'd appreciate that." Laying some money on the table for her dinner, she scooped up her purse and made her way toward the door with Alex a few steps behind.

Jessica unlocked the car door and threw her purse into the passenger's seat. Alex stepped close and hovered for a few seconds. He moved back and pushed his hands deep into his pockets, but he didn't fool her intuition for a minute. The wanting that passed between them was thick enough to cut with a knife. His mouth twitched as he moistened his lips.

"Well," he said, stepping closer. "I'm sure we'll see each other again before you get that—story of yours finished. Maybe sometime—." He stopped short as if the words caught in his throat. Drawing back, his eyes went first to his boots then back to her.

"Yes." Jessica looked up at him and smiled expectantly.

"I was just going to say I may be around for a while."

"Me, too." She shifted on her feet and glanced around feeling awkward. "Thanks again."

He leaned forward, moved his face across hers. His breath whispered across her mouth but his lips never touched hers. He stepped back and shot her a wink. "The pleasure was undeniably mine."

Jessica slipped behind the steering wheel and Alex closed the door. This had been an unexpected turn of events. Her head was reeling. Maybe this was a good thing for her story and her career, maybe not.

Alex walked across the dimly lit parking lot. What the hell was he doing? He never should have asked her to dance, but what else could he do? That drunken cowboy was making a pass.

If he were going to stay in control of her story and her nosing around, they had to get better acquainted. Why was he lying to himself? He'd enjoyed every minute of it. But he couldn't let himself get involved, not again. It was just when she was close she seemed to have some kind of spell over him. He glanced around as a shiver ran through him. Or maybe this whole place had some kind of spell over him.

Jessica drove the ten-mile stretch of highway back to the cutoff to Mesa Verde, savoring the warm schoolgirl glow left from her dance with Alex. And chastising herself for not trying harder to get something for her story.

Dammit. She couldn't afford to let a bunch of badly neglected hormones get in the way. She wasn't any more prepared to deal with this than some age-old spirits, or whatever they were. This story was way too important for her to be swayed by all these distractions. It was time to get a grip.

As she turned onto the winding road to the mesa, something stepped from the darkness and into the road. Swerving and hitting the brakes, the flash of a large white animal passed through the headlights and ran off into the distance. The white wolf, she thought, pulling back onto the highway and scanning the dark roadside for another glimpse of the animal. Again she hit the brakes. Standing in the center of the road was the familiar figure of a man with long black hair.

"Nechi." She rolled down the window and he stepped around to the driver's side of the car. "What are you doing out here?"

"Flat tire." He motioned several yards up the road to where a black jeep was parked in the next turnout. "No spare."

"Can I take you somewhere?" she asked without hesitation.

"Back to Cortez." He was already halfway around the car before he finished the sentence.

"Sure. I owe you one." She snapped the automatic locks and Nechi climbed into the passenger side, a huge smile on his face.

"Glad you came along. It's a long walk back to town."

"No problem." She hesitated then looked at him curiously. "Don't you need to take your tire?"

"No," he said unconcerned.

She shrugged and turned the car around in a sandy turnout. They'd just pulled back out onto the highway when Alex's green SUV swished past.

"Great," she said.

"Pardon?" Nechi looked in her direction questioningly.

"Nothing," she said. Alex was probably wondering what she was doing driving around in the middle of the night with a strange man in the car.

"So is the pretty journalist lady about through with her story?" Nechi grinned and winked at Jessica.

"Hardly. I'm only getting started."

"You having problems?"

"Let's say I'm finding people a little less than cooperative."

"Maybe the lady doesn't see the real story here."

"What does that mean?"

"Maybe there's more here than meets the eye. Perhaps there are many stories buried here if one knows where to look."

"You're talking in riddles again. You seem very good at that."

He nodded. "Perhaps. But some of us write the stories, some of us tell the stories and some of us live the stories. Do you not agree?"

"Yes, of course I agree. Maybe you could be a little more specific."

"I know a story, if you'd like to hear it."

Raising an eyebrow in suspicion, Jessica nodded. "Sure why not. Is this one a riddle, too?"

"Not a riddle. A legend."

"Fine. Tell me your legend."

"Oh, it is not my legend. The legend belongs to the people."

"The people?"

"*Our* people." His eyes narrowed. "It belongs to all who dare to come here and ask of their past."

His look intimidated her, so she didn't argue. His choice of words gave her goose bumps. "Well, I'm investigating the past, and I'd like to hear your legend. But it's not very far back to town." The corners of her mouth turned upward in a stifled smile. "You'd better get on with it."

Nechi nodded. "Long ago, long before any of the dwellings existed here on the mesa, a small tribe of nomadic ancients traveled the deserts of the southwest. The people traveled many years after leaving their homelands."

"Do your people believe your ancestors came from the north rather than the south?" Jessica interjected. "I've heard opposing versions of that story."

"This is a legend, not a white man's history lesson," Nechi said sarcastically. "If time is so precious to you, it would be best to make good use of it."

"Sorry," she said, somewhat surprised by his reaction. Obviously this was serious stuff to him.

Nechi nodded then continued. "They were led by a man of great vision, a spirit leader who was guided by the spirits of the earth, the fire, the sky and the worlds beyond our own."

Jessica raised her eyebrows, struggling with the logical part of her mind, as Nechi seemed to transform himself into someone wise beyond his years. "Interesting," she commented.

Nechi shot a glance in her direction. "Before you leave this place, you will understand some of our spirit world that you now have so much difficulty accepting."

A chill ran down Jessica's spine as she glanced at Nechi, meeting his eyes for a moment. "Oh, so you're a mind reader, too?" she quipped, in an effort to break the tension.

"Do you doubt such powers exist?" he asked.

"Certainly not," she responded. "There are a lot of things I can't explain, it doesn't mean I deny their existence."

"It is good you are open to such possibilities. It will be useful in the days to come. Now, I will tell you the legend."

Jessica eyed him suspiciously. He'd made several references to her visit here. What did he know that she didn't?

Nechi went on. "Guided by the leader's visions, the tribe roamed in search of a beautiful green valley where they were destined to end their nomadic life and make a permanent home."

Nechi's eyes shone, and his face took on the expression of someone in a trance as he spoke. "The leader was told he must find a towering green mesa and there under its mighty protection would lay a plentiful valley. Led by a powerful vision, the leader found just such a mesa and the tribe arrived in the valley as the last of the spring snow melted from the greening grasses in the meadows. It was a place where game was plentiful and the soil rich and fertile."

Nechi looked down at his hands, which he held palms up forming a bowl and seeming to visualize the protective valley he spoke of. "Within the valley that spring, along with the rebirth of nature, also came a rebirth of the people. They would wander the plains and deserts no more and live here in the valley the Earth Mother had so graciously provided for them." He passed one hand over the top of the imaginary valley he held in the other and smiled. "The spirits of good shone down upon them like rays of sun and the people built a village in a canyon to the east, near the base of the mesa where they would be protected from the winter winds."

"East side. Wouldn't that be near the new site?"

Nechi put a finger to his lips, commanding Jessica's silence then continued. "A large and very beautiful cavern existed in the canyon and the people were so grateful to the gods for their generosity they declared it a sacred place of the spirits. They constructed a great temple at the cave's opening where the people came daily and praised the gods for their new found homeland and all its blessings."

"A temple. Hmm."

"The tribe lived in the village and worshiped the gods at the temple for many, many seasons." Nechi crossed his arms with fists clenched and put them to his chest. "And with each new generation, came a new and strong descendent of the spirit leader. The wisdom and goodness passed from father to son each learning the knowledge they needed to keep the tribe prospering and at peace."

"Okay, this is starting to sound like a fairy tale." Jessica waved her hand, emphasizing her point. "I know some of the history here. If everything was so perfect in the valley, why would they have moved to the dry mesa top?"

"If one is to hear what the legend has to offer, it is best to close the mouth and open the ears."

She raised an eyebrow at his scolding. "I guess I'm forgetting it's a legend and I'm trying to weave it in with facts."

"Do with it what you will, writer lady. But hear it to its end before you decide."

"Fine. Please go on."

"You must know where there is great good, great evil will always be lurking. A hideous evil spirit had followed the people from the North." Nechi's face became clouded with lines of displeasure. "It was the evil who put so many great stumbling blocks in their paths as they searched the deserts. It had plagued them with bad weather, misled them and inflicted much turmoil as he tried to stop them in their conquest." Nechi raised his fists in a gesture of victory. "But the leader's wisdom and visions had led them to the valley in spite of the evil one's efforts to stop them. His leader was the stronger one. Now the evil one sat high upon the mesa overlooking the valley and waited for his chance."

"Of course, every fairy tale has to have a villain," Jessica said.

Nechi shot her a disapproving look, and his voice became low and wicked sounding as he spoke barely above a whisper. "The construction of the temple had intensified the evil's challenges to destroy the goodness that existed. It would wait for its chance. It would wait for some weakness to show itself, no matter how long it took.

"The people continued to worship, listening to the lessons of the forefathers, of the hard times they had been through and of the gratefulness for their newfound life. All the while, the evil one sat upon the mesa and watched, biding its time."

Jessica pulled the car into the parking lot of Mountain Jeep Tours. "Well, I guess we're here," Jessica said hesitantly.

"We have arrived at our destination, but the journey for you has not yet begun. In your haste to arrive, you could miss much."

"Let's suppose for a moment I'm not in such a hurry as you believe me to be in. What then?"

"Then I would believe you were willing to take the time and learn the lessons you and your soul are seeking answers for."

"All right. I'm intrigued by your legend. Tell me more."

"If you want to know the legend, then do not merely listen to the words. Feel it with all your senses." Nechi turned in the seat until he faced her. He raised his hand, almost touching the car roof, ran his fingers down her forehead and closed her eyes. "*Dahiina*. Let it come alive."

After a moment of silence, he went on. "As with all things of this earth, change is inevitable and none of us can be protected from evil forever. As I said, many generations passed and life was near paradise in the valley. Then, on a warm summer evening, a beautiful new son was born to the tribe's leader."

As Nechi's words droned in Jessica's ears, the pictures of the story began to form in her mind. Deep behind closed eyelids, she fell into a dreamlike state as the story played in her head. "The pale blue eyes of the infant boy foretold his destiny even then, the sign that had marked each child's fate, generation to generation. The baby would one day lead the people as his forefathers had."

Behind Jessica's closed eyes, a picture formed.

A baby squirmed and cried in his father's hands, his tiny voice pierced the night sky and called out to the round golden moon that hung high over his head. The father's words went up into the darkness as if floating on the billows of smoke from the fire that burned before them. The child shivered and the chieftain tucked him carefully into his mother's arms. In the folds of a buffalo robe that encircled her shoulders, he sought out the warmth of her body and the nourishing milk of her breast.

"Eagle Song," the father whispered as he ran his hand over the tiny one's head. "Eagle Song—"

Jessica became aware of the pressure of Nechi's fingers on her eyelids. Grabbing his hand and pushing it away, she opened her eyes. An eerie feeling ran through her when the full yellow moon that had risen just above the horizon greeted her. She spoke in total amazement. "How did you do that?"

"Do what?" he asked.

"Put those pictures in my head. I felt like I was there. I could smell the smoke and feel the night air. What sort of cheap trick was that?"

"It was no trick. The pictures in your mind are your own. I cannot put them there. I can only open the doorway for you. You must find your way through it alone."

"He was a beautiful child, the baby, I mean. Tell me the rest of your legend. I want to know what happened to him."

"As children do, the child grew. On his seventh birthday the child began his training to follow in his father's footsteps."

"But he was only a child. What sort of training did he have to do?"

"Slow at first. A learning of the old ways. It would have taken many summers to teach the young man all the elders had learned over the centuries."

"So his training was almost a life long thing. How old was he when it was completed?"

"He was to have taken his father's place on his twenty-first birthday, had fate not intervened."

"What do you mean by that?" Jessica asked suspiciously. Nechi had done his hocus pocus on her, and now she had invested her emotions in the young man's story. This better have a happy ending.

"Before you know that, you must also know that in the beginning of his seventeenth summer, the young man began to feel the stirring of manhood. He met a maiden, a beautiful girl with long flowing dark hair. She was fragile as a tiny turtle dove and the warrior only wanted to love and protect her." Nechi frowned and shook his head. "His father was not pleased with this for she stole the young one's heart away. He spent much time thinking of her when he should have been learning his lessons of leadership."

Jessica glanced at the clock on the dashboard. It was close to midnight. Remembering she had an interview with Mrs. McCabe at eight the next morning, she felt compelled to try to speed Nechi along. "It's getting kind of late, can we skip over some of this and get on to the part where they get married and live happily ever after?"

"Oh, there is no happiness in the end of this story."

"What? You mean I've been listening all this time so you can give me some tragic ending?"

"It is true of the legend. Sometimes it is true of life. At the end of the young one's nineteenth summer his father was killed. The young man was frightened by his new responsibilities and did not believe he was prepared to be the leader."

"I'm not going to sit here tonight while you tell me another hour and a half of this stuff and then bash me with a miserable unhappy ending. Short and sweet, how does it end?"

"The evil one took over the village and paradise ended for the people of the mesa."

"I'm sorry, I don't mean to be impatient. This really is a great story, and sometime I'd like to hear the rest of it." Jessica rubbed the back of her neck in fatigue and frustration, wishing she hadn't been short with Nechi. "Can I have a rain check before my coach turns back into a pumpkin?"

Nechi grinned. "There is no doubt you will hear the rest of the story. It is something that must be."

She looked at him oddly. "Yeah. Okay. I'm a sucker for love stories and I'd like to hear about how the two lovers get together in the end. Promise me you'll finish that part before I go back to Denver."

He opened the car door and stepped out into the night. "When you are ready, I will be there."

"Wait a second," she stammered. "You said something earlier—something like—some write the stories, some tell the stories, some live the stories. Why did you say that?"

"Before your journey here is done, you will have done all three." With that he closed the car door and walked away.

Jessica backed up the car and started toward the street, glancing behind her at the vacant parking lot in the rear view mirror. Startled, she stopped and scanned the dimly lit area. Nothing stirred. It was as if Nechi had disappeared into thin air.

She shook her head, let out a heavy sigh and pulled back out onto the street. There were no logical explanations for the things that were happening to her. But she had to ride it out and see where it ended.

During the silent drive back, she replayed the story and the odd attachment she now felt for the young man in the legend. Somehow Nechi had brought him into her reality. She thought of the young maiden she'd met on the mountain. Could she be connected?

Was it possible? She vowed she would find an answer to these questions before she left this place.

The woman reached up and touched his face. Her hands were warm against his skin. He wrapped them in his own large fingers and kissed them. Her long dark hair flowed from beneath a band of rawhide where three gray feathers were tied and lay softly on her dark tresses. The white buckskin dress she wore was decorated with tiny red, blue and yellow beads.

As he bent to kiss the full beautiful lips, the woman evaporated in his arms, changing to a blue-tinged cloud of mist within his very grasp. He stood for a moment clad in a leather loincloth as the sweet-smelling moist haze hung around him then moved away. The stone was cool and hard beneath his moccasin-covered feet as he scanned the chamber of a cavern. An odd light illuminated the walls and the cloud now hung over his head.

Within the cloud a face formed, the solemn beautiful face of the Indian maiden he'd held only moments ago.

"You must help us." Her voice vibrated in echoes as if it came from some distant place.

"Why?" he asked.

"You are the only one who can," she replied. The features of her face changed form into the face of Jessica Sinclair then vanished into nothingness.

Alex sat upright in his sleeping bag, a cool mist clinging to his shirtless body. He ran his hand through his hair. Whimpering, Yellow Dog raised his head as he lay in his usual place next to Alex.

Alex patted the dog's large head in the scattered light of moonbeams that filtered through the half-open tent flap. "Sorry, boy," he whispered.

Alex rolled from the sleeping bag and stepped out into the moonlight, wondering at the dream he'd just experienced. The woman's touch had been real to him. He ran a hand across his face recalling the feel of her.

Standing here with the soft rays of the moon on his body, he felt a kindred spirit with the loin-clothed warrior he'd been in the dream. High above him on the rocky cliff of the canyon wall, the silhouette of a wolf appeared. Raising his woolly head to the sky, he let out a mournful howl that raised goose flesh on Alex's arms. The white fur of the animal illuminated in the bright light of the full moon and he stood there regally before walking away into the night.

A surge of animal kinship coursed through Alex's veins and an overwhelming urge rushed through him to join his wild brother in his song to the night. He stood beneath the same moon his native fathers had worshiped, stood upon their soil in the heart of their ancient lands. How could he help being stirred by their primitive history and feel his own connection to their past—his past?

It was only a dream, but something in him was stirring that had never been aroused before. Who was the beautiful maiden in his dream? Why had she melted away into Jessica's image? The thought of Jessica made his own savage blood pulse harder in his veins and warm his hungry loins.

What the warrior felt for the maiden was not so different from his own feeling for Jessica. He rubbed his chest where Jessica's head had laid just hours before when they danced. He could still feel the imprint of her next to him.

Did the dream have some meaning? Who was the maiden and why had she asked him for help? He again stifled the urge to call out to the round moon and ask what it was he was being called to do.

A dream, just a dream, he thought and stretched his body before the glowing orb above him hoping somehow to absorb understanding from the light. An understanding not only of his dream but also of his churning insides as unexplored feelings washed over him.

CHAPTER SIX

Jessica climbed the stairs of the immaculate front porch and rapped on the door. The porch was surrounded with pots of colorful flowers and adorned with an old-fashioned porch swing covered with bright daisy-patterned cushions. Jessica observed and smiled. It all spoke of the house's occupant.

A woman peered through the lace curtains on the window then opened the door a few inches.

"Mrs. McCabe?" Jessica asked.

"Yes."

"Jessica Sinclair, from the *Colorado Explorer*." She offered the older woman her hand.

"Oh, hello." Mrs. McCabe opened the door and warmly accepted Jessica's outstretched palm. "Please come in. I've been expecting you."

Mrs. McCabe was clad in blue jeans and a bright plaid shirt and motioned for Jessica to enter the small feminine living room. The smell of fresh baked bread hung in the air, reminding Jessica of her Aunt Helen's kitchen when she was a child.

The room was decorated with white wicker furnishings and bright floral fabrics. Flowers and houseplants were tucked into every nook and cranny.

"You have a lovely home," Jessica commented.

"Oh, thank you. Sometimes I think it's a bit much." She waved her hand toward the room. "All the flowers, you know. But I do love flowers. Jonathan never liked so much frill."

"It's beautiful." Jessica smiled at the petite woman who stood before her.

"I was just making some tea. Would you like a cup?"

"That would be nice." Jessica detected a nervousness about the little lady.

Mrs. McCabe hurried into the adjacent dining room and lifted a tray from the lace-covered tabletop.

"Please have a seat, anywhere you're comfortable." Mrs. McCabe sat the tray on the coffee table and rubbed her hands together.

"I appreciate you seeing me." Jessica took a seat on the sofa.

"It's no problem, my dear. I only hope I can help you. You know it's been several weeks since I left—since I moved off the ranch." Mrs. McCabe's face clouded as she checked the neat gray bun at the back of her head for stray hairs.

"I understand. I'm mainly interested in the discovery of the site. I believe you were still there when that happened."

"Yes—yes, I was." The woman put a small hand to her tanned and deeply lined face. Her brow creased and she glanced down at the floor.

"It must have been an exciting time. Your husband being the first to find it and all."

Mrs. McCabe poured the tea into two dainty teacups. Her hand trembled slightly. "Exciting, yes. You know a small corner of it actually is on the ranch. But it's caused more turmoil in my life than I ever thought possible."

Jessica reached into her briefcase and pulled out a pad, pencil and a small tape recorder. "Do you mind if I record some of our conversation?"

Mrs. McCabe glanced at the small black box and shrugged. "Reckon that would be okay."

"You said it caused turmoil, Mrs. McCabe. What kind of turmoil?"

"Oh, please call me Dorothy. Everybody does. We're pretty informal here in Cortez." The woman turned and settled herself into the wicker rocker across from the sofa. Some of her nervousness seemed to subside.

"It was Jonathan," she said as if letting out a long held sigh. "That place seemed to take control of his very being."

"You mean he was—obsessed with it?"

"Obsessed, yes." Mrs. McCabe seemed to weigh her words. "Maybe possessed would be closer to right. He'd be gone for days sometimes. He wouldn't eat, wouldn't sleep. He smoked like a chimney and shook—Lord, he had the shakes worse than anybody I've ever seen."

"I take it this was unusual behavior for him?"

Mrs. McCabe wiped the palms of her hands across the legs of her blue jeans and shifted in her chair. "Oh yes, dear heavens, my Jonathan is—was, the best husband a woman could have asked for. He was gentle, loving, never made a fuss over much of anything."

A tear glistened in the corner of Mrs. McCabe's eye as she spoke. She reached into her shirt pocket and pulled out a dainty white handkerchief and dabbed it away. "You see I was sick, real sick, several months before all this happened. Near died, I did.

Jonathan was there every day, every single day I was in the hospital. Then when I came home, he took care of me better than any two nurses could've managed. And never once complained. Told me he only cared that he still had me here with him."

"Sounds like he is—was—a very kind man."

"Oh yes, not only kind, but a hard working man, too. He loves that ranch more than anything–well maybe not more than he used to love me—yeah, used to." Dorothy twisted her handkerchief then went on.

"Guess my point is, something changed him. Changed him into somebody I don't know anymore. I had to get away. Not long ago I'd have bet my life I'd never leave him. But now he's different, like somethin's gone wrong with his soul. I'm sorry. I don't mean to ramble on about him. I know you didn't come here to listen to me carry on."

"What about the site, Mrs. McCabe—Dorothy? When did your husband realize what he had found?"

"Oh, it's been three months or more. Jonathan come up on the site when he was out lookin' for one of the cows. If there was anything Jonathan took care of as good as me, it was his cows. Lord knows he loved them one and all." Dorothy shook her head and looked at the floor. "Anyways, he was out lookin' for one of them. We had a pretty little heifer, not more than six or seven months old. She wandered off up in that canyon." She pulled her gaze back to Jessica. "You see the fires last summer barely touched that one corner of our land. My goodness, we was lucky. All it burned was some old brush and dead trees. Can't hardly see any sign of the fire now. Well, it must've uncovered this place and the cow had got herself caught in some sort of hole. She'd been missin' for days."

"Is that when Mr. McCabe found the ruin?"

"Oh, yes, that's when it started. He come home all excited carryin' some stuff in his coat. An old pot and some sort of stone axe or somethin' he'd found. He took 'em over to that cultural center on the edge of town."

"The Anasazi Center?"

"That's the one. He talked to some fella he knows over there. It was afterward he started actin' strange. Actually, it was the next day he went out to that place and didn't come home for days. When he finally did, he was actin' real peculiar."

"Peculiar in what way?"

"Mumblin' to himself, all shaky like. His eyes looked real funny and wild. He kept mutterin' 'bout all the money he was gonna get for the stuff."

"If you don't mind my asking, were you in need of money?" Jessica asked, curious about McCabe's motives. "Some sort of desperation must have fueled such an extreme reaction."

"Oh Lord." Mrs. McCabe put her hand to her heart. "Everybody in these parts knowed we was hurtin' for money after all them hospital and doctor bills. I spent near a month in ICU."

"I'm sorry," Jessica said, offering a sympathetic smile. "Did he share with you why he thought he was going to make so much money?"

"No. He never told me anything. He took some of the stuff into town and tried t' sell it. It was right after that he got a call from the folks at the University in New Mexico. He was hoppin' mad. Said them folks had no right to be stickin' their noses in this. Started carryin' a rifle in his truck and said he was gonna shoot 'em if they showed up."

Jessica's eyes went from the notepad to Dorothy. "But the site is only partially on the ranch, the rest is on government property. Isn't that right?"

"Oh yes. But that didn't seem to make no difference to Jon. He thought since he found it, it was his. I'm afraid somethin's gone wrong in his head."

A tense feeling gripped Jessica's throat as her mind went to Alex alone at the site. McCabe could be even more dangerous than she had first feared. "It seems he had a pretty violent reaction to all of this. Was that something unusual for him, too?"

"It was, up 'til then. Jonathan ain't that kind. Why, he could hardly bring himself to shoot them coyotes that was hecklin' the calves last spring. I finally called the fish and game service to come out and take care of the problem. Relocated 'em they did."

"Why do you think he was so angry?"

"I guess cause of the money he thought he was goin' to make. Don't know for sure, but he called some man from out at the Anasazi Center and he come right over to the house. Him and Jonathan spent a long time sittin' in the parlor up at the house and talkin' in real low voices."

"Any idea what the meeting was about?"

"No. Like I said, Jonathan never told me anything." Dorothy sat back in the chair and looked sadly at her hands now folded in her lap.

"I'm sorry, you know, about your marriage." A surge of compassion welled up in Jessica's throat. "I know how hard it is to lose someone you love."

"Ain't nothin' to be sorry for, girl. That's life, you know. Things like this happen. Oh, here I go again. Would you like some more tea?"

Jessica held out the cup as Dorothy poured more of the steaming sweet smelling tea. Bad things do happen to good people, but this woman seemed to be having more than her share of hard times.

"These cookies are wonderful," Jessica said as she nibbled at a tiny sugar coated lemon cookie.

"Oh, thanks. They're Jon's favorite, you know."

"No, I didn't know, but I can see why."

"Seems to be about all I do these days is cook and rearrange the dust in this place. I really miss the ranch. Can't seem to get it out of my blood."

"Do you think you'll ever go back?" Jessica asked, unable to hold back the emotion washing over her. This woman was so much in love with her husband, and her broken heart was evident.

"I'd go back to my old life in a heartbeat, girl, if I could have things back the way they were before Jon found that miserable ruin." Dorothy's cup rattled in the saucer and it was obvious she tightened her grip to stop it.

Jessica nodded. Seeming to sense the depth of Jessica's compassion, Mrs. McCabe rose then knelt on the floor next to Jessica's feet. Reaching out, she placed a warm hand upon Jessica's arm.

"There is somethin' I've got to tell you." Dorothy's voice was low and shaky. "This probably sounds silly, but when you called me yesterday—" She paused and bit her lower lip as she searched Jessica's eyes.

"Yes." Jessica reassured, squeezing Dorothy's hand as it lay upon her arm.

"I got the strangest feelin' that somehow you were goin' to be the one who made things okay again—" Dorothy stared down at the floor then stood and adjusted her clothing nervously. "I'm sorry. I'm babblin' nonsense. I hurt so bad without him, I guess I'm prayin' for a miracle and I hoped you'd be it."

An irresistible urge came over Jessica. She rose to her feet, put her arms around Dorothy and hugged her. She caught the sweet smell of perfume, the scent of fresh cut flowers and sunshine. The same scent her aunt always wore. Dorothy was about the same age as Aunt Helen—if—if Aunt Helen were still alive.

"You know, Dorothy," Jessica said, "I can't explain it, but I think there are some things greater than ourselves at work here." She paused and gently squeezed Dorothy's shoulders. "And I have a feeling too—call it intuition if you like—but I think somehow things are going to turn out okay." If this beautiful lady had hope, Jessica would be the last to take it from her. No matter what she'd been through, she'd never let herself stop believing happy endings were possible, even if it didn't always happen that way.

Dorothy stepped back and smiled, dabbing her eyes with the lace handkerchief. "I sure hope you're right, my dear. But I've enjoyed the company anyway. Not many folks come to call on me these days. Jonathan's run off most of our friends."

Jessica winked and gathered her belongings from the coffee table. "I've enjoyed our visit, too. And I know I'll have more questions along the way. Would you mind if I came back?"

"Oh, my dear, I'd love to see you."

Stepping outside, Jessica descended the stairs and opened the car door. She tossed in the briefcase and waved to Mrs. McCabe who stood on the front porch. She wasn't sure why she'd told Dorothy everything would be okay. Her own words seemed to have come from someone else's mouth.

As she sat in the car, the voice of the spirit in the kiva rang in her ears. *"You are called now to help the souls of many."* She'd come here with her own important purpose, her own dream, and she wanted it badly. But somehow it kept fading into the background, swallowed up by some immense force, pulling at her heart.

Had this opportunity come her way by chance, the opportunity to launch herself into a new career? Or was something else at work here, something with a greater purpose? It haunted her, made her uncomfortable and she was damn well determined to find out if it were true. She needed some answers to some deeper questions and she knew there was only one place she could go to get them.

—◆—

Jessica sat cross-legged on the cold stone floor of the kiva. The rays of morning sunlight peeked through the opening in the kiva roof overhead. The air was crisp and still and the faint sound of two scolding magpies echoed through the canyon and the surrounding trees. She looked around warily and took a deep breath. Frankly, this wasn't her choice of places to be, but it was the only place she dared ask the questions of her heart. God, would Miriam love to see this.

Closing her eyes and focusing her mind, she extended her palms and rested them on her knees. After several more deep breaths, she spoke. "Oh, spirit. I am here to listen," she crooned.

She waited in anticipation, listening for some sign of the spirit's presence. The birds up above had quieted their chatter and not a sound could be heard. This time she whispered. "Spirit, are you there? I've come back."

Nothing but heavy silence hung in the room. She settled herself again on the stone floor, squared her shoulders, and whisked back a strand of hair. "I'm ready to hear more."

Jessica listened intently. Not a leaf rustled, not a bird made the slightest sound. Suddenly she felt silly. Good God, she hoped no one had seen or heard her. If they had, there would be a padded truck and some guy with a straight jacket waiting at the top of the canyon. She'd been contemplating McCabe's sanity maybe she should be concerned about her own. She rose to her feet and glanced around the darkened room. Stonewalls. It was just a cold stone room and the only thing in it was her and her overactive imagination. She turned back to the ladder and grasped the rung.

"What has brought you back?"

Jessica stopped and whirled around. "Are you there?"

There was no answer. "You told me I'd come when I was ready to hear more." She moved away from the ladder and moved back toward the center of the room. "Well—I'm ready. And I have questions."

"The questions you can keep for later, but I know what you seek." A small iridescent lavender cloud rose from the spirit hole and grew in size as it moved in a circular motion above the opening. A cool damp wind whistled around her, and at last, the cloud formed into the old shaman's face. This time his headdress was the image of an enormous eagle. Sharp eyes stared ominously at Jessica.

"Why an eagle?" she asked.

"The eagle flies high and is the messenger of the gods. I have come to deliver a message to you. Be silent and allow me to speak."

Her mind reflected on the vision from the night before. The child had been named Eagle Song or something like that, a messenger to the gods. What his father had said made sense now. "Do not be dismayed. As streams flow together and become rivers then flow to become the oceans, so will the small pieces of what you have seen come together. But you must be the one to see it as an ocean. No one can do it for you."

"Your answers only bring more questions. Everyone here seems to talk in riddles."

"Riddles, perhaps. But they, too, are part of something of greater meaning. You have met the man with the blue eyes?"

"You mean Alex?"

"Alex is what you call him. I know him by a name much older, but he would not recognize it."

"Wha—?"

"The blue eyes, they have much meaning for him. They mark him as a chosen one."

"A chosen one. What kind of mumbo jumbo is that?" Jessica stopped as her words hung in the air and she remembered the blue-eyed baby in her vision.

"I know only what the blue eyes can foretell for this man. And be sure that his enemies know this as well."

"Enemies?" Jessica's mouth dropped open.

"The one of the spirit world and those who it controls."

Jessica stared at him. She wasn't sure she wanted to hear any more.

Before she could speak, the spirit answered. "You have come to seek me out. I assumed you want to know."

"I do want to know. I want to understand. But I came here hoping to comprehend my own feelings—and all of the things that have crossed my path in the past few days. I didn't come to add to the confusion. I want to know what it all means?"

"Look to the seventh direction and you will find your own answers. Why will you not allow the words of the spirit in? Your heart knows the truth, but your mind and mouth seem to constantly question its reality."

"What do you mean look to the seventh direction? Aren't there only four?"

"Our people believe in seven. North, South, East, West, upward to heaven, downward to our Mother Earth and inward to oneself. You need to look inward, that is where the answers to your questions lie."

"But I have my own reason for being here. This was to be my chance to do something for myself—at last, something for me."

"Doing for oneself is merely that. Not that it is wrong, but it is seldom rewarding, unless it also benefits others. Each of us has our own unique purpose in this world and our own soul will tell us when we find it."

The spirit's words began to hit home. "Well—if I look inward, I wonder if some of these things are happening for a reason. I feel them so deeply, and I want to help. But where do I begin to find and understand such a purpose, if that's what it is?"

"It is as I said of the oceans. Many streams will lead you there. Some of this time, some of the past, but before you are through with this journey, all will be one. Do not forget that, and the answers will become crystal clear."

"This is all very confusing," she said, rubbing her temples. "Let's go back to what you said about Alex. Two things you said still bother me. You said something about his enemies. Is he in some sort of danger?"

"For now, the enemy's only worry is that Alex will discover his own identity."

"Hmm. Then wouldn't he be better off if he didn't know?"

"His ignorance of the truth will only protect him for a while. The greatest danger may be to those who try to show him the way."

Jessica raised her eyebrows. She didn't think she wanted to hear any more on that subject either. "This brings me to my other question. You called him some sort of—chosen one?"

"Alex's coming to this place has very special meaning in the spiritual realm. But he does not know of the things that are his only by his birthright. For you see, Alex's blood is still strong and pure, not thinned so much by the mixing of many races. He has been far removed from his heritage, set on a path generations ago by a force that wished the destruction of his bloodline."

"Are you saying his ancestors lived here?"

"Many, many seasons ago, his family called this land home. The blood of his ancestry mingles with the sands of these mesas and canyons."

"Does he know this? Is that why he gets angry with me when I try to talk to him about the site?"

"No, child. His confusion comes because he is disconnected from his past. He feels it in his spirit but he does not understand the fire that burns in his soul."

"Why don't you tell him this, instead of me? He's the one who needs to know."

The shaman's image bowed his eagle-shrouded head and sighed. "If it were only so easy. When the spirit is closed, so are the ears. Only a willing soul can speak with those who hold its destiny. He is not to blame, his destiny was foretold generations before his birth and much has been done by those who opposed him to steer him away from what can belong only to him."

"But if he can't hear you, how will he ever know what his purpose is to be? And how do I fit into all of this?"

"You are an interesting child, you answer your own questions with more questions." The cloud that held the spirit grew thin and translucent and an image of a couple emerged, a beautiful young Indian couple, holding each other and looking into each other's eyes.

"I saw her—." Jessica whispered. "I saw her on the hillside above the ruin. Who is she?"

"If you look closely, you will know," the spirit said.

Leaning forward and squinting at the hazy image of the two lovers, the faces began to crystallize. The faces were Alex and hers. She gasped then sputtered in protest. "Wha—what are you trying to show me? I'm not her, she's not me—I mean we're not them."

"What once was will be again. That which lives eternal, is sometimes born again, if not in the flesh, then in spirit alone. Think about it, my child, it seeks to speak to you. Two things should speak to you from this vision."

"I'm the one who has to help Alex?" Jessica heard the words come from her mouth, but they seemed distant. The problem was, she didn't know what she was supposed to help him do. The rest of the question spilled out like a runaway pony. "Why do you show us as lovers? How could you know such a thing, if even I don't know?"

"As I said before, you hear my voice, therefore I know. I know the truth, before you know it is truth."

"But what about the Indian maiden? You haven't told me who she is. And that young man—"

"In time, you will know. The story shall be revealed to you soon enough."

"The story—you mean the legend? Is it possible? It's not just something someone made up?"

"Only you can be the judge after you have heard and experienced the story for yourself. Then and only then, will you know why you have come here. For the past, for the future, only you will find the truth." The wind began to whistle once more and the cloud spun in its large circular pattern, sending particles of dust and dirt in Jessica's direction.

"Where are you going?" Jessica demanded. "You can't leave me now—"

As the spinning cloud dispersed into a tiny pinpoint of light in the spirit hole, the shaman's voice echoed. "I am always at hand. I am never far away, fear not. Go the way you are taken and listen."

Jessica was now on her hands and knees staring down into the blackness of the spirit hole. "Wait. You can't—" she cried, as the light disappeared. A feeling of desperation clung to her heart as hope vanished in a twinkle of light. Sitting back onto the stone floor, she gave a huge sigh of frustration.

"Dammit," she whispered. She'd come here seeking answers and hoping for comfort. Now she felt worse than ever. He'd given her just enough to make it next to impossible to concentrate on her article. If he were right, there was something a lot bigger going on here than met the eye.

But she wasn't going to stop writing her story. Nothing would stop her. She still had a chance at what she wanted. Even if she did have to slay a few dragons along the way, she wasn't leaving until it was finished.

How dare the old shaman make a crack about doing things for herself? He hadn't been where she'd just come from. She'd paid her dues. And she still had the mental power to deny any of this ever happened, if she chose to—and it damn sure was her choice. Even he'd said that himself. *Subconscious grief that's all you are. You aren't real.* Tears burned the backs of her eyes. Why in God's name had it chosen her and why now?

If she agreed to this, how the hell could she help Alex find the truth? "Truth?" She snorted. She and Alex couldn't even talk about the ruin.

How could she teach him about his ancestry from the mesa? And if she did, what was she supposed to tell him? "Open your ears, sweetie, this spirit's got something he wants to say." *Good grief.*

After a few minutes she climbed out of the kiva and into daylight. She certainly wasn't going to find any more answers here, today. It seemed like a giant jigsaw puzzle. Trouble was, the more pieces she had in her hands, the more confused she became.

———◄———

Alex brushed the soil from the shard of pottery and held it out of his shadow and into the late afternoon sun. It was more of the same common Anasazi pottery. Nothing similar to the pattern he searched for. With his gloved hands, he placed it on the fabric spread on the ground next to him. These were more advanced patterns, definitely from the end of the Anasazi occupation of the mesa.

Something troubled him about these pieces. They were too near the surface and their condition wasn't conducive with where he'd found them. Buried in the earth for eight hundred years, they should have shown more signs of discoloration and deterioration from moisture.

Leaning back on his heels as he kneeled over the fresh dig, he put his hands on his hips and scanned the surrounding area. He couldn't quite put his finger on the feeling he had.

As he moved forward, he began working a small adjacent area where his explorations had gone deeper into the earth. Under the shelter of a rocky overhang, he hoped to find better preserved clues to the past.

Brushing at the sandy soil, his eye caught a glimpse of something. He parted the grains of sand, bit by bit a small rawhide pouch revealed itself from its hiding place in a tiny pocket next to the stone.

Gently, he removed all the soil then laid the pouch upon the fabric next to the pottery pieces. The rawhide was stiff and discolored, but out of the top of the tiny pouch protruded the end of a polished bone.

Using great care not to damage the pouch, Alex removed the object and laid it on his glove-covered hand. The tiny piece of the past lay in his palm in near-perfect condition. *An eagle bone whistle.* He recognized it at once, having seen one at the university during his studies. The modern version on display there was still used at the Native American Sundance.

That one had not affected him in the same way as this one. Something about the piece spoke to him, touched his memory somewhere. It glinted in the rays of the sun, polished to a beautiful shine and preserved in a state of perfection. Reality clicked in his mind as he scrambled for a bag to place the pouch and whistle in, out of the sunlight and air. His eyes did not want to leave the piece, as he placed it in a plastic bag and wrapped it in a strip of dark cloth.

Cradling the piece in his gloved hands, he carried it to the back of his vehicle and proceeded to pack and catalog it. Tucking it safely away, he pulled up the tailgate. Yellow Dog, who lounged in the shade of the truck avoiding the midday heat, rose and lifted his ears. He turned his head from side to side and listened intently. A low growl came from deep in his throat. "Whatta you hear, boy?" Alex glanced down at the dog. A high-pitched noise came to his ears, and he stopped in his tracks and looked around. The whistling sound grew louder and began to weave itself into a sad bone-chilling melody.

Alex looked in every direction then realized the sound came from behind him. It was almost hypnotic and Alex became obsessed with finding its source. He rummaged through the pile of personal effects in the back of the vehicle. Finally, his attention focused on the folds of fabric protecting the bagged artifacts. He reached for them but quickly realized the sound came from a cardboard box next to it. Pulling the open box closer, he looked down at the bubble wrap covered kachina and the small cloth shrouded object he'd inadvertently laid on top of it moments earlier. The realization sent a shiver up his spine.

"No, it's not possible," he whispered. Goose flesh raised on his arms as he picked up the object and moved back the cloth from the small plastic bag that held the eagle bone whistle. Picking up the bag, the melodic vibration and rhythm pulsed in his hands. He dropped it and stepped away in disbelief. He ran a hand through his hair and rubbed the back of his neck, not knowing what to make of this. He raised an eyebrow in the direction of the box, a renewed uneasiness at its contents surfacing.

Within a few minutes the music stopped. Alex picked up the bag containing the whistle and removed it from its wrapping. It lay majestically upon its aged pouch, glistening in the sunlight and whispering Alex's name. There was no logical explanation for its effect on him nor could he explain the music it had played moments before.

He was a skeptic, but in his years at the temples and altars of the ancients, he'd learned not to doubt the possibilities of anything. With a creased brow, he put the tiny object back into its sanctuary and into its proper place among the other artifacts.

"Maybe we've been out here alone too long, huh, boy?" he said to Yellow Dog. "Or this heat has gotten to our brains. How about we have some dinner?"

The dog yapped and wagged his tail. Alex closed the tailgate as insurance the piece and the kachina were both out of sight and earshot.

———

Alex tossed and turned. He pounded his fist into the sleeping bag, trying to find a place where he was comfortable. But tonight any comfort he could find for his physical body was being overridden by images dancing in his mind and the sound of the whistle echoing in his ears. He couldn't seem to turn it off, until at last somewhere in the early hours of the morning, sleep claimed him. Then the dreams began.

The young man moved back from the cliff's edge as the warm wind whipped the rawhide loincloth that covered him and threatened his balance. A high-flying crow swooped down, his raspy squawk echoed through the crannies and crevices below.

Beside him the old chief stood at the rocky edge, unflinching. As the chief spoke, the wind stilled and the scolding crow fell silent. "Look out over the lands, my son. For this will soon be your kingdom." The old chief waved his hand before him as he looked out into the distance.

"It's beautiful, Father, but it will be a long time before this is my land to watch over." The young man smiled in amusement at the idea.

"Perhaps not, my son." The old man's eyes narrowed. "I have had a vision that brings me much concern for the future."

The boy turned abruptly toward his father. "What is it you have seen?" The young man's heart pounded harder.

"You are very young. You have much to learn, but the time is near when you must lead the people without my help."

"But, Father, I'm not ready. You've said so yourself and you have promised me more summers to learn what I must know."

"It is not up to me, my son. The gods have decided my teaching shall only bring you this far. There is much you do not know." The father shook his head. "I can only ask the great one to guide you. I have been foolish, for I have no control over what the creator of all decides will be."

The boy's heart was in his throat. The ugly hand of fear grasped at his belly. "Then you must teach me all you know. We must work harder. You must help prepare me for what is to come."

"I think there will be little time for such teaching." The old man's chin seemed set against a quiver. "And I regret that your preoccupation with the woman has kept you from learning as much as you should."

The young man flushed as his father acknowledged his secret. But he refused to feel shame for what he felt in his heart. Silence fell between them. At last, the boy spoke. "I'm afraid. I can't do this without you."

From beneath the rows of adornments that hung from his neck, the chief removed a rawhide string that bore a leather pouch. The shells and beads covering it announced the contents as precious. The young man's eyes widened. From out of the pouch the chief took a lavishly decorated whistle and a rose colored stone that hung from a string of rawhide.

"You must always remember this. The power of the spirits is yours, but only if you believe it is so. If the power fails you, you must always keep these near. The whistle will help you summon the spirits of good. The amulet will protect you from the evil that is sure to follow. Use them well, use them wisely, and you must

always keep the two of them with you. Good and evil have been together since the beginning of time, you will never find one without the other close at hand. Good has the power to prevail, but evil lurks at every turn in the path."

The boy took the whistle and amulet and held them in his hand. He fought back the fear and sorrow that choked at his throat. No words would come to his lips.

The old man's eyes shimmered with moisture as he gave the boy a half smile. "Look to the spirits, my son. Depend upon the gifts of the fathers for they shall be all I can leave with you now. Look out upon the valley, look behind you at the grandness of the mesa. It is your heritage."

The father turned, took several steps and the rocky mass beneath his feet crumbled away.

"No—" the boy screamed as his father fell from the top of the craggy point to the bottom of the canyon below, spreading his arms as he fell like an eagle in a deadly dive.

Alex sat upright in his sleeping bag. His heart hammered so loud he could almost hear it echo through the canyon. Beads of perspiration ran down his back. He ran his hand down his own bronzed bare chest, so much like that of the boy in the dream that he sat there and stared down at it for a moment. The boy's raw manhood spoke to Alex, both were afraid of change, both afraid of the unknown, both at the threshold of some spiritual journey.

Alex knew this dream had some deeper meaning for him. Something out there in the wild beyond was trying to speak to his soul. Like the boy, he needed to teach himself to hear what it had to say.

CHAPTER SEVEN

Jonathan McCabe lowered the binoculars and spat on the ground next to his dusty stained boots. "Dammit, woman. What the hell are you doing out here?" he growled through clenched teeth. "Don't you know what's going to happen to you if you don't stay away from that bastard archaeologist?"

McCabe stood on the opposite side of the canyon and ground his heel into the dirt in frustration as he watched Jessica perched high on a rock overlooking the site.

His tiny glimpse of coherency was short-lived as the fury built inside him once again. Heat rushed to his face and he choked for breath, as he struggled to push the fire back into his core. The blood raced in his veins and his heart beat fiercely within the walls of his rib cage. He wanted to stop this thing that grabbed hold of his insides and brought out the hatred, the obsession that took total control of his being. It refused to be stifled. His hands shook so badly he could no longer hold the binoculars to his face.

A groan came from deep down as the force consumed him. His mind flashed. Mental and physical pain flooded through him. A picture of the person he used to be blazed in his mind's eye then was extinguished by a flood of rage.

"I won't let you come between me and my prize." The gravelly inhuman voice rode on a ribbon of hatred and flowed from his core. "This place is mine and so is that fool's soul. No matter what." His dry lips turned upward in an evil grin as he remembered something he'd found earlier in the day.

He cackled with wicked pleasure and with long hurried strides, climbed the incline back to his truck. Opening the door, he looked at the rifle hanging on the rack in the back window. He could easily pick her off from up here, but that damn archaeologist would hear the shot. Then he'd have to shoot him, too, and he couldn't afford to do that, not yet. The time wasn't right.

He let the truck roll then popped the clutch. Driven by his mission, he picked his way through the sagebrush and scattered piñon pines.

—⋘

The warm sun baked its heat deep into Jessica's back as she sat, head in hands, contemplating everything swimming in her mind this afternoon. She raised the camera, zoomed in and snapped a few shots of Alex working at the ruin.

The truth was, she was distracted and her heart wasn't in her work today. She'd come here to be near Alex, closer to the feel of his soul. A desire burned to know what was going on inside of him. An amusing thought, considering she wasn't sure what was going on inside of her own depths at the moment. If she were smart, maybe she'd call Simon and tell him she couldn't get the story. She could get into the car, drive away and never look back. It would be that simple.

But it wasn't that simple. Not anymore. What had started out to be an exciting assignment and a stair step to her dream job had gotten very complicated. She could go back to her mundane life and hope and pray another chance like this came along. Maybe another one would come her way. Maybe Simon would forgive her. If he did, could she forgive herself?

But it was Alex who was the real issue here. A few hours with him might put the story together and she could be gone. It was a daydream. He didn't want to talk to her about the site. And truth was, she didn't want to leave. She wanted to be around him, with him—in more ways than one. They'd danced, they'd touched, he'd held her close and she wanted more.

How could she possibly ignore the ancient spirit's words about Alex? The haunting message had a hold of her—soul deep. Could she walk away from this experience and never look back? Never wonder about the outcome if she ignored the things she'd seen and felt in the last few days? Could she leave and never know what happened to Alex? Or more important, never know what would happen here if she stayed?

She'd been told she was the one the spirit awaited for seven centuries. *Gee, no pressure there.* While her logical mind was going into convulsions, deep down there was a place that knew it was true. She had to follow her heart even if it didn't make any sense, even if the cost was more than she was prepared to pay.

And then there was Dorothy McCabe. A woman she barely knew who had captivated Jessica's heart with her plight. She'd honestly believed Jessica was here to help. Why? Where had that come from? If she walked away, she'd never know, nor could she ever forget the look in Dorothy's pleading eyes.

Common sense told her to have nothing to do with McCabe. There was danger there and she wanted to steer clear of it. She'd damned near been killed leaving his property. That was omen enough. But she was drawn in by Dorothy's story. Something about this ruin had changed him, changed him completely.

The ruin did have a magnetism about it, not just for McCabe, but for Alex, too. She could feel it, a drawing in of the soul. A connection to a long, lost past that threatened to be all consuming. What was it that McCabe had come across that had such power over him? She wanted to know.

Maybe that was why she'd chosen this profession over the one that had chosen her. Her idea of fun was to dig around in things, find out what made them tick, take them apart, touch them, and feel them. Then, once absorbed into her soul, she spit them out onto the page for the rest of the world to share. Sometimes it was a blessing. Sometimes it was a curse.

Nechi and the legend, the Indian maiden, Jonathan and Dorothy McCabe, Alex and she were all connected somehow to this place. In the spirit's words, they were the streams that came together to make an ocean, but right now it was a big murky pond. Each with their own story, each with their own reasons, and it seemed it was up to her to connect the dots and decipher the code.

She was fooling herself to think she could walk away. It was part of her now. She had to see it through to the end and pray she found the story of her dreams along the way. Gathering her belongings and placing the camera into her backpack, she started back through the wilderness to the park.

The time alone had helped clear her mind and she was feeling more at peace with her decision. Making her way through the sagebrush and yucca plants, she headed for the thick bushes and piñon trees that lay between the ruin and the park boundaries, half a mile or more ahead. The trail crossed a small ravine a few yards from the forest's edge. Carefully navigating the gravel slope, she made her way toward the bottom.

As she took quick short steps down the incline, a hissing sound came from the dip in the trail.

"Sssssss—" This time it was louder. Looking up from the path to search for the source of the noise, her heart stopped. She froze in her tracks stifling the piercing scream that tried to escape her lips. Less than a yard ahead, a gray and black snake was coiled, ready to strike.

The snake's beady eyes stared ominously. Its shaking tail displayed an unmistakable row of rattles. Cold beads of sweat formed on Jessica's brow. She stood motionless before the deadly reptile. Her breathing was shallow. Terror gripped her throat. She was afraid to swallow for fear the sound might set the snake off.

She could try to run, but any movement could cause it to strike. The incline behind her was too steep. No way could she climb it fast enough. Moving only her eyes, she scanned the rocky draw. Clumps of yucca and sagebrush surrounded her. Nothing was close enough to afford protection from the venomous fangs. Her foot slid a fraction of an inch. The snake's head rose. She'd never make it.

Her heart pounded like a base drum. Her ears thrummed. She struggled to keep her shaky legs in control. The snake moved its head from side to side. It waved its forked tongue, exposing the two long fangs, fangs that could hit their mark at so much as a twitch.

A movement to the right of the coiled creature caught Jessica's eye. She dared not look. A second snake slithered out from behind a neighboring rock. Menacingly it followed suit with its counterpart.

"Good God," she whispered. There were more? What if she'd walked into a whole nest of them? What if they were all around her? The beads of perspiration trickled down her upper lip and tickled the corner of her mouth. Her hand wanted desperately to brush it away. She forced it into stillness.

Her mind raced. What should she do? Any reaction could bring a deadly strike from either or both of the snakes. A pebble rolled down the embankment behind her. The snakes raised their heads and moved closer.

The blood raced through Jessica's veins. Light headed, she rocked ever so slightly back and forth. She willed herself not to faint. Not now. Her survival mechanisms were maxed out. Her brain ached as she forced it to think of a way out. Inside, she prayed.

Something screeched overhead. She dared not look. Loud rustling and a rush of air preceded a second deafening scream. A powerful mass of strength and feathers reared back massive wings and swooped down. Its great force knocked her back against the gravel hillside.

She looked on stunned as the mighty talons of a huge bald eagle pierced the flesh of one of the coiled snakes. The bird carried the reptile skyward, dangling and squirming in its claws. Its massive wingspread blocked the sunlight for a moment then disappeared into the distance.

Flinching, she pulled herself a few inches up the hill with her elbows. Her eyes were glued on the second snake that seemed as surprised as she. Perhaps realizing the bird posed a greater danger than Jessica, the snake lowered its head deeper into its coils. The reptile's beady eyes were on Jessica. Its ominous tail still rattled.

A loud crunch came from behind her. The gravel rolled beneath her and two large hands grasped her underarms. In one swift motion, she was dragged up the side of the ravine and out of the reach of the snake. Wary of the eagle and pelted with gravel, the snake uncoiled and slithered toward a neighboring yucca plant.

Jessica looked up at a towering muscular frame standing over her. At this moment the form seemed at least a hundred feet tall. In a matter of seconds the image crystallized and she realized it was Alex.

"Wow." He bent over, placing his hands on his knees and gasping for air.

"Oh, my God." She sat up and buried her face in her trembling hands.

"I've been running all over this hill tracking down that scream of yours." He struggled to regain his breath. "I couldn't see you down in this ravine."

"How'd you get up here so fast?" she asked.

He motioned to his vehicle parked a short distance away. "What in the hell are you doing out here?" he asked in an annoyed tone.

She hesitated. This time his scolding stung her emotional state and threatened to bring her to tears. "Research," she managed a defiant reply and brushed at the dust and bits of rock clinging to her jeans. "But that was a close one," she reluctantly admitted under a relieved breath.

"Close one." His hands on his hips punctuated his displeasure. "You damn near got yourself snake bit."

"No kidding," she retorted. No matter what he said, she wasn't going to cry.

He rolled his eyes. "Are you all right?"

"Fine, aside from being half scared out of my wits."

Perhaps he began to understand how scared she really was. He seemed to contemplate for a moment then a half-smile crossed his face, mixed with a look of amazement. "You know, I got here just in time to see that eagle snatch up the snake. That's how I found you."

"Pretty wild, huh?" She felt a little sick thinking of how lucky she had been.

"Wild." He snorted. "You must have a guardian angel who took wing and turned into a bird. Unbelievable."

A chill ran through Jessica's body and tiny goose bumps raised on her arms at his words. It was unbelievable, every bit as unbelievable as walking away from the Jeep accident.

Alex offered a hand and helped her to her feet. "You know, if you're so damn set on getting this story, maybe you should come down and have a look around." His hesitation and creased brow told her he was uncertain about the offer. Picking up her pack, he put a steadying hand in the small of her back and brushed the dirt from her shirt.

She paused. Had she heard him right? "I'd be very grateful for your help." She faltered for words or maybe she choked on the crow she was about to eat. She wasn't sure which. But the sting of his earlier words melted in the warm rush from the touch of his hand. It appeared he was giving her what she wanted, but for some reason that frightened her. There was sure to be a catch somewhere. As she walked along next to him, she toyed with the thought.

"You don't have to pretend to be shy and appreciative," he said, motioning her in the direction of his SUV. "I've worked with the press before." He flashed her a cocky smile. "I know under that pretty exterior is a shark looking for fresh meat."

She gave him a sideways glance, not sure how to interpret his comment. "I've been called a lot of things," she said, "but never a shark." She walked a little faster. If she addressed the remark with the fire that wanted to jump straight from her mouth right now, she'd never get to the site. She gritted her teeth, swallowed her anger and went on.

"Nothing personal," he grunted, coldly apologetic. "If you still want to, I can give you a quick ten cent tour and you can be on your way. That is, if you think you can keep from getting yourself killed before we get there." He threw her a smile somewhere between annoyance and mischief. Opening the door, he quipped, "Besides after this scare, you could probably use a stiff drink."

"I think I'll take you up on that one." She tossed her backpack into the car. Whatever it was about this site that made him so uptight, she was going to find out. This guy switched from hot to cold so fast, she was getting whiplash. If life was intent on giving her a new assignment, it could have picked someone a little less difficult to read.

The angry scream echoed through the forest and canyon and was muffled by the noise of the vehicle as the engine started and the SUV wound its way back down the canyon. Jonathan McCabe stood a few yards away, hidden by the cover of the scraggly trees at the forest's edge.

"What rotten luck," he growled. "Damn woman, must have nine lives or somethin'."

He lit a cigarette and threw the smoldering match into the dirt, grinding it with his heel. Making his way down the ravine, he kicked a rock and grumbled, "I'll be a son of a—"

He was running out of ways to make this look like an accident. He'd even wasted the boulder he'd been saving for Alex on her. It was time for stronger tactics.

He kicked the yucca bush where the rattler had taken refuge and laughed as the snake slithered down the gulch. "Go ahead an' run you scaredy cat," he chanted like a mocking child. "Before I turn your worthless behind into a hat band."

All he had accomplished was bringing the two of them together. One step closer to what he was trying to prevent. Alex, by himself, seemed easy enough to fool, but this pesky woman was the real problem. Given time, she'd have Alex thinking. Thinking too much. She had to go, one way or another. Scratching at his unshaven face, he turned his thoughts back to the site. Things weren't moving as fast as he'd like them to. With Alex out here all the time, getting at what he wanted was tough. And it would be impossible if he didn't finish before that crew arrived in two weeks. He cringed. The place would be crawling with people.

If he'd been working alone, it might've been easier, but he didn't have a way to sell the goods without Tom Wilson. Wilson was the one with cold feet. If it wasn't so complicated, he'd get rid of them all. He smiled. Maybe that was what he'd have to do anyway.

CHAPTER EIGHT

Alex navigated the vehicle over the rough terrain back to camp. Jessica sat quietly in the seat next to him. He observed her out of the corner of his eye. She was very pretty, with her dark hair, high cheekbones and those hazel eyes that seemed to see into his soul. Something about her was innocent and sincere. She was relaxed and charming but carried herself with an air of wisdom and grace–even when he'd had to pick her up out of the dirt. Maybe, if he had met her in a different way—

Her looks distracted him. He had every right to be annoyed. Maybe it wasn't fair, she must have been terrified by those rattlers. But she was repeatedly putting herself in danger to get some stupid story. He'd never understand reporters but, okay, he kind of admired her for being so passionate about what she was doing. He just didn't have time to keep babysitting her. He had work to do.

Alex hoped he was doing the right thing by taking her to the site. It was better if he were in control of what she released to the press. Besides, she'd get her story and go on back where she came from. He hoped he was doing the right thing. Just then the dog poked his head between the seats and attempted to give her a kiss.

"Sit, Yellow Dog," Alex commanded. Great, now the dog was going to get in the act, too. As if his emotional traitors weren't enough. "Sorry, he's not usually a nuisance." Yellow Dog shot him a wide-eyed look then ignored his order completely.

"Don't worry about it. What a beautiful animal." She smiled and stroked the dog's ears. "He has an unusual name."

"Actually, he had a Spanish name when I got him, but it translates into Yellow Dog."

"Interesting. How long have you had him?"

"Two years. I was working at the Mayan ruins in Mexico and an old man gave him to me as a gift."

"I'm surprised anyone would give away such a gorgeous dog."

"It was a little odd, I guess." Alex shrugged and maneuvered through the sagebrush and piñons. "He asked my name then handed me Yellow Dog's leash and mumbled something about the gods wanting me to have him."

"Really?"

"Yeah, pretty strange, but believe it or not, weird things sometimes happen around old ruins. At least that's been my experience." And he added to that experience every day.

"I don't find that hard to believe at all," Jessica replied. Her matter of fact tone caused Alex to cast her a sideways glance and raise his eyebrows. He wondered what that was about. Slowing to avoid a rock pile, he made his way down into the canyon. His main concern was for her safety.

"You know, I still can't believe you were lucky enough to walk away from that accident. And now this." He couldn't get it out of his mind.

"It could have been luck. It could have been fate." She shrugged and grinned at him.

He didn't like her flippancy about it, but he couldn't keep from returning her infectious smile. "Yeah, if that boulder had landed on you, I'd never have had a chance to dance with you."

"Or pull me away from a rattlesnake. I guess we could say you've rescued me twice, huh?" Jessica quipped.

Alex shook his head and laughed. "You could say I saved you from two snakes. One with a rattle and one in a cowboy hat. What do you say, let's try and leave the snakes alone from here on out? Agreed?"

"Agreed."

Alex didn't believe her for a moment. He'd had a feeling she'd be trouble from the beginning, but it sure wasn't working out the way he'd imagined.

The SUV stopped next to the rock formation at the head of the canyon and Jessica stepped from the car. "I can't get over how beautiful it is out here," she said, breathlessly.

"Yeah, it's pretty awesome." Alex opened the rear door and Yellow Dog jumped out.

Jessica took a deep breath, seeming to inhale something from the land, as she looked down the canyon. "Can I ask you something?"

"Depends on the question." *Now what.* He stepped near her. Plunging his hands into his pockets, a hint of a smile tugged at the corners of his mouth.

"Oh, it's nothing personal. Well, it is in a way." She hesitated then glanced in his direction before continuing. "Is there something unusual about this place? I mean the whole mesa seems to emit some sort of feeling to me. It's very strong right here. Something I guess I can't describe."

He watched her, taking in the smooth curves of her body as the wind whipped the denim shirt tight to her breasts. Her full perfectly shaped lips formed the words as if she feared something she did not want to say might spill out at any moment.

She glanced at him, perhaps uncomfortable with his all-encompassing look then turned back toward the canyon. "I'm sorry," she said. "I must be rambling."

"Don't apologize. I was just watching you, the way your eyes lit up when you were talking. Something here must touch you very deeply."

"It does. Maybe sometime I'll be able to find the words for it and I can share it with you."

"I'd like that. I'd like it very much." Their eyes met again, punctuating the tiny pact between them.

Alex stepped away and motioned toward the small camp he had set up on the opposite side of the site. "Well, I don't have much to offer you in the way of creature comforts, but I have some cold soda or something stronger if you'd like."

"A cold drink of water would be fine, thanks," Jessica said surveying the camp.

Stepping into the tent, he pulled a plastic cup and a small folded towel from a box of camping supplies. He filled the cup and moistened the towel with some water from the spigot of the large plastic storage container that sat on a metal folding table. Handing her the towel first, he said, "Thought you might want to wipe a little of the dust off while you were at it."

Jessica smiled and accepted the cloth, wiping her face and neck. "I must be a mess." She looked down at the brown residue she'd wiped off.

"Not really." He passed her the cup of water. "A little dust doesn't diminish the quality of the merchandise."

Jessica stopped in the middle of a swipe across her face and gave him an odd look.

"I only meant considering you've been rolling around in a ditch with a couple of rattlesnakes, you look pretty darn good to me." *Oh, Alex, you've got such a way with words.*

"Well, thank you. I think." A slight blush came to her cheeks.

Alex glanced toward the sun that was sinking toward the horizon. "We don't have a lot of daylight left. If you want me to show you some of the dig, we should probably get on with it. That is, if you have your wits about you again."

"Sure. I'll get my gear from the car," she said as she walked away from him.

He waited with arms crossed, admiring the view of her snug fitting blue jeans. From this angle he had to remind himself she was a reporter and he needed to be cautious. If he wasn't careful, he was going to put himself right back in the same old vulnerable position he was in last time. He swore he'd learned his lesson in Mexico. He couldn't afford to let his guard down.

Jessica pulled her pack from the car and returned with her camera and small recorder. "Okay, let's get started." Excitement bubbled in her voice.

"It might help if I knew what you hope to find here." Alex shifted his boots in the sandy soil, arms still crossed, and aware of the serious change in his demeanor. "I mean, what sort of article are you writing?"

"Like I told you, I've been sent out here to find out more about this particular ruin. Specifically, the fact it predates any others in the area." She clicked on the recorder, as she too seemed to switch into business mode.

"Okay, stop right there." She wasn't going to lead him anywhere. He was in control here. "We have no proof it predates anything on the mesa and we've found nothing to suggest it does. Radio carbon dating involves taking samples and sending them to the university lab. It takes weeks, sometimes months. I won't commit to anything until I have those results."

"Then what started the rumor? Why was the archaeological community excited enough about this for the university to send you out here?" Holding the recorder in the palm of her hand, she pushed it closer to him. "I've read about the hundreds, maybe thousands of ruins that have been uncovered because of the fires, and I know the university doesn't have people at all of them. What makes this one so special?"

"We're only doing preliminary testing. I'm here to investigate the possibility and that's as far as it goes." Placing his hand over the machine in her hand, he frowned and pushed it back toward her. "Would you mind turning that thing off?"

"I'm sorry," she said. "I assumed—you said you'd worked with the press before."

Alex shook his head and turned toward the ruin, trying to keep his frustration from showing on his face.

"And you don't like it very much, do you?" She turned off the recorder and slipped it back into her pack.

"Why would you say that? Maybe I just don't like being recorded."

"Come on. That shark comment you made earlier didn't exactly ooze of respect for my profession."

He looked at the ground contemplating his response, arms folded across his chest. "Let's just say my experiences haven't been good and leave it at that."

"Please don't judge me on your past experiences. Reporters are human beings and some of us have scruples, while others don't." Her eyes seemed sincere, and he was having a hard time not being drawn in by them.

"You'll have to prove that to me." Her intuition was so right on, it was spooky, but he was sticking to his guns. He hadn't gotten where he was without demanding proof, and he wasn't about to get soft headed now.

"Then why did you invite me down here at all?" Her jaw was set and her head was tilted defiantly.

"Because it seems to me you have more than your share of accidents out here. I don't want to feel responsible if something happens to you."

"That's very noble. But I think there's something deeper than that going on. Forgive my frankness, I know we don't know each other very well, but you seem totally different toward me when you address me as a reporter." Her hard-nosed side was shining through. "You aren't the same person who just pulled me away from those snakes and danced with me the other night. Every time we talk about this place, you turn from Jekyll to Hyde."

"That might be true," he said, turning to face her as their eyes met. "I take my job seriously. And until you win my trust in you as a professional, don't expect anything but the facts when we're discussing my work." By God, he was drawing his line in the sand with her right here. "My work is a separate world and out here we're in a different place. If you can understand and agree to that, I'll be able to give you some things you can use in your article."

He dropped his arms to his sides, trying to change the brick wall posture he knew he exuded. "If you've come here for a story on the age of this ruin, I can't help you. I can't give you supporting facts, and facts are all I am willing to base my statements on. I will not speculate."

His demeanor softened. "If you're interested in some of what I've found and how we try to put together the history of a site using our information then you may have some ground work for a story. Anything else will be released by the university at a later date."

Alex rubbed his neck against his shirt collar, a reaction of relief for releasing his pent up hostility. He was a little uncomfortable he'd let it all go at Jessica. It had to be said. He waited for her reaction.

"That's fair enough. I appreciate your being candid with me." She squared her shoulders and raised her chin. "I'm here after a story. It's what I get paid to do. But, for the record, I'm not someone who would write a pack of lies in order to sell an article or promote my own career. Not at the expense of someone's professional integrity, and particularly not when that person may have saved my life."

She wet her lips and glanced down at the ground, before looking him square in the eye. "Maybe I'll never make it as a reporter, I don't know the answer to that. I write because I love to write, because it enriches me as a human being. If this kind of writing requires me to be underhanded and deceitful then it doesn't serve the purpose I want to accomplish."

He gave her a nod of approval. He liked her answer. Frankly, he'd have been disappointed in anything less. She was on the road to winning his respect and a bit of his trust, but words were only words. He expected her to prove it. That was who he was.

The ice between them melted a little, now they'd found mutual ground. "Why don't you step on over to where I'm excavating?" Alex turned and motioned for her to follow him. "I think some hands-on experience would benefit you more than anything."

Jessica followed him through the maze of stakes and caution tape as he threaded his way to the small mound of fresh dirt. He steered her around the screen laying where he'd dropped it when he'd heard her scream. Smiling, he pointed to the hole where he'd been working. "Well, here's where I spend my days." "You've been here *two weeks*?" Jessica asked, surprise evident in her voice.

"Excavating something like this is a slow and painstaking process. Progress is limited to about ten centimeters at a time. First the location has to be mapped and the artifact photographed in situ. It's a repetitive process. Go down ten centimeters, level the floor, photograph, then remove the artifact and continue down another ten centimeters."

"Wow. I had no idea it required so much time."

"It does. And it's kind of like being a detective. If you're not extremely careful, you'll destroy the tiny piece of evidence that can bring it together for you."

"Interesting," Jessica said, snapping a couple of shots of the hole. "What do you think was here? What sort of building, I mean."

"Hard to say, yet. But judging from some of the markings I found down the canyon this morning, there may have been a whole village here at one time."

"Really?" Jessica's eyebrows went up as if she found his words surprising.

"It could have been a good sized one, maybe even as big as the Yellow Jacket ruin."

"Yellow Jacket?"

"Another ruin over by Cortez. They estimate three or four thousand people could have lived there at one time. This one may not be quite as big, but it was sizeable. Although I'm suspicious this one may have had a second habitation."

"Second habitation? You mean it was abandoned and then people moved into it again, sometime later?"

"Possibly. I've found some unusual contradictions here indicating the possibility."

"Thought you weren't going to make any speculations."

He threw her a glance and was met with a vixenous smile. "That isn't a speculative comment you could hang me with." Here was a test for her. "But if you have the integrity you claim, you won't put it in print until I give you confirmation I've proven my theory."

"And how long could it take for you to prove your theory?"

"A matter of days, I hope. Maybe a week at the most."

"Hmm. I might have to extend my stay here until you've done some more work."

"An intriguing possibility," he said, giving her a sideways grin. That could be reason enough for him to slow the process, or at least the flow of information to the "press."

"What makes you think it was inhabited more than once?"

"You see the first area here, it's much more shallow than the second." He pointed to the hole at their feet as she continued to take periodic snapshots of the hole and surrounding area. "What I've found in the first area differs considerably from what I've found in the second." He pointed to the adjacent pit, which was at least two feet deeper than the first.

"That's pretty simple. Wouldn't that in itself tell you what you need to know?"

"Yes and no. I'm not convinced yet. It's more a matter of analyzing the materials to determine what I've found. I've done some tree ring dating, where we use the rings of the support timbers to help identify the age of the ruin, but there are several inconsistencies between those findings and what the other excavations have turned up."

"Mind if I ask what sort of inconsistencies?"

"Well, strictly off the record—" Was she listening or not? "I'm not satisfied the newer pieces haven't been disturbed in some way."

"Meaning?"

"When something lays in one place for centuries, or even for a shorter time, it takes on certain markings from the soil, or whatever it has been buried in. Things like colorations consistent with where the dirt has lain on it. Water marks on a certain area, if it happened to be in a depression where moisture gathered and sat against it for a period of time. Simple stuff, detective work, nothing technical."

"And you're bothered by those inconsistencies, aren't you?"

"Enough that I wouldn't be able to give a definite answer right now as to what went on in this spot seven hundred or more years ago."

"Have you found some things older than that?"

"I wouldn't like to comment on that yet. More testing needs to be done."

"Is that what you do with these so-called pieces of evidence you find here?"

"Yes, and that could be the next part of your tour. I have most of them packed in boxes in the back of my vehicle. Want to have a look?"

"Of course."

She followed him back through the maze of stakes and tape to his truck. Opening the back, he pulled out a cardboard box and opened the top, displaying its fabric-wrapped contents. Though drawn to it, he avoided the bundle containing the eagle whistle. He'd not be making any mention of it to anyone. As he folded back the layers of fabric, the tiny, bagged bits and pieces of the past lay exposed.

"Wow," Jessica commented. "You mean you can take a few pieces of a broken pot and tell me how long it's been here?"

"How long it's been here, what it may have been used for and what it looked like when it was in one piece."

"That's pretty amazing."

"No. It's my job. But most of the in-depth analysis is done back at the university."

Alex picked up two of the small plastic bags and held them out for Jessica to examine. "See the

differences I was telling you about?" He pointed to the
first bag that contained a shard of pottery. "This is a
typical piece of pottery, very common in the later part
of the occupation of the mesa, white surface with black
design. I've found several pieces like this in the layers
of earth in the shallow pit."

Jessica listened as she turned the bag over in her
hand.

"The problem I have with this piece is it was
partially buried in the dirt. Look at it closely. There
aren't any markings or discolorations. The marks it
did have, came off with just a touch of my finger. After
seven or eight hundred years, that wouldn't be the
case."

"Hmm. How does this support your theory of a
second occupation?"

"I'm not sure it does. But when I look at these
pottery pieces," he said, opening his hand and laying
the second packet on it, "they are a totally different
style. This is a much cruder pot. Made from ropes of
clay wrapped in a circular motion. Much less
sophisticated and from an earlier time." He rubbed his
hand gently across the surface of the plastic covering.
"This piece came from the deeper pit."

"That's why you believe the Anasazi may have left
and then come back here."

"Let's say it's what the evidence would indicate. It
isn't unusual, a very simple deduction, really. Several
of the other sites around the mesa appear to have been
occupied more than once. I'm not questioning the
possibility."

"Then what is the question in your mind? I can see
it in your eyes." Jessica seemed to have caught the
excitement.

"Like I said earlier, something just seems all wrong
here. The question is in my own head, I guess." Alex
turned back toward the box of folded fabric. He wasn't

ready to share his notion that the site had been disturbed in some way.

Picking up a piece wrapped in double layers of fabric, he pulled a tiny wooden object out into the sunlight. This was one of his favorite pieces. "Look at this. I believe it's some sort of ceremonial piece." He held the tiny figure enclosed in its plastic bag. The fact it was likely to be hundreds of years older than any of the pottery, must remain his secret, but he couldn't resist showing it to her. He'd made a real issue of not having any information on the age of the site. *Best not to reveal that to her yet.*

"This is wonderful," she exclaimed.

Turning it over, she moved the tiny bag to get a better look at the small figure of a deer constructed of split twigs and strips of willow, perfectly preserved for centuries.

"If it hadn't been back in the shelter of the rocks, it wouldn't have survived."

Jessica paused then gave him an odd look. "You said it was ceremonial. Do you think there may have been some sort of religious structure here? Say, maybe a temple or something?"

Alex stopped and raised an eyebrow at her question. "Nearly every structure here has at least one kiva. Religious ceremonies were performed in them on a daily basis. Modern Pueblo tribes still use kivas."

"I understand that. But perhaps one of these groups of people may have constructed a temple for their gods."

The odd comment struck a cord in Alex. Why would she have said such a strange thing? "That's an interesting theory. Mind if I ask where it came from?"

Jessica paused and looked away. "Just a thought, something I heard— Never mind. I was rambling."

Alex placed the objects back in their protective wrappings and tucked them away in the SUV. Closing the back door of the vehicle, he turned to Jessica and smiled. "Well, that's the tour. I hope some of it helped you."

"It may have. Thanks." Jessica said, distractedly.

The sun was disappearing behind the mountains and Alex was struck by an impulse. He didn't want Jessica to go. "I'm not a great cook, but if you aren't in a rush to get back, I could make us something for dinner." He must be crazy. Asking her to have dinner with him here. What was she going to think of a dinner cooked over a campfire, with a rock for a chair and him and a dog for company? She was probably from the city. She'd think he had a screw loose.

"I can't think of anything I'd like better," she said with a smile.

Well, he'd opened his mouth, nothing to do now but follow through. He needed to face the truth. He was lonely. A little companionship for a change might do him some good. What could it hurt?

CHAPTER NINE

Alex spread a blanket on the ground for Jessica. She watched with some amusement as he dug through a box on the table next to the tent. A flash of a smile that could easily have melted her heart followed the clatter of pots and pans. If she let him in, what would it cost in the end?

She studied him. Who was Alex? Was he the angry man who had sent her away from the site that first afternoon, or the gentle hero who had chased her down after the accident to be sure she was okay? Was the real Alex the man who had rescued her from a drunken cowboy and pulled her from harm's way just hours ago? Or was he the arrogant insulting archaeologist who believed she was a shark. He was complicated and she was puzzled.

What about his chilling warning about the ruts in the road the day of the accident? Had it been coincidental, were they words he'd said in anger, or did he know something about what happened that day? His entire demeanor said otherwise, but still it nagged at the back of her mind.

She had the remnants of a story, all Alex wanted her to know. He was holding back. It was obvious. But why had he been so defensive at first then decided it was okay for her to come here? If what he was doing was as routine as he wanted her to believe, why had he been so protective? There was something here that ran deeper, something driving him that he wasn't talking about. Did it have anything to do with the visit from McCabe she'd witnessed earlier? Surely he wasn't mixed up with that slug.

She was attracted to him, but his signals were more confusing than an out of service traffic light. He wanted her to go away then he wanted her to stay. It was as if he liked her, but hated what she stood for. She'd had no problem squaring off with him over her own integrity. How the hell could she sell Alex, who relied only on absolute proof, on the idea he was here for some spiritual purpose? It was laughable.

She hadn't known the definition of "challenge" until this afternoon. The story still seemed to have greater hope than getting Alex to open up. Sad and pitiful as it was, at least it had more possibility than her mission with Alex.

The clatter of Alex's pans brought her back to the moment. The spirit's suggestion that Alex and she had some sort of destiny together kept rolling through her head. She wasn't sold on that one there were a few too many unanswered questions to let her heart approach such a thing. Right now she had an opportunity to ask a few of those questions. Best to jump on it before he changed his mind again.

"How did the university find out about this site anyway? Didn't it start when some unusual artifacts surfaced?" she asked.

"A few months ago some artifacts surfaced at a shop in Cortez. The shopkeeper called the university about them." Alex moved on to a new box and assembled some canned goods next to the pots and pans. "The stuff was unusual and was traced back to a man named McCabe, the man who owns a ranch next to this site. He said he found the stuff on his property."

"I understand part of the site is on his land."

"Yeah. A very small corner of the site itself. Anyway that's how the university got involved and that's how I ended up here." He frowned. "I hope you're not expecting a gourmet dinner. Yellow Dog and I eat pretty simply while we're working."

"Whatever you have will be fine." Jessica kept her smile in check as it tried to push its way out into a chuckle. She returned to the question tugging at her mind. "What do you think of Mr. McCabe?"

"Stay away from him, Jessica." Alex turned toward her and abandoned his dinner project.

"I'd thought about an interview with him, but—"

"Don't go anywhere near him. Please. Something's not right with that man. Promise me you'll steer clear. Okay?"

Jessica raised her eyebrows, surprised by his forceful reaction. Why was he so intent on keeping her away from McCabe? She shrugged. "I can say one thing for sure. He was nasty enough the first time I saw him. I'm not anxious for a second helping of his ugliness."

"Good. Then leave him alone." Alex let out an obvious sigh of relief. Running his hand through his dark hair, he glanced down at his boots. "Guess I'd better get a fire going."

Jessica didn't like the tone of his last demand. She had no intention of obeying his orders. But his relieved reaction interested her, and she'd really like to know what it meant.

In the waning light of dusk, Alex assembled wood for the fire and stacked it in a circle of rocks a few feet from Jessica. She sat in silence with her arms encircling her knees and wondered what Alex was thinking. As she watched him, she contemplated the words of the spirit.

Tiny orange flames licked at the pile of logs in the fire pit. The smell of wood smoke tickled her nose as the shadows grew long and darkness crept into the camp. "Tell me about yourself."

"What do you want to know? I've already shown you what I do."

She couldn't resist the urge to pry when he answered as if his job were all there was to him. "You said you worked in Mexico, but what about before? You know. Where did you grow up and what made you choose this profession?"

Alex smiled as he knelt next to the fire and stared into the flames. "I grew up in Los Angeles."

"L.A.?" Disappointment filled her. The spirit had invoked images in her mind of Alex as a child running bare-chested and wild on a reservation.

"Yeah, how about you?"

"Oh. Denver. What about your family?"

"They've been there for a very long time. Dad's a professor at the University of California and Mom's on the City Council. My brother, Nate, is a lawyer in San Francisco and my little brother, Jimmy, is fighting forest fires in Southern California." He stirred the flames, sending sparks into the darkening sky. "Does your family still live in Denver?"

"No," she said. Had she been wrong? Was Alex the person the spirit had talked about?

"They live far away?"

"No. I don't have any. I lost my parents in an accident a long time ago."

"I'm sorry," he said, looking up from the fire with sympathetic eyes.

She bit her lip. "Thanks. It was difficult for a while, but I had a wonderful aunt who helped me through the worst of it. I don't know what I'd have done without her." Nor did she know what she would do without her now.

"It's good to have someone you can lean on when you need them."

"Yes. It is." She looked down at her hands, not wanting to revisit that part of her life right now.

"I never had a chance to know most of my extended family. I visited them a few times in Arizona, when I was a kid."

"The rest of your family lives there?" she asked, relieved to have the focus of the conversation back on Alex.

"My grandparents lived near Phoenix."

"That's nice," Jessica said absent-mindedly, mulling over the spirit's words.

"Grandpa'd roll over in his grave if he heard me tell you some of my relatives still live on the reservations in the northern part of the state."

Jessica snapped to attention. "You have relatives on the reservations?"

"Yes, on my dad's side of the family." He nodded and looked at her curiously.

"So you do have American Indian ancestry?"

"You seem surprised." His eyes narrowed.

"Not surprised, interested." She didn't mean to make him feel uncomfortable. "But why wouldn't your grandfather want you to tell anyone?"

"As a child, it was forbidden for me to even ask about it." He looked into the fire as if he were gazing into his past. "Don't get me wrong. It was something that came from a generation before, and was passed on to my grandfather, then my father. A kind of shame and prejudice that never should have happened."

"Shame? A shame for their own heritage?"

"My great-grandparents met at what was called an Indian school. Do you know your Indian history?"

"I know some. I've heard of the schools, but weren't they set up to educate Indian children?"

Picking up a piece of wood, Alex placed it on the fire. "That was their misguided intent and the way it was written in the history books. But from the way the story is told by my family, it was much different. Did you know that the children were taken against their will, against their parent's will? Did you know they were taken by force, from the lives and homes they had always known?"

Jessica's mouth went dry. "No—no, I didn't realize—"

Alex's eyes were cold and steely, his jaw tight. "When the children arrived at the school, their hair was cut. Yet another misguided "favor" since long hair was symbolic in their spiritual culture. From there, they were stripped of their native dress, scrubbed with lye soap like diseased animals, and turned into the white man's idea of civilization."

"How humiliating for them." A cold emptiness settled in Jessica's stomach at the thought.

"They were forced to stay at the school." He snorted. "Educated in ways the white man thought fit for savages."

"For what my opinion is worth, it wasn't the Indians who were the savages. How could they take children from their parents? That was cruel."

He shrugged, the solemn look of sadness deep in his eyes. "For some, it was years before they saw their families again." Alex let out a heavy sigh. "Many died. It's said they believed it was the only way they could go home."

"That's heartbreaking." Jessica swallowed the lump forming in her throat. "And your great-grandparents?"

"They were part of another group who never went home. They were stripped of their heritage and too ashamed to ever go back. My great-grandparents were proud people, silent people who carried a lot of hurt inside them. The white man did a grave injustice to them and many others. They made them ashamed of who they were. Turned them into people who neither fit in their own world nor in the white world."

"That's awful." Jessica felt stunned.

"It was awful. But a huge number of Native Americans of their generation ended up that way. They passed their feelings of separation and shame on from generation to generation."

"But they didn't pass it to you, did they Alex? You live in a different time. You should be proud of your heritage."

"What they left me, Jessica, was no feeling at all about my heritage. You know, until I came to the mesa, I hadn't thought about it in years. But something here—."

"Yes." Jessica could sense his passion surfacing.

He grinned at her and tossed a stone out into the darkness. "Could be that feeling you were talking about earlier."

"Maybe, or something even stronger."

He gave her an odd look, shrugged and rose to his feet. "That's enough of this walk down memory lane. I better get on with dinner or there won't be any."

Jessica sat by the fire and tried to absorb what Alex had shared with her. No wonder he didn't know how he felt about his roots. Not surprising he'd turned a deaf ear to his ancestral spirits. He came by it honestly. But she'd seen it. Beneath the shield of confusion over his heritage, burned a flame that was her glimmer of hope, and a new understanding of why she had to help Alex find his way home.

In moments, Alex had thrown off the weight of their emotional conversation, but then he'd lived it for a lifetime. It was nothing new to him.

He walked to the table and returned with an armful of pans, several cans and a handful of utensils, including a can opener. Picking up a grate from beside the fire, he dropped it onto the hot coals in the fire pit.

Deep in her thoughts and with renewed, although questioning, faith in the spirit's guidance, Jessica watched as Alex placed a blackened iron skillet over the fire and sliced a can of Spam onto it. The meat sizzled as it hit the hot surface. Yellow Dog laid near Alex's elbow, occasionally sniffing the air as the food cooked. A second pan was placed on the rack and Alex emptied a can of pork and beans into it.

"Told you it wouldn't be fancy," he said as he returned with a loaf of bread in a bright yellow wrapper.

"I think anything tastes good when it's cooked over an open fire."

"Then you've camped before?"

"Lots of times. I love the outdoors. I spend a lot of time hiking."

A pleased smile formed on Alex's lips as he stirred the pot of beans and then scooped them onto paper plates and accompanied them with generous slices of the fried meat.

"I had you figured for a city girl," he teased.

"Hey, you're the one from L.A. What got you interested in this kind of life anyway?"

"I started out following in my dad's footsteps. Got a teaching degree, taught for five years and hated it. Couldn't stand being in a stuffy classroom all the time. When I took an interest in archaeology, I got my degree and the rest is history."

"How long ago was that?"

"Seven years. Then they sent me to Mexico on my first dig and I've been there and in South America most of the time since. This the first time I've worked in the states since I graduated."

By the time the food was ready, Jessica was starved. She ate the simple dinner in silence and enjoyed every mouthful in the fresh night air. The feeling of sadness that had crept into her soul over Alex's family history was replaced with a satisfaction that washed over her as the pieces of the puzzle regarding Alex began to fit into place.

"Do you plan to research your own past now that you've been here?" she asked.

Alex shrugged as he wrapped a piece of bread around his meat. "I don't know. It's never been a priority for me."

"Oh," she said, somewhat disappointed. She'd thought it would be the next logical step, knowing what she did from the spirit. "You mean you aren't curious?"

"I guess I just have more important things on my mind. You know, the dig and all."

If she could have reached out and slapped some sense into the man at this moment, that's exactly what she would have done. His nonchalance annoyed her. Here he was with this incredible heritage and a secret unknown destiny, none of which she could tell him about, and he seemed to be wrapped up in his own little world. In his own blasted career. Well, she'd have to bite her tongue on that one. But how was she ever going to lead him on the spirit's path? He had his big dirty boots planted so deeply in terra firma and he wasn't even willing to consider what was in his very hands? Didn't he grasp what he'd told her was in his heart?

After a few minutes, he asked. "Everything okay? I mean the dinner wasn't too bad, was it?"

"No, it was very good," she answered contemplating the enormity of the challenge she'd been handed. "Is that offer still good for a drink?"

"Sure. I've got a couple of beers and a bottle of wine."

"I'll have some wine. Let's see. Does red or white go with Spam?"

"Red, no doubt. Coming right up, madam," he joked. "Only trouble is, you'll have to drink it out of a plastic cup."

"Oh, what the hell. Why not."

A few sips of wine helped to melt some of her frustrations. Deep in thought and cozy by the fire, she sipped some more. It tasted good. Was it the night air or the company?

Alex sat next to her on the blanket and leaned back as he looked up at the clear night sky. "Ever notice how many stars there seem to be out here, away from the city lights?"

"I know. Seems like a million, huh?" She leaned back too far and lost her balance. She toppled into Alex.

"Sorry," she said as she pulled away and righted herself. The wine must be going to her head.

He put his hand on her arm. "Don't be," he said, his face was close to hers. His breath was soft and warm on her skin, his touch gentle as he pulled her near. He placed his strong brown arm around her shoulders and pointed at the sky. "I can't recall ever seeing the moon stay full for so many nights in a row. Isn't it something to see out here?"

"I've noticed it, too." She remembered its beauty from the night before when she'd seen, in her mind's eye, the chieftain offering his child to the great god of the moon.

"It's even haunted my dreams," he said barely above a whisper.

Jessica turned her head from the great expanse of night sky and met Alex's eyes. "Is the moon what you dream about?" Her lips were inches from his.

"Not always." Something in his eyes looked distant, soft yet intense in the flickering firelight. He covered her mouth with his, stealing the breath from her, both from surprise and pleasure. His hand caressed her cheek and her heart quickened as his mouth remained on hers, his lips parted, soft, moist and wanting. They moved sensually over hers. Then as suddenly as he'd drawn her to him, he pulled away.

"I should be getting you back to the lodge," he said after a long moment of silence. His hand reached and held hers, a hint of a smile on his face, but his eyes refused to meet with hers.

"Okay," she said, finding herself at a total loss for words. She was mystified by his actions and what was going on in his mind. His kiss was so passionate and sensual and all she wanted was more. It seemed he hadn't intended for it to happen either. She wanted to turn off her churning insides so she could hear what her head was thinking. Now wasn't the time to act like a horny college girl, but damn if her libido wasn't screaming out that very thing.

Alex stepped away and waited in the vehicle while Jessica gathered her belongings. He had to put some distance between them. He wanted to turn off his feelings, turn on his mind and understand his reactions. The wine was a bad idea. He couldn't afford for things to go there. Everything was on the line. Jessica's lips drove him wild. They were so soft and he could feel the wanting. How could he have resisted? But a strangeness lingered. It was as if the woman from his dream had revisited him. As if that kiss had happened again. He felt like he was living the passion of that vivid dreamscape. What was going on here? The memory of the moment when his mouth met hers, when their lips parted and he'd drunk of the nectar of her being, filled his mind.

He moved uncomfortably as the warmth surged through his body. The desires of the dream warrior pulsed beneath the surface, held back only by the thin thread of reality.

Alex rolled down his window, breathing in the night air and trying to smother something he'd never felt before. A passion so strong, that if he allowed it life, he didn't know what would happen. Now was not the time.

The image of the warrior, who stood naked before the moon, called by his wild brother, remained imprinted in his brain. He feared his own feelings. The call of something primal tugged at his insides. He didn't know if he dared release it.

CHAPTER TEN

Alex was restless. Thoughts of Jessica had coursed through him all night and given him a fitful sleep. As he stood in the bright sun, he kicked at the rocks in the gulch where he'd pulled her from the snake. Something about what happened here yesterday was bothering him. But he couldn't quite put his finger on what was wrong. Uneasy and out of sorts, even the smell of fresh mountain air couldn't soothe what was eating him today.

Alex called to Yellow Dog who came bounding out of the clump of trees above the dry wash. "What you doin' up there, boy?" Patting the dog on the head, he playfully rubbed him behind his ears.

Attracted by something white laying on the forest floor, Alex walked up the hill and into the stand of timber. He approached and kicked at a white pillowcase. *Odd place for it to be.* There wasn't any civilization around for miles. Campers? *Pretty doubtful, way up here.* One thing for certain, it couldn't have been there very long. It was too clean.

He started to walk away, and something caught his attention. Something familiar. It was the imprint of a man's boot with a distinctive star shape in the heel. He squatted and put his fingers into the earth wishing it could speak to him and tell its story.

Alex rose and walked back into the trees, picked up the pillowcase, and looked inside. Along with some dry grass and tree needles was something unusual. He pulled it out and it crackled between his fingers. The tiny piece of dry, scaly material was almost transparent in the sunlight. He knew, beyond a doubt, what it was. Snake skin, the dry outer membrane shed by a reptile. Looking into the pillowcase again, he could see several more small fragments.

His gut knotted. This was a stupid trick if that's what it was. Dump a couple rattlers in the path and wait for some unsuspecting person to come along. *Unless, of course, they were intended for someone in particular.* Who was he kidding? There wasn't anybody else up here. Him and Jessica—and an occasional two-legged reptile named McCabe. Finding one snake out here was likely, two together could be insurance for a madman's corrupt plot.

The thoughts in his head made his belly sick. Anger caused blood to rise to his face. Clutching the linen, he walked back to his vehicle with Yellow Dog close behind. He'd had enough. He wasn't turning his head this time.

Unsettled, Jessica browsed the notes from her interview with Dorothy and decided to check out the Anasazi Center. As she drove, she couldn't turn off her mind. She'd dreamed all night of Alex, about his stories of the Indian schools. Every time she thought about it, the injustice caught in her throat. It was one more of the miserable details about Native American history she didn't really want to know.

Small wonder Alex seemed to be so far removed from his roots. The spirit said the evil had done his work well in separating Alex's family from their destiny. Even the children of a shaman would be hard pressed to overcome the mental and emotional torment of such a separation.

What could she do to help heal the spiritual wounds passed generation to generation? Wounds that were soul deep. She wasn't sure she could do anything. Hell, she wasn't sure she should try. Alex seemed to have come to grips with his past. What business did she have trying to interfere? Why was she even pursuing the possibility? Because her heart wouldn't let her stop, it wouldn't leave her alone.

She had to get herself back on track with the story before she got lost in this thing. Parking in front, she got out and strolled toward the circular building as the sun hung halfway up the morning sky. Its warm rays reflected in the large windows spanning the front of the structure. Her reflection in the glass caught her eye. Was she the same woman who came here a few days ago? Did the things running rampant in her mind, show on her face?

She pulled open the door and stepped inside, removed her sunglasses and scanned the many exhibits. Immediately, she began to examine the displays and dioramas. There was a complete history here of the Anasazi people that offered a step-by-step tour of their occupation of the mesa.

Pottery, stone axes, fragments of yucca fiber sandals and an array of lifelike models pulled her even further into the reality of their existence. She jotted down some notes and sketched a few drawings of objects in the display cases.

As Jessica leaned over a glass case near one of the windows, a flash of light from the outside caught her attention. It was the reflection off of the side mirror of a black pickup truck as it pulled around the side of the building. She recognized the truck. It was like the one she'd seen Jonathan McCabe driving. Maybe she'd see where he was headed.

She followed the truck along the inside of the building. It pulled into a loading area right below where she stood. Sure enough, Jonathan McCabe stepped from the vehicle. He was met by a man dressed in a suit. The stranger's red hair and beard caught the morning sun in a golden red glow. He tugged at the lapels of his jacket and adjusted his necktie as he glanced around nervously. At the sound of muffled voices, Jessica stepped closer. What luck. The lower panel of the window, only three panes away, was open. She'd pretend to be enjoying some fresh air and maybe she could hear what they were saying.

The red-haired man looked around warily before he spoke. "This was a bad idea." His voice was tense and he sounded agitated.

"Dammit, Tom, there's only so much night and day and we're runnin' out of both," McCabe snapped, not appearing to care who heard him.

The man called Tom, motioned for McCabe to keep his voice down. Jessica leaned forward and strained to hear his words. A spring breeze played in her favor. "I don't like having you come here in broad daylight."

"I told ya. Make up a story for 'em. They'll believe anything you tell 'em." McCabe narrowed his eyes and hissed back.

"Yeah, right. Let's get on with it. Just play along." Tom seemed angry as he jerked open the door of the truck.

With that McCabe grabbed a cardboard box from inside the cab and shoved it toward Tom. Then McCabe grabbed another one and they both disappeared into a doorway next to the loading dock. Jessica shrugged, wondering what that was about. A few minutes later, they emerged carrying two more boxes and quickly tucked them into the truck.

"It's good and dark by eight thirty. See if you can't get yourself there on time tonight." McCabe said.

"Great. Get the hell out of here before somebody sees you." Tom spoke in a hushed voice.

McCabe climbed into the truck. "Now, don't be late," he cackled as he pulled away.

The man ran his hand through his hair in obvious relief as he watched McCabe leave. Then he disappeared through the door by the loading dock.

Jessica stood there for a moment, contemplating the strangeness of their meeting. What were the two of them up to with those boxes?

Quietly, she made her way down the hallway, wondering how she could get down to the lower level. As she rounded the corner at the end of the hall, she saw a metal stairway. She descended the stairs with quiet, rapid steps. At the foot of the staircase was a large stainless steel door. A sign across it read "Employees Only Beyond This Point." She pulled on the door. It was locked tight. She raised on tiptoe and peered through the tiny window in the door.

The room beyond was filled to the ceiling with cardboard boxes, carefully labeled and stacked. It appeared they were marked with dates and locations. Before she could see any more, a face appeared in the window and the metal door swung open. She found herself face to face with the red-haired man who appeared to be as surprised as she.

"Can I help you?" he barked, obviously displeased by her presence here.

"Oh—I was looking for—the ladies' room," she sputtered.

His look of surprise changed. His eyes narrowed and recognition seemed to cross his face, followed by a flash of something resembling fear. "Upstairs and on your right." He herded her up the stairs then pushed past. As he did, she caught a glimpse of his name badge. It read, "Tom Wilson, Museum Curator."

Wilson threw a glance back over his shoulder as she hesitated at the top of the stairs. "Employees only down there. If you don't obey the rules you'll be removed from the museum."

Thrown out for trying to find the bathroom? That was an interesting policy. Must not have landed this job with his customer service skills.

She gave a quick glance at the room below then decided to pursue the man. Walking after him, she called out. "Could you wait a moment? I'd like to ask you some questions."

"The information desk is next to the book store. Ask them."

My goodness, for a museum curator, he certainly was rude. "But—" she sputtered. Before she could get the words out, he doubled back and was down the staircase in a flash. By the time she reached the top stair, the steel door had slammed shut. She stood there for a few seconds, contemplating her next move. Almost instantaneously, what appeared to be a white sheet of paper covered the window she'd looked through. Well, that was strange behavior. But what did it mean?

—◆—

Alex leaned against the door of the deputy's patrol car knowing full well he blocked the man's intended escape route. They stood toe to toe in the gravel parking lot behind the sheriff's office where Alex had approached him only minutes before.

"But, Dr. Nakai, I'm real short-handed with the sheriff gone on vacation." The deputy shifted on his feet.

"You could at least go out there and check those footprints. I know there's a connection."

The deputy scratched his chin. "With all this rain, it ain't likely them tracks are still there."

"You don't seem to understand. Whoever was on that mountain and sent that boulder down the hill, had on the same boots as whoever planted those snakes in the ravine." Alex stepped in front of the deputy's face, towering over his short chubby frame. "Short-handed or not, I don't see how you can deny the connection."

"Well, you know, that boulder came down on Mr. McCabe's land," the deputy whined.

"So. What happens on his land isn't exempt from the law, is it?" Alex flushed. "Owning a piece of property doesn't give him license to try to kill anybody who comes out there."

"Them are awful strong words, Dr. Nakai. You can't go accusing people of tryin' to hurt somebody unless you're sure. And you know this might be nothin'."

"And the only way to be sure is to get evidence. Right? And the only way to get evidence is for someone to get their lazy backside out there and compare those footprints."

"Well, even if I did take my lazy backside out there, as you say, it still don't prove nothin'. And I ain't no fool. McCabe carries a rifle in his truck, and I ain't crossin' him without cast iron proof. When you've got that, call me."

"Oh, now I see. Being a madman makes you above the law in this county."

The deputy looked down sheepishly as he kicked at the dirt with his freshly shined black shoes. "I reckon it makes folks a little leery."

"Well then, if the law's afraid of him, what other course of action does that leave me?" Alex narrowed his eyes and looked at the deputy point blank.

The deputy looked away.

"If you won't enforce the law, then maybe I'll be forced to take the law into my own hands."

"I wouldn't advise you to do that, Dr. Nakai," the deputy weaseled.

"I didn't ask for your advice. I asked for your help. Obviously, I'm barking up the wrong tree." Alex slammed the door of his vehicle and sped away.

Several hours later, Alex sat by the campfire. The flames danced, creating shadows around him that lit up the desert floor. His gut gnawed in anger. That damn useless deputy had gotten to him. He was losing his focus. Too many things were getting in his way and his frustration level was at its peak. He didn't have time to go chasing all over this godforsaken place, trying to keep some careless reporter and some madman from running into each other.

Maybe it was a coincidence. Maybe the deputy was right and he was making something out of nothing. Another day was gone, part of it wasted. Picking up a small stone, he tossed it out into the darkness. It was time for sleep again, and again he knew it would evade him.

Alex sipped at some of the wine left from the night before, but it only reminded him of Jessica, the sweet taste of her lips and the soft scent of her hair. Even the dancing light of the flames reminded him of the fire in her eyes. Damn, he couldn't get her out of his head. He lay down in his sleeping bag and hoped the liquor would do its job. Tomorrow he had to make some progress, and nothing could stand in his way. Holding that thought in his mind, the wine finally kicked in and he drifted off to sleep.

The woman stood at the water's edge, cool crystal droplets splashed on her bare feet and legs as the water plummeted from the rocky ledge and cascaded into the pool below. Its splashing sent ripples and shimmering drops in all directions from its core and the resulting waves lapped at the bank of the pool, making sounds resembling a thirsty dog's tongue on a hot day.

Gracefully, she extended a toe and tested the temperature of the water. Dropping the rawhide dress from her shoulders, it slowly made its way down her body and fell with a swish to the ground.

He watched her from behind a bush, a deep groan came from somewhere deep inside him. A surge of heat coursed through his veins as she dropped her garments and revealed the soft curves of her bare shoulders and buttocks. His eyes followed the sweet undulations of her bronze back, down to the long silky legs and thighs. She waded out, causing little ripples of her own as she immersed herself. Her naked beauty disappeared into the crystal clear pool.

Rising from his hiding place, he walked to the edge of the water and dropped the loincloth that shrouded the evidence of his wanting. She looked in his direction, first with surprise then raised her eyebrows in approval as she looked upon him for the first time.

He stepped into the water, following her path to where she stood. She parted her full moist lips as he pulled her to him and tasted of a passionate wet kiss.

"We mustn't. You know it is forbidden." Her objections came beneath bated breath.

"If it is forbidden, it should not feel so right," he whispered. Even the tepidness of the pool could not cool the heat that had burned, denied in his loins for such a long time. He drew her to him, the silkiness of her wet body next to his, heightening his desire for her.

Alex awoke suddenly, his body drenched in sweat from the intensity of his dream. He sat up in the sleeping bag and pulled himself free of its flannel-lined jaws. Crawling from the tent, he rose to his feet, begging the cool night air to wash over him. His heart still pounded in his chest, his muscles ached with tightness. He picked up a small pan and ran some cool water into it from the container on the table. He washed his face, splashing the cool liquid through his hair and onto his bare chest, its icy coldness at last breaking through the heat that clenched his body. A deep cleansing breath released more of it.

Who were these people who haunted his dreams, this young man who took over his body in the depths of his sleep and filled his mind and soul with these feelings? When he awoke, there was always one thought on his mind. Jessica.

Alex ran his hands through his hair as questions raced through his head. What was she doing to him? Was he ready for this relationship in his life? Was he ready for the intensity of what he felt for her? His body said yes. His conscious mind wasn't so sure.

CHAPTER ELEVEN

Jessica pulled into the turnout at the Sun Temple Ruin pondering the oddity of the empty parking lot. Strange that each meeting she'd had with Nechi had been like this, with no one else around. She stepped from the car, an uncanny silence hung in the air.

There had been a message at the lodge for her. Nechi wanted to meet with her here at Sun Temple. His only explanation, it was a matter of great importance.

She skirted the ruin and noted the craftsmanship of the structure. A plaque was inscribed with some information about the ruin's history. She scanned it briefly. Compared to the other structures here, this one struck a note in her mind. Never inhabited, it appeared its sole function was a temple to the gods. Perhaps a grateful people built it in thanks for their abundance. But another possibility haunted Jessica's mind. What could have created a need so great for the help of the higher powers that a simple people would have dedicated a building this massive to such a purpose. Considering the size, it would have been something important, indeed. People who had only their backs to carry stone and their hands to shape this enormous construction into existence built this. Whatever the reason, something great must have motivated such an outpouring of human effort.

Turning from the plaque, she scanned the area. Nechi stood at the edge of the forest, his arms folded, apparently observing her. He waved his hand, motioning for her to come. As Jessica walked toward him, he moved deeper into the piñons and scrub oak that formed the perimeter around the ruin.

Jessica lost sight of him. "Nechi." She pushed through the dense junipers and wild currant bushes.

"Nechi." Making her way to a large rock a few yards ahead, she laid her arm on its rough surface and searched for movement in the undergrowth. She walked around to the far side of the massive boulder and stopped short in surprise. Seated on the ground before a circle of stones was Nechi.

"I thought I'd lost you." Annoyance pushed into her voice. "Why didn't you answer me?"

"I was never lost. I have always been right here, with myself." Obviously he wasn't bothered by her frustration.

"Well, I couldn't see you. You could have answered."

"Could have. But some worlds you must find entry to on your own, without anyone's help."

"Oh brother, did I come out here to play another game with you?"

"It's not a game. Sit and you will understand why you have been called to this place."

Dropping her backpack, she seated herself on the ground on the opposite side of the stone circle. The sun filtered through the trees and brush, casting patchwork shadows on the dirt and on Nechi's face. Today he was hatless with a thin strip of rawhide tied around his head. He was wearing his typical light colored denim attire. Jessica couldn't keep from smiling, yet she couldn't explain why. He was a source of frustration and comfort rolled into one.

Resting her forearms on her knees, she looked intently at Nechi. "Now what is so important? Do you have something for me about the new site?"

"Yes and no. What you call the new site is to me a very old and disturbing place. Once sacred, its rich history is forever tainted with sadness and the shadows of evil from centuries ago."

"It's just a figure of speech. I know it's old." Jessica frowned, sidestepping his comment about the evil. A cold chill played down her spine.

"You know this, but you do not really understand. You do not understand the story that once lived within its crumbled walls. There is still much you have to learn."

"The legend again? I've heard most of it already."

"You have heard it, but you have not felt it. You have not allowed yourself to connect with what took place here hundreds of years ago."

"Well—" She didn't know how he could be so sure of himself, but she was curious. "Maybe I don't really understand what it's all about. Or maybe I just don't understand what it has to do with me."

"You can go no further until you answer that question." Nechi spoke with wisdom beyond his years. "We must go back to where it all began."

Nechi raised his hands above the circle of stones, and closed his eyes. The small pile of wood in its center ignited. "How did you do that?" Even to herself Jessica's voice sounded strange and high pitched with surprise.

"By myself, I do nothing. It is the Great One who works through us all." He passed his hand above the flames, each time a new color flashed in the fire, first yellow, then black, then red and white. With that he answered the unspoken question on Jessica's lips. "The colors are sacred, symbols of the four directions. Some believe they bring wisdom and power."

Jessica nodded, mesmerized by Nechi's calm sense of connection with what lay beyond the physical world. Her presence here suddenly seemed of greater significance, she wouldn't chastise him again for his reasons. She felt compelled to listen to what he had to say.

"A few days ago, I told you the legend. The tale of a young man destined to be a chieftain. Today, you are here for yet another story. A love story."

"A love story?"

"Two young lovers lived here many, many seasons ago." Again, Nechi moved his hand over the fire and a cloud of purple smoke formed in the air. Thick and heavy, it blocked her view of Nechi for several moments before it dissipated. She rubbed her eyes and coughed then waved her arms to fan the smoke from her face.

The smoke cleared. On the opposite side of the fire, a cloud-like image of the beautiful maiden she'd seen on the mountain sat next to Nechi.

"Oh my," Jessica gasped. "Who are you?"

"In life my name was Snowcloud. It is my story the gods wish you to know." The maiden's voice was clear and sharp. "You've heard the legend of our mesa, of how we came to be here. Now I will teach you the truth of its people. It began when I was a child. That was when I met the man who was destined to become my one and only love."

"The lover you called to on the mountain?" Jessica asked.

Snowcloud nodded, a distant look upon her oddly glowing face. "Song of the Eagle was his name. He was a beautiful, perfect child. His round face was like that of an angel and shone with something beyond this world. Something about him was different from the rest of the children, as if he were grown long before his time. Perhaps, because of his calling, it was as though he were already an elder inside. Song was never allowed to be a child. He walked among the villagers dressed in the finest buckskin, covered with colored beads and precious shells, treasures gained in trade with other tribes. Feathers of the eagle adorned baby fine black hair that shone in the sun with the blues and blacks of a raven's wing. Song only wore the feathers of the eagle, symbolic of his connection to the gods. A rawhide headband bore the turquoise image of an eagle. All his adornments told the people of his special place in the world.

"Song's eyes were blue, the color of the palest crystal blue sky above the snow-capped mountains." She raised her hand skyward, a far away look was on her face, as if part of her were somewhere in a distant place. Jessica thought of Alex's eyes. They too were deep and knowing, almost ethereal.

Snowcloud went on. "His soul called my name, called me to him with unspoken words. Even as a toddling child I was drawn to his beauty and perfection. I wanted to touch him, to bring the glow that shone from his face into my being and drink of its peaceful light.

"Song's father was a fine, proud man. He, too, carried himself with the dignity of a leader, and bore the love for his people in the depths of soft blue eyes. No one shrank from them in fear, but rather drew near wanting to touch the essence of spiritual peace that emitted from their presence.

"Our childhood was a happy time. The people of the village went about their daily lives with no fear or worry. The crops grew well and the people of the mesa had full stomachs.

"As Song grew into a man, he stood tall and proud beside his father at the ceremonies. His chest had grown broad and on warm summer days I could not keep my eyes from his glistening brown skin that rolled over his rounding muscles. The childlike chin faded and grew strong. The round features of a boy passed and gave way to high cheekbones and a determined set jaw. His hair grew long, a symbol of his power and strength.

"In spite of all this, he did not lose his softness, but along with it gained wisdom and a look that demanded respect. He walked in his father's footsteps, intent upon becoming a leader. I watched him from the crowd and noticed his eyes often wandered to me.

"If I acknowledged his admiring looks, he turned away. I, too, was growing into womanhood and became aware of the changes in my body. At first, I felt uncomfortable when I knew his eyes were on me as I walked through the village, but then I learned to watch for him, to want his eyes upon me. If I could not touch him, this was the next best thing.

"When we both had reached our seventeenth summer, I saw Song of the Eagle leave the camp one day with his father. Breaking all rules, I followed them, being careful they did not see me. His father left him in a clearing, telling him he must learn to pray to the gods in solitude. It was essential to his role as a leader to call upon the spirits without help from the elders. I watched him for a while then came to him. He did not acknowledge me at first. He acted as if I were not there.

"I followed you," I said to him, trying to get him to look upon me.

"I know," Song said, at last nodding and accepting my presence, but avoiding me with his eyes.

"Why do you not look at me?" I asked.

"I have come to pray. My father has bidden me to do so."

"I thought perhaps you found me unpleasant to look at. I have seen you turn away from me many times."

"You are not unpleasant," he said, softly. "It is not allowed."

"Not allowed?" I asked him. "So you are forbidden, exalted one, not only to be among us, but forbidden to look upon us, too?"

"That is not all truth. You have seen me many times among the villagers. My father speaks with the elders and walks among the people."

"I have seen, but I do not feel that you are one of us."

A sad look came upon Song's face. "Perhaps we are different."

"I think not," I retorted. "You are of flesh and blood just like we are. What makes you so different?"

"I am destined to be the leader of the tribe one day. I must learn all that I can, for one day I will carry the awesome responsibility of bringing the words of the spirits to the people."

"Does that mean you are a god? Or are you flesh and blood like us?"

"I am very much flesh and blood," he said. "Do you not understand that I have longed to be like you, allowed to play and run in the meadows of the valley? As I sat in cold dark kivas and listened to the drums and the words of the elders, I thought many times of your freedom. When I walked the village and others looked upon me as if I were something different, something strange to them, it was I who felt I was not your equal. It was I who felt lonely and chastised by your world. It was you who was free to live, to speak, to touch—"

The maiden stopped and looked at Jessica. "I recalled a day when we were small children and I had drawn too near. He looked at me as if I were a wonder to him and he reached out to me with his tiny fingers and carefully touched the ends of my hair. I was snatched away by my scolding mother, but I had never forgotten the look in his eyes. A look of great sadness, and now I saw it in his eyes once again. Until I met him in the clearing, I did not understand."

"I am sorry I followed you here," I said. "It was wrong for me to interrupt your prayers." I started to walk away into the forest and Song called out to me.

"Wait," he said. "Do not leave. I have dreamed of a time I might have a chance to speak with you, to be alone with one of the people and be treated as one of you. Would you sit with me for a while and talk to me as you would one of your own?"

"I sat, feeling again the sadness I'd seen in a lonely little boy's eyes. We talked for a very long time that day."

"Is that when you realized you were in love with him?" Jessica asked. She had sat nearly motionless and mesmerized by the girl's story.

"It was then that something changed between us, something far stronger than the looks that had passed between us over the years. I became Song of the Eagle's connection with the ordinary world. A world he'd been denied entrance into, and he became my eyes and ears into the world of the spirit.

"For many days we met at the clearing. When he came to pray, I would make excuses to leave the camp. I would go to gather berries, or bring water from the pool by the waterfall. But, I lied. I had gone to meet with the young chieftain, to hear the stories no woman had heard before. Stories of ceremonies held deep in the kivas where only men had ever entered. Stories of his father's magic and of the calling of spirits through the spirit holes."

A cold chill ran bone deep through Jessica's entire being. It was both an acknowledgment of her experiences and a confirmation of their origin. She grasped her arms and sat in silence, catching the watchful eye of Nechi.

The tiny maiden continued. "He told me of magic concoctions that kept evil from our village and conjured up the images of leaders from the spirit world. He spoke of a power of goodness so strong it had brought peace among the people for centuries. I knew nothing of such things. My life had been one of great peace and the stories I'd heard of anything different were centuries old, of ones ancient, even in my own time.

"The evil I'd heard spoken of was something I could not imagine, and fool that I was, I believed it could have no relevance to me." She stopped and looked down upon her small bronze hands and rubbed them together. A tiny light shone in the palm of her hand and she first looked at it then put it next to her heart.

"Song of the Eagle became the light of my life. We met in secret for many months. Even on the coldest of winter days, I would make my way in stiff leather moccasins to be with him for a little while. We sat in the snow and warmed each other's hands and hearts with stories of the other's life. I would tell him of warm summer days in meadows of knee deep green grass and wild flowers, and he would speak of the heat of ceremonial fires and of the heavy costumes worn in the dances to praise the gods. While the stories helped warm our bodies from the cold, in our hearts a fire of another kind was burning and growing daily.

"Song was a strong man, and he was obedient to the wishes of his father and of the gods. But by the summer of our eighteenth year, those wishes were dim next to the desires festering within us. One day, it was not I who followed him into the forest, but he who followed me to the pool by the waterfall. I loved him so and he loved me and we were meant to be together. Perhaps the fact our love was forbidden made it burn all the hotter. For once it began, we had no power over it. It controlled us, we did not control it."

"Sometimes when things are forbidden, they seem all the more desirable until we have them," Jessica said.

"True," Snowcloud said. "But such was not the case between us. Please do not misunderstand. That which Song and I shared was beautiful. It was the heart and soul of my existence. It was what breathed life into me, and it was the same for him. We wanted only to be together, but I did not realize that he could never truly be mine for he was already taken. Betrothed to a life as a spirit leader and though it was permitted for him one day to marry, it was not permitted for him to have the distraction of a woman in his life until his training was completed."

"And when was that to be?" Jessica asked.

"Not until his twenty first summer. And I had been a great distraction to him for a long time. He was further from being ready for his position of leadership than anyone in the camp knew."

"But didn't he have a long time still left to learn? I mean hadn't he been training all his life to be strong enough to lead?" Jessica struggled to understand.

"Perhaps everything would have been fine, if not for two events that occurred in his life. Shortly after he and I—" She paused, her eyes filled with longing, then she continued. "One day Song went with his father high onto the mesa, for what was to be his first vision quest. But before it ever came to be, a tragic thing happened. Song's father fell from one of the cliffs on the mesa and was killed.

"It was a terrible day. I still remember the sadness and fear on my young chieftain's face as he came back into the village, bearing the broken body of his father upon his back. He tried very hard to convince the people that all would be well and they were safe in his hands.

"Perhaps Song convinced everyone, except himself in the first days after his father's death. He sat upon the altar of the temple as the villagers mourned their dead chief. He did not let them see the anguish tearing at his soul, but I knew. It was only before me that he allowed his tears to fall, to mourn the passing of his beloved father, and to express the doubt he felt in his own abilities.

"It was during this time of turmoil I became aware I was with child. Our love had been forced to remain a secret and I knew this too must not be known by anyone but myself and Song. The superstitions of the people ruled their lives in those times. They believed if the leader should conceive his blue-eyed offspring before his own training was completed, the knowledge necessary to be a leader might be lost forever. The child would be seen as an act of evil spirits trying to steal the magical knowledge of the ancients.

"This was the reason they were forbidden contact with the outside world. I felt ashamed before the people, but it could not destroy the joy I felt at the growing symbol of our love growing in my womb. In Song's sadness, I believed the news of our child would help to heal the wound left by his father's death. And I believe it did. Song was very joyful to know we had conceived a child. He knew the villagers would not be pleased, and it would create doubt among them. We agreed it best to tell no one.

"We devised a plan that in a few months, when the child's coming became evident, Song would hide me away in his chambers. It was a special chamber, in the great cavern behind the temple, where only the great chief and his family were allowed entrance.

"In the meantime, the days of mourning for the great chief continued, and on the day of the chief's burial, something happened no one ever expected or imagined. A great dark cloud formed at the end of the canyon and a horrid smelling stench blew into the village and hung there for many days. No one could explain its source or its meaning.

"The elders met with Song and told him of their fears. Something in the cloud smelled to them of evil. It was weak, indeed it seemed to be hindered by the influence still left of their great chieftain, but they didn't like the look of it. They had great fear in their hearts. This was an omen of the things to come and they believed that Song must now call forward the spirits of good with his own powers and frighten the thing away.

"Song was reluctant, but agreed to call forth the gods to drive the thing from camp. A great ceremony was held and Song sat in his father's place before the fires and called upon the forces of good. The elders seemed satisfied with his ceremony and left.

"I met him later and there was great fear in his eyes. Song had convinced the elders he had spoken to the gods, but heartsick, he confided in me that nothing had happened. He had not seen the spirits or received their guidance. He had not done so in the forest on those many days we had spent together and now he could not do so for the people. I calmed him, I told him he had the power, he was grieving for his father, and expecting too much from himself. If he did not try so hard, and he prayed to the gods in solitude, they would surely come to him for they certainly knew of his destiny. He was the new leader.

"Song decided he must have solitude and went into hiding for many days. Before he left, he gave me a beautiful rose-colored amulet his father had given him. He said that it was to protect me from evil. Because I had seen it around the neck of the dead chief, I wore it hidden beneath my garments. I kept it close to my heart where my chieftain always dwelled.

"Song went into seclusion by day, praying from dawn to dusk. Under the cover of darkness, I would visit him in his chambers. I would keep him aware of what went on in the camp. We stole golden moments of passion together, one another's only clear vision of what the future held. But on the outside, things were far from perfect. The gray cloud lingered over the camp for many weeks, and it became obvious a change had come over the villagers.

"It began with idle gossip among the people, questions about why their leader had hidden himself away in the cavern. And it grew. Soon the whispers among the camp carried the sounds of doubt.

"One of the tribesmen, a strong and quiet man named Raven, began to talk with the villagers. Raven talked too much, of things he knew nothing about. He began to behave strangely, as if something from outside his own being were speaking through his soul. Rumors started of terrible things that were going to happen if Song could not lead the tribe. Fearful whispers spoke of the loss of the care and protection from the gods, which was eminent if Song could not pull himself together.

"Vicious things were said. Song of the Eagle was far too young and had not completed his training. The elders scolded the people for their lack of faith. They believed he could follow in his father's footsteps, but as time went on I could see the clouds of doubt forming even in the eyes of the wise ones.

"Raven was not an important man in our village, but he was capable of doing great harm. He planted the seeds of doubt in the minds of many and daily he added fertilizer to those seeds. Raven preyed upon the young men and told them they were responsible for the survival of their families. Raven convinced them the village would parish without the leadership it needed and that when it was gone, there would not be enough for everyone. As the days passed, his influence grew ever stronger. And through Raven's evil words, spread the voices of fear.

"I did not speak of it to Song at first, for I believed it would pass. But as time went on, it was clear the panic would lead to terrible things. At last, I told Song. I did not want to take him from his prayers because I, too, believed he must find his connection to the spirits or the tribe would face great trouble. Song went immediately before the people to tell them things were all right. He told them to fear not at his weeks of seclusion, for he had been speaking with the gods. Then Raven confronted him before the village. Raven demanded he show his power, then and there. Song told them he was not a magician, but a spirit leader. If those who doubted did not wish to follow him, they must find their own way.

"Perhaps his words were too harsh for those who lived in fear and doubt. For Raven now had a large following, and upon Song's dismissing of their concerns, they departed the camp. Surprised by their actions, but believing the situation was done, Song went back into hiding.

"Things might have been different if the tribe had been experienced with war and hatred, but centuries spent as a peace loving people had left them nearly oblivious to its existence. The news first came of attacks on the mesa top. Those who had always come to the temple stopped, fearing being ambushed by the ostracized band of what had now become warriors. They attacked the single-family dwellings and small offshoots of the village across the valley, stealing food and destroying homes. Anyone who tried to stop them was killed.

"The drums of war thundered through the camps and canyons by night and no one slept. Fear was on the lips of the people across the valley. Even the villagers remained in their dwellings, fearful of leaving the larger group. I, too, was afraid, but my fear was not fully realized until one evening when I visited Song. Song sat before his ceremonial fire in full war paint. I tried to speak with him, but he would not listen. Song was a loving man, and our child and I meant more to him than anything else.

He was determined to protect us from what was going on at any cost. He had come to the realization that his spiritual powers were not strong enough to fight whatever evil had invaded his camp, and the only other means he had of fighting it was with force. He vowed to stop the band of marauders from their campaign of terror. I know now it was his decision that weakened his spirit and led him into the dark days that were to come.

"I kissed Song that night before he went to the people to propose his plan to stop the killing, and it was as if I were kissing a stranger. The strong, proud look of a spirit leader had faded from his face, and the softness in his eyes had been replaced by fear. He had the true spiritual gifts, but in desperation he was reaching out to his human instincts to protect what he held sacred. Over the objections of the elders, a small band of warriors, led by Song, armed themselves with their hunting spears and went out in search of those who would destroy the peace of our valley.

"Many months passed and as the child grew within my womb, I heard stories of fighting across the area as more and more of the people of the village joined with the warring bands. Some went to Song, but others doubted his strength and joined with the evil ones. It was a difficult time. I hid myself away in Song's cavern just as he had said, away from the eyes of the already troubled village. Song came back to camp regularly, expressing his need to be with me and to see what had happened in the village. Distress covered his face these days, and it was clear he hung only to the hope of his unborn child and my undying love for salvation." Snowcloud paused. A trail of tears trickled down her bronze cheeks.

Jessica's heart shared the pain this woman felt for the man she loved, a pain that stirred questions. Was it foretelling her own pain and frustrations with Alex? Men choose their own path and women support them, because they believe in the man they love. Could she make this kind of commitment to Alex? And in the end, could she succeed where Snowcloud had failed and convince Alex to listen to his own soul?

CHAPTER TWELVE

The cloud of mist holding the image of the maiden floated above the flames as she continued her story. Jessica hung on every word. The mental pictures evoked by the maiden's story pulled her into the heart and soul of two ancient lovers. Their world of long ago left her wondering how it paralleled the questions in her own mind.

Snowcloud's words fell softly on Jessica's waiting ears. "As the months passed, it became time for the birth of my child and as it grew near, Song came more often. In the depths of the night and in the shelter of the cave, Song watched the birth of his new son. We leaned forward together, in the light of the torches, as our small beautiful baby opened his eyes on the world for the first time. We looked to one another for answers when the tiny squinting eyes stared back at us, a beautiful pale blue. What we feared most had happened.

"The newest leader of the people had been born in secret, and born of a father who was, by the elders' beliefs, untrained to lead his people. If we brought our baby son to the people, the ancient superstitions would not only taint, but possibly end his life. He could never be brought to them. Song had no faith or support from them and this would surely bring an end to everything.

"I had heard stories of tribes to the south of us. I could not keep my child in hiding forever, so I must try to find a place where he would be safe. As I prepared for my journey to the south with Song's help, yet another devastation came upon us.

"In recent days, the cloud that had hung for months over the village appeared to grow in density. As it hung ominously over the people, the stench from it became even stronger. I heard a great commotion in the village on the eve of my departure. Stepping out into the dim evening light, I saw the dark cloud growing in size and whirling above our heads.

"It brought with it a fierce hot wind, and a devastating odor that nearly overpowered me. As I stepped out into it, I could see Song standing near the temple fires. I knew he had been deep in prayer. I tried to reach Song, but I could not make my way through the fierce wind and flying debris. The thing came down upon us with unrelenting force then the whirling mass stopped before Song.

"So you are the pitiful new leader." A deep and frightening voice spoke from the black cloud.

Song stood there, too stunned to speak.

"Your father was a powerful man. It has taken months for me to break through his force and get into your camp."

"Who are you?" Song demanded.

"I am everything you have ever feared and more." An evil and horrible laugh came from the cloud, and the people shrank in terror. "Your forefathers were strong men of the spirit world and I have waited centuries for you. I knew if I waited long enough, my chance would come."

Song squared his shoulders and stood tall before the hideous thing. "What is it you've come for?"

"Half my job is already done. For though you are strong of spirit, you are weak of mind. You did not see

those among you who I slowly pulled away. Now they have left you. Now they kill the others who might pose a threat," the cloud barked. "Because you have been a fool, you have played into my hands. When your village began to break apart, you did not rely on your spirit world. You relied on the forces of your own foolish body. Many have died and many more will be killed."

"You. It is you who have caused this. I have smelled your stench before, deep in the kivas when you tried to enter into our ceremonies. The great ones never allowed you in. I have been a fool or I would have known you were the one behind this."

"Oh, poor soul," the evil one chided. "Now you see the error of your ways. Now when it is too late, you see the truth."

"It isn't too late," Song cried out. "It isn't too late, as long as I am alive to fight you. I will never let you have the people of my village."

The evil thing roared with laughter. "Since you are so determined, perhaps we can make a deal."

"What do you mean?" Song asked angrily.

"You say you won't surrender your people, but what of the bodies scattered across the land and in shallow graves."

"Of what concern is that to you?"

The immense dark cloud of stench oozed lower and hovered above the ground. "You are a weak spirit. I should like the pleasure of stopping you and this sickening goodness once and for all."

"The people have lived here for centuries, in peace until you came." I could feel the fear I knew burned in Song's chest, but he did not flinch as he confronted his enemy. "What do you want to leave this canyon, this mesa, forever? What is it I can give you to leave us in peace once more?"

The evil did not respond for a moment, then he spoke as a violent wind that screamed through the canyon and vibrated from its walls. "Bring me your dead. I want to see the bodies of the people you hold so dear. I want to see the tears fall upon your face and hear the sobs of your fathers before you. Then I will be content. I want you to know there is a power greater than good, greater than the power that led this tribe for so many years."

Song rubbed his chin in thought. "I will not give you the souls of our dead at any cost."

"I did not ask for the souls, young fool. I ask for the bodies. The souls have left them many days past and their fate has been decided. My power is limited to the souls of the living. I have waited many seasons for this day. I want you to look upon the death and sorrow that has overtaken your good people." The evil one cackled. "Then you will know your power is useless before me. Bring me the bodies and place them in the cave behind the temple."

Song thought hard about the evil one's request. I know he too believed they were merely bodies, the empty shells of the dead. "I will grant your request, if it will rid the living of the plague of your presence. Go now. Return in five days. I will have accomplished your request."

"That night, Song sent a messenger out to the small bands across the mesa. If they were to be rid once and for all of the horror of this evil, they must bring the bodies of their dead to the canyon.

"As I left the village early the next day, the people had already begun to bring the dead, wrapped in ceremonial blankets of turkey feathers and yucca mats. Ceremonies were to be held at the final resting place. Pottery and prized trinkets were brought and placed in the cave to ward off the evil and carry the loved ones on to the next world.

"It was a sad picture that remains in my mind for eternity. But I could not risk staying at the village, for my own son's life hung in the balance. I knew I must keep my secret hidden from the evil and from the people, if he were to survive.

"I took my son to a place two days walking to the south. A woman there had many children, some her own and some the maimed and crippled her village had abandoned. For the people of my time believed those children were possessed of evil spirits. Because she had taken them in, she was forced to live some distance from the rest of her tribe.

"This made it a safe place for my son to grow, away from the prying eyes of others. One day he might be forced to leave because of his blue eyes, but for now, he was safe with the woman who had more love to give than she knew what to do with. Others, too, had brought their children to her to save them from certain death at the hands of the superstitious tribesman. She cared for each of them as she did her own. There, with my heart breaking, I left that tiny piece of my soul and made my journey home to Song." With that the sad little maiden faded away.

"Where did she go?" Jessica asked, stunned by her sudden disappearance. "What happened to Song and the village? What about the child and Snowcloud?"

"You were here today to hear of their love. Has it touched you?"

Jessica looked down at her hands folded in her lap and took a deep breath. "Of course it has. How could it not?"

"Many things of late have not so much as scratched the surface of your heart. You have been inside yourself, inside a shell that would not let you feel." Nechi's words cut deep. "Now you must experience what is being put before you. Your destiny and the destiny of others call to you. You can no longer deny the existence of things outside your own being." He raised his hand and pointed at her then closed his fist. "The hand of fate is closing around you. You can choose to remain uninvolved, but by doing so you will live in the shell you have built until it becomes your tomb."

God, he was so right. How did he know these things? This was the first time in the months since Jessica had first realized her aunt was going to die, she'd allowed herself to feel compassion for another human being. She'd crawled into her own little world of self-pity, hiding from the inevitable fact that she would be alone. The fact was, she had no family, no one who cared if she lived or died. Since she'd been here, she'd felt the pain of others deeply. They were pulling her from her internal refuge and forcing her to share their pain.

In all the months of arguing with herself, she'd lived in her own private quandary over quitting her job and following her dreams. She hadn't been able to reach beyond her own fears and insecurities and let herself experience the world from another perspective. Her doubts in herself, her abilities and her own spiritual beliefs had manifested and changed her into someone she no longer recognized.

Now she was feeling. Feeling it all. The tears streamed down her face, completely beyond her control. She cried for her aunt, she cried for herself and her own emptiness. She cried for her frustrations over her career. She cried for Dorothy McCabe and what she had lost. She cried for two young lovers, ages ago, whose love was so deep, and the unfairness that kept them apart. She cried for the frustrations of a young chieftain whose failure was only to believe in himself, so much like her own struggle.

She cried at her own lack of faith, her inability to believe. She looked across the flames of the fire and into the eyes of Nechi.

"It was here you had to arrive," he said softly. "The journey isn't over yet, but you've come a long way."

"I'm sorry," she said brushing the salty tears away from her eyes with her fingers.

"Tears are not a sign of weakness. They are the waters that cleanse the soul. They do not make us weak, they only make us stronger."

Her lips quivered as she searched his face. "You know, Nechi, you've taught me a lot. Strange. What you've taught me is about myself."

"This is how it was intended for you. As you follow the path before you, you will understand."

"I think I'm beginning to."

For the first time she noticed a squirrel had come to sit beside Nechi. It twitched its tail and looked at her. To his right a small wild rabbit wiggled a velvety nose and nibbled on a tender green leaf. A blue jay swooped down and came to rest on his shoulder. They sat in silence and peace as if they'd been hypnotized by the soft sound of his voice.

There was something different about Nechi. He was as unique as the place he lived in, as connected to the earth as the creatures themselves. She marveled at his slow easy talk and the energy he seemed to emit. He was as comfortable with nature as the birds that floated on trusted wing through azure skies on invisible currents of freedom.

Nechi was part of this, part of the earth's body and soul, part of the wind that stirred or was stilled at his command. Fire jumped from nothingness with the wave of his hand and showed in a rainbow of colors when he beckoned it. Somehow, she was not surprised by the animals that now sat next to him. Wanting to be in his presence, fearless of his closeness and the fire. It was such a natural and easy flowing part of who he was.

Was he man or spirit? Probably much more the latter than the former, but certainly not someone of an ordinary world.

"Nechi," she whispered.

"Yes."

"Will I ever know how this legend ends?"

"You will find the answers in your own time. And you must find the way there alone."

"Sounds like another riddle," she smiled, wiping the last of the moisture from beneath her eyes.

"The answer lies in a message written long ago. I can tell you no more. You have found the seventh direction, now you must learn what it means to you."

The flames rose and shot a cloud of black smoke high into the air. Jessica put her hands to her face to shield it from the heat. As quickly as it arose, it dissipated leaving no evidence of the fire. All that remained was the empty ring of stones.

Nechi rose to his feet. "Go now and find your answers."

Jessica nodded and picked up her backpack. His actions left little to be said. As she walked back toward her car, she glanced behind her. Nechi was nowhere to be seen. Somehow that didn't surprise her.

Jessica was on the steps of the research center when the pretty blonde woman turned the key in the door and opened for business after lunch.

You must be Miss Sinclair." The woman extended a hand in welcome.

"Oh, you remember my call," Jessica said, warmly accepting the greeting.

"We get lots of calls, but some are of more interest than others." She motioned for Jessica to come in. "I love to read your magazine. I was very pleased to hear from you. I've pulled quite a few items I think may be of use to you."

Closing the door behind them, she pointed to a large pile of books spread on an adjacent table.

The building was rustic and smelled of old wood and age. Jessica guessed it had been built in the early 1900's when the park was established. The wood floor creaked as they crossed to a row of tables and chairs. Glancing around, Jessica noticed the surrounding shelves piled high with books and journals.

"This is wonderful. Thanks for pulling these." Jessica placed her backpack on the floor and seated herself in one of the mismatched chairs.

"I hope they're helpful. There are several here that give detailed descriptions of the early excavations on the mesa. Personal accounts and the like." She smiled pleasantly and motioned toward the stack of books. "You can have a look then let me know if there's anything else I can help you with. Oh, and there's a pot of coffee brewing if you'd like a cup."

"No, thanks." Jessica pulled out a large yellow tablet and settled herself in the chair. "I'll just get to my work." With a nod of her head, the woman walked away and went into her office at the opposite end of the room.

Jessica leaned back in her chair. This felt like a moment of truth in many ways. Her head was swimming. This morning's meeting with Nechi had only added more questions to her already overwhelming list. She'd spent most of last night searching her feelings about this story. She knew she had to buy in or get out. The connection she'd felt with the mesa from the beginning was something she couldn't explain. Now she walked among the ancient spirits of this place. They spoke to her soul and she must somehow understand their message. A message, in Nechi's words, that was written long ago.

Poring through the books spread on the rough wooden table it wasn't long before she was absorbed in her reading. Pulled, once again, into another time and place.

She read the accounts written by Richard Weatherill and Gustaf Nordenskiöld, the first men to explore the mesa. Pouring over their accounts of the excavations of graves, caused goose flesh to rise on Jessica's arms. Their stories burned the maiden's words into her soul. Snowcloud's word paintings had been very good—and chillingly accurate.

Nordenskiöld's story of the unearthing of the tomb of five warriors and three infants brought a sadness and lump to the pit of her stomach. The detailed descriptions of other ruins seemed to speak to her of a time of unrest, of a time when the people did not feel safe.

The high-laddered entrances and rocky refuges accessible only by hand and footholds chinked in the rock, told their own story. Something had changed on the mesa from its humble and peaceful beginnings. They began as people who farmed the mesa tops and valley, living in pit houses on the mesa. A scattering of nomadic people whose families once felt safe living apart, suddenly massed together and retreated to the canyons to build structures intended to keep out their enemies.

Nechi's story rang in her mind, rang of truth, and now rang of possibility. The people who lived and farmed in the area were ruled by the great spirit leader for centuries. They lived in peace and harmony and worshiped at the temple in the canyon. The trail, she had followed to the canyon seemed to be beaten into the earth by centuries of bare or moccasin-covered feet, making their way to the center of their tiny universe. They had come to a carefully crafted temple, built to thank the gods for their abundant gifts.

Even now, centuries later, their imprint remained in the earth and stone. It had only now occurred to her, though she'd walked the path many times. What if the path hadn't been cut by hiking tourists, but by ancients? Perhaps their spirits walked that pathway still.

She mulled it over. Something had changed, something of great significance must have happened in their lives. Something had placed fear in their safe world, brought on tribal wars, drought, hunger— possibly something evil was responsible. Thoughts whirled in her head.

Badly in need of a break, she rubbed her eyes and stepped outside. Her lungs filled with the clean dry air, laced with smells of sagebrush and juniper. A complete contrast to the smells of the city she was used to outside her Denver apartment building. Across the road was the building that housed the park's museum. Days ago, she'd have considered the building old. Today, she had a new perspective.

A few people milled around the parking lot, but did not muffle the sounds of a chattering jay. She strolled over to the open doorway to the museum, taking long easy strides and enjoying the warm rays of sun. The inside of the museum was rustic with floors made of light polished wood.

She smiled and nodded to the ranger behind the information desk, avoiding conversation that would pull her from her thoughts. Browsing through the model villages and re-creations of what modern man believed was here centuries before, she snorted softly.

"A guess, a scientific guess." Made by people like Alex Nakai.

An elderly man looked over his dark rimmed glasses at her in distaste at her comment, but she ignored him. She was coming to realize the pieces she'd seen here were only someone else's vision. Her own was probably almost as viable. No one would ever be able to duplicate the events of the past.

A civilization had vanished, or they had left and intermixed with surrounding peoples, but no one would ever know the real truth of the fate of the Mesa Verdans. It was pure speculation, educated guesses, based on bits and pieces, like a huge jigsaw puzzle with three quarters of the pieces missing.

If something happened on this earth, today, at least the written historical record existed. There had been no such thing for this band of true Americans. The spirit had spoken of her own ancestral ties to the mesa, and in her soul she believed it to be truth. It was her ancestry, her history. Maybe that was it, more than anything else, she felt cheated. She'd spent years in American schools, being taught the European version of American history. And now, years later, she was learning this big piece of truth had been omitted.

This was America, before anyone from across the ocean ever set foot on her soil. Before it was contaminated by greed and destruction. This was the history of her family, the history of her own spirit and she'd been cheated out of it. The white man had stolen far more than the land from the Indian. He'd robbed him of his heritage and stolen his God-given right to what had been his for centuries.

Anger boiled in her gut, but there was no direction to turn it toward. It was just a cheated feeling that she knew someday she'd put into words on their behalf because they hadn't had the skill or knowledge.

Rounding the corner and stepping down into another room in the museum, she stood before a glass case that contained small slabs of stone with figures carved into them. There were tiny stick-like pictures of animals, birds and people etched into the rock. She read the words printed on the display board. *Petroglyphs.* Next to it was a painting of a man scratching designs into a cliff wall with a sharp piece of stone. They called him a storyteller. She smiled and started to turn back toward the main museum then stopped in her tracks as Nechi's words echoed through her head. "The answers lie in a message written long ago."

Fool, she mentally scolded herself. She'd spent hours combing through books looking for a written record without realizing the record came from the hand of the Anasazi ages ago. If the legend was true, someone may have recorded it on the walls of the canyon, or the walls of the cave. The realization sent her mind spinning in new directions. Was it possible the proof of the legend's truth could be found somewhere in the canyon?

A vision flashed through her mind, so strong she staggered from its impact. The mental picture of a wall, overgrown with heavy bushes, and along with it a feeling of foreboding and a surge of fear. It didn't matter, she had to go there and find it. She'd come this far there was no turning back, no matter what the costs.

CHAPTER THIRTEEN

The sharp needles of the juniper scraped against the bare flesh on Jessica's wrists. She pulled hard on the tree branches and scrub oak. Something behind the mass of vegetation called to her. A limb sprung back and caught her in the temple. She rubbed at the painful sting then tackled the branch again, more determined than ever to reveal what lay hidden beneath nature's cloak.

Firmly placing a boot on the wiry brush, the snapping of twigs announced her success. At last, the undergrowth fell aside defeated, revealing a wall of stone beyond. Her jaw dropped in astonishment. The exact replica of the vision she had experienced lay before her in reality.

Blinking her eyes in disbelief, she ran her fingertips across the rows of petroglyphs imprinted on the stone, ages earlier. Even to an untrained eye, a story unfolded in the etchings. Vertical stick-like figures were scattered in all directions from the center of the drawing, some clutched their heads while others, drawn horizontally were scattered about like matchsticks. Tracing from figure to figure, she followed the ribbon of story to its end, where a stab of pain hit her heart at the last picture.

The last imprint was of a human hand that trailed down the wall in a smear of finger marks, as if the author of the drawing had shown an ending of

tremendous pain. In her mind she visualized the hand
of a dying man, and read the message etched in
stone—bloody fingers dragging—depicting the end of a
life—or many lives. A cold chill ran through her and
tiny bumps raised on her arms in spite of the warm
afternoon sun.

She observed the drawings for several minutes,
studying the small crude figures and absorbing
emotion from the picture. A dark heaviness swept
through her chest. A deep feeling of sadness grew
inside her, followed by a foreboding she could not
explain. And yet the picture beckoned to her, seemed
to pull her toward it.

Kneeling, she opened her hand and spread her
fingers. She placed her palm over the handprint,
wanting to feel the closeness and absorb its message.
Warmth radiated through her hand and up into her
forearm as she pressed it hard into the stone image.
The heat became intense and she attempted to pull
her hand back, but to her surprise it wouldn't move. It
remained upon the imprint as if somehow melting
itself into the stonewall.

Perhaps fear should have taken over then, but it
didn't enter her mind. Instead she stared at the glow
forming around her hand and felt a pulsating
sensation begin in her palm. The feeling spread
through her body, finally reaching her head. Her body
vibrated and her mind became a blur of bright light.

Something behind her eyes generated a yellow-
white radiance brighter than the sun itself and
swallowed up all possibility of thought. She seemed to
float in an inner world beyond her own imagination.
Suddenly, she was engulfed in blackness.

The floating sensation continued then stopped
abruptly. Warmth turned to cold, the buoyant softness
to hard stone against her back.

Opening her eyes, she blinked against the piercing
brightness and rubbed her nose as a smoky, musty
smell invaded her senses. The light of several torches
burned in a narrow stone room. Standing before her,
watching with wide eyes, stood a small man, a near
replica to one she'd seen in a book at the research
library. His face and body were painted in a black and
white striped pattern. From the top of his head a
plume of stiff black hair emerged, spiking up wildly.
The black loincloth covered his private parts and was
the only clothing on his body. A well-wrapped wooden
torch blazed in his hand.

He looked at her strangely then circled as if sizing
her up. At last he spoke. "Well, you are finally here.
Let's pray you have not come too late." His high-
pitched cackle offended her ears. She lay there,
dumbstruck and apprehensive on the cold stone floor
of what appeared to be part of a cavern.

"Who are you? Where am I?" Jessica tried to clear
the cobwebs from her head.

He scowled. "I am the one whose medicine brought
you here. And I have waited many sunsets."

Jessica sat up and looked at the small painted
figure of a man. His shadow on the stone wall behind
him, loomed large and frightening in the flickering
light of the torches that surrounded them.

Jessica had experienced about one more illusion
than she could handle. Running her fingers through
her short hair, she looked at the medicine man in
bewilderment.

"There is no time to sit, there is much to do. The
chieftain and I have asked the spirits to send us help
on this night. And here you are."

"What—?" she sputtered.

"But I fear much suffering will come to my people
before this spell is broken." He shook his head and
surveyed her doubtfully. "You do not look like a magic

one—and you are a woman. Are you a witch woman?"
he challenged.

"I'm not a witch," Jessica answered shortly. "You're
babbling nonsense. I don't understand what you're
saying."

He put a hand to his chin and circled her one more
time. "No witch woman? Well, if you are what the
spirits have sent me, I will have to make do with you."
He turned his head to one side and squinted. "You
wear a strange robe for a magic one. It will never do."

He reached down beside his feet, picked up a piece
of buckskin and tossed it in her direction. "Cover
yourself with this," he said. Holding up the large shirt,
she looked at it questioningly.

"I was expecting a warrior. One who is capable of
great things is most likely a warrior. Put it on. Cover
yourself. We must walk among the people." He shifted
nervously. "We must go now. Things are not good. The
great one has gone into hiding and the others speak of
war."

Pulling the pungent smelling rawhide garment over
her clothes, she followed the medicine man. As she
moved through the chamber of the cavern, a sickening
odor reached her. She covered her nose and mouth
with her hand and gasped.

"What's that horrible smell?" she asked.

"It is the stench of death. The smell of fear, is what
sickens you. The smell of what we all fear."

Nearly gagging, she followed him out into the night.
Drinking in the fresh air as they emerged from the
cave, she had to walk quickly to keep up with the tiny
man as he moved along a rock formation that led down
a slope and into a canyon. The crisp night air was
filled with the sounds of drums and chanting. They
rounded a rocky corner and before them rose a huge
stone temple, alive with activity.

Light from many fires illuminated the altar of the temple on the upper level, throwing sparks high into a moonless night sky. One level below, men draped in hides and animal heads, their faces painted, performed a sort of ritual dance. They moved in circles around three rough pine ladders that emerged from the square openings of three kivas.

Light came from the openings. Smoke clouds filled with tiny sparks shot like fireflies into the great dark beyond. The smell of burning juniper filled the air. Dancers circled the ladders of the first and last kivas. Then one by one, as the light's reflection cast ghostly images, they disappeared down the ladders and into the ceremonial chambers below.

Jessica stood silently, in complete awe of the scene before her. She looked at the medicine man that was about a head shorter, and could not find words to speak.

"Come," he said simply. "There is not much time."

She trailed behind him as they picked their way through rows of women and children who sat cross-legged along the perimeter of the temple. They all sat, heads down, speaking a mournful sounding chant that raised goose flesh up Jessica's spine. She touched her rawhide covered arms and rubbed them to calm the chill and check her own reality. The feeling of floating persisted, as if she were here and yet she was not.

Stepping carefully through the gathering of rawhide and animal skin covered figures she glanced down, avoiding a small child who sat with head down clinging to his mother's arm. The boy looked up at her startled then his face calmed and he smiled. With a jerk from his mother's disciplining hand, he bowed his head once more and resumed the chant in his tiny voice. She glanced at the medicine man.

"It is forbidden for them to look upon you," he said. "You are from the spirit world. They fear your magic."

"I have no magic," she said loudly then bit her lip as the people moved restlessly. She repeated it in a low voice, close to the medicine man's ear.

"I prayed for you. I asked the great spirits to send us our salvation, and they have sent you. If I believe this, you must believe it to."

"But—" Jessica stammered.

"The spirits are using your soul for some purpose. It would be wise of you to follow me to see the great leader."

Arguing seemed useless. Jessica followed the small man over to the temple wall where rows of hand and footholds led the way to the upper tiers.

"This way," he said, and scurried up the wall. In the dim light, she noticed the rings of sand caked around his small calloused feet. The reality of that detail pierced her senses. How could this be a dream?

Placing the toe of her boot securely in the first notch and grabbing hold of two higher ones with her hands, she followed him up the ten-foot wall to the first tier.

After scaling the wall, they moved quietly across the side- wall and toward the front of the temple where the ceremonial dancers filed one by one into the kiva openings. Eerie sounding flute music floated on the night air and ceremonial drums vibrated to the beat. The feet of the brightly clad dancers pounded upon the stone. They danced, casting long shadows in the flicker of the firelight. Mesmerized by the scene, Jessica stopped.

A tiny hand tugged on the sleeve of the musky smelling buckskin shirt. "Follow me. The Great One is here." The medicine man pointed to the center ladder and swung his tiny frame around and down into the square opening lit by the flickering shadows from the fire below. Rapidly, he descended and disappeared into the hole. Jessica was close behind, her mouth dry, her heart pounding as anticipation grasped her.

At the foot of the ladder, Jessica turned to see a young man clad only in a loincloth, sitting cross-legged by the fire. Shadows danced against the wall in an odd light as the boy looked at her and nodded. "So you have come to us at last," he said, a great sadness evident in his tone. Firelight illuminated his face where a look of age appeared deep in his features. The haggard look of an old man hung in his eyes and face, yet he appeared to be little more than a boy.

Jessica instantly felt compassion for his sorrows. She nodded her reply, casting a quick glance at the medicine man.

"Please. Sit with me," he said, motioning her to a place beside him at the fire.

She did as he asked, the medicine man followed suit. The two men exchanged a glance across the flames and nodded. The medicine man untied a thin rawhide cord and removed a leather pouch that hung at his waist. He opened the pouch and poured a small handful of dried herbs into his palm.

He chanted as he scattered the mixture over the flames. It responded in an assortment of colors. Deep reds, purples and yellows replaced the orange blaze in the fire pit. Flames rose higher and snapped in response. The heat grew more intense. A flush rose to Jessica's cheeks and a sweet smoky smell filled the room.

The young leader and the medicine man looked toward the ladder as the feet of yet another appeared and descended into the kiva.

The young man looked up as a figure stood over him, and attempted to rise. "Who are you? And why do you come here this night?" The stranger put a hand on the young man's shoulder, gently pushing him back to his place on the floor. As the man turned and took in the other two at the fire, the light reflected off of his pale skin, making him seem eerie, almost translucent.

He spoke in a soft gentle voice. "I came from a village far, far from here. I am sent to deliver this message. Passed to your hands by your father is a healing power used by your forefathers."

"What would you know of my father?" The boy screamed. My father is dead.

"Joining him will not help your people." The stranger's look was stern. "Look beyond your own fear and anger. Though the evil is near, and surely tragedy awaits, you must use the power of your father's gifts."

The young man's lips trembled and the fire of anger burned in his eyes. "I do not know who you are. You are not of my clan, not of my people. I dare not trust anyone. Leave me. Go back where you came from."

"I beg you to listen to my message. It is all I am allowed to share if you chose to hear no more." He looked in the boy's angry face. "And you have made your choice. I will leave as you ask, for sadly I can do no more." With that the stranger climbed back up the ladder and was gone.

The boy's eyes turned accusingly to Jessica. "Do you know of what the stranger speaks?"

Jessica shook her head. She sat in awe of what transpired, not understanding any of the scene playing out before her. The young man's anger and fear was so overwhelming, she could not comprehend why he would turn away the stranger who seemed to be offering help.

"Very well. We must proceed." With that, he turned his eyes to the medicine man and nodded. Then both turned their faces toward the rocky ceiling, closed their eyes and lay their hands with palms open on their knees. Jessica imitated their actions. The smell of the potion filled her nostrils and her head felt out of focus.

"Aiiya, aiyoo, aiiya," they chanted. The young chieftain sang the words over and over in a near mournful tone reminiscent of a coyote's sad yelps. "Aiiya, aiyoo."

The sound filled the room and Jessica's mind floated in a haze. The room seemed to spin. At first she fought it, then gave herself to the sensations. The rhythmic chant vibrated through the chamber and out into the night air. Integrating itself with the clouds of smoke that wrapped around her and filled her head with the sweet pungent odor of the sprinkled mixture.

Through a fog, she realized the chanting had stopped and the high-pitched notes of a whistle reached her ears. It played over and over with a subtle melody. She allowed her eyes to open. Seated in front of her were the faint shadow of four images, in full ceremonial dress. The young warrior blew into a small, decorated whistle. Four ancient faces stonily observed his actions.

The shadowy onlookers were clad in an array of buckskin garments, lavishly decorated with beads and feathers. Silver-white hair flowed from beneath headdresses as different as the wrinkled faces beneath them. One wore the great head of a grizzly bear atop his headdress, while another the black curled horns and brown curly wool of a buffalo.

A third had the fur and head of a lynx draped over his shoulder, the cat's eyes were empty, but its open mouth revealed the sharp fangs of the animal. The ancient gently stroked the fur as he sat with an expressionless face and watched the young man play the whistle.

The fourth ancient wore an enormous breastplate made of bones and claws. A headdress of long eagle feathers began just above his forehead and flowed from the center of his head to midway down his back.

Their aged, lined faces showed deep concern. They watched the young man then looked from one to the other. "Again, he does not see us," spoke the spirit draped in the lynx fur.

"It is not important that he see, only that he hears what we tell him to do," said the man with the feathers wisely.

"He has no power before the evil if he cannot use us in the fight." The ancient beneath the buffalo horns shook his head in obvious sadness.

"The boy is scared, it is his own fear that holds him back. It is what keeps him from hearing us. The boy's heart does not believe. Not in us and not in himself," the lynx spirit retorted.

For the first time the bear spirit spoke. "You are all wrong. The boy does not know how to use his own power. As you witnessed, he refuses to listen to even those in the physical world. He understands the whistle, but it is the amulet he needs or he will never keep the evil from affecting him."

"But he does not have the piece. How could he use it, if he doesn't have it. His lessons were not learned, his ears did not hear," the lynx spirit persisted.

Through the conversation among the ancient ones, the boy sat deep in his trance, alternating between chanting and playing the eerie tune on the whistle. The medicine man sat with eyes closed. Both seemed oblivious to the bantering conversation of the spirits.

"It is good that we have brought the woman," said the spirit of the bear.

"She is our hope for the future. We have no hope for today." The old spirit continued to stroke the lynx's fur.

"It is true. But we cannot interact with the human world unless the young chief hears us speak to him." The eagle-feathered spirit seemed more interested in the boy.

"This woman you have brought, she comes from many hundreds of seasons in the future. What help can she be to the people?" the bison-clad spirit interjected.

"I fear she cannot help them now. Her lesson and her journey lies in what is yet to be." The spirit of the bear shook his head.

"But what of the people's fate, until then?" asked the eagle spirit.

The one with the buffalo horns showed great sadness. "He is right. There is little hope. The fighting, the wars, and the evil will continue until nearly all is lost. The people will endure much suffering."

"Then why this woman?" The eagle spirit seemed skeptical.

"It has taken seven centuries for the blue-eyed one to return. And it has taken years beyond that for us to find her, to find one in this modern world who could hear our voices." Eyes of the four ancients turned from the young warrior to Jessica.

She opened her mouth to ask why they spoke of her in this way, but no words came from her throat.

"The woman has no tongue," the spirit with the lynx chortled. "This is a great improvement for the future."

"Be silent, fool," the bear spirit barked. "She is not here for your entertainment. She is in the highest state the human spirit can obtain and remain living, therefore, she has no command of her physical body."

"But how will she remember what she has seen?" the eagle spirit continued his skeptical questioning.

"She will remember. Her heart and soul will not let her forget." The buffalo spirit had now joined with the bear. The spirit of the bear spoke directly to her. "Woman, you are about to witness the fate of the people. The peace they have known is about to vanish from the earth for many, many moons. The hands of good are now tied and controlled by an immense evil. Learn well for a time will come when the evil will rise again. You will know when you see it." His wisdom and words of doom echoed in her head.

"The young man has not the power to overcome this thing alone, and he is our only hope for intervention. What you shall see tonight cannot be changed, the souls of these innocent people are about to be taken and ruled by the mighty chief of darkness. The dead will be entombed and not allowed rest. The living will carry the evil one's curse with them for centuries to come. This is their destiny, and we cannot change it. You are the only hope we have had in all these years and here is the mission you must carry out."

He now looked at the young man. "The man, Alex, is the chosen soul. He carries the blue eyes like the young one before you. He has the powers of the forefathers, the power of the great ones who led the tribes for thousands of years of peace and goodness." Turning back, his eyes met hers. "You must help him. Alex cannot hear our voices, but you do. You must help him to free the spirits whose souls are trapped for eternity in this awful place. Beware, we have said Alex is our last hope, but other blue-eyed ones have come. The evil has destroyed and misled them, just as it will destroy this young chieftain before you. You must help the man called Alex to find his powers, for it is he and he alone who has the special gift that can release these spirits."

The buffalo spirit spoke to her. "We know you will have many questions when you go back. Do not be discouraged. Answers will be given to you when you are ready. Now prepare yourself to witness the horror that is about to overtake this village, when the force of evil returns here this night."

The ancient images spoke no more, they folded their arms across their translucent chests and sat in silence.

"Do you see them yet?" the medicine man asked in a weak, half-frightened voice.

Exhausted, the young man held his head in his hands and spoke through choked-back tears. "It is no longer of any use. The spirits have deserted us. We must face the evil one, alone."

A stricken look came upon the faces of the two men. At last the medicine man spoke. "But what of the woman, great one? Is she not magic? Can she not help to save us from the stinking beast?"

"We can only hope she has powers before his wickedness. It was you who conjured her up."

Jessica's heart sank to the pit of her stomach. She had been told she could do nothing. She could not give them false hope. Finding her voice again she spoke softly, "I have been told, I am here only to watch. I have no power against your enemy."

"It is as we feared." The young one hung his head.

"I'm sorry," Jessica said. "I would help you if I could."

"You must not be sorry. I have not the power to call forth the good. And those who come to me speak of things they know nothing about. It is I who failed my people."

But you do have the power. Why won't you listen and believe? She wanted so badly to scream the words to him, but her voice left her.

"It is forbidden for you to intervene. You cannot change our history." The ancient with the eagle feathers warned her sternly. She nodded, her throat loosening as she accepted his words into her heart.

The buffalo spirit spoke again. "What you have been brought here to do is not easy, and you will not leave unscarred. It is only by witnessing the horror firsthand that you will be able to help the man Alex fight his battle in the future. All who have seen what really happened have been gone for many, many seasons. No one who witnessed this thing had the power against it."

"Living it is what will bring you strength when you need it most," the lynx spirit said.

Jessica lowered her head. Why had they chosen her, and why did they assume she was willing to take on the awesome responsibility to help Alex find his way?

The spirit of the bear read her thoughts and spoke sternly. "We know that you have accepted this in your heart or you would not be here. For it is only your will and strength of spirit that has allowed us to bring you to this place."

"Alex's plight has become part of your own destiny. You have accepted it as your mission, and only you can change it. Just as with this young chieftain, it is not the good spirits who command his fate. Fate is controlled by the willingness of the person to give himself to the spirits and allow them to lead."

"You have allowed us to lead you here, in that your will is superior to the will even of this spirit leader. This man has allowed the evil one to touch his soul, to drive him to turn to wickedness himself when he believed good had failed him. He has the power, but the fear, another work of the evil one, prevents what must happen to turn the events around."

"Before us is proof that the fate of all mankind can be forever changed by one man's shortcomings, as the fate of a civilization of people will change this night. By his fear, his doubts, and his failure to trust and believe in both the powers of the spirit world and himself, he has unknowingly turned his back on his own destiny and his people."

Jessica rubbed her hands over her face, pulling her fingers gently over her eyes, wondering if when she opened them again, this scene would have vanished. She opened them slowly, and still she sat before the licking yellow flames of the open fire. The smell of juniper and pinion pungently mixed with the sweet powder from the medicine man's bag.

The vision of the spirits had gone and the harsh reality of the hard stone beneath her backside was enough for her to know the powder's influence had subsided. The hand of the tiny medicine man patted her knee gently.

"We must go now and leave the great one to his work. Perhaps there is still hope he will reach the spirits and receive their guidance."

Jessica looked at the little man solemnly. She shook her head, and clenched her jaw to keep from speaking and drowning his hopes. He seemed to intuitively know what her unspoken actions meant. A look of sadness and distress came upon his face as he looked into hers. "Come," he said. "I will take you back to the cave."

Turning to the young chief, she met his gaze. His eyes foretold both sadness and acceptance of his fate as he spoke to her. "The rest is in the hands of the gods. You were our last hope and now we know you can do nothing. I do not understand why they have sent you here. Nor do I understand why, if they have such great power, they will not help me to save my own people." He leaned back and raised his chin and arms skyward, as if pleading his case one last time to the heavens. "I know in my heart I am not strong enough to do this. I know I am not worthy, but I have pleaded with them to intervene and help me against this evil thing that lurks in the canyon."

He looked back to Jessica. "Perhaps my own terror will be the downfall of my people. It is too late, the time has run out. The evil one will return this night when the moon is high.

"I have done as he asked and brought the dead to his cavern. He has promised this would be his trade for the lives of the hundreds outside. But now, I do not truly believe he will take this and leave us in peace. He is a horrible wicked thing. I have no power before him. I cannot compete with his power to control the people.

"So many of them have turned to his teachings and wish only to kill and bring suffering upon the handful who have chosen to stay and follow the old ways. I had no idea this fate would come upon me. The death of my father would not have devastated the people so badly, if I had been more mindful of my studies. If I had learned the powers of the ancients, instead of breaking the sacred rules they set forth. If I had not disobeyed my father and ignored the ancient vows, the people might have been spared."

Jessica held in her words behind a clenched jaw. The young chief was blaming himself, but for the wrong reasons.

The tiny medicine man stepped to the side of the warrior and placed a hand upon his shoulder. "You cannot blame yourself for the evil that has come here. We have all made mistakes, but we do not all have the same destiny. The mistakes of the powerless do not affect the world, the mistakes of the powerful reach far beyond their own house. You have spoken the words yourself. Our future now lies in the hands of the gods. May they be merciful to us and the people."

The medicine man reached into his pouch and pulled out a handful of crushed leaves. He held them up as if offering them first to the gods then threw them into the fire. "We leave you to your prayers." He turned on his heel, and taking Jessica's arm motioned her to the ladder.

Looking back only once and permanently burning the distraught figure by the fireside into her memory, Jessica climbed the ladder with a heavy heart.

CHAPTER FOURTEEN

Jessica pulled herself through the kiva opening. The dancing figures still circled the ladders, now emerging from the chambers, one by one. The drums beat, sending vibrations to the pit of Jessica's stomach and reverberating in her soul. Her head was heavy and achy, her mind slow. Exhaustion weighed her steps, drained by her encounter in the kiva. Somewhere deep inside she knew she must not question what she was experiencing. There was more she needed to learn and she must not allow the other side of her spirit to intervene.

"Wait, wait," called out a female voice from the crowd below. Jessica squinted in the dim light of the fires. The petite figure of a young girl rose from among the bowed heads of the women and children and scurried up the handholds toward Jessica.

The young woman's face caught the light of the fires and Jessica recognized her at once as Snowcloud.

"We meet again," Jessica said.

The girl looked at her then shook her head, an odd expression in her eyes. "I have something to give you," she said breathlessly. In the dim light, the girl pulled something from around her neck and placed it in Jessica's palm, casting a wary glance over her shoulder as she did. Her petite fingers grasped Jessica's and closed them over something cold and hard. Jessica pulled away and opened her hand. A

shiny pink stone reflected the light of the fire. A thin
strip of rawhide was threaded through a hole at the
top of the clouded rosy piece.

"Take it, magic one. If you see my son, you must
give it to him. Tell him it came from his father."

"What—?" Jessica stammered.

The girl put her lips next to Jessica's ear and
whispered. "I have hidden the child away. No one must
ever know this. They will kill him." Moving her head
away from Jessica's ear, the girl's eyes met Jessica's.
"The piece has some magical power for the chosen
ones. The young chief was given it by his father and
Song gave it to me." Tears rolled down her cheeks as
she spoke the words. "I fear it will soon be all that is
left. This piece and my son."

Jessica looked down at her hand that the girl
clutched tightly closed. "But I will never see your son."

"Perhaps you never will, but I believe some day you
may. But, for now, if you are the one sent to save the
people, perhaps you can understand its power."

As quickly as she had come, the girl scurried back
down the side of the temple and disappeared into the
sea of bowed heads. Jessica looked at the piece and
tucked it into the pocket of her jeans.

A hand pulled at her sleeve. "This way," the
medicine man said impatiently trying to drag her
along with him. Just beyond the adjacent kiva, he
stopped short. "Listen," he whispered. A low roaring
sound began in the distance. "We have lingered too
long. Prepare yourself, for it comes down the canyon."
He clung to her hand and stood rigidly as he looked
out into the blackness.

Slowly the roar built. The outpouring of dancers
from the kivas stopped and the beat of the drums and
music of the flutes died away. The soft, murmuring
chant continued and the people joined hands making a
protective ring around the temple's base. Those who

stood on the temple walls turned to the growing noise coming from the darkness.

Jessica saw a small orange light some distance away. The roaring sound grew louder, and the orange ball increased in size. Growing larger and louder, it came closer. An almost unbearable heat and brightness came from the great burning orb. Shielding their faces with their arms, they tried to look at the thing that grew nearer. An overwhelming stench filtered into the air, forced out the smells of the juniper and piñon fires and replaced it with a putrid odor, resembling burning hair and fresh manure. The smell permeated the air, and the gathering of people on the temple choked and gagged as the rancid smell engulfed them.

Out of the ball of flame emerged a dark formless shape. A terrifying voice vibrated from inside the dark mass. "Where is he? Come out, Song of the Eagle. Oh, Great Leader, show yourself to me."

The dark head of the young leader appeared on the ladder as he emerged from the center kiva. "I am not hiding from you, you worthless beast," the young man barked.

Jessica felt a surge of pride at the bravery the young man showed before the monster. He had confessed to her of his fear, but he did not show it in the face of great danger.

The evil thing let out a hearty laugh that sent fiery, putrid-smelling flames toward the gathering on the temple. Many fell to the floor, while others staggered and shielded their faces. Jessica stepped backward and pressed herself against the wall behind her. Tiny pieces of stone rolled down the wall as the people on the upper level scrambled to escape the heat and stench.

The young man stood before the beast in full war paint. His chest gleamed with perspiration in the light of the fiery glow. "So you have returned."

"I have kept my word, but only to see if you have kept yours." The dark mass moved from side to side as it spoke.

"I have done what you asked." The young man stood defiantly. "The bodies have been brought to the cavern."

Jessica put a hand to her mouth, remembering the awful smell in the cave. Her stomach turned over and she choked back the urge to vomit. The thought of it and the stench of this beast were more than she could take. The medicine man's hand tightened on her arm and he put a finger to his lips. She knew he feared the beast would pick her out of the crowd. Forcing back her physical response, she ground her fingertips into the wall.

"So you have followed my instructions," the beast cackled. "You have brought me the bodies of your dead."

"Yes," Song replied, his voice heavy with emotion. "I have done this thing to please you. Now you can look upon the spoils of your evil influence, reap your satisfaction and leave us alone."

A wicked laugh came from the dark form. "Leave you, oh, I will not be leaving."

"But you said—"

"I said I would be done with you. That's not the same thing."

The young man clenched his fists and cried out. "I knew it. I knew you would not keep your word, even when I violated spiritual law and disturbed the graves of the dead to please you. I brought you the bodies. I went against what I believed was right. What more do you want from me?"

"Don't be so hard on yourself. You have done well. I am well pleased." The thing snickered. "You have brought me many souls. I could not have done this without you."

"No. I have brought you bodies. Only bodies— You said it yourself. These are the discarded shells of the spirits who have passed to the other world."

"Do you know that for sure? Do you know that the souls have left the bodies? How could you be sure of such a thing?"

"I will not allow you to play these games with me. The soul leaves the body when it dies, our fathers have always known this."

"Oh, but your world has been for many centuries without evil. Those who die a peaceful death may leave quietly, but it is not in your experience or your forefathers to know what a soul does when it is possessed of evil. Or what could happen to a soul, even a good soul, if an evil influence were to say–hold it hostage within its body."

Song stared at the evil image. He was silent then he spoke in a disbelieving voice. "Is what you are telling me true? Have you tricked me into selling the souls of my own people to your eternal wickedness?"

"Oh, you are perceptive, young leader. It's unfortunate you are so slow." The evil laugh echoed through the canyon. "If you were not so stupid, you would have known that you lost the battle to me long before this."

"What?" Song asked.

"You were mine when you first raised your hand against your own people. When you gave in to fear and killed the first one of those who were entrusted to your care."

Song's face paled and a look of stricken horror claimed him. "But it was war. They were killing innocent people. It was all I could do." The young man dropped to his knees and sobbed in his hands.

"And you did it my way," the evil hissed. "You were clay in my hands. And now you've saved me this work."

Screams of pain and anguish rolled out into the endless expanse of black sky for what seemed a long time. Silence hung over the rest of the village and the temple. Finally, Song rose to his knees and sobbed to the heavens. "I am no leader. I have been stupid. I raised my spear against my own people. And sold the souls of those I was assigned to care for, to the god of the underworld to save myself. I have failed you, my forefathers. I have failed my people. I do not deserve to live."

"No need to worry. I shall not deny you a fate any different from what you gave to them." The evil's voice was mocking in its tone.

"Kill me. I am ready to die. You have destroyed my soul." The young man lay down on the stone and held his hands up to the heavens.

"Surely you do not believe it will be so painless, you fool."

"It matters not." The young man lay with eyes closed and arms crossed over his chest. "Let the living go. You have many souls and you have me. Do as you will with me and let this be done at last."

"The living shall go. They will be of use to me later for my further amusement. They have no force of goodness to lead them now. And I rather enjoy letting them wander and suffer in their human way. Eventually they will come to me."

With that, many in the gathering below scrambled away, breaking the protective circle and deserting the young man to meet his fate, alone. A few in the circle remained, attempting to restart the chant, holding to the hope of keeping the evil from destroying the leader.

"Fools," the evil barked. "Do you think your pitiful howling will save what the spirits themselves have thrown aside and denied? This is why I find such joy in making your lives miserable. You are weak and pathetic." With that the chanting stopped and the bowed heads of the figures at the temple's base dispersed into the darkness. The evil cloud above them took on a human facial appearance. Dark and ugly, it had the look of a giant black warrior as it loomed large and heavy above the second story of the temple.

A figure brushed past Jessica in the darkness. Knocking her aside, the buckskin clad form rushed to the warrior who lay upon the temple's second tier.

"No," Snowcloud screamed. "No." Throwing herself upon the chieftain, a fierce combination of fear and anger showed on her face. Snowcloud turned toward the mass that hovered overhead. "You cannot kill him. He has done what you have asked. You cannot kill him because of your lies and deceit."

A wicked smile curled on the face that formed in the cloud. "And who is this who vows to protect you?"

"I am his wife. I love him and I will give my life to save his. Take me in his place, but let him live."

Jessica gasped, my God, she should have known this was Song of the Eagle.

With that Song rose from the floor and enfolded Snowcloud in his arms. The dancers moved forward and encircled the two in a protective ring.

The evil looked on, a smirk of pleasure crossed his face. "How sweet. The woman wants to save her lover. And the rest of you want to join her. How humanly sickening of all of you."

"You must go. You should not have come back," Song said to Snowcloud in a hushed voice, barely audible to Jessica's ears. "I will not leave you. If you are to die, I will die with you. It is my place."

"But what of—" The maiden raised her hand and put it to his lips to silence him. She shook her head and looked into his eyes.

"If he is to send you to the world of the Great Spirit then I will go with you. We are one, for eternity. I will not let death separate me from you." The young leader pulled her to him and kissed her deeply. The two moved apart, looked into each other's eyes and then kissed again. He stroked her hair. "For eternity," he said. "For you, I will fight him."

"Oh, please," the evil form sneered. "You think this sentiment will change anything? Put it up against this."

With that the evil form puffed out its gigantic cheeks and blew. All the heat of a blast furnace came at them in an unbearably strong burst. A hurricane force wind with the heat of a thousand fires blew down upon the small group left on the temple tier.

Jessica covered her head and face with the large floppy sleeves of the rawhide shirt, thankful for the protection it offered. She felt a pang of pain at the cries of the shirtless medicine man and reached forward, pulling his small head close to hers and under the protection of the shirt.

Peeking from beneath the folds of leather, she could see the dancers had been blasted backward and hovered next to the wall to her left. Screams of anguish pierced the night air as the burning wind foretold the greatness of the force they stood before. The young leader and the maiden clung to each other and tried desperately to stand. Its searing force at last collapsed the two into a heap and the evil's fiery breath closed in on the bare flesh of the leader's back. At last, the hideous thing stopped, leaving the group lying in a crumpled mass upon the temple.

"Do you doubt my power, stupid humans?" the great hovering beast bellowed.

Summoning the last of his strength, the leader rose wearily to his feet. Pushing the sobbing maiden behind him, he stood before the evil.

"You will not fight me fair and square. You will not meet me on my own terms. I have no power equal to your own. I have lost, but I only ask that you spare my wife." Song's voice was steady as he pleaded with the unflinching monster. "You have said you will not kill the living. You have let them go free, and I ask only that you spare her as well. She does not know what she says when she asks to die with me. Please, please give her life."

"Sniveling does not become you and your war paint. I expected you to rise and give some great final fight against me. Perhaps I need to pull it from you." With a mighty force, the maiden was whisked from behind Song and thrust upon the temple's altar on the third tier.

The warrior scrambled up the hand and footholds to the maiden and covered her with his body. She lay silent and motionless on the stone block. The color had drained from her face. It took on a spooky translucent glow in the light of the torches burning upon the altar. Pulling themselves away from the wall, Jessica and the medicine man followed the crowd to the altar and huddled against the wall behind Song.

"So you still think you have power over me? You are a fool, but you do not quit easily. Give up. I have won. The spoils of victory are now mine to enjoy, and I have saved the best for last." From out of the boiling cloud emerged a black warrior. "Raven," Song whispered. "He has taken your soul—"

Jessica's eyes flew open at the mention of the name of the evil warrior from Snowcloud's story. Within seconds, Raven had scaled the walls of the temple and loomed large and dark over the woman on the altar. He reached out a dark muscular arm and thrust it toward Song who was obviously hit by some unseen force. It threw him several feet into the air and he landed flat on his back several feet away. "Now watch, fool, as I take from you all you have left." This time the words came from Raven's mouth.

"Noooooo," Song screamed as Raven pulled a long crude knife from his belt and plunged it hard and fast into the heart of the maiden on the altar.

Jessica stood aghast. The medicine man gasped in horror. Song cried out in anguish, apparently pinned to the ground by the evil's dark powers.

"How can you be so wicked," Song sobbed, choking back his pain in short breaths. "If you have any pity in your soul, kill me. End this. I can take no more."

A deep evil laugh permeated the air. "Kill you, I shall, but your fate will be the same as those you have brought to me."

"No," Song cried. "Please, no. At least let me tell her goodbye."

"Tisk, tisk. You are all such cowards at the end." Raven pulled the blood-covered knife from the body of the maiden and gave it a disgusting smirk. Wiping the blade upon the stone of the altar, he put it back into his belt. With the whisk of his hand, he pulled Song to his feet and thrust him into the kiva he had emerged from earlier.

Jessica's knees wobbled beneath her as the medicine man pulled at her arm. "We must go quickly. Back to the cave," he said near hysteria.

"One moment, just one moment," Jessica mumbled. Driven by some unknown force, she pulled Snowcloud's amulet from her pocket and hobbled to the blood-drenched altar where the maiden's lifeless body lay. Holding the stone in the palm of her hand, she pressed it hard to the maiden's chest.

A glow began between her fingers and burning warmth spread through her hand. Trembling, she held fast to the stone as it vibrated. A mist rose from the maiden's body, and an air-like image of the woman drifted several feet above her. She looked down upon her remains and then back at Jessica.

"Thank you," she whispered and floated away. The medicine man looked on in disbelief, his mouth hung open in awe. "You magic woman," he said softly.

Jessica looked down at her hand still pressed tight against the woman's chest and the world began to spin. Dizzy. Spinning round and round, then moving toward a bright light, she left the stench and the evil one behind.

CHAPTER FIFTEEN

Alex pulled the sheet of clear heavy plastic over the top of the pit as a fine mist of rain started to fall from the evening sky. Tiny drops pattered in the dusty glaze that covered the plastic, its chemical odor at odds with the smell of fresh earth and rainwater.

A flash went through his mind, a picture he couldn't quite grasp, as a distinct feeling of uneasiness washed through his chest and mid-section. Standing erect, he looked around, listening intently. He scanned the hillside above the ruin. A small voice called to him somewhere in his mind, but he couldn't make out what it was saying. He glanced at Yellow Dog who was on his feet, ears at attention, and looking up the slope next to the rock formation. The dog reared his head back and sniffed at the air. He looked at Alex and a silent message passed between them. Alex stepped out into the open, farther away from the ruin and studied the hillside next to the mass of stone. "Come on, boy," he said, and pulled his shirt collar tighter around his neck as the raindrops fell harder. Dusk was nearing and the cloudy sky hastened its onset as he climbed the incline with Yellow Dog close at his heels.

A hundred yards or more up the slope, the formation jutted out and a scattering of junipers had grown up. Rounding the protrusion, he stopped in his tracks as his eye caught a magnificent wall of petroglyphs partially hidden by clumps of broken bushes and piñon tree branches. He was stunned for a second by what he saw, but a flash of color on the slope pulled his gaze away. Next to the broken bushes and trampled limbs, Jessica lay sprawled in the damp earth.

"Jess." Rushing to her side, he dropped to his knees next to her. His heart raced. "Jess, are you okay?" He spoke louder this time. He patted her damp face and brushed aside the strands of hair that clung to it. Pulling off his shirt, he raised her head and tucked his shirt beneath it. Her head fell back limply.

"Oh, my God," he whispered. "What's happened to you?" He felt for a pulse in her neck and then put his head to her breast, thankful to hear a soft steady heartbeat. Looking her over, he could see no outward signs of injury.

Her eyes half opened as she squinted up at him. "Alex? What are you doing here?" Her gravelly voice was music to his ears.

"Are you hurt, Jess?" His brow furrowed in deep concern.

"I don't think so." She raised her head weakly. Her gaze seemed disoriented and confused. "I'm just cold."

"Lay still. I'll get you out of here." Scooping her up against his bare chest, he started back to camp. He turned to see Yellow Dog standing next to the petroglyph wall. The dog stood with ears raised, looking as if he were listening to something behind the stone.

"I know, fella, we'll check it out tomorrow," Alex called to him. He was curious about the dog's behavior, but much more concerned with the precious cargo he held in his arms. The dog yapped twice then reluctantly followed Alex as he navigated his way through the scattered rocks and yucca plants on the steep hillside.

Alex searched through the pile of firewood for dry logs. With a hatchet, he chipped away some kindling and arranged it in the circle of rocks. The flame from a lit match soon spread to the slivers of fresh wood. In no time, the flames were licking orange and blue around two piñon logs. Thankfully, the rain had dwindled to a drizzle.

Jessica sat wrapped in a blanket, still looking a little dazed as she sipped a cup of water.

"I think you should let me take you into town to see a doctor." He poured a can of soup into a blackened saucepan and placed it on the fire.

"Alex, I appreciate your concern. But I'm fine. Honest."

"Okay." He shrugged. "I guess you're the one who would know." Kneeling beside her, he reached up and pulled aside a few strands of wet hair. "The fire will help dry you out." He paused, unable to hold in a half-exasperated smile. "What the heck were you doing up there anyway? Didn't your last two trips out here teach you anything?"

"I was looking for something." Her eyes widened in her pale face. It was obvious troubled thoughts ran through her mind. "I'm just not sure I can explain it to you right now."

He patted her damp shoulder and retrieved a flannel shirt from the tent. "Here, put this on before you catch cold. You're soaked to the skin."

She took it and gave him a half-smile. He turned politely and stirred the fire with a stick, but couldn't resist a quick look from the corner of his eye. Stripping off the wet shirt without hesitation, she slipped the clean one over her fair petal soft skin and sports bra. She buttoned the shirt and pulled the blanket around her.

Turning toward her again, he smiled. "Better?"

"Yes. Thanks." She held the palms of her hands to the warmth of the fire and rubbed them together.

"What happened to you up there? Did you fall?"

She looked into his eyes, her brow fraught, her face disturbed. "I'll tell you about it. I need to tell you about it." She bit her lip. "Right now I'm too exhausted to know where to start." She offered a weak smile. The heavy sigh that followed only made him more curious, but brought him to the realization he had to let her do this in her own time.

He wanted to question her about the petroglyph wall, too. She reminded him of a pathetic soaked kitten as she sat by the fire and tried to get warm. The wall was an exciting archaeological find. It could be a major breakthrough. With nightfall upon them, he was anxious about it, but he had more important things to attend to here.

The soup bubbled in the pot and he poured her a mug full of the hot liquid. Her hands trembled when she brought the cup to her mouth. Aware he was watching her she offered a tired smile. "I can't seem to get warm."

"Come with me." He extended his hand and pulled her to her feet. With one hand in the small of her back, he walked with her to the tent and pointed to his sleeping bag. "Wrap yourself up in there for a while and drink some hot soup." Shivering, she hesitated then climbed into the inviting rolls of warmth in the heavy sleeping bag.

Alex glanced up at the sky as darkness fell and lit the Coleman lantern hanging from the center bar of the tent. "There are still a few minutes of light left. I'm going to have a look at that wall." She gave him an unconcerned nod and took a sip of hot soup.

Flashlight in hand, he moved up the gravel slope with long strides and dug in the toes of his boots for traction. As he stood before the wall, he maneuvered the beam of light from one figure to the next. There was more here than an ancient hunter's story. He'd studied prehistoric artworks many times before, but this one had some unusual figures and depictions. Repeated stick figures seemed to represent many people, then arrows or more likely spears. The final streaked handprint stopped him, ran a chill through him.

Shivers ran down his spine. He cast the beam of the flashlight around and an eerie feeling came over him, as if a cold dark presence had crept up behind him. He sniffed the air. A foul stench wafted its way around him, a smell like something dead and rotten. Hideous pictures flashed through his mind, quick, like a bolt of lightning. A flash of a decaying heap of bodies followed the picture of a bloodied body. He put a hand to the side of his head, as a dizzy feeling overcame him.

A spray of gravel hit him from out of the blue, knocking him from his haze. The flashlight flew from his hand. The side of the mountain exploded in screams and snarls. Alex groped for the flashlight in the darkness. His heart hammered. Fear gripped at his gut. His first thought was that Yellow Dog had tackled a mountain lion. The sounds of a vicious battle continued. Wildly cascading pebbles pounded Alex. He crawled on his hands and knees searching for the light. At last, he found it. The sounds stopped as suddenly as they had erupted.

Pushing the button on the light, he pointed its beam out into the darkness. He half expected to find the mangled body of his treasured pet. He moved the light frantically around. It came to rest on a white wolf that sat on the hillside above him. The animal licked its nose and tossed its head then ran back up the mountainside. Another quick scan of the hill revealed nothing.

Hurriedly, Alex made his way back to camp. He pulled back the tent flap. A flood of relief washed over him as he saw Yellow Dog lying protectively at Jessica's feet.

"Everything okay here?" His words fell on deaf ears. Snuggled in the warmth of the sleeping bag, Jessica lay fast asleep. Yellow Dog opened a sleepy eye and wagged his tail.

Alex poured himself a cup of the warm soup. He sat by the fire for a while and contemplated the event on the mountain and Jessica's mysterious appearance tonight. Fatigue won out as the soup warmed his stomach. The incident on the mountain had unsettled him, but being here with Jessica nearby, brought him back. He put another log on the fire. It was best to keep a fire burning. Whatever the white wolf had encountered on the mountain, he wanted it to stay away from camp.

Watching from the door of the tent, he could hear soft noises coming from Jess. She was dead to the world, head back, mouth open and making raspy little sounds. He smiled and whispered under his breath, "Damn, I finally find the girl of my dreams and she snores." He wouldn't wake Jessica to take her back to the lodge. Let her sleep here tonight and get some rest. Pulling some extra blankets from a roll in the tent, he spread them out next to her, took off his boots, and crawled beneath the covers.

Yellow Dog peeked his head through the tent flap, his tongue hung out expectantly. "Sorry, boy. Your spot's taken tonight." Alex whispered. Yellow Dog whined once and laid down outside with a heavy thud. "You're lucky it stopped raining." Alex added in an amused tone.

A fragment of the moon peeked from behind a cloud and shone through the tent flap. Alex moved closer to Jess who snuggled her head into his shoulder. "Lucky

I'm such a nice guy, Jessica Sinclair, or I might take advantage of you." He kissed the top of her head. If she'd known how much he wanted to, she'd have been afraid to close her eyes. The truth was, he'd settle for this any night.

———

Jessica opened her eyes then closed them to the intrusive light. Wow, she hadn't felt this bad in the morning since her college days. Squinting, she glanced around and gasped. About twelve inches away was Alex's smile. Propped up on one elbow, he obviously had been watching her sleep. "Alex—" She rubbed her eyes in confusion. "Where am I?" She rose and started to crawl from the sleeping bag. She stopped short and made a quick check to be sure she was decent.

"Don't you remember? It was quite a night," he chortled in amusement as she scrambled out of the tent.

She frowned at him then looked down at the oversized shirt she had on. Her head cleared. "Yes, I remember," she said, in an annoyed tone.

"I was only having some fun," he said with a big cheesy grin as he rolled from the blankets and pulled on his boots. "You always wake up this grumpy?"

"You always wake up chattering like a magpie?" She blinked against the bright morning light and tried to tame her fly away hair with her hands.

"Ooooo," he teased as he climbed from the tent. He brushed past her and poured water into a blue enamel coffee pot.

She forced a smile as her mood softened and the fog in her head lifted. "Sorry." She looked down at the ground. "Guess I got up on the wrong side of the tent this morning. Thanks for everything you did last night."

"No problem." He stirred the red coals in the fire pit and lay in some twigs.

"Did you keep a fire going all night?" she asked. "Those coals look pretty hot."

"Just protecting you from the lions and tigers and bears."

"Oh my," she quipped.

"I heard a pretty vicious animal fight up on the mountain last night. I was just playing it safe."

She nodded and flashed him a smile.

"Feeling better today?"

"Definitely." She rubbed her temples. "But I woke up with a killer headache."

"Probably need a good strong cup of coffee."

Jessica eyed the big blue pot sitting in the fire. "I'll bet you make a mean one."

"Well, I generally drink it from a lead lined cup, but I made it a little weak this morning since I had company."

"Thanks, I appreciate that." Wrinkling her nose, she gave him a flirtatious grin.

While Alex busied himself with preparing bacon and eggs, Jessica sat by the fire next to Yellow Dog. She patted his head and he responded with a good morning kiss. His nose stopped and sniffed curiously at something between her breasts. Her hand went instinctively to push his muzzle away and came upon a solid object under her shirt. Pulling it out, she looked down at the rose colored amulet that hung from her neck. "Oh, my God," she said aloud. Her heart stopped and her breath caught in her throat.

"What did you say?" Alex asked from the nearby woodpile where he was collecting another log for the fire.

"Nothing," she stammered and pushed the rawhide cord and smooth rose crystal back inside her shirt. Yesterday's experience had at first seemed like a dream to her, but it couldn't possibly have been. She wore the proof around her neck.

A little stunned, her thoughts ran the Indy 500 in her head. The voices from her vision echoed in her mind. Alex was wonderful, he made her laugh, he made her relax, but the spirits and ancient dead would not leave her alone. After yesterday there was no doubt about what she had to do. The time had come for her to lay some track with Alex. It wasn't clear yet, what Alex had to do with all of this, but she knew inevitably it would come to her from somewhere.

If she didn't start to bring him into this unbelievable world along with her, she wasn't sure she ever could. The further it went, the wilder and more far-fetched she felt it would sound to someone else. And the more real and believable the revelations became.

Up to this point, nothing the spirit or Nechi had told her had been wrong. It had all played out. She thought of Snowcloud and shuddered at the horror of the young girl's fate. Somehow Alex had to help the poor sad maiden, whose spirit still walked the mountain. But first Jessica would have to act as the bridge between their worlds.

She cleared her throat. "Alex."

"Yeah." He scooped fried eggs from a heavy iron skillet on the fire and laid them next to strips of bacon on two thick plastic plates. "Hope you like 'em over easy." Grinning, he handed her a plate.

"They look great." She bit her lip. This wasn't going to be easy.

He poured her a cup of coffee and placed it next to her on the ground. His smile faded as he observed the serious look she knew was on her face.

Where to start, where to start. "Do you remember the first time I came out here?"

"Sure, I do."

"I told you about the strange feelings I get from this place."

"Yes, of course, I remember that conversation." His brow creased into a frown.

Alex watched her expectantly. *Hell.* She couldn't tell him she'd sat in a kiva and talked to a ghost. That she'd flown through time zones into another world. He'd have her committed. She looked away. *Okay. Try a different approach.* "Well, someone told me about this ancient legend and I wondered if there could be any truth to it."

"There are lots of legends around." He gave her a curious look and took a mouthful of eggs.

"I mean, being an archaeologist, I thought you would know if it was possible."

He frowned and shrugged. "I'm not sure what this has to do with how this place makes you feel, but lay it on me. I'll tell you if I think it's plausible."

She picked at her food, taking a few small bites. "It seems there was a tribe that lived here a very long time ago."

"There were lots of people here hundreds of years ago, Jess. Maybe as many as thirty-five thousand at one time."

"I know," she said. "But let's go back even further. Let's say these were the very first people who lived at the mesa.

"Okay. I'm with you."

She relayed the brief history of the people as Nechi had told it to her. "It could have happened like that. It is possible. Right?"

"Well, you said it was a legend, but it certainly could have happened."

"Is it possible, too, that this ruin was some sort of temple?"

Alex gave her a puzzled look. "Well, I don't know. You mentioned that before. I haven't found anything to make me believe it was. It has the appearances of being a village."

"Oh, there was a village here, too," she blurted then stopped herself. "I mean the legend said there was a village—and a temple."

Alex grinned. "I see where we're going. You're trying to connect this legend with the site. Okay, I'll play along."

She let out a frustrated sigh. "This legend is about an Indian maiden and her lover who used to live here. You'll probably think it's a lot of romantic nonsense, but it's really bugging the hell out of me, Alex." She was suddenly aware of the deeply emotional rush that spewed from her. Tears welled up in her eyes. She blinked wildly to keep them from falling.

"I'm sorry, Jess," he said, in a serious tone. "Something about this means very much to you, I can see that."

He set his plate aside and grasped his mug of coffee with both hands, giving her his full attention.

"I don't know, Alex, maybe I'm losing my mind. The people in this story I—heard. They seem to be coming to life. You know, haunting me or something." Great. Now she'd convince him she was mentally disturbed.

"It's okay. I don't think you're nuts."

"I'm sorry. I'm carrying on like a lunatic. It's just some of these things I've seen—in my head, I mean. They seem so real."

"Tell me about it. I'm listening."

She wasn't sure if he was interested or playing shrink. "The young lovers lived here. Somewhere at the mesa. He was a young chieftain. His father died. Fell from some cliff and was killed. The young man took over as leader of the tribe."

Alex's jaw dropped and his expression took on a look of surprise. "The father fell from a cliff?"

She nodded. "There was a lot of awful stuff going on. Some terrible things happened here. They died here, Alex, and some horrible thing is keeping their souls—"

"Slow down, Jess. It's okay." He put his arm around her and pulled her close. "It's all right."

"It's not all right?" She looked at him in wonder. Did he believe her or was he consoling her insanity? "Alex, this girl needs—I'm sorry. I shouldn't have tried to tell you about this. I can't explain it because I don't understand it myself." She picked up her plate and stuffed in a few mouthfuls. "This is very good, by the way. Thanks," she muttered through a bite of breakfast. She wasn't the least bit hungry and she had no idea what it tasted like. But he'd gone to all this trouble and she wasn't going to disappoint him.

"Calm down, Jess. You okay?"

"I'm fine, just a little upset and confused. Maybe I've been working way too hard on this article. You know, getting too caught up in all of this."

He shrugged and looked at her, his eyes full of questions. "Maybe, maybe not."

"What does that mean? You don't think I'm ready for a straight jacket?"

"Not yet anyway." He smiled and fell silent.

She wondered what was on his mind, as he poured another cup of coffee and retreated into a world of deep thought. Maybe she'd said too much, or maybe she hadn't told him enough. At any rate her afternoon had laid out its own plan for her. She had to find the spirit in the kiva and ask him where to go from here.

CHAPTER SIXTEEN

Jonathan McCabe stared out the front window of his rambling ranch house. Shadows of the past lay long and haunting on him today. Whatever hell that lived in his soul now was sporadic. He'd have preferred it not allow him flashes of what he used to be.

He'd risen early to a house empty of the love that used to dwell within the walls he'd built with his own two hands. A house he'd built for his Dorothy. He missed the smell of a home-cooked breakfast almost as much as he missed the touch and sweet smell of her between the sheets of the bed they'd shared for thirty years.

He was a fool. He'd traded his life with the woman he loved for wickedness, hatred, and greed. Things never imagined before, now played constant games in his soul, except for occasional moments like this one. The house was filthy. Dorothy would have never allowed so much as a cobweb to collect in the house she loved. She'd cry if she could see what he'd done to it.

Then it began again, the shaking hands, the burning in the core of his being. It never let him go too far down the road to the past without tearing him back. Ripping him from what used to be reality into a world where something beyond himself controlled his mind and body. A tear trickled from the corner of his eye.

As the thing overtook him, all resemblance of the man who once was Jonathan McCabe drained from his inner being. He did not give up easily, and with trembling hands reached for the pack of cigarettes on the table next to the chair. The lighter rattled against the dust-covered tabletop that still bore the spotted evidence of the polished shine Dorothy kept on it.

"Curse this damn place," he screamed. "I should burn it to the ground."

A car outside brought him to his feet and his hands to the Winchester rifle that sat nearby. Peeking through the curtains of the front window, he watched Tom Wilson, his wretched colleague in crime, step from the car. He hated Wilson almost as much as the rest of them, but he needed Wilson, too. It was Wilson who had the connections, Wilson who knew the rich Europeans. But if he didn't need him, he'd damn sure be sizing him up through the sights of his rifle.

McCabe put aside the gun and answered the soft rap on the door.

"Getting awful trigger happy, aren't you?" Wilson asked, apparently catching a glimpse of the gun barrel as it met with the incoming rays of sunlight.

"What the hell business is it of yours?" McCabe snarled, spitting out bits of tobacco from the unfiltered cigarette butt.

"If there wasn't a profit in this for me, I'd never put up with the likes of you." Wilson shook his head and pushed past McCabe.

"Let's get down to business," McCabe spat. His lips curled as his fingers itched to strangle the bastard. "The sooner the better."

Clad in blue jeans and gray sport coat, the bearded Wilson breezed over to the sofa and distastefully brushed aside a cigarette ash before sitting. "What a slob," he said under his breath.

McCabe huffed and ignored the remark. He ground his cigarette out in an overflowing ashtray on the debris-covered coffee table. "Well, did you get the money?"

"Part of it." Wilson pulled a wad of bills from the pocket of his jeans.

"Part of it? What the hell?" McCabe roared. "You said they were gonna pay on delivery."

"They'll pay when they get more stuff. I told you it would take time. If I start shipping out too much, we'll find both our butts in jail."

"Yeah, right," McCabe snorted and leaned over Wilson trying to draw the man's gaze into his own. The heat in McCabe rose. "In the meantime, I'm holdin' off them two nosy bastards at the site. You leave that archaeologist there long enough and he'll blow this whole deal all to hell."

Wilson squirmed and tried to look away. "I'm not worried. We planted enough stuff out there to keep him confused for a long time. Those people work at a snail's pace anyway."

"Right, smart ass, eventually he'll find something if he keeps nosin' around." McCabe's lips curled as he drew Wilson's eyes to his again. Using his evil power on Wilson brought him a sick kind of pleasure.

"Then we'll take care of him. Keep an eye on where he's digging." Wilson twitched and pulled at his shirt collar. "You and your itchy trigger finger should enjoy it if he gets too close."

Now Wilson was coming around. McCabe pushed him harder. "And what about that snoopy woman reporter. You waitin' for her to put our faces on the front page of the paper?"

"I'm not the one who's waiting," Wilson snapped. "You're the one who got nervous about her."

McCabe closed in. "She's a bigger threat than the guy from the university. It would've been a lot simpler if that boulder had got her to begin with."

"That one was on you, not me. I don't get it. Why are you such a bloodthirsty bastard anyway? I don't understand why you want to kill her or anybody else. That was never part of the deal."

Wilson was going to put up a fight after all.

"You're in this with me, Tom." McCabe's voice was low and croaky, the words ripped from his throat as the internal force used him as a tool. His eyes burned from heat and dryness as he pulled Wilson in again. This time, he saw the change in Wilson's face.

"Then why don't you get it over with, Jon?"

"Hell, I can't help it if the woman has nine lives. I've been tryin'. I ain't spendin' life in prison. If you want to risk it, you should be the one who gets rid of her."

"You and your notion you're some kind of snake charmer didn't help." Wilson scratched at his short red beard and looked thoughtfully toward the front window.

McCabe had him. He drew Wilson into eye contact and held it this time. Wilson tried to avoid it and moved nervously on the couch. A long silence followed.

"Somethin' on your mind?" McCabe growled, sensing what was at work in Wilson's head.

A hint of a grin crossed Wilson's face. "I was just thinking. Maybe you're trying too hard to make it look like an accident."

"What you got in mind?" McCabe scowled at him.

"I mean some crazy drifter could wander into the park. Who knows what could happen if he decided to rob her." A deep throaty laugh parted his snarled lips. "Fiery bitches that some women reporters are, things could get out of hand."

Bingo. McCabe had him. Wilson was putty in his hands. It was easier than squashing a bug. A smile tugged at McCabe's dry mouth. "You mean knock her in the head and steal her purse?"

"Maybe the car, too. Roll it off a cliff somewhere on that steep road to the mesa. Who'd ever be the wiser?"

"Hmm." McCabe grunted as he scraped his fingers across the roughness of his five o'clock shadow. He winced as somewhere deep beyond his soul's hearing, a tiny voice cried, "Nooo— You can't do this." As quickly as it rose, some unknown evil strangled it back and extinguished it with a wicked flame that ignited a new wave of hatred in his being. He looked at Wilson with a crooked smile and nodded his head.

A thought flashed through McCabe's mind as he stumbled behind Wilson toward the door. What the hell was he doing? His life was coming apart at the seams. But he was going to fix it. When he got the money, everything would be fine. He just needed the money—he'd make it okay with Dorothy. Oh, God, if he carried through with this, would he ever be able to make things right again?

But it was too late. The trembling seeped back into his bones. A wicked laugh parted his lips as he stood on the porch and watched Wilson drive away. He was in too deep. It was useless to fight what was happening to him anymore.

—◄—

Jessica sat cross-legged on the cold stone floor of the kiva, her face buried in her hands, asking herself what the hell she was doing. She shook it off. It was way too late to turn back. She'd come to the mesa hoping to get over some of her grief, and, frankly, she hadn't thought about it in days. The story she'd hoped would launch her into her dream career consisted of a few pages of notes and two paragraphs scratched on a notepad in her room.

These past few days had seemed more like a ride through the fun house than anything else. How had she gone from having serious doubts about an afterlife, to being on this far-fetched mission to help a ghost and chase an ancient spirit around in a kiva? And why in the hell had she paused to analyze it? For the second time in her life, she knew she was better off if she didn't ask why.

"You seem troubled." The familiar voice came without any beckoning. "Your visions have disturbed you."

"Disturbed me? Holy sh—"

"Much has happened in a short time."

"That's an understatement." Jessica scooted nearer the spirit hole as a dim light illuminated the area around it.

"But you are still here. More important you have come again."

"There's not much chance I'll walk away now." She shook her head. "Especially after yesterday."

"I am sorry you had to experience such suffering first hand, but it was the only way."

"The only way? What do you mean?"

"That you would understand. The only way it could become important enough for you to risk so much to help Snowcloud."

"Snowcloud. That poor tragic girl. Her spirit cannot rest." Jessica could still see the image of the slain maiden upon the altar. "Please tell me what I can do to help her."

"You cannot do the deed that will allow the maiden's soul eternal peace. The man Alex is the only one who can help her." The spirit's voice came from the spirit hole, apparently he had chosen not to show himself today.

"You told me that before, but I still don't understand what I have to do with this."

A great sigh filled the kiva, one Jessica knew was brought on by frustration. "You have done your work, and done it well. Do you not see where it leads?"

"No. I'm sorry you find me so inept in all this, but I'm not exactly a seasoned spirit chaser you know."

A low chuckle came. "That was obvious to me from the start. Had I been the great hand from beyond, you would not have been the flower I would have plucked to serve such a grave purpose."

"Well, excuse me," she snorted. "I'm certainly feeling special after that comment. After seven hundred years, I didn't think you'd be so choosey."

"You speak the words of truth and wisdom, young one. But you must admit you have not made it easy for me."

"Easy for you? I'm the one who's been riding a runaway train through hell's alley. I don't know what it is you spirits do, but from my side, I'm not feeling too sympathetic."

"It was not I who sowed your roots or created your destiny. I am only here to work with what the Great Creator of all things has given me."

"Whatever Mr. High and Mighty Spirit." He was getting on her nerves. "While you're making chitchat about my inadequacies, my butt's freezing to this slab of rock. I came here with questions, not to be told I'm an inadequate piece of putty."

The chamber filled with hoarse laughter, deep and intense. "You have passed the test, young one. You have a fiery spirit. You sit here unafraid and speak to the symbol of goodness without any qualms. You must stand before the symbol of evil in the same fearless way."

"Symbol of evil? No! Not the hideous thing that came to the temple. Oh, no."

"Oh, yes, his spirit lives and remains strong."

"But that was hundreds of years ago. It's not possible."

"As goodness has endured, so has evil. His powers have changed over the centuries. He has made the ruin his own, the center of his domain. He makes his rumblings there, but still he seeks a human form. That is where he draws his strength." The spirit paused. "Just as he inhabited the body of the warrior, Raven, years ago, and forced the man to do many hideous acts, he now lives in the body of another."

"How will I know who he is?"

"When the time comes, you will know."

Jessica raised her eyebrows. She wasn't nuts. "Well, I'm not going to go out and look for this thing."

"No need. He will find you."

This was getting scary. "Can we get back to the maiden? You're giving me the creeps."

"The maiden is another problem. You have no power to help her."

"You said that before."

"You are the link between her and her lover. You are her connection to the man you call Alex."

"Alex is a special man, but I don't think I'll ever be able to get him to buy into this." She'd made no headway in her first two attempts.

"You must. So much depends upon you." The voice thundered.

"Then stop all the mumbo jumbo and just tell me. Between you and Nechi, I'm not sure what the heck is happening here." Now she was mad.

"I will tell you. You will listen."

She scooted back from the spirit hole a little. Apparently, he was a little perturbed with her. "Yes, I will. But tell me everything this time. No more games."

"The man Alex is the chosen one. He, and only he, can free the spirits of the native people that were trapped in the cavern by the evil one. The evil one still lives there. And, mind you, it still is very powerful. This wicked force will do all it can to prevent Alex from doing what he must."

"Can you tell me again, why you are putting this on me instead of Alex?" It was almost too much.

"You must understand you are the link. For the man Alex, the inherent pain around his heritage has caused him to build a wall around his spirit. He protects that side of him with his logical mind." The spirit sighed. "Alex only allows in what he wants to hear, then he molds it into what his heart can accept. He has inherited the belief he is letting down his lineage if he walks back into the Native American world."

"But he's an educated man. Surely he knows better than that."

"This is far more a matter of the heart than of the mind. Emotion does not feed from intelligence or education. Many men carry the pain of their elders in their hearts, and it does not come from logic, but rather from upbringing. These things are among the hardest for them to change about themselves."

"Swell," Jessica muttered under her breath and ran her hand through her hair.

"Make no mistake, our voices have tried to break through to him. We have whispered to him by day and stalked his dreams by night. Now he has come to his moment of truth and still he does not hear us."

"And now it's my turn." Jessica buried her face in her hands. "As you said, that's why I'm here."

"At last you understand." The spirit sighed again, this time as if he were relieved. "We have helped you by planting the seeds in his mind, but his is not a spiritual nature. He is one who must touch and feel and smell to believe. Bring him proof of what you know, lay it in his hands and in time he will connect it with what has been put in his mind by the spirits."

"You mean the legend. I have to convince him of its truth."

"Again, you understand."

"But what of freeing these souls."

"Once Alex knows, he can find the way. First, he must free the ancient chieftain. When the chieftain's spirit is free, the evil one's spell will be broken and the rest of the souls will follow."

"Song of the Eagle." She'd nearly forgotten to ask about him. "The evil one threw him aside after the maiden died, but I did not see what happened after that."

"The chieftain was sealed alive in the kiva, in the ceremonial chamber where you visited him. The evil one wishes to keep his soul there for eternity." There was a brief silence, allowing her time to comprehend. "Alex is a descendent of Song of the Eagle. The final hope. The only one alive who can break the spell and free the chieftain and his people."

"This sounds crazy. Like something from a fairy tale."

"You can say that, after all you have seen?"

"No. Of course not."

"But what about the spirit of the maiden? I've seen her, spoken with her. How did she break free?"

"You do not know?"

"No."

"You freed her, young one. You held the amulet to her bosom."

"No. That was part of a nightmare or something."

"Call it what you will. The proof hangs around your neck."

Jessica was silent, staring at the amulet. What had really happened to her?

"It is time for you to go. You have much to do."

"But wait. How will we free the chieftain? You haven't told me that."

"It is forbidden that I tell you. The man Alex has the powers of the ancients, and like the young chieftain, he must find his fate through his spiritual power." His voice softened. "The secret has been revealed to him, just as it was to Song of the Eagle. Let us pray he can find it for himself."

"But what if he can't?"

"The evil prevailed in those ancient days. He has the power to do so again."

"You mean—Alex could be—"

"Next." The spirit's words echoed in the kiva and in her ears.

Jessica's head spun. She didn't like where this was leading. Questions bombarded her brain. What if she couldn't get Alex to believe her? What if she failed? If Alex didn't know, maybe nothing would happen to him. The spirit read her thoughts.

"If you do not tell him, his soul is lost already, along with the hope of yet another generation. Listen to your inner voice and use the tools you have been given." With that the room grew foggy and the dim light faded, leaving the final parting thought in Jessica's mind.

She grasped the amulet and squeezed it. She'd seen it snatch the maiden's soul away from the evil. Too bad it couldn't force the spirit's words into Alex's thick logical head. Truthfully, she didn't hold much hope for that. It seemed it was up to her to hammer it in on her own. Maybe she just needed to use a bigger hammer.

CHAPTER SEVENTEEN

Another night had come and Alex tossed and turned in his sleeping bag. He drifted in and out. At last, sleep claimed him and pulled him down that endless river and into another world.

The maiden lay deathly still upon the altar. Her raven black hair picked up the glow from the torches around her. The young man's heart pounded in his chest like a thundering herd of buffalo. He struggled against the unseen force that held him back. The pain in his muscles was unbearable. But he did not, and could not stop. He must get to her.

The black painted face of the massive warrior loomed over her. An evil smile curled his lips. The warrior's face portrayed his sadistic joy. Raising the knife high over his head, he grasped it tightly in both hands. Then plunged it toward the gently heaving bosom of the beautiful woman.

The young man looked on in horror. His gaze went to her. For a fleeting second she opened her eyes. She looked at the plummeting blade that sped toward her breast. A blood-curdling scream that tore from her lips pierced the night air before it was silenced forever. The knife blade struck the stone after passing through her body. Its sound hit the young man with an impact as forceful as the deadly blow itself. Falling to his knees, he was released from the invisible force that had held him. Released—too late.

As he fell, a ball of fire raced through his insides. It surfaced in an agonized scream he had no power to contain. He collapsed then dragged himself to her side. Tears streamed down his face. His breath came in short painful gulps.

"My princess," he gasped, running his hand through her soft raven hair. His fingers caressed her bronze face, now pale and opalescent in the firelight. Softly, he kissed her blood-spattered cheek.

A flash of lightning lit up the sky. Alex shot straight up in his sleeping bag. The following boom of thunder rattled through the canyon. The ground beneath him vibrated from its force.

His heart raced. Beads of sweat ran down his face and back, bearing all the wetness of the threatening downpour outside the tent. Alex wiped the moisture from the corners of his eyes realizing the intensity of the dream had brought him to tears. He held his head as the devastation of the dream warrior ran through his body, no less intense than the first time. He choked back a sob that tried to escape. Still caught in the surreal world, he looked at his hands, half-expecting to see the maiden's blood dripping from them.

A spattering of raindrops hit the canvas of the tent. Alex dragged himself out into the storm, struggling to pull himself from the horror. He lay face down in the dirt. The softness of Yellow Dog's nose on his ear brought him plummeting back to this world. There, in the quickly muddying soil and drenching rain, he sat cross-legged looking up at the sky, asking for meaning in the wave of emotion and fear that clenched his gut.

Mother Nature's shower chilled his skin. A second clap of thunder brought him to his feet. The devastation faded, but the fear still remained, only grounded now in reality. One thought had immersed him in a premonition of what he feared most. Jessica was in danger.

McCabe twitched nervously and pulled out another cigarette. Hunkering low behind the steering wheel of the truck, he struck a match and inhaled. He watched the flame disappear into the tobacco then return to the match head. Blowing the puff of smoke through his nostrils, he shook out the match and threw it on the truck floor. Nothing was going to be left as evidence tonight.

A flash of lightning illuminated the sky and the dark end of the parking lot. McCabe sunk in the seat again. What luck, a storm. He could damn near read the paper by that bolt. A few drops of rain spattered on the windshield. He pulled the dark jacket around his ears.

The light in the room blazed brightly. *Doesn't the woman ever go to bed?* In the lodge parking lot, only one dim street lamp burned tonight. A blessing of sorts, but it deprived him of the light to see his watch. He'd lost track of time. It seemed to drag. The knot of anxiety gnawed at his gut.

Tremors racked his weary body. Somewhere deep within, a distant voice called to him, telling him he wasn't capable of murder. Good God, of course he wasn't, but the evil thing kept strangling back the man inside. The struggle within his body and soul exhausted him. Tonight, the real Jonathan McCabe was fighting harder than ever to escape. But it was a useless fight.

Whatever power possessed him was mightier than he was these days. Maybe in the beginning he could have fought it, but now it was too hard, too tiresome. Maybe that was why he had given up. Why he sat in a parking lot waiting to kill someone he didn't even know.

The feverish heat surged through him again causing his rib cage to clench, drowning all hopes that a flame of goodness still flickered within. The beast inside him wanted her dead, no matter what the man himself thought.

He rolled down the window, letting out the smoke and allowing in the smell of rain. "Come on, bitch," he whispered. "Turn off the light. Let's get this over with."

As the rain plummeted down, a near blinding flash of lightning hit. This time plunging the whole area into blackness.

"Hee, hee," he cackled with pleasure. "I've got some help after all." Whatever force drove him must be stronger than her protector after all. This was proof.

From the seat of the truck, he picked up a screwdriver and Dorothy's old silk scarf. His hand went to the leather scabbard on his leg to be sure his hunting knife was in place. He grasped the cold metal of the door handle with a clammy hand, and pulled up on it slowly. The soft squish of his boots in the muddy soil seemed inaudible in the pouring rain. He stopped as a tiny flicker of light appeared in Jessica's window then was gone. He'd wait a minute to let her settle into bed. Then he would strike. The pouring rain ran off the brim of his cowboy hat and down the back of his jacket as he stood beneath the eave. Quietly, he jimmied the lock with the screwdriver.

The door squeaked open then was lost in the sound of a vehicle barreling up the turns to the lodge. "Curses," McCabe whispered and retreated to his truck, slithering away soundlessly into the storm and the night.

Alex rounded the turn at the top of the hill, the wheels sliding on the slippery surface of the road. Whipping the vehicle into the space next to Jessica's car, his SUV screeched to a stop. Everything was immersed in blackness. He fumbled for a flashlight, swearing under his breath when the batteries failed.

The tightly drawn drapes of the cabin where Jessica's car was parked gave him no clue of what was happening within. Alex knocked, the door opened at the first firm rap of his fist. His heart leaped to his throat as he pushed the door aside and walked into the dark room.

"Jess?" he said, softly at first, then louder. "Jess, where are you?"

He felt his way across the room, tripping over Jessica's shoes and finally reaching the bed. Frantically, he riffled through the blankets until he was satisfied she was not there. "Jess, where the hell are you?" Turning from the bed, he was pulled to a dim flickering light beneath a closed door.

"Jess." He felt his way across the room and reached for the knob. The door swung open.

"Wha—" A surprised Jessica sputtered and tossed aside the headphones of her hand-held CD player. There in the candlelight, up to her shoulders in a bathtub full of bubbles, was Jessica, naked as a jaybird.

A sigh of relief left him that came from the toes up. "Good God. You scared me to death."

"I scared you?" Jessica blurted, her eyes the size of saucers. "What the hell are you doing here?"

"Never mind." Relief washed through him like a tidal wave. He stepped to the side of the tub and dropped to his knees. Placing his large hands around her damp hair, he pulled her to him and kissed her firmly. "You should lock your door," he scolded. "I thought someone had broken into your room."

"But it was locked," she sputtered and started to sit upright in the tub then seemed to remember her absence of clothing.

At the moment, Alex could have cared less what she was saying. He pulled her face to his again and placed his lips over hers. This time he took the softness of her mouth into his own. Emotion of the night's events had built inside him and he felt no inclination to stop it as he let it flow from him. Beads of moisture on her face and lips pulled his mind and emotions to the dream he'd repeated a thousand times in his head. The smooth supple body of the maiden who bathed in the waterfall, the intensity of the warrior's wanting. It ran through his own body all over again. Only now Jessica was here, in his hands. When he kissed her a third time, he let go of the feelings he'd kept at bay for so long.

She gasped, the intensity of his kiss left her panting softly. The droplets of water trailed from her hair down to the water that splashed against her breasts. He kissed at the trail, following it with his tongue, but stopped just above her half-exposed breast.

Her breath escaped in a gush. "Oh, Alex."

He sat back on his heels and bit his lower lip, attempting to corral the rush of emotion as he realized where it was leading him. A runaway freight train of passion held back by a thread. "Thank God, you're okay," he whispered. With raised brows he looked into her somewhat stunned expression.

Pulling himself back under control, he knew he must stop. The vision of Jessica half naked in the candlelight, peaked his wanting more than he cared to acknowledge. He must be a fool for walking away from her, but he couldn't let it happen. He had to be sure it was the right thing for both of them, not driven by his own intense feelings and exhaustion. The only thing he wanted more than to be with her, was not to hurt her.

Maybe age had made him more careful. Or maybe it had made him a fool. He wasn't a young kid anymore, waiting for the chance and wanting just the pure pleasure. He had to consider the consequences it could have in both their lives. Why did this seem to be such a fragile relationship? Perhaps it seemed fragile because it was so devastatingly important in his life.

He leaned forward and kissed her one last time. Then shook his head at her passionate response and grasped her wet hand as she reached for him. He squeezed it softly. "We have to talk. I'll see you tomorrow."

With all the emotional strength he could muster, he rose to his feet and walked to the door. With one final glance back at her glowing skin in the candlelight, he said, "I'll be sure the door's locked when I leave." Then he turned and left her, checking the front door before he stepped out into the pouring rain. He hoped its cold pounding wetness had the power to calm the fire raging in his heart and soul.

The scent of something evil was in the air. Something he couldn't explain. Everything seemed quiet. Hopefully, his surprise appearance had thwarted anything if it were afoot. The unlocked door bothered him but he wasn't sure if Jess had left it open or— Or what? Maybe his wanton hormones and the nightmare were wreaking havoc in his head. Clear thought evaded him. His emotions had taken control of his good sense.

Alex paused as he turned the key in the ignition. The rain ran in little rivers down the windshield and he reached for the wiper switch. He didn't want to leave her, but he dared not stay. His emotions were raging in his gut like a bull pawing the ground, trying to break through a gate.

This wasn't like him. He wasn't sure what had come over him. Part of him liked it, the other part wasn't sure. All the feeling was there inside him for Jessica, but he couldn't risk letting it go until he was sure. Certain she felt the same. Certain she was who he believed her to be. Mind shattering emotion ran through him, passions connected to life, death and destiny—capable of shattering the mind, but even more deadly to the heart. Especially, if he was wrong.

He wasn't sure he understood what had happened to him since he'd come here. It had begun with an emotional education about his own heritage, his own connection with the ancient people of this place. It seemed he'd lived their very lives. And now he was forever connected to them by these vivid and unforgettable dreams.

More important, he'd learned to know himself. For the first time, he knew what he wanted in his life. He hoped to hell he was right about Jessica. He wanted her, wanted her to be with him, and to love him. He wanted to be there, to hold her, care for her, to heal the loneliness in her life. And what he hoped most was that he was right. Something in his soul told him she was meant for him. Something in his dreams connected them to an ancient world and wanted to bring it into this one. Spiritually connected. Soul mates. He'd heard all the terms, but up until now they'd meant nothing. Tonight they were reality, tonight it was *his* destiny being written.

Jonathan McCabe pulled up next to the dark green car parked at the side of the road. The rain-streaked window went down and the face of Tom Wilson appeared, a scowl deeply implanted in his brow.

"Where have you been and where's the broad's car?" he called out as McCabe rolled down the passenger window.

Raindrops spattered into the truck as McCabe yelled to him. "Never mind. Get out of here."

"What the hell are you doing, Jon? Either give it up, or get it right before we both end up in the slammer."

As McCabe pulled back onto the road, he heard the last of Wilson's remark and sped away. The rain poured in through the open window. A blinding flash of lightning lit up the road ahead and the headlights of Wilson's car appeared in his rear view mirror.

"What the hell *are* you doing, Jon?" McCabe repeated Wilson's words under his breath as he took the sharp curves at break neck speed. His trembling hands gripped the steering wheel tightly and an occasional raindrop hit his arm. He sped on contemplating the question. He couldn't answer, but he knew he couldn't stop until it was done, until he had the money from the artifacts and Alex and the woman were both dead.

His heart pushed hard in his throat as a picture flashed in his mind, the image of his truck going over the side of the twisting road and down to the bottom on this rainy night. It was an escape, one he wasn't sure would be a bad thing. He pulled the wheel to the right thinking it would be a quick end, but some force held it back, held the wheels fast on their path around the sharp curves of the winding road.

Something wasn't going to let him out that easy. McCabe let go of the steering wheel. It turned sharply on its own. The truck navigated the corner smoothly without any help from him. He put his hands back on the wheel, knowing he wasn't in control. But somehow, it made him feel better. This thing that ruled his life and being was frighteningly powerful. Now he knew. The only way out for him was to see it to its end. And whatever ending this evil had in mind, is the way it would be.

CHAPTER EIGHTEEN

Jessica popped the door lock and grabbed Alex's note from the car seat. As she surveyed the scattering of people in the park, she didn't see him. She rubbed the slip of paper nervously between her fingers then read the message for the thousandth time since she'd found it on her car window this morning.

"Jess - Please meet me at the city park at 7:00 p.m. tonight. We need to talk."

After their encounter last night, she was uneasy. The intensity of her feelings had taken her by surprise. In spite of her own logic, or what she had believed was logic only a few days earlier, she'd have made love to Alex last night if he hadn't stopped his advances. There was no doubt in her mind she would have; no doubt she would have done so more than willingly.

Alex was different from any man she'd ever met. There was something inside him. Something in his heart she'd found nowhere else. Tenderness she couldn't explain. He was real, without pretenses, solid and secure in himself. Most of all, she was falling hopelessly in love with him.

She'd come here with a different goal, a goal that benefited only her, but along the way everything had changed. Withdrawn in her own emotions, she was sorry for herself because she felt so alone. The spirit had knocked her from her shell and made her realize a much bigger picture existed. Among these age-old ruins, her life had expanded beyond her own heartache and moved into the mysterious realm that crossed the expanse of time. She'd started out wanting to help and now Alex's future depended on her playing out her role in a centuries-long battle between good and evil.

Her heart pounded as she shifted from one foot to the other and watched the growing crowd that gathered for the nightly Indian dancers. They assembled, spreading blankets on the ground and unloading lawn chairs around a concrete slab. Several men, women and children adorned in brightly colored Native American dress milled around the cement pad preparing for their performance.

Jessica let out a long breath. She had no idea what Alex had to say to her. Even worse, she had no idea what she would say to him. Out at his campsite, everything was slow and easy. There had been only the two of them and the open spaces, no pressure, no divulgence of what they were feeling. No pressure to identify their relationship. They should have made love out there for the first time. It would have been different, easy and natural. Talking about it changed things, turned on the self-consciousness and made her feel awkward. Last night it would have been perfect, spontaneous and unexpected.

Maybe she should duck into the ladies room and make a quick check in the mirror. As she darted around the corner, she took one last look to be sure Alex hadn't shown yet. Once inside, she stared back at her reflection and shook her head. Here she was checking her lipstick and worrying about what Alex was about to say to her when she should have been concentrating her energies on the real issues.

She had to find a way to tell Alex about the rest of the legend. Alex was the descendent of some special spirit leader, the fate of two lost souls lay in his hands and she had been chosen to explain that to him. She buried her face in her hands. That was the real issue, and her own heart was double crossing her.

Her deep-seated feelings for Alex had captured her focus because of her selfish fear that she would get Alex to fulfill his destiny and their time together would be over. She'd go back to Denver and he'd go his way, to whatever the hell he was supposed to do when this was all over. It wasn't fair.

If she'd taken on this awesome task, listened to the nagging, haunting forces, and done what they'd asked, wasn't it only fair she should be allowed her moment with Alex? Even if all it ever could be was a moment. She was entitled to that much.

Brushing aside a stray hair and touching up her pale lipstick, she tossed her head and walked back out into the park. The last rays of the setting sun streamed between the trees in patchwork patterns on the grass. She took a deep breath and a quick left around the concrete block wall that protruded several feet from the entrance to the restroom. Without looking up, she took several determined strides. A tall thin figure of a man stepped from behind the building and into her path, stopping her abruptly. Looking up in startled astonishment, she stood toe to toe with Jonathan McCabe. The smell of stale cigarette smoke and perspiration wafted from him as he stood uncomfortably close, his face only inches from her own.

His eyes were wild and fearful like those of a trapped and frantic animal. He grasped her upper arms and squeezed them tight enough to hurt. McCabe searched her face for several seconds. His voice was low but his terrifying message was clearly understandable. "You have to get out of here before it's too late."

"Out of the park?" she stammered, taken off guard.

"No." He shook her and pulled her closer. "Go back where you came from, while you're still alive." His eyes widened and a tremor ran through his hands that shook him so hard it ran through her as well.

"No. Noooo," McCabe moaned, his voice sounded sad and pitiful. He released his forceful grip and fell to his knees. "Don't you see I can't stop it?" he wailed. Then with a surge of effort, he rose to his feet, clinging to his arms and shaking violently. Jessica watched in terror and amazement, as it seemed an internal battle took place inside McCabe. A wicked gleam pushed its way into his eyes.

"Go," he screamed and ran toward the street. She watched aghast and open-mouthed as McCabe jumped behind the wheel of the black pickup truck parked on the street.

Trying to swallow the hard lump in her throat, sheer terror gripped her heart. She'd witnessed the face of evil, a wild man driven by some unbelievably wicked force—and bearing a frightening warning. Jessica's eyes darted toward her car as pictures flashed through her mind. The boulder plummeting down the hill, the snakes rising hideously before her, ready for their deadly strike and Alex's warning about the door she knew she had locked. *God, what am I doing?*

It was all she could do to keep from running to the car. An uncontrollable feeling of foreboding engulfed her. The spirit had warned her of the evil one's appearance and his intent to stop her. He'd not prepared her for the fear that tightened her chest or the evil glow in McCabe's eyes. A frightening battle had played out in McCabe's soul as he fought against the hideous force. There was no doubt in her mind. McCabe was the human form the evil had chosen. Dorothy's story now rang with new meaning.

Terror washed through her, erasing everything but fear for her own safety. Her heart hammered in her chest. Jessica forced her trembling hands to still enough to get the key into the door lock.

In one quick motion she slid into the driver's seat and locked the doors. Her knuckles turned white as she squeezed the steering wheel. Beads of cold sweat pushed their way through her pores. With a shaking hand, she maneuvered the key into the ignition. As her fingers turned it, a large hand covered her own. A startled jerk of her head brought her eyes to the stern face of Nechi who leaned over from the passenger seat. "Wait," he commanded.

Jessica looked at him stunned, having no idea where he had come from. Nechi's familiar face was a welcome sight. For the moment, she didn't care how he'd gotten here. Helplessly, she was drawn to his peaceful eyes.

"I can't do this. I can't," she blurted.

"Stop and listen to me." His hand still covered hers and she twisted nervously at the key. She closed her eyes and clenched her jaw, drew in a deep shaky breath and tried to still her trembling body. As she released her grip on the key, Nechi spoke in a soft calming voice.

"So you choose to run away?"

"Yes. No. I don't know."

"The evil one is closing in."

Jessica cast him a fearful glance, but did not respond. Resuming her icy stare through the windshield, her body remained a steel rod of tension.

"You are a greater threat than Alex himself."

She looked back at him, this time with a questioning eye. "If Alex has some special power, why is it me this evil thing wants?"

"Because it is you who will come between the evil and what it wants." Nechi moved her hand from the key and gripped her fingers in his own. "You have planted the seeds of question in Alex's mind. Now the evil one stalks your path."

"How the hell did I get mixed up in this thing anyway?" She pulled away from Nechi and rubbed her hands across her cheeks.

"It was not of your choosing. But staying or leaving is up to you and you alone."

She pressed her lips together and surveyed the dashboard. "And why should I be stupid enough to risk my life for this?"

"Stupid is an interesting choice of words. That is a question only you can answer." Nechi squared himself in the car seat and looked straight ahead.

"And if I leave, then what?" She looked down at her lap.

"Alex will lose the second and third most important things to him."

"What do you mean by that? What will Alex lose?"

"His soul and his life."

"My God, you mean he could die?"

"The evil one awaits Alex's breaking of the most sacred of rules among his people. If you do not intervene and bring him to understanding, his own scientific and logical mind will be his demise. The evil one will use it against him. The spirit of darkness will do what it did in the past and find victory again."

Jessica's mouth went dry. "You know this isn't fair. You must know how near I am to falling in love with Alex." Her mind and heart tugged at one another. "I have to stay and help him, no matter what the cost."

"I know," Nechi said. "I have seen it in your eyes."

Pressing her forefinger tight to her lips to hold in the sob that wanted to escape, she looked intensely at Nechi. "You said Alex's soul and his life were second and third. Surely his work isn't more important to him than his own life."

A smile turned the corners of Nechi's mouth. "Alex has found a passion stronger than any other, but it is not for his work." Nechi's eyes turned toward her.

"Oh, my God." Jessica put her hand to her mouth and tears welled in her eyes. "I have to find him." She grabbed the door handle and smiled at Nechi. "Thank you," she whispered.

Alex scanned the crowd that formed in the evening shadows beneath the park's tall trees. The smell of fresh cut grass mingled with the fragrance of lilacs in full bloom. A feminine smell, a woman's scent, like Jessica, sweet but fresh, clean and honest. An honesty he'd doubted in the beginning but now knew was genuine. He'd been with women who smelled of expensive perfumes. Frankly he preferred those that smelled of the freshness of the earth. Jessica was that kind of woman.

The air had cooled and the sun touched the blue western horizon. But a heat burned between his heart and stomach as fiery as the crimson clouds that announced the great red orb's departure for the day. A primal fire of passion consumed him, a need unlike anything he had ever experienced before. He had to constantly quench it, keep it in check and not allow it to override his mind, his good sense. He'd known Jessica just over a week, a handful of days, and yet he felt as if she'd been part of him forever.

Something familiar burned in this passion he felt for her. A familiarity, perhaps tied somewhere to the ancient past. He stopped himself short. There was no logic in that. Where were these feelings coming from? All consuming feelings, fed by a seemingly endless flow of dreams and ever-changing emotions ran through him constantly in this ancient spiritual place. They were transforming him, taking possession of an unexplored corner of his life. A place he'd never allowed himself to go, a place in the depths of his own soul.

Perhaps he'd been frightened of the emotions both love and the great beyond evoked in him. Now he only wanted more. Both were at odds with his scientific background. Logic, scientific fact; all things could be proven, had basis in fact and reality. Perhaps that was what made the workings of the human spirit so frightening to him. He couldn't hold it in his hands, but he was coming to know it was as real as the artifacts and fragments of ancient civilizations he'd spent years studying.

Alex leaned against an elm tree as he gathered his rambling thoughts and searched the crowd. Maybe she wouldn't show. Maybe he was moving too fast for her. Maybe she would run like a scared rabbit.

Indian drums began a slow steady beat, the sound was low from this distance. The dancers practiced and paced nervously in anticipation of the performance. The drums beat with the pulsation of his body, the anticipation blended with his own as he ran the words over in his mind. Words he had to speak to Jessica. He had to tell her what he was feeling. He wanted her, but only if she wanted more, more than a fling, more than a one-night stand. He wouldn't put himself through it if she didn't.

Maybe he was a fool, but this was too intense, too meaningful to him. If all they could have was one night, could he? Would he walk away? Alex shifted on his feet, kicked at a clump of grass and pushed his back hard against the rough bark of the tree.

"Alex." A soft voice was followed by a gentle hand on his arm.

He closed his eyes at her touch and forced back the surge of warmth in his loins. "Jess," he whispered. He placed his large fingers over her small ones and savored the softness. Her sweet smelling hair pressed against his shoulder. The long pause told him she was enjoying the moment too.

"Jess." Alex pulled her around to face him then drew her to him and kissed her honey sweet lips.

She stopped him. "Alex," she whispered.

"We have to talk."

"No, not here." The answer came quickly. Her eyes darted.

Tilting her chin, he looked at her questioningly. "What's wrong?"

Jessica shook her head, but offered no explanation. He studied the tension in her face as she glanced around like an apprehensive animal expecting its predator.

On the wings of a heavy sigh, the air of hope left him. Was Jessica afraid of what he was going to say? Did women's intuition tell her what he was thinking? Was she unsure of how to let him down easy? She must not feel what he did. Otherwise, what was bringing on this fear he saw in her?

Turning, she scanned the crowd anxiously, standing close to Alex.

"What is it, Jess?" His mouth was close to her ear.

"Let's go somewhere else. The site—" She answered barely above a whisper. "Can we go there? Now."

"Yeah. Sure. Are you okay?" Alex sensed her fearfulness was grounded in something other than him.

"I'll take my car back to the lodge. Can you follow me and we'll go from there?" Her eyes never stopped searching the milling crowd.

"Whatever you say." Alex scanned the people, too. He wasn't sure what Jessica was searching for, but he'd absorbed a growing sense of uneasiness.

"Stay close. Please." She glanced up with a half smile.

"No problem. I'll walk you to your car then follow you. Okay?"

"Yes. *Now.*" Jessica pulled at his hand and guided him away from the crowd. Following her to the car, his own mission was forgotten momentarily. Alex clung to her hand, feeling like something between a bodyguard and an obedient puppy. Mystified by her actions, he found himself more than willing to take a chance on whatever her motives were. A flash of hope burned that she had passionate reasons for wanting to go out to the site, but was dampened by a sense of concern over her behavior. Something had her very disturbed.

Alex closed the car door behind her. She immediately locked it. Perhaps his fears for her last night had not been wrong. The breeze that caught at his shirt seemed to carry a sense of impending danger. The same breeze that carried the scent of lilacs moments ago, had turned cold, harsh and full of the unknown.

He glanced in both directions. A black pickup truck was parked along the south side of the park. That ominous black truck he identified with McCabe. Was it McCabe making his skin crawl? Was it McCabe who was at the heart of Jessica's fear? Alex couldn't be sure, and he couldn't explain it. He only wanted to get Jessica away from here. *Now.*

CHAPTER NINETEEN

Jessica was silent as they drove the rutted road from the highway to the site. She didn't feel like talking. Alex was reading her mood and she was glad. Where was she going to start? When Alex stopped, she got out. Using the headlights, he found a Coleman lantern. Gathering several twigs and a split log, he lit a handful of chips and dry pine needles then sat back and gazed into the fire.

With her hands in her hip pockets, she stood across the fire from him. "I'm sorry."

"Nothing to be sorry for." He glanced at her then stared into the tiny orange and blue flames that licked at the wood. "But would it be too much trouble for you to tell me what's going on?" He seemed to take Jessica's odd behavior in stride, but she detected a tone of sulkiness in his demeanor.

Jessica shook her head, searching for words.

Alex's expression changed from casually patient to hard and determined. He rose and approached her. "Dammit, Jess. What the hell *is* going on with you?" He squared himself in front of her. "It's only us now. Tell me."

She searched his eyes and knew she must risk it all. The truth and the whole truth, nothing else would do. As their eyes met, the fire of passion ignited again and Alex pulled her to him, bringing her mouth to his. She fell into his arms and his wanting. Heat surged through her and the soft sensuous feel of his kisses brought her own needs rushing in, choking at her breath. They were soft, moist, harder now, his mouth taking in hers.

He pulled her mouth to his over and over. Fumbling with the buttons on her shirt, he undid the first two. His kisses trailed down her neck, toward her half-exposed cleavage.

The sound of a car in the distance made her tense. She placed a firm hand on his shoulder and scanned the canyon rim.

"What's wrong, Jess? You're nervous as a deer?"

"I'm sorry."

"Dammit. Stop apologizing for everything."

"I'm sor— It's craziness, Alex." She couldn't go on. If she shared McCabe's threat with him, how would he react? Would he go after McCabe? If Alex was in danger, she refused to add fuel to the fire. Her only out was to act fast. To bring Alex full circle into the middle of all this spiritual mayhem so he would be able to defend himself, fully aware of what was at stake.

"Look, if this is about us, we're both adults. We need to talk about this before you drive me crazy."

"Us? Oh God, no, Alex."

"Jess. I want to understand whatever it is that's going on inside you." He grasped her forearms and pulled her close, his face nearly touching hers.

"I'm not sure you really want to know the truth."

"If you mean you don't feel the same, I'd rather know."

"No, no, no. We aren't talking about the same thing." She pressed her fingers to his lips. "Stop. Please stop."

Alex stepped back. His eyes were intent and hard. "Okay. Talk to me. Tell me what's going on!"

"Some strange things have happened since I've been here." She chose her words carefully. She stopped. "Promise me you won't think I'm a lunatic."

He raised his eyebrows and gave her a sideways nod, skepticism evident in his face even in the dim firelight.

She had her work cut out for her. There was no doubt. "You remember the legend I told you about at breakfast the other morning."

"I remember."

"Well, there's a lot more to it." Jessica was buying time, searching for the right way to tell him, a way that didn't sound so far fetched. "Remember the young lovers I tried to tell you about?"

"I recall that it upset you." His brow furrowed. "But I don't understand why you're so caught up in some story you heard."

"Look, you asked for answers. Please step outside that damn logical box you live in for a minute."

He held up one hand and nodded.

"I know you think it's some story someone made up. Humor me for a moment and enter the realm of possibility, just this once."

"I don't see what this has to do with anything."

She looked at him in exasperation. "Alex, I guess it could mean almost anything. From nothing to everything." She buried her face in her hands. Why did it all seem so real and so clear when she spoke with Nechi or the spirit and completely insane when she tried to bring it to the analytical Alex?

She wanted to burst into tears and run away. The fear that McCabe might show up, forced her to hold onto the tiny piece of her brain that wasn't swimming in utter turmoil and confusion. "God, there's so much I don't know how to share with you. Too much that's very hard to explain to someone who isn't open minded."

A flash of hurt crossed his face. "I don't see myself that way. Not the way I used to." He ran his hands down his face. "Jess, I live in a world of scientific fact, not a world of fairy tales. My life, my job, doesn't give me room to fly off on wild goose chases. Give me something solid, one thing, and I'll follow you as far as you like into that realm of possibility you believe in so strongly."

"All right." A strange force seemed to slip into Jessica's being. A sense of determination shrouded her doubts and overtook her concerns about what Alex thought. "I happen to believe this legend—actually happened. And I think I can prove it."

"How could you possibly prove it?"

"If the legend is true, a temple stood on this very ground hundreds of years ago."

Alex shrugged his shoulders.

"Behind the temple was a cavern. Within the cavern was a room where a young chieftain and his forefathers slept and conducted ceremonies." Jessica turned and pointed up the hillside. "The cavern is somewhere on that hill."

"Good God, Jess, you don't even sound like yourself. First you tell me this is all new to you then you sound like some sort of self-taught expert on the subject."

"No, Alex. I'm just an emotional sap who couldn't walk away when I had the chance." She waved her arms in animated exasperation and struggled to keep from shouting her words. "I'm a not-too-bright reporter who has totally lost sight of my own mission and somehow taken on a monumental task I don't really understand. And now I'm doing my best to carry it through and you damn sure aren't making it easy for me."

Alex's blue eyes widened at her outburst.

"Now, if I can find the cave, I know is on that hillside, you'll have your proof, and we can get on with whatever the hell it is we're supposed to be doing out here." Turning on her heel, she prepared to march out into the darkness.

"Wait a minute. It's pitch black out there."

The distant sound of a vehicle and the thought of McCabe washed cold, fearful dread through to her bones. She spun and shot Alex a hard determined look. "We don't have anymore time to waste. We need to find it now." After her meeting with McCabe and Nechi at the park, she couldn't be sure what would happen in the next few minutes, much less by morning. She gave his shirtsleeve a sharp jerk.

"Oh, all right." Alex pulled away muttering. Grabbing the lantern, he followed her out into the darkness with Yellow Dog close at his heels. At the foot of the hill, Jessica stopped and surveyed the slope.

"How do you know so much about this cave?"

Jessica whirled to confront him and as the lantern light eerily illuminated their faces, she spoke in a voice that seemed to come from deep within her being. "The picture in my mind is as clear and real to me as the two of us standing here."

His mouth dropped open and an odd expression crossed his face.

"Don't ask." She stopped the next barrage of questions before he could utter them. "Just come with me."

Groping in the darkness, they followed the rock mass up the hill on the opposite side of where she'd found the petroglyph wall. Jessica's mind would have dictated to go back to the petroglyphs, but this time she was following something else. A picture burned in her mind of an ancient place but its source was a mystery to her. It was a place she had seen in a vision or in some mysterious reality. For the first time in her life, she was relying on feel, straight from the pit of her gut. She allowed an ancient spiritual voice to guide her path and trusted in something she could not see or touch.

Jessica climbed the slope, stumbling over rocks, scrub oak and sagebrush and pushing aside the prickly stems of the yucca plants that grew out of the rocky hillside. Alex followed close behind, and held the lantern high so it illuminated the path she cut. Driven by whatever force pushed her on through the darkness, she went on, seeking something that called to her soul.

"You'll never find it in the dark," Alex scolded. "At least let me ahead of you with the lantern."

Jessica pressed on, this time ignoring Alex's grumbling. The gravel beneath her feet slid and she fell to her knees.

"You're going to get hurt." Alex reached to help her, but there was no need. She was already on her feet.

She'd have given anything for a pair of jeans and her hiking boots. The thigh length pair of khaki shorts she'd chosen for a rendezvous in the park weren't of much use to her now. She brushed the gravel from her stinging knees and fought back the sharp bushes and tree needles. Thankful for the sweat jacket she'd slipped on, she forged ahead, unable to afford the luxury of self-pity.

The scent of damp musk carried on a soft breeze and registered somewhere in her mind. She shot a quick look at Alex as he stopped and held the light high. His keen eye searched the wall several feet up the hill from them. The twitch of his nostrils told her he had picked up the odor.

"I'll be damned." Alex kneeled and pulled away a mass of sagebrush and some clumps of wild grass. Jessica knelt beside him. The bush fell away revealing a three-foot opening in the rock.

Jessica's eyes met Alex's. Not a word was spoken. She sensed Alex had absorbed some of the spiritual energy she was feeling. His hard look of skepticism faded and a light of unexplainable origin took its place.

Yellow Dog shoved himself between them, his nose to the ground, and started into the dark hole.

"Hold on, boy." Alex leaned forward with the light, trying to see what was inside. "There could be wild animals or bats in there." He gave Jessica a curious look. "It could be anything, you know. Don't get your hopes up."

Irritated by Alex's constant skepticism, she pushed toward the cave opening and met his resistance as she grabbed for the lantern. "Sit here and analyze it all you want. I'm going to have a look."

Yellow Dog shot Alex an "I'm with her" look and pushed his way past and into the opening. The sound of scrambling feet and falling gravel was followed by a soft thud that told them there was a short drop off.

"Yellow Dog," Alex scolded. "Damn. I swear the two of you are working together. Why can't this wait till daylight?"

"Because what's in this cave, you need to see, and you need to see it now," came her fiery response. "What the hell difference does it make? It's always dark inside a cave anyway." She was flat out of patience with his doubting attitude and his constant questioning of everything she tried to tell him.

He didn't respond but rolled his eyes and gave her a stubborn look.

"You know, Alex, even if I told you why, you'd never believe me. This one you'll have to see for yourself." This time she snatched the lantern from his hand and raised it high, holding it inside the entrance to the cave.

"There's your proof." She pointed to a row of crude brown figures written on a sandstone background just inside the entrance.

"Pictographs." Alex took the light and turned toward her. "All right. We're going in. Watch your step and stay close."

Yellow Dog stood on the cave floor about three feet below them. The dog's tail wagged and his tongue hung out as he shot Jessica a pleased look. "And you can keep your comments to yourself," Alex grumbled to the dog, observing the interchange between his comrades.

Alex dropped to the cavern floor then turned and helped Jessica down. Her bare legs brushed against the soft insides of his strong arms. "You're not exactly dressed for this expedition, are you?" he commented as he let her slide down the front of him.

"Well, I guess it will have to do."

Alex stopped and examined the markings on the wall. He raised an eyebrow in the dim light. "Looks genuine to me."

She walked close to him through a small passage where the cave split in four directions. Alex raised the lantern and surveyed the options and the stone roof above them. "Guess we're lucky tonight. The bats must be out sucking someone else's blood."

"Alex." Jessica punched his rib cage with her elbow. "This is serious."

"I know. I am serious. But I want you to lighten up a little. It's not brain surgery."

Both could mean life or death, if only he realized what he was saying. "You don't know how important this really is."

Still holding the lantern high, he shone the flickering light into a small chamber. It was a tiny room with a visible fire pit at its center. Cold chills ran through Jessica as a ghostly familiarity hung over her.

Alex kicked the charred remains of what appeared to be a torch. He knelt, shining the light of the lantern onto the pieces of a small twig figure that lay next to the fire pit.

"Ceremonial." He picked it up and poked at it in his hand. Then he walked to the corner and prodded at a heap with the toe of his boot. Jessica let out a soft gasp as Alex moved what appeared to be the remains of a rawhide shirt away from the wall. "You okay?"

She nodded. "Yeah. There's just something too familiar about all of this."

"Huh?" he asked, but was so preoccupied with the two items he'd discovered, her words didn't seem to sink in. "I don't want to disturb this stuff," he said carefully laying the pieces of the stick figure back on the cave floor. "I'll come back tomorrow and pack and catalog them properly."

Jessica cast a glance back into the eerie chamber she was certain she'd visited earlier. The picture was still distinct in her mind of the black and white painted medicine man with his torch, who had guided her through a vision so powerful—so real. Alex tugged at her arm. "Come on. Let's see what else is here." His voice pulled her from the floating sensation that was washing over her and brought her back to the moment.

"Over here." Jessica pointed at a long corridor across from the room.

Alex sidestepped some rock scattered on the cave floor. "Watch out," he cautioned as he made his way toward the dark chamber. With the light, he observed a myriad of black patterns on the roof over their heads. "Smoke black," he said. "There have definitely been fires in this cavern."

The next chamber curved to the left. The wall by its entrance bore the same crude markings as the outer wall. This one included the distinct outline of a bird. As the light danced in long shadows, they moved silently into the chamber.

Alex raised the lantern and illuminated a room containing a fire pit and several dust-covered animal hides. Pots of varying sizes and shapes lined one wall. Pictographs surrounded them on all sides, as the ghostly light danced on them and seemed to transport them back thousands of years in time.

"I'll be damned," Alex whispered. "This chamber hasn't been touched in centuries."

"Just as he left it." The words spilled out of her without a second thought.

Alex shot her a quick glance, but was obviously entranced by his surroundings. He shone the light on the assortment of animal hides, the fur still surprisingly intact.

Jessica's mind darted to the picture of two young lovers, making passionate love nestled in the warmth of the furs. Their energy was still here, the essence of their intense emotion lived on in this chamber. For a moment, she felt as if she were intruding on their torrid and forbidden love affair.

She looked up at Alex, who stood very near. Close enough she could feel his breath on the nape of her neck. His silence caused her to wonder if his feelings matched her own. Catching his eye, she was certain he felt it, too. How could he not?

"The chieftain's chamber," she said, both respect and sadness filled her voice.

"How could you have known this was here?"

"You'd never have believed me if I told you, Alex." A surge of courage ran through her. She needed to talk about it. "I've been through a lot of strange and miraculous experiences since I came here last week. I don't know what they were, or where they came from, but they led me here. They led you here." She took a step closer to him, needing to feel him next to her, although she couldn't look at him. "Talk to me, Alex. Tell me what you're feeling. You have no idea how important it is."

"Jess." He hesitated. "There's something here. You told me when you first came out to the site that you felt something, and I understand. I've been feeling it, too, growing with it, changing. Almost transforming— inside, I mean." He cleared his throat. "It's like the spirits are incredibly strong here, so vivid. They haunt me in my dreams, they talk to me, pull me to them. But I don't understand what they want, or what they're trying to say to me."

The catch in Alex's voice pulled her to him. She embraced him and held him tight. "I know," she whispered. A soft sob came from deep down inside him as he clung to her, holding her with an embrace that spoke of something between deep longing and overwhelming fear. She could feel his passion. He was feeling it all. It was pouring through him and into her.

A connection of their spirits began as they held each other. Tears filled her eyes as he clung to her, allowing the spiritual energy to absorb him for the first time. The tension left his shoulders and he leaned into her embrace. She knew he'd given in and allowed it to take him. He trembled in her arms, his faraway look seemed to teeter between worlds; between the physical and the spiritual, between the past and the present. It engulfed them both, and their souls burned for a bright moment as one light and then—

Alex pulled himself together, something brought him back into the now, into that logical scientific being. His trembling stopped. The hard gulp from deep in his throat told her he was swallowing the emotion that had almost swallowed him. He had come close, and he had neared a threshold she knew he'd never crossed before. But she knew he'd come back to her disappointed.

He'd fought back the spiritual force that had finally reached him, and he had, if only momentarily, let go of his soul. In the depths of her heart, she knew he'd come back to the physical world because it was the only place where he felt safe. What would it take for him to cross into that other realm? She didn't know, but she damn sure had to find out.

CHAPTER TWENTY

Alex swallowed hard, aware of the gentle heaving of his chest against Jessica's breasts. The flicker of the lantern cast dancing shadows on the cave walls. Soft sounds of their breathing were all that broke the silence. His mind struggled to comprehend what he had just experienced and yet he knew. A spiritual awakening was taking place in his soul. Like the tiny skeleton in the grave, barren of life's baggage, Alex's soul was being stripped clean and was beginning again on a new foundation. It terrified him, and yet it was time.

A new aspect of his personality was surfacing, a part of him that needed to be loved that was dependent on another human being. He pulled Jessica nearer and held her to his chest. Neither spoke, as a vibrant energy still seemed to pass between them.

His head reeled. His emotions were raw from purging a lifetime of denial. An internal war raged between this new awareness and his scientific side, but he wasn't willing to give *that* up. Not yet. Perhaps somewhere in the process the two would make amends.

Drawn into the dimensions of a world beyond the five senses, he was being asked to see and hear with his soul, to feel with his heart and trust in things he could not physically prove. It was different for him, a new realm. And it grew stronger daily. What he had just experienced pulled him into a place of the spirit.

Surprisingly, it had drawn Jessica into its power as well. She still trembled against him. Soul had spoken to soul. He'd felt it distinctly, her emotions and energy blended with his own. He'd read her thoughts and merged momentarily with the essence of her soul, a bright and beautiful soul. He could have let go then, let the force take him, but he had to admit the strangeness of this new feeling frightened him. He'd gone liquid in her arms, lost his grip for a moment. For him it was uncharted ground.

Maybe it wasn't manly to be afraid, but damn it all anyway. Damn all the things he'd had ingrained into his being. Be a man, don't show your emotions and be silent about what you feel. Deny your ancestral roots because that's what your family has done.

Damn all the baggage that had been handed down and taught as gospel. No matter how much he loved his mother and father and his grandparents, he would no longer be denied his heritage. Not because of things that happened generations before. What had been their truth didn't have to be his.

Jessica pressed herself hard against him, still awkwardly clenched in his arms. The lantern hung precariously in his grasp. He pulled from the depths of his own thoughts, forcing himself to regain his composure from the emotional storm that raged in his soul.

Jessica's touch, her presence brought him back to a state of calmness. Sighing, he kissed the top of her head taking in the sweet smell of her hair. He was glad he'd bared his soul to her, glad he'd opened that door and let her in, even if only a little. Jessica was part of all this, part of the mystery of this ancient place and the voices that called to him in his dreams.

Only now had he realized the strength of that connection.

"You okay?" she whispered as Yellow Dog nudged the back of his knee and whimpered.

"Yeah, I am," he answered, letting go of her at last. "Maybe we should go and come back tomorrow."

"Sure." Jessica hesitated at the room's entrance. "You do believe me now, don't you?"

He nodded, gave her a half-smile, and walked over to the fire pit. The lantern cast ghostly shadows on the walls of the cave. It brought pictures to his mind of what the room must have looked like ages before by the light of blazing torches.

Kneeling, he picked up an oddly shaped piece of a small crude pot that had probably been a ceremonial vase of some sort. A strange feeling passed from it into his hands, an energy perhaps left from the ancient who last held it. He savored it, tried to absorb it, tried to pull it into his being and search for some message it carried from the past.

"Jess, I think it's very possible some ancient tribe, like those in your legend did live here. I think we need to go back to camp and you can tell me more." Reaching down, he filled the bottom of the tiny vessel with ashes from the fire pit. Searching his pocket for a small plastic bag he'd placed there earlier, he carefully secured the tiny treasure. Here was something he could use to help prove or disprove her theory. He would test them later.

"So you're open to the possibility now?" She watched him prepare and tuck the bag into his shirt pocket.

"Let's just say I'm open to a lot of things I was never open to before."

She turned back toward the main entrance of the cave and Alex admired the view of her backside in the skimpy khaki shorts as she walked ahead of him.

Yellow Dog walked at his side, sniffing at an occasional stone and panting contentedly seeming to be satisfied with some accomplishment. Alex shot him a curious look, wondering at his intuitive and all-knowing demeanor at times. Who could say, maybe the dog had been having dreams of his own.

Alex placed the lantern on the embankment at the cave entrance where ages of rock and dirt had washed down the hill and partially covered its entrance. Grasping Jessica around the waist, he boosted her up next to the lantern and out into the cool night air. The light of the lantern illuminated her soft skin and high cheekbones and brought out the green in her eyes. The look in those mysterious eyes was one he'd not seen before.

A depth of new understanding was forming, as if earlier their spirits had touched and something had passed between them. Recognition perhaps of something higher, a fleeting glimpse of a power at work far greater than the limits their physical world allowed.

He leaned toward her, his lips wanting for the soft touch of hers, aching to capture the closeness of her. She leaned into him bringing her mouth to his, moist and ready.

A loud blast pierced the quiet night. A whistle and a ping followed. Something hit the rocks above them a split second later.

Alex came to a dead stop. "What the hell." His mind raced to interpret the noise. The second blast followed close behind. This time it struck the rock next to Jessica's shoulder.

The gunshots registered in Alex's unsuspecting mind. Adrenalin hammered through his senses. Grabbing Jessica, he dragged her from the ledge and back inside the cavern. Stumbling backwards, she tumbled down upon him. A third shot rang out and hit somewhere near the opening. Yellow Dog made a single leap and landed somewhere outside.

"Yellow Dog!" Alex rose to his feet and grabbed the lantern. The animal cleared the embankment and kicked gravel back onto Jessica and Alex.

Alex could see the dog's hindquarters disappear into the nearby bushes. The dog paid no heed to Alex's call.

Alex helped Jessica to her feet from where she squatted next to him, huddling low.

"Somebody's shooting," she gasped.

"Come on. Get back further into the cave." He shoved her along, looking over his shoulder at the entrance.

"What about Yellow Dog?"

"What about us? I don't think they were shooting at him," he answered quickly then saw the concern on her face. "Don't worry. He'll be all right." He hoped he was fooling Jessica. He wasn't convincing himself.

Alex raised the lantern as they came to the dividing point of the cavern's chambers and stopped.

Jessica pressed herself to him, trembling and out of breath. "What should we do?"

"Wait. We'll wait here a minute and see if we hear any more shots. It could be a poacher. We're in the back country here." Alex held her to him, hoping he was calming her. At the rate his heart was hammering, he doubted he was soothing her much.

"Alex, whoever it was shot when they saw the lantern. I think those bullets were meant for us."

He shook his head. "Probably somebody target practicing. Or maybe some hoodlums raiding the camp for a thrill." His insides knotted and instinct pulled him toward the cave entrance. Jessica pulled him back. "I know who it is. It's McCabe." Her eyes were wide and her fingers clung tightly to his shirt.

Alex didn't respond. His mind raced like a runaway train. *McCabe?* That fool always carried a rifle with him. Who else would be out here in the middle of the night? Maybe McCabe had finally slipped a cog. Lord knows he was close enough most of the time.

"How can you be so sure?" Alex asked. There was no doubt in his mind McCabe was conniving and treacherous, but would he really have the balls to come after them with a gun?

"Alex, I'm sure all the way to the soles of my shoes." Jessica's eyes were fiery now. "It's *him*."

Hell. It was that madman. Alex knew it. That boulder didn't come down the mountain all by itself, and those rattlesnakes were more than a coincidence.

Damn. Why hadn't he forced the law to do something? Now it was more than a hunch. It was in his face, outside taking potshots at them.

They pressed together, listening intently. The only sound was the unevenness of their breathing. Alex's heart hammered in his ears. He let out ragged breaths. Waiting. Wondering.

A scuffling sound drove instant tension into their bodies. Yellow Dog barked in the distance. Angry voices and another gunshot echoed through the caverns. Alex's gut wrenched. He prayed his dog would be wise enough to stay clear, but right now he had to save his own behind—and Jessica's.

"They're coming this way," Alex whispered. Turning, he surveyed his four options with darting eyes. There was no place to hide in the two chambers they'd been in. He'd take a chance on one of the others. Maybe there was another way out.

Alex's hand held tight to Jessica's. He pulled her down the passage to their left. Some twenty feet ahead, the passage was blocked by a pile of rock and dirt.

"In here." He whirled, nearly dragging Jessica along, and ran into the chamber that was his final option.

The lantern lit up the walls of a small stone pocket. Alex eyed it. His mind was stunned by what it was taking in. The room was filled with stacks of cardboard boxes piled three and four high. The sound of falling gravel echoed through the stone walls. It came from the cave entrance. His worst fear was realized. He had to hide them. And do it fast.

"Here." Stepping into a space between the boxes and the cave wall, he turned out the lantern and laid it on its side behind a box. He slid down until he was sitting on the floor. His feet were stretched straight in front of him, and he was hidden from view. As he went, Alex pulled Jessica, who faced him, along with him. She landed on her knees, straddling his hips. Her body pressed tight against him, her face inches from his.

The sounds from outside in the cavern were muffled. Footsteps walked softly. Boots on stone weren't easy to keep quiet. Alex's blood boiled with hatred for McCabe. He fought the raging of his wildly pounding heart. If he didn't know the bastard had a rifle–if he weren't more concerned with Jessica's safety than his own–he damn sure wouldn't sit here and be terrorized by this madman.

A loose rock rolled somewhere outside. A dim glow lit the cavern right outside their hiding place. Jessica trembled in his arms. Her shaking hand grasped his shirt. In the darkness, he brought his hands up around her face. His thumbs gently pressed her lips fearful she might make a noise.

The sounds grew closer. Alex knew the uneven steps couldn't be one man alone. The perpetrator's breathing echoed in the chamber, heavy and excited, like his. He prayed the cardboard around them would absorb the soft sounds they couldn't control. Jessica lay stiff and tense on top of him. He pulled her near and pushed her face into his shoulder, further muffling the fearful little sounds that came from her. The room lit up from the beam of a flashlight. Alex watched it circle the room.

"Damn it. Where could they have gone?" The unmistakable crackling voice vibrated through the space. Alex twitched and clenched his fists tight against Jessica's back. The boxes slammed against them from a loud blow Alex knew was delivered from the kick of McCabe's boot. Alex held his breath as the lantern rolled. It teetered precariously above his head, threatening to fall from its hiding place.

A second voice spoke, this one at a lower pitch. "They're probably outside on the mountain. You don't know if they were in here."

"They were here," McCabe snarled. "I can still smell 'em."

"You fool," the other voice snapped. "Only an idiot like you would take potshots when all you could see was a light. How the hell do you know who you were shooting at?"

"Look, you coward, we can't let them find this stuff or the jig is up and you know it."

"I don't think they were ever here. I think you've just blown this whole thing wide open. You put a noose around both our necks this time." The other man pounded a box with his fist.

"They were here," McCabe adamantly defended his position. "And when I find 'em, I'll bury 'em here."

"Great. Now we're talking murder one."

"If they're out on that hillside, I'll find 'em before daylight. They won't get far in this rugged country in the dark. And if they dare turn that light on again, I'll pick 'em off. And I damn sure won't miss this time."

"Christ, McCabe. You're the craziest thing I've ever seen walking around on two feet." The other man walked away in disgust, heading toward the main part of the cavern.

McCabe shoved at the boxes again and spat on the ground. "Maybe I'll shoot you, too, just for good measure," he hissed then cackled to himself.

The sound of McCabe's boots on the stone floor was no longer muffled, suggesting to Alex he was sure they weren't in the cave. The footsteps grew fainter and the last of their words faded away into the night.

"You watch this cave. We don't want 'em doublin' back on us and hidin' in here," McCabe yelled.

"Yeah, yeah. I'll keep an eye on it. You go run through the brush like a rabid coon hound," the other man snorted.

With that final bit of conversation, Alex realized his plans were set for a while. They dared not move from where they were. The entrance was nearly a hundred feet away, but any loud noise or light could bring them back in on top of Jessica and Alex.

Pressed tightly together in the pitch-blackness, holding each other, they gradually let themselves breathe again. Jessica clung to him like a frightened little girl. For several minutes they lay clutched together listening for any sound of the intruders.

At last, Alex felt it was safe to speak. "He's a madman," he whispered.

"What was he talking about?" Jessica choked, in a barely audible voice. "Why is he after us?"

"I don't have any idea. Do you think he's after somebody else and it's all mixed up in his head?"

"God, I wish that were true. We've done nothing to him— but he was the reason I was so afraid tonight." Her hushed voice filled with emotion. "I saw him in the park. He was trying to warn me. Alex, he turned into some wild trembling maniac in front of my eyes."

"What did he say?"

Jessica let out a heavy sigh. "He told me to leave or something terrible would happen."

"Why didn't you tell me? You should have called the police."

"McCabe ran away. And Nechi told me I had to find you because you were in danger."

"Nechi? You're babbling nonsense. Go back and start at the beginning and tell me what happened," Alex whispered.

"It's not nonsense. I had to bring you here. I had to convince you. I know it sounds crazy, Alex, but I think McCabe is possessed by something evil."

"Oh, come on, Jess."

"Please. Shut up and listen to me this time. Hasn't this whole thing gone far enough for you to need some answers?"

"Okay, okay. As long as we keep our voices down so those two crazy men don't hear us." His finger found her soft lips in the dark, trying to calm some of the anxiety that had built between them. "I'm your captive audience. We won't be going anywhere for a while. Beats going stir crazy in the dark."

In low whispering words in the blackness of the ancient cave, Jessica began her haunting tale. "Nechi is a young Indian man I met when I first got here."

"Oh?" Alex tried to keep a hint of jealousy from his voice.

"He's the one who told me the legend. There's something about him." Jessica paused.

"That's great, but what exactly did he tell you?"

"According to the legend, hundreds of years ago, a tribe of nomads made their home at the foot of the mesa. They built a temple here next to the sacred cavern. They deemed it sacred, because they found evidence in the cave that it had been inhabited by even earlier beings."

"They probably felt much as we do," Alex said as a feeling of kinship flooded through him. "Connected in some way to the people who lived here in the past."

"I know. I feel it, too."

"And you know it's very possible. I believe man has inhabited the North American continent a lot longer than any history books tell us."

"It's sad, isn't it. All we are taught in school is the European side of American history." Jessica sighed. "The real story is here. This is *our* history. This is *our* ancestry."

"We've been cheated. I've been cheated. It makes me angry." Alex wrestled down the knot of heat growing in his chest. He would have to deal with his feelings later. He nudged her. "Go on."

"These people were led by a family of spirit leaders. You know, generation after generation. Father to son and all that." Jess rested her chin on his chest. "According to the story, the people were led by the gods through these leaders."

"You mean they acted as a kind of a conduit for the Great Spirit."

"You've got it." She slapped his chest softly. "You're even getting the hang of the lingo."

Alex laughed. "But Jess, there were lots of shaman and spiritual leaders among all the tribes. A lot of superstition, too."

"That's part of their culture. How can we doubt their beliefs when we haven't experienced their way of life?"

"My grandfather used to say, never doubt a man till you've walked a mile in his moccasins."

Jessica shifted around. "Do you think we can get up now?"

"No way. I want to be sure we're safe. You heard McCabe's sidekick say he would watch the cave."

"But it's so dark in here. What if there are animals—you know bats and things." She hunkered closer to him.

"All the more reason to stay here, together," he said, pulling her tight against him. Although he was much more concerned about the evidence of a cave in down the other corridor than he was about wild animals, he knew they dared not light the lantern. Jessica moved nervously. "Keep talking to me," he whispered. "Then it won't bother you so much."

"Okay. Where was I? Oh yeah, shaman and such. Anyway, it seems that along these people's way, something tragic happened. The Old Chief was killed before his young son was ready to lead the tribe."

"You mentioned that the other night. You said the old man fell from a cliff."

"Then you were listening," she scolded. "Why did you pretend you didn't hear my story?"

"It was an odd coincidence. I wanted to think about it." He softly cleared his throat, as they both still spoke in voices barely above a whisper. "I had a dream like that when I first came here. A man falling from a cliff—an old Indian chief."

"Alex, can't you see. It was an omen. You should listen to these dreams. They're trying to tell you something important."

"Shhhh," Alex cautioned. "Let's go on, okay. You can nag me later."

"Ahhh," she grunted in exasperation, blowing air between her lips. "Don't you see? The legend tells of this poor young chief who didn't understand the ways of the forefathers. He was preoccupied with other things as most young men are. But for him, something terrible happened. After his father died, this evil came into their village and he was young and frightened and didn't know how to fight it."

"Well, no legend would be complete without an evil spirit," he guffawed softly.

Jessica tensed. "Don't laugh until you've looked into McCabe's eyes," she said sternly.

A cold chill ran through Alex, pulled back to the moment and the situation with one cold slap of her words. He swallowed hard, understanding the look she spoke of far too well. And the lunatic had a gun and was hunting for them outside on the mountain. He had to keep Jessica busy—and himself. They were in for a long wait. He wasn't about to venture out into the darkness tonight, not with a crazed man stalking them. A man capable of God only knew what.

"Go on with your story," he encouraged. "I want to hear everything."

"I'm not sure I want to talk about it anymore," she whispered. "It doesn't have a happy ending. In fact, I think it's too frightening to tell." He felt her shudder.

"Well then, tell me the story of the lovers you were carrying on about before." Alex tried to soothe her by patting her gently on the back and changing the subject.

"They were so much in love, Alex. They were so young." There was a long silence. "Alex, you're the only one who can help this young maiden's spirit be reunited with her lover."

"Come on, Jess. You must be sniffing some old Indian's peyote in here." What kind of nonsense was she muttering?

"Stop it. Stop with your skepticism and your wise-ass attitude. You told me you dreamed about an old chief and his son. Don't you think that was pretty odd in itself?"

"Well—" Truth was he did. It had stopped him short the first time he'd heard it.

"Then tell me what else you've dreamed. You told me you'd been haunted in your dreams. Let's hear some of them, if you're so sure they have nothing to do with the legend," she challenged.

"Don't get all excited. I'll tell you about them." He pulled her gently toward him. At first she stiffened against his tugging, then relented and snuggled her chin into his chest and listened. "Sometimes I dream about a beautiful young woman. She reminds me of you, Jess." He ran his hand through her hair and kissed the top of her head. "And a young man. I'm always dreaming in his head, not mine. When he watches her, I know what he's thinking. He intensely loves this girl."

"Alex, he's trying to tell you. His soul is trying—" She was growing excited. "A warrior possessed by that evil thing killed the maiden. Sacrificed her on an altar. I saw it. I saw it, in my mind—somehow."

Alex's heart jumped into his throat as the devastating dream washed back over him with the force of an incoming tide. His heart filled with the emotions of the young man's tragic loss all over again. Vivid images of the dying girl clouded his head. The black-painted face of the warrior loomed over her limp body and delivered the blow that ended her life. His stomach jumped to his throat. If he'd dared to move he believed he might wretch. How could a mere dream remain so vivid in his mind's eye? It was so vivid, and so detailed.

Hearing it from Jessica's mouth made the reality of it almost unbearable. While it had existed only in his own mind, he could keep it under control. He could pretend it existed only in a dream world, no matter how real it had seemed at the time. He was breathing heavy, choking back all the emotion of the nightmare.

"Are you okay?" Jessica whispered. "What's wrong with you?" Her voice grew louder.

He pulled his hands up and covered her mouth, unable to speak, but fearing she would reveal their cover. "I'm okay," he sputtered. "You have to keep quiet."

A rustling noise outside the cave entrance sounded as if someone were sliding down the hill. Rocks and gravel spattered into the cavern and echoed through. The sound forced Alex back to the moment. They both lay stiff, tightly grasping onto one another, listening until they were sure no one had come inside.

"I'm sorry," she said, barely above a whisper. "You scared me. You were making all sorts of funny little noises. What happened?"

"I—I dreamed about your maiden," he stammered. "I had a nightmare. I was afraid you were in danger. That's why I came to you last night."

"I guess that wasn't too far from right either," she said, a quiver evident in her voice. "That crazy man is after me—after us now." They fell silent and she began to sob softly on his chest.

"Jess, Jess. It's okay." Holding her to him, he rubbed his hands up and down her back. "We're all right. They're out there and we're in here. They didn't find us." All he wanted was to comfort and protect her.

"I know, Alex, but what if they come back. If they find us, if they kill us, I'll never get to—" She stopped and sniffled before her emotions could escape. Raising her head, she kissed him, long and hard. Taken by surprise, he didn't think about his response. He pulled her closer and placed his mouth over hers, drawing in her soft full lips and hungrily tasting them.

"You'll never what?" he asked, between kisses. "Talk to me, Jess."

"Oh, Alex. What about us?"

In the pitch-blackness, and the absence of all things visual, his other senses came alive. Her soft moist lips, warmed from his kiss, slipped gently, sensuously and hungrily across his. Parted now, he drew them into his mouth.

The heat from her kisses spread through his body igniting the pent up passion that smoldered. It had filled him in his dream state with its wanting by night and haunted the alcoves of his mind by day. He'd kept it in check like a soldier in boot camp, forced it into submission, because this time he wanted commitment. This time he wanted forever. Now it broke free like a captive wild pony. He struggled as he prepared to let it go.

"Jess, Jess," he whispered as he tugged at the zipper of her sweat jacket in the cramped space. "I wanted to talk to you tonight." They couldn't stop kissing as their choppy words filtered in between the unleashing passion.

"I know," she mumbled as her lips pulled at his. "Please talk to me."

"Jess, I love you. I'm so much in love with you."

"Oh God, I love you, too. I knew it from the night you danced with me in that sleazy little bar."

Finally fumbling the jacket zipper free, he pulled the tank top up. His hands found their way under the sports bra she wore. The sensation of his fingers on her smooth skin quickly brought urgency to the fiery flood that rushed through him. Reaching down, she undid the button of his jeans. He placed a shaky hand on hers.

"Jess, I don't just mean I love you for now. I don't want a one time thing."

She stopped, her breath wavering, then she kissed him again hard and wanting.

Pushing her back, he whispered breathlessly. "I mean if I let go of everything that's burning inside me, it's got to be forever." He prayed, wished he could see the revealing green eyes, and know what she was thinking as she stopped, panting softly in the darkness.

"Don't say it because you want me now," he went on. "I want to make love to you again and again. For the rest of our lives." He gulped. There he'd said it. His chest heaved up and down and he ached for more of her hot uninhibited kisses.

At last, she found the words his ears wanted to hear. "Alex, I feel like you've been part of me for as long as I can remember and beyond. I mean your soul and mine. I feel like there's no other way it could ever be, but for us to be together."

"Oh God," he moaned, pulling her to him. Passion flooded his body and mind as she completely freed him from the confines of the growing tightness of his jeans. Pulling aside the loose crotch of the shorts and the silkiness of her panties beneath, with a soft groan of pleasure, she maneuvered to allow him entry.

Smooth and moist, his mouth covered hers. The smell of her hair and skin pressed to him in the dark chamber only heightened his ecstasy. The sound of her breathing was hard and fast as soft sounds of pleasure escaped her full and fevered lips. A light inside his head passed behind his closed eyes as Jessica quivered and gasped echoing his own release of imprisoned desire. His head filled with white light and made him dizzy.

Jessica's hands were wrapped tightly in his shirt as she lay trembling. Her breath came in ragged little spurts. Flashes of a warrior and maiden making love the first time in a pool at the waterfall played on a tiny movie screen in his head. His body quivered with pleasure and oneness with the woman he'd been waiting all his life to find. If this moment of passion was driven by impending danger, he didn't want to know. Would its meaning fade in safety and the light of day?

CHAPTER TWENTY-ONE

As Alex opened his eyes, the rays of morning sun parted the darkness at the cavern door and cast a dim light into the chamber. It was a visible blessing that brought hope. Their long night's siege had come to an end.

Waking in the cramped space after being pressed together all night, he cared only that Jessica was next to him. "Good morning," he whispered.

Jessica moved and stretched where she still lay curled on top of him. "Aw—" she moaned softly. "I think my knees are part of this floor by now."

Alex could almost hear her clearing the cobwebs from her head. He chuckled and pushed against her, helping her rise to her feet. He pulled himself up between the boxes, his backside cold and stiff from sitting on the stone for so long. In the dim light that came from the entrance, he felt around for the Coleman lantern then pulled a book of matches from his pocket. "Think it's safe?" Jessica stretched her achy limbs and rearranged her rumpled clothing.

"It's daylight. I'm sure they gave up and left hours ago. If not, at least we can see them." Alex held the lantern and looked her up and down.

She smiled at him in the flickering light. "Why are you doing that?" She pulled her hair back self-consciously.

"You're beautiful, Jess." Warmth flooded through him. She rolled her eyes and looked away. He stepped close and bent to kiss her. "Still feel the same in the light of day?"

Jessica pushed him back. "Go see if it's safe to go out, so I can at least wash my face."

"Yes, ma'am. I'll draw you some water." He winked at her and pushed her in the direction of the cave entrance. "Right after I call the sheriff on my cell phone and report those two lunatics. Stay here a few minutes while I have a look around camp."

"Wait a minute." Jessica surveyed the boxes. "Bring the light over here."

Alex stepped close to the pile of cartons. "What is it?"

"I've seen these exact markings before." She pointed to the label fixed to one of the boxes. Alex leaned closer with the light. She read the print aloud. "The Anasazi Cultural Center."

"Doesn't mean anything to me."

"Well, it means a lot to me. I saw McCabe and the museum curator loading boxes in McCabe's truck over at the center a few days ago. What do you think?"

Alex's eyes narrowed. "We're about to find out." He pulled open one of the boxes. Reaching inside, he retrieved a carefully wrapped pot.

"What is it?" Jessica asked.

As he tore a piece of the wrapping material away, he could see the familiar black and white markings of a common Anasazi pot. The wrapping bore a tag with a catalog number on it. "These are artifacts from another site." He squinted to read the handwriting.

"What are they doing here?"

"I'm not sure. But I'm going to mention this to the sheriff." Alex was hesitant to share his thoughts. His mind had clicked on a possible connection between these artifacts and what was troubling him at the site.

Maybe someone was salting the ruin to lead him astray. Maybe that someone was McCabe or his buddy.

Alex made his way down the hill, nervous and wary. He kept low and quiet. Everything was still at the camp. An uneasy feeling gripped his gut, but there was nothing visible to back it up. He let out a half sigh of relief, opened the passenger door of his SUV and reached for his cell phone.

"Stop there, pretty boy," a voice hissed and cold hard steel pushed into Alex's neck. A knot twisted in his gut. A rush of fear ran through him only to be overtaken by anger. His breath became a conscious thing, quick and deep. He struggled to keep it under control. His very life depended on it.

The barrel of the gun vibrated against the soft tissue of Alex's neck. The shaking hands of a madman grasped the butt of the rifle. Wild-eyed and trembling, McCabe commanded, "Back on outta there." McCabe jerked at Alex's shirt collar with his free hand.

Alex reluctantly moved his hand back across the car seat. It had stopped inches from his phone. Following McCabe's orders, he backed away from the open door. His jaw was clenched, taught as steel.

"Sit," McCabe snapped and pushed Alex. He stiffened at McCabe's action and fought the desire to throw a punch. Turning, he squatted then sat cross-legged in the dirt. The barrel of the gun rested below his cheekbone.

A coarse laugh came from McCabe. "I've been waiting for this," he cackled.

"My ancestors would have cut your heart out," Alex seethed through clenched teeth.

McCabe's face instantly lost its look of amusement. His eyes flashed. He pushed the gun barrel harder into Alex's cheek. "Get your hands behind you," McCabe barked.

Alex's face was hot with anger, but he was at the mercy of a crazy man. Watching McCabe with steady eyes, Alex did as he was told. McCabe fumbled a piece of thin rope from his pocket. He stepped behind Alex, pushing the gun barrel into Alex's neck at the base of his skull.

With the quickness of an experienced calf roper, McCabe wrapped the rope around Alex's wrists and tied them off. Alex knew McCabe was precariously holding the rifle under one arm. At this angle he wasn't willing to risk being paralyzed for life or worse. The way McCabe handled the rope, he just might be quick enough to pull the trigger.

"So where's your girlfriend hiding?" McCabe gave the rope one final jerk and pulled it painfully taut around Alex's wrists.

Alex went tense as a steel rod at the thought of McCabe finding Jessica. He pushed hard against the ropes holding his hands. Its coarse bristly fibers cut into his skin. The wild dark eyes of McCabe gleamed with an unnatural light. He seemed to find great joy in Alex's anger.

"Scoot back," McCabe commanded.

Alex resentfully slid toward the vehicle until his back touched the front tire. "You bastard," Alex said under his breath, knowing Jessica couldn't see them from the hillside. McCabe crouched in front of him, leaned close and hissed into Alex's ear. "I know your little friend is around here somewhere. You spent the night with her some place on this mountain, didn't you?" McCabe snorted. "Well, the party's over, lover boy."

Alex jerked forward, rage and disgust boiled in his gut. He stopped abruptly as the gun barrel pressed hard into his chest. He glared at McCabe, rolling the muscles of his clenched jaw. A wicked gleam burned in

McCabe's eyes. The corners of his mouth turned up in a dingy smile.

Just then loose gravel rolled down the mountain. Alex's greatest fear was rapidly approaching.

"Alex," Jessica's voice called out. "Alex, where are you?"

McCabe shoved the rifle barrel harder into Alex's chest, defying him to make a sound. Torn between anger and fear for Jessica, he bit his tongue to keep from calling a warning to her. He had no doubt McCabe would pull the trigger. And he was sure he'd shoot Jessica, too, if he were pushed to the edge. Soft footsteps in the sand told Alex that Jessica was getting closer.

"Alex," she called again, this time from just behind them. McCabe twitched like a jungle cat, waiting for the precise moment that would leave her no escape.

In one quick sweep, McCabe rose to his feet and pointed the barrel of the rifle in her direction. A stifled scream came from her. Alex tried to turn to see her, mentally flogging himself for allowing her to walk into this situation. Hell, he couldn't have stopped it. Not if they were both going to get out of this alive.

As McCabe dragged her around the truck by her arm, Alex could see the terror on her face. He swallowed hard. "It'll be okay, Jess."

"It'll be okay, Jess," McCabe mimicked then laughed wickedly. "Don't worry, your big strong boyfriend will save you." He spoke in the voice of a taunting child. "Not much chance, turkey."

Alex gritted his teeth and rage built in his chest. His pulse pounded so hard he could feel it hammering in his neck. "Look. Whatever you want, you can have."

"Really," McCabe bellowed at him. "What I want is your head on a plate. And I've already got that." McCabe's eyes narrowed and his lips curled. "You think I'm some cheap robber? You dumb ass." He shoved Jessica against the door of the SUV and pulled a second roll of rope from his pocket. As he lashed her hands together, the rifle teetered, grasped under his arm. Giving the last knot a quick pull reminiscent of a roping competition, he whirled Jessica around and pushed her into Alex with the sole of his boot.

"Don't you dare hurt her, you bastard," Alex snapped. He couldn't catch Jessica without the use of his hands. She tumbled into his lap.

"And what are you gonna do about it, pretty boy?" McCabe circled them, pointing the rifle at them all the while.

Jessica slid from Alex's lap and pulled herself into a sitting position next to him.

"You're too cowardly to give me a fighting chance, aren't you?" Alex taunted, hoping to find some way to make a break.

McCabe's lips tightened in a snarl. Alex's heart jumped into his throat. McCabe raised the rifle and looked through the sights at him.

"What the hell are you doing now?" a voice called. McCabe's accomplice scurried down the hillside behind them, scattering pebbles in all directions.

McCabe bristled and turned toward the man who confronted him. "Leave me alone, Wilson. This ain't none of your affair."

"You lunatic! Taking them hostage in broad daylight," Wilson seethed. "What the hell are you going to do with them?"

McCabe raised the rifle barrel. His hands trembled, making the gun shake. A deep throaty and unnatural voice came from McCabe. "Don't try to stop this. Leave me alone," he bellowed. Wilson's eyes opened wide. A flash of fear was evident. His eyes darted from McCabe's face to the cold steely barrel of the rifle. "Calm down, Jon," he said. His voice changed from rage to a soothing tone as he tried to calm the madman. Wilson's face took on a curious look. His brow creased and a stunned, but troubled look replaced his anger.

How different it was for Wilson when the gun was turned on him, Alex thought. He flashed a look at Jessica, whose eyes were big as Frisbees. Her jaw was taught with fear.

"Don't do something you're going to regret for the rest of your life, Jon," Wilson went on.

"Shut up! Shut up!" McCabe raged. "I'll kill you, too, if I have to."

Wilson rubbed his short red beard nervously, his eyes fixed on the gun.

"You really plan on killing these people, don't you?"

Alex sensed Wilson was testing McCabe, sizing up the chances McCabe would pull the trigger.

"Jon, how are you going to do this without going to prison? You shoot them out here with all this evidence and the law will know you did it." It was obvious Wilson was laying the groundwork for a mind game with McCabe. He was searching for McCabe's weakness.

"Well—" McCabe hedged, his voice returning to normal. His eyes seemed less glassy at the mention of life in prison. "I—I ain't gonna kill 'em here. I'll take 'em up on the hill and roll 'em over the side."

"There's a chance they could survive that." Wilson kicked at the dirt with his boot toe.

"I'm gonna set their damn truck on fire," McCabe bellowed. Rage spread across his face. He seemed to teeter in and out of his inhuman state, as if something inside was trying to talk sense to him. "Then I'll push 'em over. They won't survive that," he said with satisfaction.

"Hmm," Wilson said, rubbing his finger across his lower lip. He tugged at his beard, as he appeared to contemplate McCabe's plan. "That's gonna be tough to do with their hands untied. Don't you think they're gonna put up quite a fight?"

"I can't untie them, you imbecile," McCabe snapped. "They can go just as they are."

"Really?" Wilson clicked his tongue. "Seems it would be some pretty ugly evidence when the sheriff found two dead bodies in a burned out car with their hands tied. It'd be tough to write that one off as an accident. Don't you think, Jon?"

"If you don't shut up, I'll shoot you dead right here." McCabe screeched, pushing the gun into Wilson's face. The click as McCabe pulled the hammer back was followed by dead silence.

Wilson shifted, but never faltered. "Seems to me that would be an awful expensive bullet." Wilson looked away and coolly shook his head. "There's a cave full of boxes up there worth an awful lot of money. Unless, of course, you have yourself a buyer without me."

McCabe's eyes narrowed as he looked down the barrel of the rifle at Wilson. Wilson never twitched. He returned the steely gaze.

Alex's jaw tightened. These two were playing more than one game and this guy was spilling his guts to save his backside. Alex watched McCabe's face go ghostly white. His eyes told the story of a tortured soul wavering between madness and moments of sanity. McCabe's fingers twitched back and forth and he slowly released the hammer. Wilson let out a ragged breath as McCabe lowered the rifle.

"I gotta get rid of 'em now," McCabe stuttered. "You gotta help me."

"Dammit, Jon." Wilson spat on the ground. "Now you've opened up a real can of worms for both of us. You've put our backs to the wall this time."

Wilson pulled McCabe over next to him and spoke in a low voice. Alex couldn't make out what they were saying. He looked over at Jessica, and noticed for the first time that a tear had run from the corner of her eye and down her cheek.

"It's okay," Alex whispered. "It's going to work out somehow."

"They're going to kill us. That must be what they're talking about over there."

"Try to stay calm," Alex said as his mind strained to find an escape route. Pushing hard on the rope that tied his hands, he felt it loosen, stretching against the pressure of his strength. He was tied too tight for it to do much good, but his silent prayers continued as he watched and hoped for a miracle.

McCabe's face was pale and drawn. The light of something uncontrollably wicked burned in his eyes and contorted his face. He lit a cigarette, shaking almost too hard to light it and get it to his mouth.

Wilson looked distraught. It was obvious to Alex, whatever arrangement he had with McCabe, this was far more than Wilson had bargained for. Wilson ran a trembling hand up his face and wiped sweat from his brow.

McCabe's eyes flashed with anger, something Wilson was saying seemed to trigger the madman inside of him back into action.

"I can't wait anymore. I can't keep 'em sittin' here lookin' at me like a couple of steers waitin' to be slaughtered. If I'm gonna do it, I have to do it now." McCabe started in Alex's direction. Wilson caught his arm with a firm hand and pulled him back around.

"You gotta wait, Jon. Why don't you take them up to your place and put them in the barn for a while?" Wilson's darting eyes told Alex he was flying by the seat of his pants to buy time. "Yeah. We could load up the stuff out of the cave in your truck and leave them up at your ranch. Hell, by the time anybody found them, we'd be out of the country. Probably all the way to South America."

McCabe ran a shaky hand across his stubby whiskers. An idea obviously bloomed behind his eyes.

"If you kill 'em here, the law's gonna come after you for sure," Wilson rambled on, nervously looking from Jessica and Alex to the quivering McCabe. "You gotta think on it or you're puttin' yourself behind bars."

"Let's get 'em to the ranch." McCabe rushed over and, grabbed Jessica's arm with one hand, grasping the rifle tightly in the other. Yanking her to her feet, he shoved her forward.

"Treat the lady with a little respect," Alex growled. Wilson's boot nudged him in the backside and he tugged on Alex's arm, helping him to his feet. Alex glared hard at McCabe and pushed abruptly on the rope that held his hands uselessly behind him.

"No need to rough her up, Jon." Wilson sounded mousy and appeasing of McCabe. Wilson's eyes were lined with red circles of fear, as he looked Alex in the face. "Just do as he says, man," he said, his voice barely audible. "And maybe nobody will get hurt."

Alex eyed McCabe's accomplice suspiciously, the man smelled of cologne and wore an expensive tweed jacket over his blue jeans. Alex wondered how two such unlikely cohorts had managed to team up.

"Put 'em in the archaeologist's truck," McCabe cackled as he half-lifted Jessica into the backseat. His rifle leaned beside him. Alex caught the eyes of Wilson sizing up the weapon. Wilson smelled of fear and it was obvious his mind was working overtime to figure out what to do next. It was even clearer to Alex that Wilson wanted no part of the way things were playing out.

Hooking his boot heel on the running board, Alex slid into the backseat next to Jessica. McCabe shoved a bony hand hard into Alex's front pocket, extracting the keys in one rough motion. McCabe cackled. The stench of his cigarette-laden breath was as nauseating to Alex as the fire of wickedness that burned behind McCabe's eyes.

McCabe threw the keys at Wilson. "You drive. I need to tend to the two of them, and you, too. Don't get any fancy ideas, I still might blow your butt off if you do."

Wilson caught the key ring and answered obligingly. "Oh, no, Jon. Whatever you say. Remember I'm with you. We're partners." Wilson's sincerity was sheer as glass.

There was a heaviness in Alex's chest as he realized McCabe's real hatred and need to destroy was focused on Jessica and himself. Wilson and whatever scheme the two of them had, seemed of little consequence to McCabe. The only thing that appeared to affect him was Wilson's warnings about his share of the money and going to prison.

Alex's thought was barely completed when an astonishing thing happened. Wilson slammed the rear door next to Alex as McCabe opened the front passenger door. Suddenly, McCabe's body began to heave and shake violently. His rifle flew about wildly as if he were in some sort of tug of war with an invisible force.

Sidestepping in a kind of dance, Wilson tried to hold onto McCabe. Wilson weaved back and forth trying to stay on the harmless end of the rifle barrel at all costs. Alex leaned into Jessica, shoving her forward with his upper body. He hoped to find her some protection behind the seats.

"Jon. Jon," Wilson repeated breathlessly. "What the hell are you doing?"

A wild-eyed McCabe blurted, "It ain't gonna let me leave here."

"What? What's not going to let you leave?" Wilson wrestled with the writhing McCabe. Finally gaining ground, he pushed McCabe over onto the front seat and leaned on him. The rifle barrel pointed over Jessica's head.

"Stay down," Alex commanded and threw himself nearer Jessica. Just then McCabe's haunting face appeared between the front seats. McCabe's dark beady eyes burned with the fire of two blazing torches. His face was drawn up in a grotesque expression. Saliva seeped from the corners of his mouth. Wilson held him down but McCabe had a death grip on the rifle.

"I gotta kill 'em. I gotta kill 'em here," McCabe raved.

Wilson had an arm under McCabe's neck, but the unearthly sound coming from his mouth was not affected. The bone chilling voice that came from McCabe ran shivers through Alex as he gazed into the eyes of pure evil.

Wilson played his cards. "Jon. We already talked about this. We can't kill 'em here. We *can't*. We gotta take 'em somewhere else." Wilson was talking so fast his words blended together, not even resembling the polished English he used earlier.

"Let go of me," McCabe raged. "Let go." It was evident pure fury was building within him.

"No, Jon," Wilson shouted, frantically. "The money, remember the money. You gotta get your share first."

McCabe's lower lip trembled. He cast a glance back toward Wilson. The fire in his eyes flickered and a tremor of torment racked his bones as it did. A grimace of pain crossed his face.

"The money. Yeah, the money," he mumbled.

"You'll go to jail, Jon. If you kill 'em here, you'll go right to jail." Wilson played the scenario to McCabe perfectly. Alex shot a glance at Wilson. The clenched jaw and cool commanding voice told Alex that Wilson was now their greatest ally. Wilson shot him a quick hard look. All their lives were at stake and Wilson wasn't giving in.

McCabe closed his eyes. Evidence of pain and weariness crossed his face, mingled with his final efforts to struggle against Wilson. Obviously weakened, McCabe roared, "Get me the hell out of here. Now." A hint of normalcy overrode the strangeness in his voice.

Wilson pulled McCabe up straight in the seat. McCabe grasped the rifle with white knuckles. Wilson looked him up and down quickly, slammed the door then raced to the other side.

"We're goin', Jon. We're goin' now." Wilson yelled as he pulled open the driver's door.

McCabe's breath was shaky. Alex let out a choppy sigh, releasing both anxiety and exhaustion for another tense situation they had survived. *Just keep surviving, one moment at a time.* His mind was trying to restore calm to his taught insides.

The SUV bounced over the rocky and rutted incline out of the canyon. Alex's heart felt like it was on a string. It bounced with every rut in the makeshift road. Wilson whipped the vehicle sharply right and away from the wagon road back to the highway.

Alex swallowed hard. They were headed for McCabe's ranch. God himself only knew what was going to happen there. He had to calm his gut and keep his mind sharp if they were going to stay alive. He shot a glance at Wilson, wishing he knew what was ticking in that mind. Was Wilson out to save his own ass or was he trying to help them? Only time could answer that question.

CHAPTER TWENTY-TWO

Jessica flinched and maneuvered herself around on the barn floor. Sharp pieces of straw poked at her bare thighs and half-exposed backside. *Damn these shorts.* A brief picture of the interlude with Alex flashed through her mind, but was quickly snatched away by fear. If she died today, at least they had made love.

She forced herself to banish the notion. It wasn't going to end here. They had too much to go on for. The sound of voices at the door announced McCabe as he jabbed at Alex with the rifle barrel and walked him into the barn. Her heart had been in her throat for so long, her stomach was sick. If not for the fact her insides were tied in a hard knot and refused to move, she probably would have thrown up.

Alex slid down the bales of hay stacked behind them and sat beside her. A black cloud of hatred hung behind his pale eyes. He watched the half-stumbling McCabe walk back toward the barn door.

Wilson stood just outside. His short red beard appeared almost gold in the rays of sunlight that peered through the mass of clouds rapidly growing in an angry sky. Wilson squinted at her beneath a troubled brow then looked away. She disliked him and felt unsure of his motives.

"Did you check their ropes?" Wilson asked as McCabe passed him in the doorway. McCabe shook his head wearily.

"Better be sure they're tied good and tight," Wilson said, purposefully walking toward them. Alex surveyed the man as he approached, his look half-expectation and half-suspicion.

Jessica watched as Wilson ran his hand over Alex's ropes. The bindings were loose, but Wilson paid no heed. He leaned over her, smelling of cologne mingled with perspiration. His hand went to hers and he pressed a small smooth metal object in her palm.

Pretending to secure her hands, he whispered in her ear. "Lady, get your ass out of here if you get a chance." His voice was laced with fear and concern. Jessica had suspected that concern was more for himself than for her or Alex, especially after his comment about murder one. She cast her eyes toward the straw covered barn floor determined not to divulge Wilson's secret.

McCabe had stepped back inside and loomed in front of the only escape route. "Come on, dammit. You don't need to tuck 'em in," he growled. "We gotta talk."

She glanced up, meeting McCabe's eyes for a brief moment. The hard cold evil she'd seen there before seemed diminished and weariness was evident in his body. Yet his quivering clenched jaw and wild look still portrayed an urgency to get on with whatever he schemed in his mind. The two walked out into daylight and turned to face each other in front of the open Dutch doors of the barn.

She looked at Wilson, feeling a surge of emotion for the man as she fingered the object in her hand. "Alex," she whispered, being cautious not to move and attract one of McCabe's periodic glances in their direction. Alex gave her a sideways nod. McCabe and Wilson were talking in low voices, their attention becoming more intent upon their own conversation.

"Wilson gave me something. In my hand." She leaned forward and held the object out with her fingers for Alex to see.

"Good God, Jess. It's a pocket knife," Alex breathed. Relief flooded his voice.

Jessica straightened as McCabe shot another look into the shadowy barn and watched them for a moment. He was thirty feet or more away and seemed to be contemplating his next move. Not wanting to meet his gaze, Jessica surveyed her surroundings.

Several high windows and the open doors provided enough light to partially illuminate the inside of the structure. Stalls lined the outer walls and discarded farming tools and riding tack were scattered carelessly about on the straw-covered floor.

Two dust-caked horse collars hung on one wall and parts from an old plow protruded from one of the stalls. They told their own story of the ranch that had passed from generation to generation. Jessica thought of the history, and of poor Dorothy and the life here that she loved. How much this place must have once meant to Jonathan McCabe. What kind of force did it take to make him turn away from it all?

McCabe surveyed the sky, rubbed his jaw then turned back toward Wilson. Jessica could hear Alex's breathing and the wheels clicking in his head. "Can you open the knife?" he asked between his teeth.

"I'll try."

"There should be a notch in the blade somewhere. See if you can get your thumbnail in it." His voice was low, his lips barely moved.

Staring ahead, her eyes on McCabe and Wilson, she struggled with the tiny object, attempting to do as Alex instructed. Bingo. Her nail found its appointed mark and she pulled gently. The blade snapped open. It nicked her finger but she held fast to it in spite of the stinging stab of pain.

"I've got it," she whispered.

A sigh left Alex as he released the tension he'd been holding while she worked. McCabe shot another nervous glance in their direction and lit up a cigarette. Wilson appeared to be pleading somebody's case. His arms moved animatedly and he paced the area in front of McCabe from time to time.

"Can't you see?" Wilson's voice grew louder. McCabe looked on, appearing to be recharging his internal battery after the mind-boggling, heart-stopping event he'd been through in the front seat of Alex's truck.

A flood of fear ran through Jessica as she maneuvered the knife blade toward the unrelenting rope that bound her wrists. The evil was building again in McCabe's eyes. She'd experienced its reality. Close up. Now she had a growing sense it might return even stronger than before. Whatever drove McCabe wanted her and Alex, wanted them both dead.

The spirit had warned her. He'd told her she would have to face the thing before it was over. "You must stand before the symbol of evil," the spirit's words rang in her head. If ever in her life she'd needed the guidance from that great and mighty hand from beyond, it was now.

The knife blade was wedged between the rope and her wrist. A half dozen tiny cuts buzzed on her hands and wrists from the sharp blade. She didn't care. Everything was trivial compared with the danger outside the door. She tried over and over to push the blade against the rope but it was no use, she was making no headway.

The dull side of the blade dug into her arm and she didn't have the strength in her fingers from this angle to force the blade into the ropes. Her hands ached, beads of perspiration ran tiny trails from under her hair and down the side of her face. She struggled to keep her effort from showing on her face, her teeth were clamped so tight she thought they'd never come apart.

"Any luck?" Alex asked after a few minutes.

"It's no use. I can't cut the rope." She let out her breath. Her chest heaved softly.

The men's voices were growing louder and McCabe appeared to grow agitated. "I'm not listening to your nonsense anymore," he shouted. "We need to get this over."

A storm brewed outside and the sounds of thunder could be heard in the distance. The light dimmed intermittently as fast-rolling clouds passed overhead. Jessica's heartbeat quickened. She wondered if her prayers had been heard as McCabe disappeared from view.

An excitedly animated Wilson followed close behind shouting objections. "Jon. You can't do this. We still have weeks of work to do. What about the money, damn it? Don't you see you could be filthy rich?" His objections were reaching a fevered pitch.

As the two disappeared from sight, Alex turned his back toward Jessica. "Quick. Give it to me."

Jessica scooted on the straw. It pricked and stung at her thighs, but she could not let it distract her. She focused her frantic attention on maneuvering the knife from her grasp into his. She gasped as the smooth handle slipped from her grip.

"Got it."

A flood of relief washed through her.

They pulled back to their spots just as the evil ragged grin of McCabe appeared around the barn door. He held the rifle in one hand and a gas can in the other. Wilson was close at his heels, babbling frantically.

Jessica shot a wide-eyed glance at Alex. His rippling jaw told her he was working furiously at his ropes.

"You can't do this." Wilson's voice was several notes higher now. He shot Jessica a "what the hell are you waiting for" look.

"Sure I can," McCabe cackled. "Just watch." His eyes shone with an unearthly light that sent chills through Jessica's body and down her spine. McCabe flipped the top from the gas can and sprinkled the pungent liquid around the perimeter of the old barn, dousing the dry straw.

Jessica's heart hammered in her throat. "Alex," she uttered.

No answer. Alex threw her a steely look filled with sheer determination.

"Don't do this, McCabe." Alex echoed Wilson's words. "You know you can't possibly get away with it."

McCabe stopped and narrowed his eyes at Alex then turned to Wilson. Wilson avoided McCabe's gaze. "Don't look me in the eyes, Jon," he shrieked. "Listen to the man. It's your barn for God's sake."

"Shut up," McCabe snapped, his shaking hands splashed the gas in larger surges. "Nobody's going to stop me."

"You're crazy! You can't be serious about this." Wilson ran a frustrated hand through his hair. McCabe poured the gas faster. The rifle bobbed uncertainly in his free hand, his finger ready at the trigger.

A huge boom of thunder echoed outside and rattled through the barn. McCabe's wild eyes lit up with an unearthly light. "I'm not only serious," he chortled, "but I seem to have friends in high places. One good lightning strike and we'll all be in hell."

Wilson took a step in McCabe's direction. McCabe bristled, dropped the can of gas and pointed the gun at Wilson's chest. "Don't try anything stupid," McCabe warned, his face resumed the grotesque look he'd displayed earlier.

The gas fumes made Jessica's head hurt and her stomach grew queasy. Another loud lightning bolt shook the ground. "Don't you see, Tom," McCabe sneered. "It's perfect. A lightning bolt hit the barn and it burned to the ground. Storms hit here all the time. They're never gonna ask any questions. I'll bulldoze it over in the morning. Bury their bones forever. Nobody will ever know."

A gasp of horror attempted to escape from Jessica's throat, but she managed to hold it in. Wilson's eyes narrowed. "You crazy bastard," he whispered, then threw an arm over his face. "Don't look me in the eyes, man. Stay away from me," he yelled. "You get nuts like this and sometimes you damn near make sense. I don't even know why you want these people dead, but I don't want any part of it."

McCabe laughed hideously. "You coward," he spat. Outside a flash of lightning lit up the yard.

"Look, our deal was just to sell the stolen artifacts and get the money. It was your insanity that brought it to this. What is it that comes over you?"

"How dare you," McCabe raged. "You were the one who came up with the last plan for me to murder the girl and ditch her car. Remember? That was your scheme."

Jessica's eyes widened, she looked at Wilson in horror and swallowed a lump in her throat. Wilson looked back then turned away, unwilling to meet her gaze for more than a second.

"You and those crazy eyes. They mix my head up with insane thoughts," Wilson wailed. "You might have had me crazy enough at one point to suggest it, but I'm no cold-blooded killer who can shoot or burn people to death. My God, Jon, they're sitting there watching you."

McCabe tossed aside the gas can and took two long steps into Wilson's face. Wilson cried out in rage, raised his arms and threw himself into McCabe. Taken by surprise, McCabe fell backward onto the floor and the gun fired. Wilson's body stiffened, his eyes grew wide.

Jessica's heart jumped to her throat. Wilson ran his hands down his chest. He looked down at his palms. Both were clean. The shot had missed him. He stood over McCabe, facing the rifle barrel again.

Jessica's body was rigid as steel and her pulse hammered in her temples. Her eyes glazed over with fear until she was not sure she was seeing clearly.

McCabe's eyes glowed as he waved the rifle barrel at Wilson. "You're awful mouthy for somebody whose butt is hanging out bigger than anybody's."

"What do you mean?" Wilson stammered.

"I mean you're the one with a cave full of boxes from the Cultural Center. I don't see my name on 'em—no finger's pointin' at me."

Wilson's shoulders sagged, his mouth moved but no words escaped. He stepped aside and sent a quick look at Jessica that read with urgency. At that moment, she knew his efforts were trying to buy them time. But he was drawing the line before McCabe shot him on the spot.

McCabe rose slowly to his feet. "I'll take care of you when all this is over," he snarled at Wilson. "Or burn your ass along with theirs." He picked up the gas can from where it had fallen to the floor after Wilson's attack. His wild eyes were glassy. His body showed signs of fatigue and his breath was short and ragged.

"Too much money involved here," he mumbled to himself, lost in some world of his own. "Kill him now. There won't be any money. Gotta kill him— He knows too much." He snarled in Wilson's direction reminiscent of a rabid animal then babbled on as he doused the area around them. "Kill them first— Don't care about Wilson. He's where the money's at— Fool." There was a long pause. "Oh God, my Dorothy will never forgive me for this."

Jessica shot a terrified glance at Alex whose jaw seemed less rigid. Instead, he watched McCabe's every move like a leopard surveying its prey before the fatal pounce. His eyes followed the gun barrel as it bobbed up and down and McCabe splashed the gas.

Jessica's mind flashed on the mental picture Dorothy had painted of her husband just months before. Now he wandered around the barn, mumbling and preparing to burn part of the ranch he loved. And commit murder in the process. She could not imagine what had brought him to this point. What kind of force had changed him to this madman? The truth of the spirit's words grabbed at her guts. Indeed she would know when she faced the evil. There was no doubt in what human form it resided.

Wilson paced nervously looking as if he were wound tight as a spring. She read his every move. He was ready to make a run for it at any second, but didn't know how without getting himself shot.

A torrent of rain hammered at the roof of the building and rose quickly to a deafening roar. Flashes of lightning sporadically lit up the sky and earth outside and rolling claps of thunder shook the barn. McCabe poured the last drop from the gas can and threw it aside. Baring his yellow tobacco-stained teeth, he leaned forward as if savoring the moment. He reached into his pocket and pulled out a book of matches.

A flash of lightning and a huge clap of thunder rocked the barn. The storm closed in on them, just like McCabe. McCabe struck the match, its light outshone only by the evil fire in his eyes.

He held the match in front of them, turning it in his fingers. His hideous smile grew wider. Terror climbed in Jessica's throat, higher and higher until she could barely breathe. The match fell from McCabe's hand. His eyes followed it to the floor. A look of astonished disappointment struck as the tiny flame flickered and went out before reaching its mark. Alex lunged, taking McCabe by surprise and sending him sprawling onto the floor. As Alex leaped, McCabe jerked the rifle butt around and hit Alex, square in the jaw. Alex moaned and fell heavily to the straw. McCabe rose to his feet and kicked at Alex.

"Your boyfriend thinks I'm real stupid, don't he?" McCabe cackled as he searched the hay for a new piece of twine to secure Alex's hands.

Jessica rolled onto her side and across the hay surprising McCabe. He stepped toward her and raised the rifle. He frowned down at the match that had gone out before it hit the gasoline-soaked floor.

As Jessica rolled again, something fell, freeing itself from inside her shirt. The amulet. In her fear, she'd forgotten the spirit's words.

McCabe hovered over her. His distorted face was all but afire. Evil glowed like two hot red coals behind his eyes. He grabbed her and pushed her back into a sitting position then checked her hands. As he did, she reared her head back and the amulet flashed with a mysterious light in front of his face. He squinted then blinked several times rubbing his eyes as he stared at the piece. From somewhere deep inside, came a low painful groan.

"No," an eerie voice spoke. McCabe raised a hand toward the amulet then stopped as if somehow losing the strength to pull it from her neck. He staggered back a step.

Wilson stood at the door resembling a deer ready to bolt.

Obviously far from McCabe's thoughts, the rifle barrel dipped low. Jessica's eye caught a movement on the floor behind him. As McCabe stepped backward again, Alex grabbed him around the ankles, toppled him to the floor and knocked the wind from him. A low moan escaped his lips and he stared up at the ceiling.

Alex stumbled to his feet, grabbed a pitchfork and held it threateningly over McCabe. McCabe's eyes glowed once more when he saw the hatred in Alex's face.

"Go ahead," McCabe shrieked. "Run it through me."

Alex winced, his jaw set tight as he looked down at the man's crazed state. McCabe's trembling hands reached for the pitchfork and tried to pull it toward his own body. Alex jerked back. McCabe groped for the rifle that had fallen in the straw out of his reach.

McCabe's hat had flown from his head and his sparse hair stood straight up. His wild eyes glowed and the distorted yellow smile oozed moisture from its corners. Jessica shuddered in both terror and disgust. He'd transformed again into a raging lunatic.

A thought flashed in Jessica's mind. He must be waging a terrible internal battle for this evilness to come over him in such waves. With one quick lunge, McCabe caught hold of the rifle. He waved it first at Alex then toward Jessica, struggling to get it into position with the pitchfork at his throat.

"Drop it or you're a dead man," Alex threatened through clenched teeth. His face was taut with fury and hatred. Alex held the pitchfork against McCabe's throat. McCabe paid no heed and now had a full grasp on the rifle. He pointed the gun dead at Alex. The two were motionless in a standoff. The click of a trigger or the push of the pitchfork would bring a terrifying end for one or both of them.

Jessica forced herself to shake off her fear. She rolled onto her knees and struggled to her feet. "Stop this," she commanded, finding courage in McCabe's reaction to the amulet.

McCabe's fingers twitched nervously on the butt of the gun.

"Don't do it, Jon," she warned.

"Go away," he raged, refusing to look at her. "I told you to leave. Why didn't you just go?" A sense of desperation seemed to be taking charge of McCabe.

Alex's eyes remained fast on McCabe, locked in a stare between the two. Jessica stepped closer, hoping to make the most of the amulet's apparent effects on him.

McCabe broke eye contact with Alex. As Jessica moved, his gaze stopped on the amulet then he quickly turned his head away.

"Put down the rifle, Jon," she said firmly. "You can't do this. It's not in your heart."

McCabe eyed the rifle as his mouth quivered. The pitchfork handle shook slightly, and Jessica shot a glance at Alex who seemed to be in some sort of daze.

"Get back, Jess," Alex called to her.

As Jessica turned toward him, the amulet spun away from McCabe. With the heel of his boot, McCabe shoved Jessica away from him, knocking her off balance and in Alex's direction. Alex dropped the pitchfork and caught Jessica in his arms.

McCabe jumped to his feet, his face filled with the distorted look of horrifying evil once more. He pulled the rifle up and pointed it at Alex.

At that moment, Wilson's body slammed hard into McCabe and the rifle flew into the air. McCabe sprawled onto the barn floor. Alex let Jessica slide down onto the straw, snatched up the pitchfork and pushed it against McCabe's throat. Jessica struggled to her feet.

Wilson rose, brushed himself off and stared at McCabe's wild face.

"Aaaarrrggghh—" McCabe groaned in anger and frustration as the three looked on at his glassy eyes and frothing mouth. "You can't stop me," the unearthly voice bellowed. "It's not over."

Alex's hands trembled and his focus was fixed on McCabe's face. Fear shot through Jessica as she watched Alex, the rage boiling inside him unnerved her. It was as if something were tugging at him, too, trying to pull him into a world beyond all reason.

"Alex," she said. His jaw moved, but he didn't break the stare. His lips tightened and he pushed the sharp tines of the pitchfork against the thin skin of McCabe's throat.

Wilson shot him a look filled with questions. "You people are all crazy," he muttered. He pulled Alex's keys from his pocket, eyed them for a moment and left through the barn door. The tension between Alex and McCabe did not ease even as the sound of Wilson driving away broke the storm-filled air. Another loud clap of thunder rattled through the barn and lightning lit up the area outside.

McCabe seemed to draw a final burst of strength from the blast and raged a closing threat at Alex. "I should have killed the girl when I had the chance. She's what you care about, isn't she? Your own ass isn't that important to you."

McCabe had found Alex's last hot button. Alex looked at the pitchfork then pulled it away with trembling hands and tossed it aside. He threw himself forward and wrapped his hands around McCabe's throat.

Jessica's insides turned over. Pushing herself into Alex's face, she looked deep into his eyes. "Stop Alex. Stop it now. No matter how bad he is, no matter how much you hate him, you can't do this."

Choking noises came from McCabe as he gasped for air beneath the forceful grip of Alex's fingers. Alex shook McCabe three times like a rag doll.

Jessica pressed closer. "Alex. Alex. What's come over you?" she screamed.

Alex eased his grip a little. His breath came in heavy, angry puffs. "I won't let him hurt you, Jess."

"He won't, Alex. It's over."

Alex looked up at her. His eyes came to rest on the amulet for the first time. He let go of McCabe's throat and looked down almost in disbelief at his open palms. His face took on an odd expression. He looked bewildered at the writhing McCabe whom he'd released from his grip.

Letting the weight of his body subdue the exhausted henchman, he looked again at the amulet then at Jessica.

She eyed Alex suspiciously then glanced at McCabe, praying it was truly over. Still shaking, she hovered between them with the amulet. She hoped beyond hope its power would end this near tragic afternoon once and for all.

McCabe's eyes opened and he stared at the object suspended above him. He winced then emitted a whimper. Jessica watched his face go from manic wildness to the frightened innocence of a child.

"No," he whispered. "What's happened here?" He looked around as if he'd just awakened from a nightmare. "No—" His lower lip quivered. The fire in his eyes had gone, a hollow look overtook them.

Alex moved his body aside, shoving the rifle across the barn floor. He rummaged through the straw and found the pocketknife and cut Jessica's hands free.

She rubbed her burning wrists and let out a sigh of exhaustion. Taking the amulet in her hand, she made sure it stayed in McCabe's view. Its effect on him was undeniable. It seemed to drain the evil from his being.

Alex touched the amulet. "Jess," he whispered. "This was in my dream." Their eyes met in amazement as the final connection shot between them.

McCabe, the most pertinent thing in their world at this moment, laid there, a horror-stricken look crossing his face. "I've done some awful things, haven't I?" he asked her, his eyes pleading and childlike.

"Yes," she answered.

His lower lip quivered and tears rolled from his eyes. Alex looked at her oddly, as she slid forward and scooped McCabe's head into her lap. McCabe began to sob.

"I nearly killed you." McCabe looked at her in horror and astonishment. "And him, too." He pointed to Alex.

"I know," she said.

"And, oh God, my Dorothy. I've lost my Dorothy," he wailed in the deep pain of his realizations. He sniffled. "Do you think she's okay?"

"I've seen her. She's fine." Jessica soothed. As McCabe trembled and sobbed in her arms, she stroked his wild wispy hair. It was the only reminder left of the raging evil on the broken man who quivered in Jessica's lap.

"I've ruined her life—and mine," he cried. Jessica's heart felt the stab of the self-inflicted pain of this pitiful soul.

"It's okay. It's over," she said, brushing aside a sympathetic tear of her own as she wondered what would become of the fractured human being weeping in her lap.

"Go call the police. I'll stay with him," Alex said, looking down sadly at McCabe.

Running a gentle hand across McCabe's head and patting his shoulder, Jessica laid his head softly into the straw and rose on trembling legs.

"I'm sure there's a phone in the ranch house," Alex said. She nodded, smiled weakly then handed Alex the amulet and walked out into the breaking storm.

The rays of a salmon sun peaked through the clouds to the west. Beneath it blazed the spectacular colored arches of a budding rainbow. The fragrance of freshly cleansed earth permeated the air. Jessica stepped between tiny transparent clouds of mist that rose from the wet ground like anxious spirits waiting to depart.It seemed this piece of the world was eager for what was yet to come.

As she walked toward the ranch house, she wanted to share in that hope and excitement, but a cloud hung over her heart. Though flooded with relief at the outcome of this unexpected twist, an icy chill of realization ran through her. Their greatest task still lay ahead of them. Alex's mission had only begun. The dark presence had been removed from McCabe, but she feared they had not seen the last of it.

CHAPTER TWENTY-THREE

The light of the moon peeked through the half-open tent flap. Alex quietly rolled away from Jessica. Exhaustion from the day's ordeal had pulled her quickly into a sound sleep as she lay next to him. The warmth of their half-naked bodies soothed him and he left her hesitantly. His own restlessness and a voice deep within made sleep evasive and impossible to capture.

Alex stepped soundlessly out into the moonlight. His bare feet squished in the sand and it oozed comfortingly between his toes. Staring up at the pale white opalescence of the glowing orb, he shook his head. The moon had surely been full every night since he'd been here, though he knew it defied all astronomical possibilities. Still, it called to him. Something in its presence carried a message to his very soul.

All was silent. Even Yellow Dog ignored him wandering out into the night. The dog opened one sleepy eye as Alex passed and returned to his world of oblivious slumber.

As Alex collected wood for a small fire, Jessica's words pounded inside his head. "You have a purpose here, Alex. The spirits have told me."

A few short weeks ago, he'd have laughed at the possibility, told her she needed professional help.

Tonight, his outlook on the world was different, both this world and the one beyond.

The terrifying evil in McCabe's eyes, the appearance of the amulet he'd seen in an ancient dream—and now the realization that those dreams meshed exactly with Jessica's legend. His head and heart were keen yet muddled. His mind was filled with questions. And his soul longed to find meaning in what had haunted his steps in the past weeks.

At last it seemed he was ready, ready to find the answers to the questions that weighed heavy. The dreams had moved him to connect with something; his roots, his ancestry, and his own identity. The time had come to give himself to it.

He piled twigs and dry pine needles in the fire pit. Allowing his mind to let go of the present, it formed a picture of his ancient kin who had done the same in this sacred canyon centuries ago. He placed the logs one upon the other, crossed them in the center and pointed them in the four sacred directions. The small circle of hot coals that still smoldered sent gentle blue and orange flames licking at the needles. The fire's awesome power turned them instantly to blackened straws. He watched the flames grow and increase. They consumed the twigs and spread to the crossed logs, leaping into the night air a foot or more above the pit. This small ritual, too, seemed somehow symbolic of his journey.

Alex stared into the fire then bit his lower lip. Smoke carried into his face as a gentle breeze swished it about. Its acrid taste came into his mouth, and burned his nostrils. But it was a smell of power, and a reminder of the fire's deadly force and the earth's many wondrous gifts that also commanded respect. He felt a kinship with the elements, with the natural powers that surrounded him, even on a calm cool night.

Alex rose by the firelight. The flames brought heat to his bare chest, sharing its energy and strength with him. Gazing up into the full silver moon, it seemed to call his name. He turned and walked to the SUV, parked a few feet away, and was fleetingly appreciative Wilson had chosen to leave the vehicle here before he fled.

Opening the tailgate, he searched through a small box of carefully packaged artifacts until he found the one he sought. The one he treasured most. The rules of his trade seemed meaningless as he reached into the plastic bag and pulled the eagle bone whistle from its shroud of protection.

He held it in his palm, feeling a sensual kinship of its touch on his skin. Its energy, the song it once possessed, reached somewhere into his mind, his soul and someplace far beyond.

Placing the whistle on the tailgate, he pulled a soft buckskin throw from the back. It was something he'd bought in Cortez. He'd been drawn to it but wasn't sure why. Now in the dim reflection of firelight, it became another piece of his destiny. He pulled a knife from its sheath where it lay in the back of the truck and cut the leather into a square, leaving two long strips of rawhide on either side.

Placing it in front of him, he tied the strips behind his back then examined his handiwork. In a quick motion, he freed himself from the confines of a pair of tight cotton briefs releasing the weight of his manhood and allowing himself to experience the freedom and wildness his ancient brethren had known.

He cut a second strip from the buckskin and tied it around his head, rubbing his fingers across its softness as he experienced the feel of it against his forehead. Grasping the whistle in his hand, he walked back to the fire and dropped to his knees on the blanket he'd spread there earlier for Jessica. Cradling the whistle in his palm, he ran his fingers over it then brought it to his lips and blew gently. A low shrill sound came from it. He pulled it from his mouth and looked at it again.

Somewhere out in the darkness, a twig snapped and a soft rustling sound followed. Alex looked out into the moonlit terrain and caught a glimpse of something moving in the distance. It came closer. He felt no fear, no tension entered his body as he first caught sight of the outline of an animal. The dancing firelight caught the flash of the white face of a wolf as it disappeared into the shadows. When it emerged again, the tall lanky frame of a man with long dark hair stood before him. Quietly expectant, Alex sat motionless by the fire.

The man nodded in his direction. "The time has come," he said.

Alex's eyes followed the slender form from the beaded moccasins and buckskin clad body, to his face and jet black hair where three silver feathers danced in the firelight. Their gazes met. A soft light played behind the young man's dark eyes as the fire cast its reflection and lit up his face. Alex nodded a silent invitation to him.

The man seated himself in the sand on the opposite side of the fire pit. "At long last, my brother, you have opened the door to the world of the spirit. A door you have guarded for a long time."

Alex nodded again, choosing not to speak.

"It has not been easy for you. You are a man of logic, but you are also a man of the earth." He reached down and picked up a handful of sand and let it trickle through his fingers. "These sands carry the blood of your forefathers, and the power of your birth right."

"Jessica—the woman—convinced me of that." Alex motioned in the direction of the tent.

The young man smiled. "I know the woman Jessica well. Without her, this night would not have been."

"This is true," Alex said. "A lot of things would not have happened without her."

The man smiled and looked knowingly into Alex's eyes.

"You have a name?" Alex asked.

"Nechi."

Alex grinned. "I might have known. This isn't the first time I've heard it. Talk to me, Nechi. Tell me what these things that have happened mean." Alex's mind flooded with questions as the tall gentle figure across the fire drew him in and embraced his soul.

"These things are about destiny. About why you were brought here." Nechi looked out into the darkness. "For centuries these lands have been home to the Pueblo, the Ute, the Navajo and many ancient tribes that came before them. The blood of both the Navajo and the Hopi flows through your veins. Your roots here are deep, Alex, and so is the inherent conflict that has burdened your soul."

Alex nodded. "I don't doubt you speak the truth, but it isn't all clear. It's almost as if the kachina from my great uncle started a landslide in my life."

Nechi's eyes flashed at Alex. A look of deep recognition passed through them. "The first of the kachinas— It is already in your hands— I should have known."

"What do you mean the first? What do you know about it?"

"I know only that it is of great significance. That its appearance and the timing of these events in your life are not a coincidence." Nechi bowed his head. "Learn what you learn, well, my brother. For you will need it in the days to come."

A profound sense of seriousness settled in Alex's soul. He shook his head trying to comprehend what Nechi was saying. "I don't get it— I just know that I've been called here for a purpose."

"You will soon enough. Tonight we must focus on the task at hand. This is but the first trial of your journey."

"Trial—" Alex nodded. His voice was calm as the two men's eyes met across the flames. The fire cast shadows all around them and enveloped them in a circle of light and warmth where at last Alex felt safe, knowing for now he must just trust in Nechi's words.

"Through your dreams you have lived the story of what happened here long ago." Nechi's voice was melodious and filled with wisdom.

"The warrior and the woman?" Alex asked.

"Yes. And the old chief who fell from the cliffs of the mesa."

"That warrior, the young chief, haunts me in my dreams. He calls to me as if he's trying to tell me something. I—I don't know what it is."

"Perhaps it is time for you to ask. The time has come for you to feel his pain."

"What do you mean?"

Nechi removed a tiny pouch from his belt and threw a handful of powder from it into the fire. A tiny puff of smoke plumed up and a peculiar sweet odor permeated the air. "Close your eyes and remember the face of the boy you saw in your dream."

Alex was reluctant but he did as Nechi instructed.

"Ask the question. Trust in the forces you cannot see."

Alex took a deep breath, held fast to the picture in his mind and sent the question out into the universe. He felt dizzy.

"Relax, let go of all else that exists and free fall into the arms of the spirit."

Nechi's voice trailed off as the vision of the young chief's face blurred and Alex's mind was pulled into the young man's head.

The world was black and the heaviness of fatigue was almost overwhelming.His raw fingers grasped a piece of rock and he pushed it into the stone surrounding him with the last of the strength his weary body possessed. He didn't know why he kept digging. It was useless and he knew it.

His body and mind continued to drive him toward survival when his soul had already given up its desire to go on. She was dead. His beautiful princess' blood was still on his hands. Although he could not see it in the darkness of the stone box where he was imprisoned. The only light came from the loose mud around the timbers in the roof. He'd lost the fight, both for his life and for his soul. He dug the rock into the stone again, feeling the small indentation in the wall that he'd made from hours of scraping.

With each pass he made across the stone, the heat and hideous visions of the evil closed in on him. Eternal damnation and fire leaped at his mind and heart, stealing even the beautiful memory of his princess from him.

The dirt on his hands could never cover the blood of his own people. He would never forgive his own weaknesses that had delivered the souls of his people into the hands of the ultimate enemy. His heart was broken. He was a fool, a fool who deserved what lay ahead of him—fire, eternal torment.

He collapsed. Weakness claimed him and he could no longer sit up. His throat was as parched and dry as the stone floor he lay upon. His hands throbbed and his body was racked with pain. He had lost. It was his time to die.

His eyelids were heavy as two stones. His chest burned and each breath brought a new surge of fire into his lungs. He would never see his princess again— not where he was going. His soul was condemned to this chamber of hell for eternity.

"His is a sad story, is it not?" Nechi's voice came from the distance.

Alex put his hand to his throat and ran it down his chest. The pain washed away. He opened his eyes. The fire blazed before him, Nechi sat across from him.

Alex rubbed his fingers across his face. Now he knew what it meant to trust in the hand from beyond. His mind was shaky, but what he had to do was growing clearer.

"Where is he?" Alex asked. His throat felt dry and constricted as he spoke. His heart rate was returning to normal.

"In the ruin," Nechi said somberly. "In a chamber that once lay between the cavern and the temple."

"Then it did happen here. This was the temple. I should have never doubted Jess."

"Forgive yourself what you must. You will have no energy for such things in the days to come."

Alex raised his brow. "What are you saying?"

"Free him. Free his people. Free their spirits."

"What? Free him? How could I possibly do that?"

"You are the only one who can. The power of the four winds and the Earth Mother will be at your disposal, but it is only you who can come to know how to use such power."

Alex paused. "I have felt this power you speak of—inside me. I know it's there, but I'm not sure I know how to use it."

"It is the power of the spirit. I cannot help you understand that which is possessed only within your own soul." Nechi looked into the flames. "The dreams come to you from a higher power. Listen to their message. The past and the future will become one within them, and within you. An ancient curse has made it so. Be strong, have faith and use your spirit's power and wisdom."

Alex frowned, trying to grasp the meaning of Nechi's message. He hoped what he felt inside him was right.

Nechi went on. "You have fought the battle with the man McCabe. The evil used his human form to try to destroy your body. In that, he failed. Now another battle must be waged." Nechi's face was stern and severe, the fire's glow reflected in the calm light of his eyes. "And this is only the first of many."

Alex moved his shoulders and let out his breath. The task Nechi was laying before him was daunting.

Nechi went on. "Your soul is the prize he seeks. Now that McCabe is no longer there, he will come after you on his own ground." Nechi's gaze pierced through Alex. "Be cautious, brother, his temptations will wear a strange costume. You may not recognize them as his. You must stand alone against him, for the place he inhabits is now his alone."

"The cavern?" Alex asked.

"He is hidden away in the chambers. You must go and seek him out." Nechi waved his hand in a wide motion toward the mountain. "Only you, because of the bloodline that courses in your veins, can release the chieftain from his eternal hell. That is why he calls to your soul. As of now, you and your brothers are the final descendents. But your powers are unique to you and theirs to them. You are his only hope, but know that your destruction would be the evil's ultimate victory."

Alex swallowed hard and ran his hand through his hair at the base of his head. His fingers grazed the rawhide band. He rubbed it gently and looked down at the whistle in his hand. His heritage. It was his ancestry, and a bizarre twist in his own life's plan. Now it was all at risk.

Nechi seemed to read his thoughts. "You could walk away. Perhaps it would be of little consequence in your life if you did."

"I wouldn't be here tonight if I could do that."

Nechi nodded and smiled. "I believed that was true. But I needed to hear it from your lips."

"You said I had to free the young chief's soul, but you also said something about freeing the people. I don't understand." "None of us know. None of us truly understand. Was our history altered by an evil that started here centuries ago and spread through our people?"

"Why do you ask me such a question? Theoretically speaking, no one knows exactly what became of the people here. Are you saying you blame the problems of our ancestry on one incident in one place?"

"Think of it not in your scientific terms. For this mission, you must leave that behind. The beginnings of many tribes flowed from the deserts of the great Southwest. This was no exception. Yours is native blood, connected to the land. This is your heartland. Many tribes formed from the seeds sewn in these soils. Over time, they scattered to the four winds. And the wind can spread many things along its way."

"But not all tribes believe what you say."

"This is true, but that is of little consequence. To some it would be of great importance, to the Earth Mother, it matters not. As with all mothers, she loves each child equally and unconditionally. Each is different, but no more or less in her eyes. In truth, those who came here were children of the Great Spirit as we all are. I speak only of destiny."

"So what are you trying to say? You believe this evil—this thing's actions went far beyond this place?"

"Who knows how broad its effects were? Or how much a part it played in our tragic history. The wars among our people, the loss of our way of life to the

white man, the reservations, the prejudices and the
poverty our people suffered for so many years."

Alex shook his head, not knowing how to respond to
Nechi's words. An ache brewed in his soul. The
thoughts left a bitter taste in his mouth, stronger than
the acrid taste of the fire. This, too, was his heritage.

"The evil began by possessing the soul of a dark
warrior whose influence changed a village, and
brought brother against brother." Nechi made a
circular motion with his arm. "It spread from here to
the mesa then to the valley." His eyes narrowed. "It
made life a hell for the living and captured the souls of
the dead, who have remained in a state of limbo for
hundreds of years. It broke a valuable connection to
the Great Spirit and brought fear and doubts, and war
to the people here."

Nechi looked into Alex's eyes. "Consider this, my
brother. Think of the effects one fallen angel had upon
the world and all of humanity, and ask yourself this
question. Who can say what might have been different
if this had not happened? We will never know."

Alex bowed his head. This young man's words
brought many questions. Questions that played in his
mind tore at his heart and shot fiery spears into his
soul.

Nechi gazed into the flames. "Make your choices
tonight. Do you believe what you have been asked to
do will make a difference? You may never know the
answer, but what you believe is truth may bring
answers for you tomorrow."

Nechi rose. "I must leave you now. Look inside
yourself. All you need exists there. Like the young
chieftain, the power of good is there for you to draw
upon. But you and only you can find your path." Nechi
raised his hand to Alex. Their eyes met and a silent
message passed between them. Nechi walked out
beyond the circle of firelight.

Alex watched him disappear into the darkness. Staring into the dancing flames, he heard the distant howl of the wolf. He looked down at his own body. Half clad in the rawhide loincloth, he'd spanned the bridge between himself and his ancient brothers. Nechi was wrong about only one thing, there was no choice to be made here. Alex had crossed over into that world tonight, and he could not return without his work being done.

He may have spoken to Nechi as a scientist at times, but only because his mind knew no other way. His soul, his very being now spoke another language, the language of an ancient and primal spirit that pulsed in his veins.

Alex closed his eyes and brought the whistle to his lips, sending its shrill notes out into the night. He was alone with the world, his soul one with the fire and a tiny circle of light in a massive universe.

Alex threw back his head and stared at the glowing moon, feeling it too shared its power with his wanting spirit. Somewhere in the depths of his heart and soul the answers lie, they would come, as he needed them. That, and a handful of other things he was sure of on this night; his own need to fulfill his destiny, his power to see it to its end, and his need to be with the woman from whom he drew his strength.

Jessica moved sleepily in the soft down of the sleeping bag as the sound of howling in the distance woke her. She smiled, listened for other sounds of the night then reached for Alex. She opened her eyes, realizing he wasn't beside her.

Looking up half awake, she saw his broad shoulders and sinewy form standing in the opening of the tent. He was staring at her, watching her sleep. The glow of

a dwindling fire and a bright moon behind him
illuminated the curves of his body, glistened on the
tanned, rounded muscles of his arms. As he stood in
the shadow, she could not see his face until he turned
ever so slightly.

Jessica blinked. Her eyes took in the rawhide strip
against the jet-black hair, the beautiful flowing
muscles of his bare chest and then stopped at the
loincloth tied at his waist. Was this her Alex?

Jessica started to speak, but did not want to
interrupt the depth of the thought and emotion that
gripped him. An air of intensity exuded from him. She
lay still as he turned and gazed down at her.

At last she whispered. "Alex?"

"Jess." He stepped through the tent opening. "Come
to me." His voice was filled with passion as he tugged
at the zipper of the two sleeping bags they'd put
together. Laying back the flannel, he pulled her free.
He peeled her T-shirt over her head then pulled away
her panties and tossed them aside.

"Oh, Jess," he whispered as he knelt over her in the
half- light of the fire and the moon. His eyes took in
the curves of her body. "I need you tonight," he
whispered, covering her mouth with his before she
could speak. His kiss drew her lips into the fevered
warmth of his own. Her heart beat faster. Her breath
was drawn away by the hunger of his passion.

"Tonight I need to really make love to you for the
first time. I want you to know how much I love you. I
want to show you."

"Yes," she whispered, loving the feel of his hands
moving gently down the length of her body. She
reached for him, running her hands across his hips.
The buckskin loincloth was soft and sensuous to her
touch. Tonight he was her warrior.

The tenderness of his mouth caressed her body, as
he kissed every part of her, stopping longingly in all

the right places. She gasped at his moves. Slowly, he covered the expanse of her body in tender wet kisses. He ran his hands across her breasts and up the insides of her thighs. Goose bumps ran down her spine as he kissed and breathed into the crevices between her shoulder and neck then pulled her beneath him.

Tonight his passion was an intoxicating mixture of tenderness and primal need, a need for a feeling of oneness with her. He moved slowly across her, the heat of their bodies grew with the intensity of their wanting. His mouth covered hers and she parted her lips. The feeling of his hardness beneath the loincloth built an ache within her.

"I love you, Jess," he whispered between kisses. "I want to spend the rest of my life with you."

"I love you, Alex."

"I want to make love to you in the moonlight every night for the rest of my life." With a small tug he freed himself from the loincloth. "You can't leave here without me now. You know that."

"Oh, Alex, do I know that," she whispered. A groan of pleasure escaped her lips as they pressed hard to his and ecstasy filled her. Her body was one with his, their souls connected and committed forever. His intensity, his power, drove her wild. Tonight there were no inhibitions, no holding back.

Just the two of them, the earth beneath them and the sky above filled with a million stars and a million dreams. They moved in rhythm with the earth itself, slow and even, and with what was meant to be. Alex drank of the pleasure of her body as he covered her in the honey of his kisses. Smothered her in a fever of passion, a passion that built until it exploded in fiery splendor and left her panting beneath him.

She clung to him, and defied the fear in her gut that this might be the last time. Tonight was the first night of the rest of their lives. No matter what happened,

somehow they both had to make it through tomorrow.
Tonight belonged to them alone.

CHAPTER TWENTY-FOUR

Alex surveyed the hillside, sizing up the mountain before him and the task ahead. Dawn had broken over an hour ago with its fiery red hope for a new day, an hour of contemplation, and an hour of preparedness. Reaching into his shirt pocket, he felt the eagle whistle nestled next to his chest. Somehow it brought him comfort and peace. It brought him present in the moment and forthright in his destiny.

Jessica rustled in the sleeping bag behind him. "You're up early for someone who kept us awake most of the night," she said in a hoarse, sleepy voice.

"I have a lot on my mind."

She pulled a shirt around her and searched the sleeping bag for her panties. He smiled over his shoulder at her. Stumbling out into the sunshine, she yawned and stretched toward the cloudless blue sky. From behind him, she wrapped her arms around his waist and pressed her face to his back. "Today?" she asked.

"Today."

"I'm going with you."

He hesitated, thinking it was better if she stayed behind, but he couldn't speak the words. She belonged with him. He wanted nothing more than for her to be beside him, especially now, in his time of trial.

He turned and pulled her into his arms, hugged her tight and took in the scent of her hair. "I made some coffee and eggs. Better have some. It could be a long day."

She smiled up at him, gave him a quick kiss and made her way barefooted to the campfire where he'd laid out a plate and cup for her. She ate and drank in silence as he turned back to the mountain; waiting, wondering, preparing himself mentally and spiritually for whatever was to come.

Ten minutes later, Jessica touched him on the shoulder bringing him from his thoughts. "Ready?"

He put his arms around her and looked deep into her eyes. "You don't have to come with me."

She ran her fingers across the rawhide strip that remained around his forehead. "The sooner we go, the sooner it will be over."

He turned and faced the hillside. "Logic tells me to go back to the cavern and search for the chamber there. My gut tells me there's something I need to know at the petroglyph wall."

"And which will you listen to?"

"My gut for a change."

She laughed softly. "I think you're getting the hang of this."

He nodded then began his ascent up the hill. Silently, he made his way through the scrub oak and yucca plants following the same trail he'd forged a few days before. Jessica and Yellow Dog followed close behind and he drew comfort from the nearness of his two closest friends.

Half way up the hillside, they came to the protruding rocks and stopped. The feeling of dread flooded Alex's memory as momentarily he relived that night in the darkness. He tried to shake it off, wondering what gripped his heart so fiercely here. His intention had been to return to the wall, but a sensation of foreboding had kept him away, unexplainable, but very strong. Nothing tangible existed for him to fear.

Taking a deep breath, he made his way around to the wall of petroglyphs. It stood there in the shadow of the rocks. The bushes that had shrouded it for so many years lay broken beneath it. Giving up their protective cover graciously, and revealing the ancient and undisturbed magnificence of the age-old message carved in stone.

Alex leaned close. He ran his fingers down the indentations in the stone as he absorbed the emotions of the author of the message. Carefully, he traced the tiny figures. The etchings were of the people—many people as the sun shone down on them. Then the people were armed with spears and bows and arrows, a huge angry cloud was drawn over their heads.

Next the people lay on the ground, tiny scratches represented tears and drops of blood flowing from them. Undoubtedly, it depicted a war and a time of sadness. The last picture in the series showed a large figure with a knife stabbing at stick figures of a man and woman. The woman was bleeding, the man weeping.

Then the handprint trailed down the wall, as if it smeared the blood of the people, in one final dying motion. *The death of a way of life. The death of paradise and the birth of evil.* The message was clear to him. Some ancient had drawn the journey Alex had taken in his dreams.

A black cloud had come over them. The evil took over and brought them to war. The evil became so strong it overcame the young chief and the maiden, slaying her, just as in the dream. The tragic end of the story had been communicated to his heart and mind. A nightmare, a vision, whatever it was, had brought him to tears and he carried its anguish in his soul. This stone still held the energy of that tragedy, the pain and the fear.

From his fingers to the depths of his spirit, it flowed through him, engulfing him in its reality, though centuries old. Pictures from his dreams flashed through his mind, banishing the distance of hundreds of years and bringing them here and present. The emotions that somehow had been sent to him through time choked and restricted his throat.

Maybe the knowledge that their blood coursed in his veins brought it to reality. Perhaps it was the intensity of the dreams that made him feel he'd both lived and died here. Somehow they'd pulled him into their minds and emotions. He could not define it, nor did he care to. As with many things of late, it simply was.

Anger at this evil force, who changed a peaceful world forever, tried to break through his pain. He pushed his fingers into his denim-covered thighs and filled his lungs with fresh air. Hoping to pull himself back a little, he knew he must return to the moment, for it soon would demand all his faculties.

He stopped and sniffed the air. It now carried the faint scent recognizable to him from his last visit, the stench of something rotten and wrong. The feeling was in his heart, the pain, the injustice, and the fury. It was enough for him to fight for. This stinking evil had deprived these people of life, and if Alex could stop it, he'd not allow it to deprive them of eternity.

Jessica stood beside him, silent. He could feel the intensity of her emotions. A glance at her face revealed her wiping a tear from her cheek. She did not touch the wall, but her response to it was as profound as his. He grasped her hand, squeezed it tightly, but did not speak. Their message passed without words.

Alex pulled his attention back. *Where was he to go from here?* The ancient inscription was clear. The next move was up to him. Alex took a deep breath. The scent was growing stronger. The wind stilled and silence swept across the hillside. Birds ceased their song, rustling bushes stopped and stood quietly. The air itself seemed tense, as if it sensed some disturbance in the spirit world. Jessica glanced at Alex, her senses obviously taking in the change. Her nose twitched and her eyes narrowed.

"We have to keep going," Alex said, determined not to be distracted from his mission. He studied the petroglyph. Part of it contained what looked like a long tunnel with arrows pointing in two directions. He pointed it out. "I think this means something."

He stepped back and studied the rock formation up the hill from the writings. His eye followed the soil along the rock's edge. Taking two long steps, he knelt and felt the dampness of the earth at the base of a small piñon tree then scraped aside some of the darker soil near the trunk.

Jessica and Yellow Dog looked on curiously. Alex rose to his feet and grasped the tree around the trunk and lifted it effortlessly out of the earth. Its root ball was wrapped in burlap. As he pulled, the soil fell away from the scrub oak next to it and revealed scraps of burlap there also. Behind them, a large open hole gaped in the stone.

"My gosh," Jessica gasped. "A second entrance to the cavern." Her eyes went instantly to a second set of petroglyphs etched around the opening to the cave.

Alex squatted and examined them, yet another part of this ancient story. Running his hand across the etchings, he was having more difficulty in interpreting their message. These were scattered, each one different, probably the work of many hands rather than just one author.

Their message was difficult to follow. They were worn more deeply than the first. His fingers felt them out. Their emotion was very different, sadness—deep sadness—grief. Suddenly, he pulled away as if he'd touched a hot cinder. Intense pain, gut-wrenching fear, dreadful evil was written in this message. Its energy was unmistakable.

No. He wouldn't allow it to touch his spirit. Whatever called to him from deep within this cave had to be found, had to be faced. He closed his eyes, centered himself, and focused his mind and body on his mission. Trying to enter the zone of his dream state and connect with the internal peace and strength, he drew upon his only weapon in this coming battle of the spirit.

Alex looked at Jessica who now held the lantern. She nodded and lit it for him. Yellow Dog let out a low growl as he sniffed at the cave opening then raised his head. His ears twitched as if he sensed something in the air he did not like.

Alex took the lantern and shined the light inside. He could see very little. "I'll be back for you," he said as he let himself down the short drop to the cavern floor.

The air was cold and damp and the wretched smell was almost unbearable. He closed off his other senses and tried to turn inward, opening himself to the guidance he hoped would come. Piles of rock lined both sides of a small chamber ten or more feet in length, leaving only a narrow path. Up ahead, he could see an opening about four feet high between the cavern's ceiling and a massive pile of stone. It appeared there had been a cave-in at some point that blocked the chamber. The tiny space near the top was the only window into what lay beyond. He placed his boot toe into the pile of stones and started to step up.

"Wait, Alex," Jessica called then clambered down the drop off. "I'm coming with you."

He turned the light in her direction as she slid down the rock and dirt ledge and landed on her feet at the entrance. Her sneakers made a soft squish on the cave floor as she landed.

Making a face, she put the back of her hand over her nose. Her eyes darkened and caught his in the dim light of the lantern. "I've smelled this odor before."

"Ignore it." He could afford no distractions.

She moved in his direction, the small rocks rolled under her feet.

"Watch yourself." He pulled her next to him before he turned back toward the pile of rock that lay ahead.

He nodded toward the heap. "I saw evidence of this on the other side. This side of the cavern was blocked off by a rockslide at some time."

She pointed to the opening above them. "What do you make of that?"

"That's where we're going," he answered without hesitation.

A spill of rocks at the entrance and a yap from Yellow Dog announced that he wasn't going to be left behind either. The dog landed on the stone floor and came toward them, keeping low and growling defensively as he sniffed the air. Alex shone the light on the animal's face, his other dedicated and determined companion.

"Easy, boy," he said softly. "It's going to be okay."

Jessica squeezed his arm, expressing her hope for that outcome as well.

Alex made his way up the rock pile to the opening. "Stay close," he called over his shoulder and the two followed him. Shining the lantern over the top, he could see a glimpse of the walls and ceiling of another chamber beyond. He pushed himself through, holding the lantern behind him so Jessica could see.

Alex crawled into the tiny tunnel and over to the pile of rock on the opposite side. Before him lay another large chamber, partially covered by rock but still accessible. He helped Jessica through and she balanced herself beside him. They made their way over the rocks and down to the cave floor on the other side. Yellow Dog made his way down the sharp rocks, following close behind.

A combination of dread and blackness flowed through Alex, an intermingling of oppression and anxiety. Like a black shroud being pulled over his heart.

"It's cold in here." Jessica shivered. "And awful," she added.

Alex raised the lantern high, illuminating the area near them. His eyes caught the metallic glint of two shovels leaned against the rock to his left. Jessica looked toward them, too. "McCabe and Wilson," he grunted, knowing full well who the perpetrators had been. It didn't take a two-bit lawman to figure that one out.

Alex shone the light to his right and took in a gruesome, but familiar sight. A human arm bone lay on the cave floor next to what appeared to be some fresh digging. In two steps he was there, dropping to his knees and carefully examining the bone and the area around it. Above it was the rest of the human skeleton, half buried in the rock. Jessica watched over his shoulder and let out a tiny gasp as she realized what it was.

Alex brushed at the soil, uncovered the bones and carefully fingered the remnants of a common and recognizable burial cloth, a turkey feather blanket. This was no incidental skeleton that was a victim of the rockslide. This was an ancient burial. Holding the light closer, he brushed at the dirt again, this time revealing a tiny shard of an ancient pot.

Rising, Alex held the light high and walked along the wall of tumbled stones that lined the right side of the cave. His foot hit something and it spun ahead of him. Casting the light in its direction, he realized it was part of a human skull. He stopped in his tracks and raised his hand in front of Jessica who walked at his side. "No farther," he told her. The floor ahead of them was littered with rock—and the remnants of human remains.

"Oh, God. This is the chamber." Emotion filled Jessica's voice. "The place where the bodies were given to the evil." As if her acknowledgment added strength to some hideous power, a faint rumble came from somewhere deep inside the bowels of the earth.

Scanning the area ahead and around them on all sides, a sickening feeling came over Alex. A mass grave. The largest he'd ever heard of in his time. Skeleton after skeleton, lay in rows ahead of him, some partially covered by the rockslide.

With the light, he quickly examined the ones that lay directly in front of him. His jaw clenched at the tiny scattering of broken pots and shells, scraps of an assortment of once treasured and sacred possessions lay around them. They'd been picked clean by grave robbers. Wilson and McCabe.

An odd sensation crept over him. His sick feeling wrestled with a burst of greed and anxiety that grew in him. Alex's heart raced. Beads of perspiration appeared on his face. His stomach was taut, his breathing heavy and fast as his eyes took in the scene and his mind absorbed the magnitude of it. A mass grave. A burial chamber containing hundreds of corpses. The archaeological find of the century. A discovery that could bear his name. His alone. A discovery that would put his name in the history books, make him world-renowned in his field. Him. Alex Nakai.

He squinted and blinked his eyes. A fire of greed that craved fame and fortune burned in the center of his gut. He pulled at his shirt collar. Heat flushed through him. He'd dreamed of this. Worked for this all his life.

Alex stopped himself. Stiffened against whatever was raging inside of him. What was happening? He tried to breathe in some air but it was stifling with its sickening stench. Something caught his eye and seemed to call to him. He wet his lips. *What could it hurt?* He was okay. He was in control.

Alex set the lantern on a rock and dug at a tiny object glistening in the light. He began gently, brushing at the dust slowly at first. Soon his breath was coming in short choppy spurts. Something overtook him. Alex dug faster. Frantically pulling away the earth and debris without any regard. He gave it a jerk. Bones cracked, then snapped, as he pried his trophy from the grasp of dead fingers. He heard Jessica gasp behind him, but something drove him on. In his hand he held a tiny pot.

Opening a trembling hand, he brushed away the layers of dirt and held it to the light. Holding it close, he could see a familiar black and white pattern. Oh, God. It was familiar, because he'd looked at it on the chip in his pocket every day for months. Oh, God. Not now. Not now.

Turning it shakily in the light of the lantern, he rubbed at the dirt, straining to make out the image on the front of the piece. Was it the image of a feathered serpent? A classic Mayan symbol?

He blinked and swallowed, rubbing at his eyes in the dim light. Was he seeing right? Was he holding this or was he imagining it? His head was fuzzy, his vision fogged. What had come over him? His stomach lurched, his insides burned. Still, he held it in his hand.

A stab of tightness and pain grasped at his chest. Wait. There was something more. The light reflected off something silver above the folded hands of the skeleton. It was a piece of jewelry of some sort. He leaned forward, and pulled at it. It was secured around the neck of its owner. His heart hammered, his head felt light. It didn't matter. He needed to see it. He pulled again. And again. And again.

"Alex," Jessica's hand touched his shoulder. "What are you doing?"

"Look at this, Jess. Just look at this." He held up the pot for Jessica. Her face was clouded with horror. His hand was wrapped around the piece of jewelry. He pulled at it once more then looked back at Jessica.

Alex stopped short, his stomach jumping into his throat for a second. He ran his hands over his face. What the hell was he doing? He sat back on his heels and took several deep breaths.

Something strange had come over him. He'd completely lost the focus of the mission he'd come to accomplish. Suddenly, his hands felt dirty. Unclean. He rubbed them together then down his thighs trying to remove whatever it was that clung to him. He reached for Jessica's hand.

"Are you all right?" she asked.

"I think so." He set the pot down carefully and pushed the palms of his hands tight to his eyes.

The storm in Alex's head was clearing. He felt woozy. What had grabbed hold of him? He pulled his thoughts to Nechi and their meeting last night. This was part of the battle he had spoken of. But God, dear God, he'd never dreamed it would hit him like this or hit him so personally.

Alex looked at the pot and the necklace. He had to move on into the chamber. What would he do about this? He wasn't sure yet. He had only fought one battle. Maybe the answer would be clear by the end of the war.

Alex rose and turned toward Jessica, turning his back to the bone-lined wall. Glancing down at the

amulet that hung from Jessica's neck, its glow drew
his gaze to it. He felt dizzy, faint and light-headed.
Something in his gut burned like a fiery ball. The glow
of the amulet in the lantern's light washed him in a
calming feeling and centered his thoughts back on
finding the warrior's tomb. Turning, he wiped cold
perspiration from his face.

What was wrong with him? Jessica must have
thought he was a ghoul the way he tugged at that
necklace. God, he was a ghoul, at least for a moment.
But the burials, the discovery, the pot. Again the
amulet's glow drew him to it. *What was it about that
stone?* He couldn't take his eyes from it now. His spirit
surged, flooding his soul with strength and power,
pushing aside all the thoughts that raced in his mind.
A voice inside called to him, coupled with many
ancient voices from somewhere far away. *"Only you,
Alex,"* they echoed. *"Because of the bloodline that
courses in your veins."* Nechi's voice was strong in his
head. *"You and your brothers are the final
descendents."* In his mind's eye, he saw a warrior,
bare-chested, clothed only in a loincloth. Strength
flowed through him, the strength and power of that
warrior. He was ready to face his enemy, unseen,
lurking here, stinking, wretched, and deceitful.

Alex held the lantern toward the opposite side of the
cave. "If this chamber adjoins the temple, it has to be
farther in that direction," he said, purposefully. He
walked forward picking his way through the debris on
the floor.

Jessica followed close behind. Grabbing a pick from
McCabe's stash, he walked along the wall on the left
side of the chamber. Something pulled at him,
beckoned him in that direction.

He squinted trying to see, opening his spirit totally
to the help he had prayed for over the past days and
nights. A glimmer of light caught his eye, but then

disappeared. Perhaps a sign of some sort. He walked toward it. At the end of the long chamber, he realized what appeared to be part of the cave-in was actually part of a manmade stonewall. The same stone construction as the remains of the walls outside at the dig.

The rancid odor sickened Alex as he reached the other end of the passage. The smell, the cold dampness, the extreme oppressive feeling, all of it engulfed him as he walked among the bones of the dead. A chill ran through his body and he prayed silently he was not leading them into the bowels of hell.

Alex placed one hand on the wall, as he held the lantern high in the other and followed the crumbled stone halfway across the chamber. Something was here, something he must find. The feeling in his gut was stronger here. His chest filled with a warmth and tension he couldn't fully define. Something was driving him on. As he reached the center, a blue-green object in the rock wall caught his eye. He knelt.

Jessica dropped to her knees beside him. "What is it?"

Alex brushed away the debris from a very large piece of silver and turquoise jewelry. "Look at this," he said breathlessly. "Just look at this piece."

Jessica leaned forward, trying to get a better look. "It's huge," she said. "What can it possibly be?"

"I think it's part of a headdress." He paused. "Maybe the headdress of a holy man. I've seen pictures of one similar to it that was found at Chaco Canyon."

"Oh." She covered her mouth with her hand. "Do you think it was his?"

Alex tugged at it, but it was caught on something. He moved away the rocks around it, one stone at a time. The first few stones revealed something threaded through it. Alex set aside several more stones then held the light close. "My God, Jess," he uttered, as his trained eye took in the sight.

"What, Alex. What do you see?"

He did not answer, but anxiously dug at the stones until he had revealed the remnants of a turkey feather blanket. Pulling it aside, he exposed the upper body of a skeleton with its arms wrapped through the headdress.

As he ran the light up and down, Jessica gasped. "Oh, Alex. I don't want to see any more."

He ran his hand down the breastbone of the skeleton to where it was nearly severed from the rib cage. Silently, he observed the strands of long black hair still attached to the skull.

"It's her," he whispered. "I think it's her."

"Snowcloud?" Jessica uttered in horrified amazement. "Alex, I don't want to see this. I can't."

"I know," he answered, lost in his deep train of thought and wonder. Rising, he looked down at the skeleton then to the wall behind it.

"Jess. This is it," he said, turning the light toward her. This must be the tomb. That's why they put her here."

"Are you sure?"

"I don't know," he said, but inside he had no doubt. He had arrived.

Alex looked down at the headdress. Something flooded through him. What was he doing? What a prize. Nothing like this had been found anywhere but Chaco. This place was a gold mine for the archaeological community. He really could be famous. Honored by his peers. The voice in his head hammered at him.

A voice in his heart cried out in indignation. *This is wrong. Look away. This isn't about glory.*

Alex wavered, a stabbing pain ran through his head and his hands trembled. The burning returned in his chest. Scattered words and thoughts raced in his mind. *The opportunity of a lifetime. This is your chance.* He rolled his shoulders and mopped the sweat from his brow, but the voices wouldn't stop. *The pot. It's proof. The link you've been searching for. You're a fool.*

A loud rumble came from behind the wall. It rocked him on his feet. He staggered. Weakened by the rush of emotion, he fell to his knees.

Yet another voice echoed inside his head. *This is a place of sanctity. These are your ancestor's bones. Leave this poor woman in peace.*

Alex grasped his head in his hands and rose to his feet. He looked at Jessica, who stood staring at him aghast. Pulling back the pick, he hit the wall hard. Pieces of rock scattered in every direction.

A wrong that was done seven hundred years ago had to be righted. Here. Today. He landed another blow. The weight of the pick seemed to increase with every swing. Still, he continued. A cloud of pictures ran through his mind, and a chorus of voices argued in his brain. He shut them out. The weight of the pick was almost unbearable now. The handle grew burning hot in his grasp.

"You evil bastard. You can't stop me," Alex screamed.

Jessica and Yellow Dog huddled near an adjacent wall and looked on wide-eyed. He focused his energy on the head of the pick, one stroke at a time. Something jerked hard against it, seeming to try to pull it from his hands. He held fast to it. With every ounce of strength he pulled it back, and away from the unseen force. He dared not stop. Bit by bit the rock crumbled away. This was a battle of pure will, both physical and mental strength. This thing was testing him on all fronts.

Sweat streamed into his eyes, nearly blinding him to his progress. Still, he did not stop. The muscles in his arms ached with searing pain, but he kept on. He had to open this wall. Behind it lay his true mission.

At last, he lowered the pick. He'd made a hole about four inches in diameter. Leaning forward, he attempted to peer inside. A belch of flaming hot gas and putrid odor blasted him backward. It hit him with the force of a cannon ball. Piercing pain nearly blinded him as his head slammed into a rock pile. Blackness hovered then threatened to pull him in. The fire in his brain tempted him to allow it to take him.

Alex lay back against the pile of rocks, his head spinning. The air had been knocked from his lungs. Pain clenched at his rib cage and shot through his back and he struggled for breath. A wave of nausea washed through him, his abdomen tightened. Somewhere in the distance a tiny voice spoke through the fog, calling him back.

Alex wasn't going to die here, and neither was Jess. It couldn't end here. A picture of the maiden on the altar shot through his mind. He damn sure wouldn't watch his one true love die—not again. He caught his breath and pulled himself up on wobbly legs. They gave way beneath him. It wouldn't stop him.

The pain of the rough stone and small sharp rocks beneath his hands and knees was almost as intense as the pain in his back and head. Alex clenched his jaw against it and crawled forward. Now was the time he must draw from the inner. The spirits must not fail him now. He had to go on.

Speak to me. Alex's inner voice screamed into the spirit world. Forcing the air from his lungs, he clenched his fists and released his own will entirely. He gave it to the only force he could trust with everything. His body and mind drained of his own power. He fell flat on his stomach to the floor.

Hold on. Hold on and believe. A voice echoed in a far distant corner of his mind. A blinding flash of light surged through him, giving him the strength to crawl again.

An intense heat burned deep in his breast. This time it was not the work of the hideous beast. Reaching into his shirt pocket, he grasped the eagle bone whistle. Crawling on hands and knees, he put his hand up and signaled Jessica to stay back. She stood clinging to the adjacent stonewall.

Alex cleared his mind and drew from the burning force in his core. Where the young man had failed, he must succeed, or there would never be another chance. He could not imagine a strength greater than the force that flowed through him right now. He rose to his feet and pushed on.

Alex was the final hope for the soul of the young chieftain. Who could say, maybe the final hope for the future of the people. His people, if he were worthy enough to stand among them. He struggled to pull back the events of the dream. The old chief had spoken the words. He had told the young man what he must remember. It had to be the key.

The thoughts of the archaeological treasure surrounding him hammered at his brain. They pried open the door he was trying so hard to keep closed. At his feet lay a treasure people of his profession would kill for. The discovery few would ever experience in an entire lifetime of digging in the sheltering earth.

Alex pushed the idea from his mind. The evil was pitting his strength of spirit against his career dream. Against the one physical thing he wanted most. But now he must allow an energy other than his own to fight it. He must not doubt the strength of the force that drove through him. He must simply let it use his human body to do its work.

Remembering the tiny skeleton he'd held in his hands on the first day of excavating, he clung to the emotion in his heart that day. It had been a tiny glimmer of temptation, a clue of what was to come as his final challenge.

Alex dropped to his knees, hoping the prayer-like position could somehow bring him closer to the spirits. Leaning into the fiery heat that still spewed from the opening, his face and neck seared with pain.

"I need your help," he whispered. He focused on the dream, pulling the picture of the old chief's face into his mind's eye. The heat bit at his ears and forced him to close his eyes. *His words—his words. What did he say?* "In the end it is the only thing that can save you. The power of—" What were the words? "The power of the two."

The picture of the old chief flashed before him. In the man's hand had lain the whistle and the amulet. "Call the spirits with the whistle, and keep the evil from you with the amulet." The rest of the words had been there all along. They had drifted in his subconscious and not until this moment had he been able to call them to his mind. The words the young chieftain had forgotten and never used to save his people.

"Jess, give me the amulet," he cried. She quickly pulled it over her head and placed it gently into his outstretched hand. "No. Don't let go of it," he commanded, suddenly realizing why she had been unaffected in the cavern. "You can't let go."

Together they grasped the rawhide strip. The amulet seemed to emit a light of its own. Warm against his skin, a new rush of spiritual power flowed through him. It filled him with the knowledge of the person he truly was. The warmth of the amulet lessened the heat from the open hole in the chamber. Cross-legged now, he faced the tomb and together they laid the amulet in his lap.

He brought the whistle to his lips and blew into it. The notes carried on the still air and hung around him. A presence seemed to hover close to him, a shadowy image of four elders appeared on the wall above the hole.

Their faces were old and wrinkled, but their eyes were keen beneath an assortment of ancient headdresses and robes. Their message passed to him, he now had the power to break the evil one's curse. He bowed his head and to his surprise spoke an ancient chant. Raising the amulet above his head, he moved it toward the wall and placed its fiery heat to the gaping hole.

White light glowed in the opening and the blast of heat ceased. He did not know the words he spoke, but their ancient meaning was clear to his heart. The glow from the amulet spread across the wall, covering the ancient faces with its blinding light.

A hum began deep in the bowels of the earth and carried through the cavern. The amulet's light illuminated the interior of the dark damp place. From out of the hole in the rock wall floated a large golden bubble, an iridescent ball suspended in the air.

All around them, smaller blue and gold bubbles floated up into the air. Alex rose to his feet, watching in amazement. The bubbles gathered and hovered near the ceiling then they floated toward the small gap at the end of the cave and out into the light of day.

"Alex," Jessica gasped. "What are they?"

"Freed souls." Alex spoke with a wisdom and knowing he could not identify, but knew his words were pure truth.

Grasping her hand, he made his way toward the hole at the entrance, following the procession toward sunlight. He stopped and looked back at the cavern, scanning the treasure of knowledge and history that lay there. He boosted Jessica toward the opening in the rock and urged Yellow Dog along behind her.

Once on the other side, they were drawn toward the door where the tiny blue lights floated into the sky. The large golden bubble stopped, changing in shape to a mist-like image of a young warrior. His long black hair adorned with the feathers of an eagle hung down on his bronze chest. Beside him appeared the image of the beautiful maiden from Alex's dreams.

He raised a hand to Alex, his message passed into Alex's mind without a spoken word. "Thank you, my brother, I will see you someday in paradise." He turned toward the maiden and as their lips met, the images faded into nothingness. Surrounded by hundreds of tiny gold and blue lights, they were carried off into the sky.

Alex turned to Jessica. Her fingers were pressed tight to her lips. A tear glistened on her cheek. "You did it, Alex. They're together at last."

"It isn't done yet," he said, squaring his shoulders and facing the pile of rock behind him. He had done what he was called to do now he must do what was right. Climbing up, he began moving rock into the gaping hole.

Jessica followed and handed rocks to him. Quickly, they piled the opening full until only a tiny space remained.

"Wait," Jessica said. She pulled her backpack around and took several pages of notepaper from it. "There," she said, stuffing them into the opening.

"Oh, Jess," he said, softly. "Your story." He hadn't thought about what effect this would have on her.

"It's okay." She looked into his eyes and passed him another stone to put into the opening. "Like the burials, the story has to remain a secret."

He stopped and looked at her. "Sometimes the right thing has to come first."

"Don't worry about me. I've traded one dream for another. Things will work out for the best somehow."

He wanted to pull her into his arms and kiss her, but it wasn't possible right now. "You know, you're quite a woman, Jessica Sinclair." He choked back emotions that wanted to spill out.

"I've grown a lot in a short time. What's important is a lot clearer now."

They piled stones until the space disappeared completely. Then slid down the rock pile and climbed out into the bright sun of the Colorado day. Alex surveyed the piñon tree and the scrub oak he'd thrown aside earlier. Pulling the burlap from around them, he planted them in the ground in front of the opening. He paused, listening for a moment. He thought he heard a rumble deep in the earth. He shot Jessica a quick glance. They both smiled as he piled the dirt as high as he could behind the bushes to help conceal what lay beyond.

"There," he said. "Think that will hold them for another seven hundred years?"

"I hope so," she said. "What are you going to tell the University?"

"That there was nothing unusual here," he said, tamping the dirt tight around the roots of the plants. "I've got a truck load of common Anasazi pottery. Thanks to McCabe and Wilson. There are thousands of sites around this area. We can only excavate the ones that hold promise. There are just too many. They'll take my recommendations."

"I hope this doesn't damage your career."

"My career," he snorted. "Seven hundred years from now what difference will it make?"

Looking at the ground, she moved her foot in the soil, a sad look came over her face.

"Why so down in the dumps?" Alex rose to his feet and brushed the dirt from his hands.

"It's over. I'm not sure where to go from here."

He shrugged. "Well, I don't know." He looked down at his boots. "But I guess tomorrow we could go into town and look at some rings."

Jessica looked up at him and a smile crept across her face. He swept her up in his arms and kissed her. "I want to marry you here at the mesa," he whispered.

Alex pulled her close, envisioning her beside him on the mesa in a white buckskin wedding dress. His dream lover, his soul mate through all eternity.

CHAPTER TWENTY-FIVE

Voices of the ancients whispered through the trees and carried on a warm comforting wind. The chill crept from Jessica's bones as she perched high on a wall at the Sun Temple watching a fiery salmon sunrise. The red stone was hard and cold beneath her, but the warmth inside made her oblivious to the outside world.

Just days ago she hadn't realized this new part of her soul existed. Neither the warm wind that suddenly swept over her nor the appearance of Nechi a few yards away, were a surprise to her. Truth was, she knew he would appear. It was time for the pretense to fall away. At last, she understood. Nechi was not of this world, at least not spiritually. The voice that spoke through him was not his own, and not of this plain.

"I'd hoped to have a chance to say goodbye," she said as tightness formed in her throat at the sight of him. His tall form approached, climbed the stones as if they were stair steps and seated himself beside her on the rock wall.

"A fitting place for such an event." He smiled a crooked smile and placed a gentle hand over hers.

"I started to go to the kiva," she said, rubbing her boot in the red dust of the hand cut building blocks.

"You now understand the connection between us. You, the spirit, and myself. Once one learns to hear, we learn that much of the universe speaks as one voice." Nechi was without expression as he spoke and his eyes followed the distant mesas. The feeling of his oneness with the land was evident. His mind seemed to circle with a hawk that floated in the sky, the early morning sunlight glistening on its wings.

Jessica struggled to hold back the lump that formed between her heart and her throat. She swallowed hard.

Glancing in her direction, he adjusted his cowboy hat and pulled it low over his eyes. "There is no need for sadness."

"But I will miss you, even though I've only known you for a short time."

"You have known me for many ages. You will know me for many more." Again the wisdom flowed from him.

"If this is true, why has it taken me so long to find you?"

"You have had a different path to walk for a while. Now you have come home. Your ears have opened to the guidance of voices that speak to you from beyond. All souls walk these paths in different ways."

"You know, somehow I've always believed in your world, but things—tragic things seem to constantly separate me from it. Why is life that way?" A tear threatened as she thought of her parents and her aunt.

"We are tested many times, but each of us is fulfilling a purpose."

"And after that?"

"We walk the paths beyond." A smile crossed his face and a peaceful light shone in his eyes.

Jessica was silent for a moment. "And do those paths cross again?"

"Many times over the ages."

"So where am I going from here?"

Nechi smiled. "That is not for me to tell you, but for you to discover. But remember that which is not destiny, is choice.""What about Alex? Is he choice or destiny?"

Nechi's mouth tightened and he stifled a smile. "Your own heart knows the answer to that question."

Jessica raised her eyebrows as a grin burst through her serious face. "This time I understand exactly what you mean. Can you tell me one more thing? What will happen to Wilson and McCabe?"

"Wilson is gone. He is still trying to run away from the only thing he can never escape—himself. Eventually, he will have to face his own conscience, no matter how far he goes. McCabe is another story. His mind now has no memory of what he has done." Nechi looked into her eyes. "Sometimes it is hard for us to understand that those who do evil things are not always truly bad people. Sometimes they are driven to do these things by mysterious forces."

"Oh, I've learned that one firsthand. I saw what was happening to McCabe. Wilson, I may never understand, but I know he saved our lives."

"Yes, he did. And I have it from a very reliable source, that the outcome of all this will be a better life for everyone involved. Love will conquer and heal all wounds. You needn't worry about that."

"Thank you, Nechi. I feel much better knowing this." She paused. "I guess the only one I haven't been able to help is Simon. I feel like he's the one I've abandoned and hurt the most." There was the matter of her writing career, too, that had been shoved aside. She had no idea where her career would go from here, but somehow she was sure she would find a way to deal with it later.

"That one, dear lady, has not been made right, but listen and trust. If it is destined to be, or if you choose to, it may right itself."

She smiled. "Okay. It hasn't failed me yet, so I'll trust it to the powers that be." She contemplated her next question for a moment. "And that evil thing, it is gone for good, isn't it?"

Nechi's eyes narrowed, he rubbed his lips together as if not wanting to speak the next words. "Evil has been with us since the beginning of time. I cannot tell you that Alex has seen the last of it."

"Oh, God," Jessica whispered. Could she ever face such a thing again?

"I am afraid this part of Alex's new life will be the biggest challenge."

Jessica ran her hand through her hair. "If it is to be, I'll have to learn to live with it."

Nechi nodded and adjusted his cowboy hat. "It is time for me to leave you, pretty lady. Go now and follow your path. Chosen or destined, it matters not. Seek love, find peace of spirit, and do the right thing. The rest will come." He rose and put his hand up to the wind, allowing it to blow between his fingers.

"I will miss you." She choked back tears through a smile she could not stop. She rose and gave him a hug.

He smiled down at her. "You cannot miss that which will always be with you. Just as the wind is always near, so shall I be." He returned her embrace then gently pulled away. "As certain as the sunrise, there is always help a whisper away. You only need to listen and let it in."

With that he jumped to the ground, creating a small cloud of red dust that rose and twisted into a whirling cloud. When the cloud disappeared, Nechi was gone. A few yards away in the fringe of the forest, the white wolf cast a look back in Jessica's direction and trotted away.

Jessica stood in the morning rays of sun, a new hope in her bruised heart and a new horizon in the distance.

A voice spoke behind her. "I was hoping to find you." Jessica turned to meet the beaming smile of Dorothy McCabe. She was radiant this morning. Years had disappeared from her face. Light danced in her eyes and pink roses bloomed in the color of her cheeks.

"Dorothy, what are you doing out here?" Jessica met her and exchanged a hug. Dorothy grasped her hands and exclaimed, "I don't know how to thank you."

"Thank me?" Jessica asked, wondering why Jonathan's arrest would have brought such appreciation.

"You brought my Jon back to me. I saw him and he's Jon again. That horrible thing, those awful fits, they're gone."

Jessica smiled, but was still puzzled. "But won't there be a trial?"

"Well, thanks to that archaeologist fellow, Alex, the sheriff said they did something called a plea bargain. Anyway, Jon has agreed to psychiatric help and community service and he won't have to go to jail."

"Really?" Jessica smiled and shook her head.

"Jon gave all the credit to you. I knew it. I just knew it when you came."

"I think the credit really belongs to Alex, and to the friend I just met here. I wish I could have introduced you to him."

Dorothy looked at her curiously. "Friend?" She glanced around the temple.

"Yes, a dear friend. His name is Nechi."

Dorothy smiled. "Nechi." She let the name roll off her tongue. "Why that sounds just like the Navajo word for spirit."

Jessica raised her eyebrows and the two exchanged a silent look of realization.

"Well, my dear, I must go. I'm moving back to the ranch today, but I couldn't let you leave without saying goodbye and thanking you." Dorothy hugged her again. As she stepped back her eyes went to the amulet Jessica still wore around her neck. Dorothy smiled and touched the stone gently with her finger.

"What a beautiful crystal. I might have known. The Navajos use them for healing. And you sure healed my Jon. You really are a very special lady." She turned and walked back across the parking lot.

Jessica watched her leave, fingering the amulet and enjoying a warm glow over the happiness the McCabe's had reclaimed. She looked around, absorbed the feeling of the mesa for one more long moment then headed back toward her vehicle. She was only a few steps away when Alex pulled up beside her.

"Jess." Alex was breathless with excitement. "I've been looking all over for you."

"Just taking care of a little unfinished business."

His face was filled with mixed emotions. "I have some news that may delay our plans. At least temporarily."

"Oh?"

"I called the University this morning and they're scrapping this project."

"Well, we knew that."

"They want me to go to work on another site. I'll have to pack up the camp and leave right away. I start work first thing in the morning."

"Where, Alex?"

"Just a few miles away. Tucked away in another canyon and only accessible by foot."

"That sounds okay, but why the rush and all the excitement."

"Jess, they suspect—cannibalism. You know I have to go."

"Of course." Her head reeled for a moment at his words. "Give me time to grab my laptop and a notebook. I'm going with you."

He smiled as she stepped forward and planted a kiss firmly on his lips. "I was hoping that would be your answer. I wasn't sure I could leave without you.

We make a pretty mean team. And I plan to make that permanent." He winked and kissed her again.

Stepping toward her car, she called to him. "I'm right behind you. Oh, and give me time to make a quick phone call to Simon. I think he's going to be interested in this one."

Alex waved and drove away. Jessica pulled out behind him. Her life had just taken another U-turn, and she had a feeling this was only the beginning.

The End

Turn the page for an excerpt from:
EAGLE DANCER
THE CRYSTAL LEGACY SERIES
BOOK TWO

CHAPTER ONE

Present Day

The girl's shoes clattered on the brick-lined path that wove through the tall trees in the city park. The sound echoed. She slowed her steps, glanced around and listened. A dark eerie feeling crept over her and held fast like the smattering of damp leaves clung to the stones under her feet. It was broad daylight, mid-afternoon in high summer, and no logical reason existed for the foreboding possessing her soul.

She would be late getting home and no doubt she'd be in trouble—again. It was a stupid choice to listen to her friends. At fifteen she should be more responsible, but those were her mother's words, not her own.

Shaking off the sensation, she picked up her pace. Crossing at the signal, she made her way down the quiet street. Distant flute music from the plaza drifted on a breeze that swept hair across her eyes. She tucked the long strands behind her ear. The music was high pitched and surreal. Normally, it made her feel wild and free, stirred something in her soul. Today it ran a chill down her spine. A heavy feeling carried on the wind and hung in her chest unlike anything she'd ever experienced.

Her feet seemed weighted, protesting their movement as if they didn't want to go this way. But some other force drew her down the street. A whispering voice seemed to call her name. An invisible hand pushed her forward, onward, ever closer—.

A large black and white magpie pecked at the brick sidewalk a few yards ahead. As she neared, it turned a dark eye in her direction. The bird sized her up then hopped into the shadowy space between two adobe buildings. Suddenly, a boy clad in black stepped from the alley and into her path. A black hat, pulled low, hovered over his eyes, blocking them from clear view. A black and white feather hung from the hat's brim partially covering one side of his face. He folded his arms and turned in her direction. She watched from the corner of her eye and attempted to sidestep him. As she did, she glanced up.

"Oh, it's you," she uttered, relief flooding her at the sight of a familiar face. The boy didn't answer. His gaze met hers, but the strange eyes that peered from under the hat's brim were like those of a wild cat watching its prey. Their odd light stopped her heart in mid-beat.

Fear grabbed at her throat, and robbed her voice. Something about those eyes filled her with terror. She must get past him. She hurried ahead. His hand caught her arm, stopping her short.

"Let go," she squeaked in protest. A flash of white passed through her field of vision. He spun her around, her head whipped back. Piercing pain and intense pressure seared her neck. It took away her breath, stole her voice before she could scream.

She grabbed at her throat. Her fingers grasped a taut cord. Fighting for air, her lungs racked with pain. The cord tightened. Spots exploded behind her eyes. Her knees buckled. The weight of her body drove the cord deeper. She struggled to her feet. Her throat seized and she fell to the ground. A sensation of slow motion masked her senses. Blackness engulfed her. She fought it at first then at last gave way to it.

In the midst of the blackness, a distant white light burned then came closer. Bright, warm, soothing. It beckoned her weary body to its comfort. A drifting feeling pulled at her. She allowed herself to move toward it, away from the agony in her throat and lungs. The pain eased.

Into the light stepped a shadow. An image emerged from the bright glow as if it had stepped through a cloud. The silhouette became a dark-haired man, broad at the shoulders and narrow at the hips. Floating around him in the light were feathers, brown and white feathers. His face cleared. Soft brown eyes greeted her. Hands reached for her, offering help. A breeze tousled his hair, as a slightly crooked smile deepened a scar on his upper lip. The intensity of the light overshadowed his face, the image faded and the pain was gone.

The icy lash of a crashing wave jarred Nathan Nakai back to reality. He shifted his feet and steadied himself on the San Francisco pier. The haunting picture of the dark-haired girl with the rope tight around her neck vanished as quickly as it had overtaken him. He loosened his tie. The pain in his throat eased and he wiped beads of cold perspiration mingled with ocean mist from his face.

Breathing in the cool salty air, his head began to clear. The girl's face was ingrained in his mind. He shook his head trying to push it away. Maybe he needed a sabbatical from this fast-paced life worse than he thought. Or maybe this was the sign he was seeking here in the darkness and solitude of a foggy night, as his discontent churned like the white-capped waves that pounded the wooden pillars and planks beneath his feet.

The unsettling emotion lingered as Nate stared into the heavy fog that rolled into the bay. He pulled the overcoat up around his ears. He glanced over his shoulder at the towering buildings and city lights of downtown behind him then looked out across the rolling ocean waters that disappeared into fog and darkness. He thought of the vast horizon beyond where sea met sky and appeared to become one and he knew without doubt—his purpose here had been served.

Gathering focus back to his purpose and his future, he reread the job offer he grasped in his hand by the light of a nearby street lamp. The letterhead read, "Public Defenders Department, Staff Attorneys District Office, Santa Fe, New Mexico."

Why the hell had he even considered leaving his successful law practice in San Francisco? He'd asked himself that question a million times and still he didn't have a clue. Some voice deep inside was calling him, something he couldn't identify, something he couldn't name and stronger tonight than it had ever been.

The cold wind that blew in from the bay suddenly shifted, and ran a chill down the back of his neck. He pulled the coat collar tighter. He only knew one thing. He had to go.

Flipping aside the job offer, he eyed the envelope he clutched behind it, the letter from his grandfather. He'd received it along with a package two days earlier. The chilling words of the strange letter haunted him and now he regretted not taking the time to open the box. He was curious, but the package was in a moving van in route to Santa Fe. Undeniably, his grandfather's words had invoked thoughts of his family, and kindled a curiosity about his own heritage.

Nate reflected on his last conversation with his brother Alex. He'd wondered at times if Alex had slipped a cog somewhere between California and Southwestern Colorado. After all the time his archaeologist brother had spent poking around old ruins in Mexico and South America, maybe something had gone wrong with his thinking.

But it was Alex's words that had started a fire in Nate's soul—a need for change that had become insatiable. An emptiness he'd never realized existed had opened up like a gaping pit in the core of his being. He sighed. *Gee thanks little brother.*

Nate rubbed his temples. He was tired, yet he couldn't put his finger on why. Worse yet, he was sickened by his own existence? Maybe it was the big city, the people, the rat race—

Or maybe he was simply sick of what his practice had become. A parade of rich people and their kids who failed to find happiness in their wealth. And who tried to buy their way out of drug charges, abusive behavior and sometimes worse. He wasn't proud of the course his life had taken; a criminal lawyer, whose clientele and lonely life left him cold as the foggy mist surrounding him.

Alex had found something that brought him peace in what he referred to as his "ancestral past." It was Nate's past, too, Native American in origin—Navajo and Hopi according to Alex's research. Nate wasn't sure how to find that kind of peace. Heritage was something they'd been distanced from all their lives. Alex could dig it out of the earth and hold it in his hands. Nate would have to find it in his own way.

He clutched the letters as the stiff ocean breeze tugged at them. "Oh no," he whispered as he tucked them into the inner pocket of his overcoat and again looked out over the bay. "I'm not giving you any more."

A spray of salty ocean water blew over him as another wave crashed against the pier. A cleansing, he thought, symbolic of the cleansing of his life and spirit.

Tomorrow he'd board a plane and within the week he'd begin a new life. A fresh start in a new land lay ahead of him—on a path paved with questions he'd never dared ask.

ABOUT THE AUTHOR

Sharon Silva grew up in the Colorado mountains and her heart does not journey far from there still. Her love for the outdoors and a "simpler way of life," are reflected in her writings. Her elementary school years were spent attending a one room school house in a small mountain community. It was in those early years that Sharon fell in love with books and the magical world of story. She began writing stories and poems of her own at the age of nine.

Sharon's favorite stories then and now have always been romantic adventures that contain paranormal elements. Her fascination with ancient spiritual places and the possibilities of mystical realms intrigue her, fuel her imagination, and inspire her stories.

The blending of Native American cultures in her own bloodlines, having three great-grandmothers descended from three different tribes, has led Sharon on a journey of research, respect and strong spiritual connection to the world and people who existed long before America was "discovered" by explorers from across the ocean. That connection was the foundation for The Crystal Legacy series.

Sharon is an awarding-winning author of several romantic suspense novels and countless poems. She lives in Colorado with her own real life hero, her husband of more than thirty years. When she isn't writing or researching a new adventure, you'll find her drag racing with her husband, spending time with family or working in her garden.

Dear Readers,

Thank you so much for reading Spirit Dancer. I hope you enjoyed the adventure. I love feedback and I love to hear from readers. Authors also love and need reader reviews so please take time to stop over at Amazon and review this book. You, the reader, are the reason we authors spend hours honing the stories of our hearts into books. For us, the reader is what it's all about so we want to connect with you.

Please visit my website at **www.sharonsilva.com** for some interesting tidbits about the series and my other works and to sign up for my newsletter. New releases will be announced there when they become available. Also keep up to date and get to know the author by connecting with me on any of the following:

Facebook: **www.facebook.com/sharonsilva**
Twitter: **sharonsilva@sharonsilva**

Eagle Dancer, the second book of The Crystal Legacy Series is now available for purchase at **www.Amazon.com** or at **www.sharonsilva.com**. The first chapter has been included for your enjoyment.

Thank you! I'll see you again soon in the pages of a new adventure.